DAUGHTER OF THE EMPIRE

Also by Raymond E. Feist

MAGICIAN
SILVERTHORN
A DARKNESS AT
SETHANON

Also by Janny Wurts

SORCERER'S LEGACY
STORMWARDEN

DAUGHTER OF THE EMPIRE

Raymond E. Feist
and
Janny Wurts

GRAFTON BOOKS
A Division of the Collins Publishing Group

LONDON GLASGOW
TORONTO SYDNEY AUCKLAND

Grafton Books
A Division of the Collins Publishing Group
8 Grafton Street, London W1X 3LA

Published by Grafton Books 1987

British Library Cataloguing in Publication Data

Feist, Raymond E.
Daughter of the empire.
I. Title II. Wurts, Janny
813'.54[F] PS3556.E446

ISBN 0-246-13226-4
ISBN 0-246-13232-9 (Pbk)

Photoset by Deltatype, Ellesmere Port
Printed in Great Britain by Mackays of Chatham Ltd, Kent

This book is dedicated to

Harold Matson

with deep appreciation, respect, and affection

Acknowledgements

We find ourselves deeply indebted to many people for much of what appears in this book. We would like to publicly offer our heartfelt thanks for their contributions, intentional or otherwise:

To the Friday Nighters, whose affection for games introduced REF to many wonderful ideas that were used in two worlds, and the many writers of those games, most especially those at Midkemia Press.

To Kyung and Jon Conning, who gave JW a red-carpet tour of their home in Korea which added immeasurably to the colour in this book.

To Virginia Kidd, for making it easy for JW to say yes, and for years of wise counsel and friendship.

To our editors, Adrian Zackheim, who started with us, and Jim Moser, who was there at the finish.

To Richard C. Freese, for caring above and beyond duty's call.

To Elaine Chubb, for making us look good.

To Daniel P. Mannix IV for both being an example of what a writer is, and for giving us a terrific place to work (the ducks notwithstanding).

And to Barbara A. Feist for putting up with one of us.

Raymond E. Feist
Janny Wurts
Frazer, PA, June, 1986

1

Lady

The priest struck the gong.

The sound reverberated off the temple's vaulted domes, splendid with brightly coloured carvings. The solitary note echoed back and forth, diminishing to a remembered tone, a ghost of sound.

Mara knelt, the cold stones of the temple floor draining the warmth from her. She shivered, though not from chill, then glanced slightly to the left, where another initiate knelt in a pose identical to her own, duplicating Mara's movements as she lifted the white head covering of a novice of the Order of Lashima, Goddess of the Inner Light. Awkwardly posed with the linen draped like a tent above her head, Mara impatiently awaited the moment when the headdress could be lowered and tied. She had barely lifted the cloth and already the thing dragged at her arms like stone weights! The gong sounded again. Reminded of the goddess's eternal presence, Mara inwardly winced at her irreverent thoughts. Now, of all times, her attention must not stray. Silently she begged the goddess's forgiveness, pleading nerves – fatigue and excitement combined with apprehension. Mara prayed to the Lady to guide her to the inner peace she so fervently desired.

The gong chimed again, the third ring of twenty-two, twenty for the gods, one for the Light of Heaven, and one for the imperfect children who now waited to join in the service of the Goddess of Wisdom of the Upper Heaven. At seventeen years of age, Mara prepared to renounce the temporal world, like the girl at her side who – in another nineteen chimings of the gong – would be counted her sister, though they had met only two weeks before.

Mara considered her sister-to-be: Ura was a foul-tempered girl from a clanless but wealthy family in Lash Province while Mara was from an ancient and powerful family, the Acoma. Ura's admission to the temple was a public demonstration of family piety, ordered by her uncle, the self-styled family Lord, who sought admission into any clan that would take his family. Mara had come close to defying her father to join the order. When the girls had exchanged histories at their first meeting, Ura had been incredulous, then almost angry that the daughter of a powerful Lord should take eternal shelter behind the walls of the order. Mara's heritage meant clan position, powerful allies, an array of well-positioned suitors, and an assured good marriage to a son of another powerful house. Her own sacrifice, as Ura called it, was made so that later generations of girls in her family would have those things Mara chose to renounce. Not for the first time Mara wondered if Ura would make a good sister of the order. Then, again not for the first time, Mara questioned her own worthiness for the Sisterhood.

The gong sounded, deep and rich. Mara closed her eyes a moment, begging for guidance and comfort. Why was she still plagued with doubts? After eighteen more chimes, family, friends, and the familiar would be forever lost. All her past life would be put behind, from earliest child's play to a noble daughter's concern over her family's role within the Game of the Council, that never-ending struggle for dominance which ordered all Tsurani life. Ura would become her sister, no matter the differences in their heritage, for within the Order of Lashima none recognized personal honour or family name. There would remain only service to the goddess, through chastity and obedience.

The gong rang again, the fifth stroke. Mara peeked up at the altar atop the dais. Framed beneath carved arches, six priests and priestesses knelt before the statue of Lashima, her countenance unveiled for the initiation. Dawn shone through the lancet windows high in the domes, the palest glow reaching like fingers through the half-dark temple. The touch of sunrise seemed to caress the goddess, softening the jewel-like ceremonial candles that surrounded her. How friendly the lady looked in morning's blush, Mara thought. The Lady of Wisdom gazed down with a half-smile on her chiselled lips, as if all under her care would be loved and protected, finding inner peace. Mara prayed this would be true. The only priest not upon his knees again rang the gong. Metal caught the sunlight, a splendid burst of gold against the dark curtain that shrouded the entrance to the inner temple. Then, as the dazzling brilliance faded, the gong rang again.

Fifteen more times it would be struck. Mara bit her lip, certain the kind goddess would forgive a momentary lapse. Her thoughts were like flashing lights from broken crystals, dancing about here and there, never staying long in one place. I'm not very good material for the Sisterhood, Mara confessed, staring up at the statue. Please have patience with me, Lady of the Inner Light. Again she glanced at her companion; Ura remained still and quiet, eyes closed. Mara determined to imitate her companion's behaviour outwardly, even if she couldn't find the appropriate calm within. The gong sounded once more.

Mara sought that hidden centre of her being, her wal, and strove to put her mind at rest. For a few minutes she found herself successful. Then the beat of the gong snatched her back to the present. Mara shifted her weight slightly, rejecting irritation as she tried to ease her aching arms. She fought an urge to sigh. The inner calm taught by the sisters who had schooled her through her novitiate again eluded her grasp, though she had laboured at the convent for six months before being judged worthy of testing here in the Holy City by the priests of the High Temple.

Again the gong was struck, as bold a call as the horn that had summoned the Acoma warriors into formation. How brave they all had looked in their green enamelled armour, especially the officers with their gallant plumes, on the day they left to fight with the Warlord's forces. Mara worried over the progress of the war upon the barbarian world, where her father and brother fought. Too many of the family's forces were committed there. The clan was split in its loyalty within the High Council, and since no single family clearly dominated, blood politics bore down heavily upon the Acoma. The families of the Hadama Clan were united in name only, and a betrayal of the Acoma by distant cousins who sought Minwanabi favour was not outside the realm of possibility. Had Mara a voice in her father's counsel, she would have urged a separation from the War Party, even perhaps an alliance with the Blue Wheel Party, who feigned interest only in commerce while they quietly worked to balk the power of the Warlord . . .

Mara frowned. Again her mind had been beguiled by worldly

concerns. She apologized to the goddess, then pushed away thoughts of the world she was leaving behind.

Mara peeked as the gong rang again. The stone features of the goddess now seemed set in gentle rebuke; virtue began with the individual, she reminded. Help would come only to those who truly searched for enlightenment. Mara lowered her eyes.

The gong reverberated and through the dying shiver of harmonics another sound intruded, a disturbance wholly out of place. Sandals scuffed upon stone in the antechamber, accompanied by the dull clank of weapons and armour. Outside the curtain an attending priest challenged in a harsh whisper, 'Stop, warrior! You may not enter the inner temple now! It is forbidden!'

Mara stiffened. A chilling prescience passed through her. Beneath the shelter of the tented headcloth, she saw the priests upon the dais rise up in alarm. They turned to face the intruder, and the gong missed its beat and fell silent.

The High Father Superior moved purposefully towards the curtain, his brow knotted in alarm. Mara shut her eyes tightly. If only she could plunge the outside world into darkness as easily, then no one would be able to find her. But the sound of footfalls ceased, replaced by the High Father Superior's voice. 'What cause have you for this outrage, warrior! You violate a most holy rite.'

A voice rang out. 'We seek the Lady of the Acoma!'

The Lady of the Acoma. Like a cold knife plunged into the pit of her stomach, the words cut through Mara's soul. That one sentence forever changed her life. Her mind rebelled, screaming denial, but she willed herself to remain calm. Never would she shame her ancestors by a public display of grief. She controlled her voice as she slowly rose to her feet. 'I am here, Keyoke.'

As one, the priests and priestesses watched the High Father Superior cross to stand before Mara. The embroidered symbols on his robes of office flashed fitfully as he beckoned to a priestess, who hastened to his side. Then he looked into Mara's eyes and read the contained pain hidden there. 'Daughter, it is clear Our Mistress of Wisdom has ordained another path for you. Go with her love and in her grace, Lady of the Acoma.' He bowed slightly.

Mara returned his bow, then surrendered her head covering to the priestess. Oblivious to Ura's sigh of envy, she turned at last to face the bearer of those tidings which had changed her life.

Just past the curtain, Keyoke, Force Commander of the Acoma, regarded his mistress with weary eyes. He was a battle-scarred old warrior, erect and proud despite forty years of loyal service. He stood poised to step to the girl's side, provide a steadying arm, perhaps even shield her from public view should the strain prove too much.

Poor, ever-loyal Keyoke, Mara thought. This announcement had not come easily for him either. She would not disappoint him by shaming her family. Faced with tragedy, she maintained the manner and dignity required of the Lady of a great house.

Keyoke bowed as his mistress approached. Behind him stood the tall and taciturn Papewaio, his face as always an unreadable mask. The strongest warrior in the Acoma retinue, he served as both companion and body servant to Keyoke. He bowed and held aside the curtain for Mara as she swept past.

Mara heard both fall into step, one on each side, Papewaio one pace behind, correct in form to the last detail. Without words she led them from the inner temple, under the awning that covered the garden court separating the inner and outer temples. They entered the outer temple, passing between giant sandstone columns that rose to the ceiling. Down a long hall they marched, past magnificent frescos depicting tales of the goddess Lashima. Desperately attempting to divert the pain that threatened to overwhelm her, Mara remembered the story each picture represented: how the goddess outwitted Turakamu, the Red God, for the life of a child; how she stayed the wrath of Emperor Inchonlonganbula, saving the city of Migran from obliteration; how she taught the first scholar the secret of writing. Mara closed her eyes as they passed her favourite: how, disguised as a crone, Lashima decided the issue between the farmer and his wife. Mara turned her eyes from these images, for they belonged to a life now denied her.

All too soon she reached the outer doors. She paused a moment at the top of the worn marble stairs. The courtyard below held a half company of guards in the bright green armour of the Acoma. Several showed freshly bandaged wounds, but all came to attention and saluted, fist over heart, as their Lady came into view. Mara swallowed fear: if wounded soldiers stood escort duty, the fighting must have been brutal indeed. Many brave warriors had died. That the Acoma must show such a sign of weakness made Mara's cheeks burn with anger. Grateful for the temple robe that hid the shaking in her knees, she descended the steps. A litter awaited her at the bottom. A dozen slaves stood silently by until the Lady of the Acoma settled inside. Then Papewaio and Keyoke assumed position, one on each side. On Keyoke's command, the slaves grasped the poles and lifted the litter onto sweating shoulders. Veiled by the light, embroidered curtain on either side of the litter, Mara sat stiffly as the soldiers formed up before and after their mistress.

The litter swayed slightly as the slaves started towards the river, threading an efficient course through the throng who travelled the streets of the Holy City. They moved past carts pulled by sluggish, six-legged needra and were passed in turn by running messengers and trotting porters with bundles held aloft on shoulder or head, hurrying their loads for clients who paid a premium for swift delivery.

The noise and bustle of commerce beyond the gates jolted Mara afresh; within the shelter of the temple, the shock of Keyoke's appearance had not fully registered. Now she battled to keep from spilling tears upon the cushions of the litter as understanding overwhelmed her. She wanted not to speak, as if silence could hide the truth. But she was Tsurani, and an Acoma. Cowardice would not change the past, nor forever stave off the future. She took a breath. Then, drawing aside the curtain so she could see Keyoke, she voiced what was never in doubt.

'They are both dead.'

Keyoke nodded curtly, once. 'Your father and brother were both ordered into a useless assault against a barbarian fortification. It was murder.' His features remained impassive, but his voice betrayed bitterness as he walked at a brisk pace beside his mistress.

The litter jostled as the slaves avoided a wagon piled with jomach fruit. They turned down the street towards the landing by the river while Mara regarded her clenched hands. With focused concentration, she willed her fingers to open and relax. After a long silence she said, 'Tell me what happened, Keyoke.'

'When the snows on the barbarian world melted we were ordered out, to stand against a possible barbarian assault.' Armour creaked as the elderly warrior squared his shoulders, fighting off remembered fatigue and loss, yet his voice stayed matter-of-fact.

'Soldiers from the barbarian cities of Zūn and LaMut were already in the field, earlier than expected. Our runners were dispatched to the Warlord, camped in the valley in the mountains the barbarians call the Grey Towers. In the Warlord's absence, his Subcommander gave the order for your father to assault the barbarian position. We –'

Mara interrupted. 'This Subcommander, he is of the Minwanabi, is he not?'

Keyoke's weathered face showed a hint of approval as if silently saying, you're keeping your wits despite grief. 'Yes. The nephew of Lord Jingu of the Minwanabi, his dead brother's only son, Tasaio.' Mara's eyes narrowed as he continued his narrative. 'We were grossly outnumbered. You father knew this – we all knew it – but your father kept honour. He followed orders without question. We attacked. The Subcommander promised to support our right flank, but his troops never materialized. Instead of a coordinated charge with ours, the Minwanabi warriors held their ground, as if preparing for counterattack. Tasaio ordered they should do so.

'But just as we were overwhelmed by a counterattack, support arrived from the valley, elements of the forces under the banner of Omechkel and Chimiriko. They had no hint of the betrayal and fought bravely to get us out from under the hooves of the barbarian's horses. The Minwanabi attacked at this time, as if to repulse the counterattack. They arrived just as the barbarians retreated. To any who had not been there from the start, it was simply a poor meeting with the barbarian enemy. But the Acoma know it was Minwanabi treachery.'

Mara's eyes narrowed, and her lips tightened; for an instant Keyoke's expression betrayed concern that the girl might shame her father's memory by weeping before tradition permitted. But instead she spoke quietly, her voice controlled fury. 'So my Lord of the Minwanabi seized the moment and arranged for my father's death, despite our alliance within the War Party?'

Keyoke straightened his helm. 'Indeed, my Lady. Jingu of the Minwanabi must have ordered Tasaio to change the Warlord's instructions. Jingu moves boldly; he would have earned Tasaio the Warlord's wrath and a dishonourable death had our army lost that position to the barbarians. But Almecho needs Minwanabi support in the conquest, and while he is angry with Jingu's nephew, he keeps silent. Nothing was lost. To outward appearances, it was simply a standoff, no victor. But in the Game of the Council, the Minwanabi triumph over the Acoma.' For the first time in her life, Mara heard a hint of emotion in Keyoke's voice. Almost bitterly, he said, 'Papewaio and I were spared by your father's command. He ordered us to remain apart with this small company – and charged us to protect you should matters proceed as they have.' Forcing his voice back to its usual brisk tone, he added, 'My Lord Sezu knew he and your brother would likely not survive the day.'

Mara sank back against the cushions, her stomach in knots. Her head ached and she felt her chest tighten. She took a long, slow breath and glanced out the opposite side of the litter, to Papewaio, who marched with a studied lack of expression. 'And what do you say, my brave Pape?' she asked. 'How shall we answer this murder visited upon our house?'

Papewaio absently scratched at the scar on his jaw with his left thumb, as he often did in times of stress. 'Your will, my Lady.'

The manner of the First Strike Leader of the Acoma was outwardly easy, but Mara sensed he wished to be holding his spear and unsheathed sword. For a wild, angry instant Mara considered immediate vengeance. At her word, Papewaio would assault the Minwanabi lord in his own chamber, in the midst of his army. Although the warrior would count it an honour to die in the effort, she shunted away the foolish impulse. Neither Papewaio nor any other wearing the Acoma green could get within a half day's march of the Minwanabi lord. Besides, loyalty such as his was to be jealously guarded, never squandered.

Removed from the scrutiny of the priests, Keyoke studied Mara closely. She met his gaze and held it. She knew her expression was grim and her face drawn and chalky, but she also knew she had borne up well under the news. Keyoke's gaze returned forward, as he awaited his mistress's next question or command.

A man's attention, even an old family retainer's, caused Mara to take stock of herself, without illusions, being neither critical nor flattering. She was a fair-looking young woman, not pretty, especially when she wrinkled her brow in thought or frowned in worry. But her smile could make her striking – or so a boy had told her once – and she possessed a certain appealing quality, a spirited energy, that made her almost vivacious at times. She was slender and lithe in movement, and that trim body had caught the eye of more than one son of a neighbouring house. Now one of those sons would likely prove a necessary ally to stem the tide of political fortune that threatened to obliterate the Acoma. With her brown eyes half-closed, she considered the awesome responsibility thrust upon her. She realized, with a sinking feeling, that the commodities of womankind – beauty, wit, charm, allure – must all now be put to use in the cause of the Acoma, along with whatever native intelligence the gods had granted her. She fought down the fear that her gifts were insufficient for the task; then, before she knew it, she was recalling the faces of her father and brother. Grief rose up within her, but she forced it back deep. Sorrow must keep until later.

Softly Mara said, 'We have much to talk of, Keyoke, but not here.' In the press of city traffic, enemies might walk on every side, spies, assassins, or informants in disguise. Mara closed her eyes against the terrors of imagination and the real world both. 'We shall speak when only ears loyal to the Acoma may overhear.' Keyoke grunted acknowledgement. Mara silently thanked the gods that he had been spared. He was a rock, and she would need such as he at her side.

Exhausted, Mara settled back into the cushions. She must rise above grief to ponder. Her father's most powerful enemy, Lord Jingu of the Minwanabi, had almost succeeded in gaining one of his life's ambitions: the obliteration of the Acoma. The blood feud between the Acoma and Minwanabi had existed for generations, and while neither house had managed to gain the upper hand, from time to time one or the other had to struggle to protect itself. But now the Acoma had been gravely weakened, and the Minwanabi were at the height of their power, rivalling even the Warlord's family in strength. Jingu was already served by vassals, first among them the Lord of the Kehotara, whose power equalled that of Mara's father. And as the star of the Minwanabi rose higher, more would ally with him.

For a long while Mara lay behind the fluttering curtains, to all appearances asleep. Her situation was bitterly clear. All that remained between the Lord of the Minwanabi and his goal was herself, a young girl who had been but ten chimes from becoming a sister of Lashima. That realization left a taste in her mouth like ash.

Now, if she were to survive long enough to regain family honour, she must consider her resources and plot and plan, and enter the Game of the Council; and somehow she must find a way to thwart the will of the Lord of one of the Five Great Families of the Empire of Tsuranuanni.

Mara blinked and forced herself awake. She had dozed fitfully while the litter travelled the busy streets of Kentosani, the Holy City, her mind seeking relief from the stress of the day. Now the litter rocked gently as it was lowered to the docks.

Mara peeked through the curtains, too numb to find pleasure in the bustle of the throngs upon the dockside. When she had first arrived in the Holy City, she had been enthralled by the multi-coloured diversity found in the crowd, with people from every corner of the Empire upon every hand. The simple sight of household barges from cities up and down the river Gagajin had delighted her. Bedecked with banners, they rocked at their moorings like proudly plumed birds amid barnyard fowl as busy commercial barges and traders' boats scurried about them. Everything, the sights, the sounds, the smells, had been so different from her father's estates – her estates now, she corrected herself. Torn by that recognition, Mara hardly noticed the slaves who toiled in the glaring sun, their sweating, near-naked bodies dusted with grime as they loaded bundled goods aboard the river barges. This time she did not blush as she had when she had first passed this way in the company of the sisters of Lashima. Male nudity had been nothing new to her; as a child she had played near the soldiers' commons while the men bathed and for years she had swum with her brother and friends in the lake above the needra meadow. But seeing naked men after she had renounced the world of flesh seemed somehow to have made a difference. Being commanded to look away by the attending sister of Lashima had made her want to peek all the more. That day she had to will herself not to stare at the lean, muscled bodies.

But today the bodies of the slaves failed to fascinate, as did the cries of the beggars who called down the blessings of the gods on any who chose to share a coin with the less fortunate. Mara ignored the rivermen, who sauntered by with the swaggering gait of those who spent their lives upon the water, secretly contemptuous of land dwellers, their voices loud and edged with rough humour. Everything seemed less colourful, less vivid, less captivating, as she looked through eyes suddenly older, less given to seeing with wonder and awe. Now every sunlit façade cast a dark shadow. And in those shadows enemies plotted.

Mara left her litter quickly. Despite the white robe of a novice of Lashima, she bore herself with the dignity expected of the Lady of the Acoma. She kept her eyes forward as she moved towards the barge that would take her downriver, to Sulan-Qu. Papewaio cleared a path for her, roughly shoving common workers aside. Other soldiers moved nearby, brightly coloured guardians who conducted their masters from the barges to the city. Keyoke kept a wary eye upon them as he hovered near Mara's side while they crossed the dock.

As her officers ushered her up the gangplank, Mara wished for a dark, quiet place in which to confront her own sorrow. But the instant she set foot upon the deck, the barge master hustled to meet her. His short red and purple robe seemed jarringly bright after the sombre dress of the priests and sisters in the convent. Jade trinkets clinked on his wrists as he bowed obsequiously and offered his illustrious passenger the finest accommodation his humble barge permitted, a pile of cushions under a central canopy, hung round by gauzy curtains. Mara allowed the fawning to continue until she had been seated, courtesy requiring such lest the man unduly lose face. Once settled, she let silence inform the barge master his presence was no longer required. Finding an indifferent audience to his babble, the man let fall the thin curtain, leaving Mara a tiny bit of privacy at last. Keyoke and Papewaio sat opposite, while the household guards surrounded the canopy, their usual alertness underscored by a grim note of battle-ready tension.

Seeming to gaze at the swirling water, Mara said, 'Keyoke, where is my father's . . . my own barge? And my maids?'

The old warrior said, 'The Acoma barge is at the dock in Sulan-Qu, my Lady. I judged a night encounter with soldiers of the Minwanabi or their allies less likely if we used a public barge. The chance of surviving witnesses might help discourage assault by enemies disguised as bandits. And should difficulty visit us, I feared your maids might prove a hindrance.' Keyoke's eyes scanned the docks while he spoke. 'This craft will tie up at night with other barges, so we will never be upon the river alone.'

Mara nodded, letting her eyes close a long second. Softly she said, 'Very well.' She had wished for privacy, something impossible to find on this public barge, but Keyoke's concerns were well founded.

Lord Jingu might sacrifice an entire company of soldiers to destroy the last of the Acoma, certain he could throw enough men at Mara's guards to overwhelm them. But he would do so only if he could assure himself of success, then feign ignorance of the act before the other Lords of the High Council. Everyone who played the Game of the Council would deduce who had authored such slaughter, but the forms must always be observed. One escaped traveller, one Minwanabi guard recognized, one chance remark overheard by a poleman on a nearby barge, and Jingu would be undone. To have his part in such a venal ambush revealed publicly would lose him much prestige in the council, perhaps signalling to one of his 'loyal' allies that he was losing control. Then he could have as much to fear from his friends as from his enemies. Such was the nature of the Game of the Council. Keyoke's choice of conveyance might prove as much a deterrent to treachery as a hundred more men-at-arms.

The barge master's voice cut the air as he shouted for the slaves to cast off the dock lines. A thud and a bump, and suddenly the barge was moving, swinging away from the dock into the sluggish swirl of the current. Mara lay back, judging it acceptable now to outwardly relax. Slaves poled the barge along, their thin, sun-browned bodies moving in time, coordinated by a simple chant.

'Keep her to the middle,' sang out the tillerman.

'Don't hit the shore,' answered the polemen.

The chant settled into a rhythm, and the tillerman began to add simple lyrics, all in tempo. 'I know an ugly woman!' he shouted.

'Don't hit the shore!'

'Her tongue cuts like a knife!'

'Don't hit the shore!'

'Got drunk one summer's evening!'

'Don't hit the shore!'

'And took her for my wife!'

The silly song soothed Mara and she let her thoughts drift. Her father had argued long and hotly against her taking vows. Now, when apologies were no longer possible, Mara bitterly regretted how close she had come to open defiance; her father had relented only because his love for his only daughter had been greater than his desire for a suitable political marriage. Their parting had been stormy. Lord Sezu of the Acoma could be like a harulth – the giant predator most feared by herdsmen and hunters – in full battle frenzy when facing his enemies, but he had never been able to deny his daughter, no matter how unreasonable her demands. While never as comfortable with her as he had been with her brother, still he had indulged her all her life, and only her nurse, Nacoya, had taken firm rein over her childhood.

Mara closed her eyes. The barge afforded a small measure of security, and she could now hide in the dark shelter of sleep; those outside the curtains of this tiny pavilion would only think her fleeing the boredom of a lengthy river journey. But rest proved elusive as memories returned of the brother she had loved like the breath in her lungs, Lanokota of the flashing dark eyes and ready smile for his adoring little sister. Lano who ran faster than the warriors in his father's house, and who won in the summer games at Sulan-Qu three years in a row, a feat unmatched since. Lano always had time for Mara, even showing her how to wrestle – bringing down her nurse Nacoya's wrath for involving a girl in such an unladylike pastime. And always Lano had a stupid joke – usually dirty – to tell his little sister to make her laugh and blush. Had she not chosen the contemplative life, Mara knew any suitor would have been measured against her brother . . . Lano, whose merry laughter would no more echo through the night as they sat in the hall sharing supper. Even their father, stern in all ways, would smile, unable to resist his son's infectious humour. While Mara had respected and admired her father, she had loved her brother, and now grief came sweeping over her.

Mara forced her emotions back. This was not the place; she must not mourn until later. Turning to the practical, she said to Keyoke, 'Were my father's and brother's bodies recovered?'

With a bitter note, Keyoke said, 'No, my Lady, they were not.'

Mara bit her lip. There would be no ashes to inter in the sacred grove. Instead she must choose a relic of her father's and brother's, one favourite possession of each, to bury beside the sacred natami – the rock that contained the Acoma family's soul – that their spirits could find their way back to Acoma ground, to find peace beside their ancestors until the Wheel of Life turned anew. Mara closed her eyes again, half from emotional fatigue, half to deny tears. Memories jarred her to consciousness as she unsuccessfully tried to rest. Then, after some hours, the rocking of the barge, the singing of the tillerman, and the answering chant of the slaves became familiar. Her mind and body fell into an answering rhythm and she relaxed. The warmth of the day and the quietness of the river at last conspired to lull Mara into a deep sleep.

The barge docked at Sulan-Qu under the topaz light of daybreak. Mist rose in coils off the river, while shops and stalls by the waterfront opened screened shutters in preparation for market. Keyoke acted swiftly to disembark Mara's litter while the streets were still free of the choking press of commerce; soon carts and porters, shoppers and beggars would throng the commercial boulevards. In scant minutes the slaves were ready. Still clad in the white robes of Lashima's sisterhood – crumpled from six days' use – Mara climbed wearily into her litter. She settled back against cushions stylized with her family's symbol, the shatra bird, embroidered into the material, and realized how much she dreaded her return home. She could not imagine the airy spaces of the great house empty of Lano's boisterous voice, or the floor mats in the study uncluttered with the scrolls left by her father when he wearied of reading reports. Mara smiled faintly, recalling her father's distaste for business, despite the fact he was skilled at it. He preferred matters of warfare, the games, and politics, but she remembered his saying that everything required money, and commerce must never be neglected.

Mara allowed herself an almost audible sigh as the litter was hoisted. She wished the curtains provided more privacy as she endured the gazes of peasants and workers upon the streets at first light. From atop vegetable carts and behind booths where goods were being arrayed, they watched the great lady and her retinue sweep by. Worn from constantly guarding her appearance, Mara endured the jostling trip through streets that quickly became crowded. She lapsed into brooding, outwardly alert, but inwardly oblivious to the usually diverting panorama of the city.

Screens on the galleries overhead were withdrawn as merchants displayed wares above the buyers. When haggling ended, the agreed price was pulled up in baskets, then the goods lowered. Licensed prostitutes were still asleep, so every fifth or sixth gallery remained shuttered.

Mara smiled slightly, remembering the first time she had seen the ladies of the Reed Life. The prostitutes showed themselves upon the galleries as they had for generations, robes left in provocative disarray as they fanned themselves in the ever present city heat. All the women had been beautiful, their faces painted with lovely colours and their hair bound up in regal style. Even the skimpy robes were of the costliest weave, with fine embroidery. Mara had voiced a six-year-old girl's delight at the image. She had then announced to all within earshot that when she grew up she would be just like the ladies in the galleries. This was the only time in her life she had seen her father rendered speechless. Lano had teased her about the incident until the morning she left for the temple. Now his playful jibes would embarrass her no further.

Saddened nearly to tears, Mara turned from memory. She sought diversion outside her litter, where clever hawkers sold wares from wheelbarrows at corners, beggars accosted passersby with tales of misery, jugglers offered antics, and merchants presented rare, beautiful silk as they passed. But all failed to shield her mind from pain.

The market fell behind and they left the city. Beyond the walls of Sulan-Qu, cultivated fields stretched towards a line of bluish mountains on the horizon; the Kyamaka range was not so rugged or so high as the great High Wall to the north, but the valleys remained wild enough to shelter bandits and outlaws.

The road to Mara's estates led through a swamp that resisted all attempts to drain it. Here her bearers muttered complaints as they were plagued by insects. A word from Keyoke brought silence.

Then the road passed through a stand of ngaggi trees, their large lower branches a green-blue canopy of shade. The travellers moved on into hillier lands, crossing over brightly painted bridges, as the streams that fed the swamp continually interrupted every road built by man. They came to a prayer gate, a brightly painted arch erected by some man of wealth as thanks to the gods for a blessing granted. As they passed under the arch, each traveller generated a silent prayer of thanks and received a small blessing in return. And as the prayer arch fell behind, Mara considered she would need all the grace the gods were willing to grant in the days to come, if the Acoma were to survive.

The party left the highway, turning towards their final destination. Shatra birds foraged in the thyza paddies, eating insects and grubs, stooped over like old men. Because the flocks helped ensure a good harvest, the silly-looking creatures were considered a sign of good luck. So the Acoma had counted them, making the shatra symbol the centrepiece of their house crest. Mara found no humour in the familiar sight of the shatra birds, with their stilt legs and ever moving pointed ears, finding instead deep apprehension, for the birds and workers signalled she had reached Acoma lands.

The bearers picked up stride. Oh, how Mara wished they would slacken pace, or turn around and carry her elsewhere. But her arrival had been noticed by the workers who gathered faggots in the woodlands between the fields and the meadow near the great house. Some shouted or waved as they walked stooped under bundles of wood loaded on their backs and secured with a strap across their foreheads. There was warmth in their greeting, and despite the cause of her return they deserved more than aloofness from their new mistress.

Mara pulled herself erect, smiling slightly and nodding. Around her spread her estates, last seen with the expectation she would never return. The hedges, the trimmed fields, and the neat outbuildings that housed the workers were unchanged. But then, she thought, her absence had been less than a year.

The litter passed the needra meadows. The midday air was rent by the herds' plaintive lowing and the 'hut-hut-hut' cry of the herdsman as they waved goading sticks and moved the animals towards the pens where they would be examined for parasites. Mara regarded the cows as they grazed, the sun making their grey hides look tawny. A few lifted blunt snouts as stocky bull calves feinted charges, then scampered away on six stumpy legs to shelter behind their mothers. To Mara it seemed some asked when Lano would return to play his wild tricks on the ill-tempered breeding bulls. The pain of her losses increased the closer she came to home. Mara put on a brave face as the litter bearers turned along the wide, tree-lined lane that led to the heart of the estate.

Ahead lay the large central house, constructed of beams and paper-thin screens, slid back to open the interior to any breezes in the midday heat. Mara felt her breath catch. No dogs sprawled among the akasi flowers, tongues lolling and tails wagging as they waited for the Lord of the Acoma to return. In his absence they were always kennelled; now that absence was permanent. Yet home, desolate and empty though it seemed without the presence of loved ones, meant privacy. Soon Mara could retire to the sacred grove and loose the sorrow she had pent up through seven weary days.

As the litter and retinue passed a barracks house, the soldiers of her home garrison fell into formation along her line of travel. Their armour was polished, their weapons and trappings faultlessly neat, yet beside Keyoke's and Papewaio's, only one other officer's plume was in evidence. Mara felt a chill stab at her heart and glanced at Keyoke. 'Why so few warriors, Force Commander? Where are the others?'

Keyoke kept his eyes forward, ignoring the dust that clung to his lacquered armour and the sweat that dripped beneath his helm. Stiffly he said, 'Those who were capable returned, Lady.'

Mara closed her eyes, unable to disguise her shock. Keyoke's simple statement indicated that almost two thousand soldiers had died beside her father and brother. Many of them had been retainers with years of faithful service, some having stood guard at Mara's crib side. Most had followed fathers and grandfathers into Acoma service.

Numbed and speechless, Mara counted those soldiers standing in formation and added their numbers to those who had travelled as bodyguards. Thirty-seven warriors remained in her service, a pitiful fraction of the garrison her father had once commanded. Of the twenty-five hundred warriors to wear Acoma green, five hundred were dedicated to guarding outlying Acoma holdings in distant cities and provinces. Three hundred had already been lost beyond the rift in the war against the barbarians before this last campaign. Now, where two thousand soldiers had served at the height of Acoma power, the heart of the estate was protected by fewer than fifty men. Mara shook her head in sorrow. Many women besides herself mourned losses beyond the rift. Despair filled her heart as she realized the Acoma forces were too few to withstand any assault, even an attack by bandits, should a bold band raid from the mountains. But Mara also knew why Keyoke had placed the estate at risk to bring such a large portion – twenty-four out of thirty-seven – of the surviving warriors to guard her. Any spies of the Minwanabi must not be allowed to discover just how weak the Acoma were. Hopelessness settled over her like a smothering blanket.

'Why didn't you tell me sooner, Keyoke?' But only silence answered. By that Mara knew. Her faithful Force Commander had feared that such news might break her if delivered all at once. And that could not be permitted. Too many Acoma soldiers had died for her to simply give up to despair. If hopelessness overwhelmed her, their sacrifice in the name of Acoma honour became a mockery, their death a waste. Thrust headlong into the Game of the Council, Mara needed every shred of wit and cunning she possessed to avoid the snares of intrigue that lay in wait for her inexperienced feet. The treachery visited upon her house would not end until, unschooled and alone, she had defeated the Lord of the Minwanabi and his minions.

The slaves halted in the dooryard. Mara drew a shaking breath. Head high, she forced herself to step from the litter and enter the scrolled arches of the portico that lined the perimeter of the house. Mara waited while Keyoke dismissed the litter and gave orders to her escort. Then, as the last soldier saluted, she turned and met the bow of the hadonra, her estate manager. The man was new to his post, his squint-eyed countenance unfamiliar to Mara. But beside him stood the tiny, wizened presence of Nacoya, the nurse who had raised Mara from childhood. Other servants waited beyond.

The impact of the change struck Mara once again. For the first time in her life, she could not fly into the comfort of the ancient woman's arms. As Lady of the Acoma, she must nod formally and walk past, leaving Nacoya and the hadonra to follow her up the wooden steps into the shady dimness of the great house. Today she must bear up and pretend not to notice the painful reflection of her own sorrow in Nacoya's eyes. Mara bit her lip slightly, then stopped herself. That nervous habit had brought Nacoya's scolding on many occasions. Instead the girl took a breath, and entered the house of her father. The missing echoes of his footfalls upon the polished wooden floor filled her with loneliness.

'Lady?'

Mara halted, clenched hands hidden in the crumpled white of her robe. 'What is it?'

The hadonra spoke again. 'Welcome home, my Lady,' he added in formal greeting. 'I am Jican, Lady.'

Softly Mara said, 'What has become of Sotamu?'

Jican glanced down. 'He wasted in grief, my Lady, following his Lord into death.'

Mara could only nod once and resume her progress to her quarters. She was not surprised to learn that the old hadonra had refused to eat or drink after Lord Sezu's death. Since he was an elderly man, it must have taken only a few days for him to die. Absently she wondered who had presumed to appoint Jican hadonra in his stead. As she turned to follow one of the large halls that flanked a central garden, Nacoya said, 'My Lady, your quarters are across the garden.'

Mara barely managed another nod. Her personal belongings would all have been moved to her father's suite, the largest in the building.

She moved woodenly, passing the length of the square garden that stood at the heart of every Tsurani great house. The carved wooden grillework that enclosed the balcony walkways above, the flower beds, and the fountain under the trees in the courtyard seemed both familiar and inescapably strange after the stone architecture of the temples. Mara continued until she stood before the door to her father's quarters. Painted upon the screen was a battle scene, a legendary struggle won by the Acoma over another, long-forgotten, enemy. The hadonra, Jican, slid aside the door.

Mara faltered a moment. The jolt of seeing her own belongings in her father's room nearly overcame her control, as if this room itself had somehow betrayed her. And with that odd distress came the memory: the last time she had stepped over this threshold had been on the night she argued with her father. Though she was usually an even-tempered and obedient child, that one time her temper had matched his.

Mara moved woodenly forward. She stepped onto the slightly raised dais, sank down onto the cushions, and waved away the maids who waited upon her needs. Keyoke, Nacoya, and Jican then entered and bowed formally before her. Papewaio remained at the door, guarding the entrance from the garden.

In hoarse tones Mara said, 'I wish to rest. The journey was tiring. Leave now.' The maids left the room at once, but the three retainers all hesitated. Mara said, 'What is it?'

Nacoya answered, 'There is much to be done – much that may not wait, Mara-anni.'

The use of the diminutive of her name was intended in kindness, but to Mara it became a symbol of all she had lost. She bit her lip as the hadonra said, 'My Lady, many things have gone neglected since . . . your father's death. Many decisions must be made soon.'

Keyoke nodded. 'Lady, your upbringing is lacking for one who must rule a great house. You must learn those things we taught Lanokota.'

Miserable with memories of the rage she had exchanged with her father the night before she had left, Mara was stung by the reminder that her brother was no longer heir. Almost pleading, she said, 'Not now. Not yet.'

Nacoya said, 'Child, you must not fail your name. You –'

Mara's voice rose, thick with emotions held too long in check. 'I said not yet! I have not observed a time of mourning! I will hear you after I have been to the sacred grove.' The last was said with a draining away of anger, as if the little flash was all the energy she could muster. 'Please,' she added softly.

Ready to retire, Jican stepped back, absently plucking at his livery. He glanced at Keyoke and Nacoya, yet both of them held their ground. The Force Commander said, 'Lady, you must listen. Soon our enemies will move to destroy us. The Lord of the Minwanabi and the Lord of the Anasati both think House Acoma defeated. Neither should know you did not take final vows for a few days more, but we cannot be sure of that. Spies may already have carried word that you have returned; if so, your enemies are even now plotting to finish this house once and finally. Responsibilities cannot be put off. You must master a great deal in a short time if there is to be any hope of survival for the Acoma. The name and honour of your family are now in your hands.'

Mara tilted her chin in a manner unchanged from her childhood. She whispered, 'Leave me alone.'

Nacoya stepped to the dais. 'Child, listen to Keyoke. Our enemies are made bold by our loss, and you've no time for self-indulgence.

The education you once received to become the wife of some other household's son is inadequate for a Ruling Lady.'

Mara's voice rose, tension making the blood sing in her ears. 'I did not ask to be Ruling Lady!' Dangerously close to tears, she used anger to keep from breaking. 'Until a week ago, I was to be a sister of Lashima, all I wished for in this life! If the Acoma honour must rely upon me for revenge against the Minwanabi, if I need counsel and training, all will wait until I have visited the sacred grove and done reverence to the memories of the slain!'

Keyoke glanced at Nacoya, who nodded. The young Lady of the Acoma was near breaking, and must be deferred to, but the old nurse was ready to deal with even that. She said, 'All is prepared for you in the grove. I have presumed to choose your father's ceremonial sword to recall his spirit, and Lanokota's manhood robe to recall his.' Keyoke motioned to where the two objects lay atop a richly embroidered cushion.

Seeing the sword her father wore at festivals and the robe presented to her brother during his ceremony of manhood was more than the exhausted, grief-stricken girl could bear. With tears rising, she said, 'Leave me!'

The three hesitated, though to disobey the Lady of the Acoma was to risk punishment even unto death. The hadonra was first to turn and quit his mistress's quarters. Keyoke followed, but as Nacoya turned to go, she repeated, 'Child, all is ready in the grove.' Then slowly she slid the great door closed.

Alone at last, Mara allowed the tears to stream down her cheeks. Yet she held her sobbing in check as she rose and picked up the cushion with the sword and robe upon it.

The ceremony of mourning was a private thing; only family might enter the contemplation glade. But under more normal circumstances, a stately procession of servants and retainers would have marched with surviving family members as far as the blocking hedge before the entrance. Instead a single figure emerged from the rear door of her quarters. Mara carried the cushion gently, her white robe wrinkled and dirty where the hem dragged in the dust.

Even deaf and blind she would have remembered the way. Her feet knew the path, down to the last stone fisted into the gnarled ulo tree root beside the ceremonial gate. The thick hedge that surrounded the grove shielded it from observation. Only the Acoma might walk here, save a priest of Chochocan when consecrating the grove or the gardener who tended the shrubs and flowers. A blocking hedge faced the gate, preventing anyone outside from peering within.

Mara entered and hurried to the centre of the grove. There, amid a sculptured collection of sweet-blossomed fruit trees, a tiny stream flowed through the sacred pool. The rippled surface reflected the blue-green of the sky through curtains of overhanging branches. At water's edge a large rock sat embedded in the soil, worn smooth by ages of exposure to the elements; the shatra bird of the Acoma was once carved deeply on its surface, but now the crest was barely visible. This was the family's natami, the sacred rock that embodied the spirit of the Acoma. Should the day come when the Acoma were forced to flee these lands, this one most revered possession would be carried away and all who bore the name would die protecting it. For should the natami fall into the hands of any other, the family would be no more. Mara glanced at the far hedge. There three natami taken by Acoma ancestors were interred under a slab, inverted so their carved crests would never see sunlight again. Mara's forebears had obliterated three families in the Game of the Council. Now her own stood in peril of joining them.

Next to the stone a hole had been dug, the damp soil piled to one side. Mara placed the cushion with her father's sword and her brother's robe within. With bare hands she pushed the earth back into the hole, patting it down, unmindful as she soiled her white robe.

Then she sat back on her heels, caught by the sudden compulsion to laugh. A strange, detached giddiness washed over her and she felt alarm. Despite this being the appointed place, tears and pain so long held in check seemed unwilling to come.

She took a breath and stifled the laughter. Her mind flashed images and she felt hot flushes rush up her breasts, throat, and cheeks. The ceremony must continue, despite her strange feelings.

Beside the pool rested a small vial, a faintly smoking brazier, a tiny dagger, and a clean white gown. Mara lifted the vial and removed the stopper. She poured fragrant oils upon the pool, sending momentary shimmers of fractured light across its surface. Softly she said, 'Rest, my father. Rest, my brother. Come to your home soil and sleep with our ancestors.'

She laid the vial aside and with a jerk ripped open the bodice of her robe. Despite the heat, chill bumps roughened her small breasts as the breeze struck suddenly exposed, damp skin. She reached up and again ripped her gown, as ancient traditions were followed. With the second tear she cried out, a halfhearted sound, little better than a whimper. Tradition demanded the show of loss before her ancestors.

Again she tore her robe, ripping it from her left shoulder so it hung half to her waist. But the shout that followed held more anger at her loss than sorrow. With her left hand she reached up and tore her gown from her right shoulder. This time her sob was full-throated as pain erupted from the pit of her stomach.

Traditions whose origins were lost in time at last triggered a release. All the torment she had held in check came forth, rushing up from her groin through her stomach and chest to issue from her mouth as a scream. The sound of a wounded animal rang in the glade as Mara gave full vent to her anger, revulsion, torment and loss.

Shrieking with sorrow, nearly blinded with tears, she plunged her hand into the almost extinguished brazier. Ignoring the pain of the few hot cinders there, she smeared the ashes across her breasts and down her exposed stomach. This symbolized that her heart was ashes, and again sobs racked her body as her mind sought final release from the horror left by the murder of her father, brother, and hundreds of loyal warriors. Her left hand shot out and grabbed dirt from beside the natami. She smeared the damp soil in her hair and struck her head with her fist. She was one with Acoma soil, and to that soil she would return, as would the spirits of the slain.

Now she struck her thigh with her fist, chanting the words of mourning, almost unintelligible through her crying. Rocking back and forth upon her knees, she wailed in sorrow.

Then she seized the tiny metal dagger, a family heirloom of immense value, used only for this ceremony over the ages. She drew the blade from its sheath and cut herself across the left arm, the hot pain a counterpoint to the sick ache in her chest.

She held the small wound over the pool, letting drops of blood fall to mix with the water, as tradition dictated. Again she tore at her robe, ripping all but a few tatters from her body. Naked but for a loincloth, she cast the rags away with a strangled cry. Pulling her hair, forcing pain to cleanse her grief, she chanted ancient words, calling her ancestors to witness her bereavement. Then she threw herself across the fresh soil over the place of interment and rested her head upon the family natami.

With the ceremony now complete, Mara's grief flowed like the water streaming from the pool, carrying her tears and blood to the river, thence to the distant sea. As mourning eased away pain, the ceremony would eventually cleanse her, but now was the moment of private grief when tears and weeping brought no shame. And Mara descended into grief as wave after wave of sorrow issued from the deepest reservoir within her soul.

A sound intruded, a rustling of leaves as if someone moved through the tree branches above her. Caught up in grief, Mara barely noticed, even when a dark figure dropped to land next to her. Before she could open her eyes, powerful fingers yanked on her hair. Mara's head snapped back. Jolted by a terrible current of fear, she struggled, half glimpsing a man in black robes behind her. Then a blow to the face stunned her. Her hair was released and a cord was passed over her head. Instinctively she grabbed at it. Her fingers tangled in the loop that should have killed her in seconds, but as the man tightened the garrotte, her palm prevented the knot in the centre from crushing her windpipe. Still she couldn't breathe. Her attempt to shout for aid was stifled. She tried to roll away, but her assailant jerked upon the cord and held her firmly in check. A wrestler's kick learned from her brother earned her a mocking half-laugh, half-grunt. Despite her skill, Mara was no match for the assassin.

The cord tightened, cutting painfully into her hand and neck. Mara gasped for breath, but none came and her lungs burned. Struggling like a fish on a gill line, she felt the man haul her upright. Only her awkward grip on the cord kept her neck from breaking. Mara's ears sang from the pounding of her own blood within. She clawed helplessly with her free hand. Her fingers tangled in cloth. She yanked, but was too weak to overbalance the man. Through a roar like surf, she heard the man's laboured breathing as he lifted her off the ground. Then, defeated by lack of air, her spirit fell downwards into darkness.

2

Evaluations

Mara felt wetness upon her face.

Through the confusion of returning senses, she realized Papewaio was gently cradling her head in the crook of his arm as he moistened her face with a damp rag. Mara opened her mouth to speak, but her throat constricted. She coughed, then swallowed hard against the ache of injured neck muscles. She blinked, and struggled to organize her thoughts; but she knew only that her neck and throat hurt terribly and the sky above looked splendid beyond belief, its blue-green depths appearing to fade into the infinite. Then she moved her right hand; pain shot across her palm, jolting her to full memory.

Almost inaudibly she said, 'The assassin?'

Papewaio inclined his head toward something sprawled by the reflecting pool. 'Dead.'

Mara turned to look, ignoring the discomfort of her injuries. The corpse of the killer lay on one side, the fingers of one hand trailing in water discoloured with blood. He was short, reed-thin, of almost delicate build, and clad simply in a black robe and calf-length trousers. His hood and veil had been pulled aside, revealing a smooth, boyish face marked by a blue tattoo upon his left cheek – a hamoi flower stylized to six concentric circles of wavy lines. Both hands were dyed red to the wrists. Mara shuddered, still stinging from the violence of those hands upon her flesh.

Papewaio helped her to her feet. He tossed away the rag, torn from her rent garment, and handed her the white robe intended for the end of the ceremony. Mara clothed herself, ignoring the stains her injured hands made upon the delicately embroidered material. At her nod, Papewaio escorted her from the glade.

Mara followed the path, its familiarity no longer a comfort. The cruel bite of the stranger's cord had forced her to recognize that her enemies could reach even to the heart of the Acoma estates. The security of her childhood was forever gone. The dark hedges surrounding the glade now seemed a haven for assassins, and the shade beneath the wide limbs of the ulo tree carried a chill. Rubbing the bruised and bloody flesh of her right hand, Mara restrained an impulse to bolt in panic. Though terrified like a thyza bird at the shadow of a golden killwing as it circles above, she stepped through the ceremonial gate with some vestige of the decorum expected of the Ruling Lady of a great house.

Nacoya and Keyoke waited just outside, with the estate gardener and two of his assistants. None spoke but Keyoke, who said only, 'What?'

Papewaio replied with grim brevity. 'As you thought. An assassin waited. Hamoi tong.'

Nacoya extended her arms, gathering Mara into hands that had soothed her hurts since childhood, yet for the first time Mara found little reassurance. With a voice still croaking from her near strangulation, she said, 'Hamoi tong, Keyoke?'

'The Red Hands of the Flower Brotherhood, My Lady. Hired murderers of no clan, fanatics who believe to kill or be killed is to be sanctified by Turakamu, that death is the only prayer the god will hear. When they accept a commission they vow to kill their victims or die in the attempt.' He paused, while the gardener made an instinctive sign of protection: the Red God was feared. With a cynical note, Keyoke observed, 'Yet many in power understand that the Brotherhood will offer their unique prayer only when the tong has been paid a rich fee.' His voice fell to almost a mutter as he added, 'And the Hamoi are very accommodating as to whose soul shall offer that prayer to Turakamu.'

'Why had I not been told of these before?'

'They are not part of the normal worship of Turakamu, mistress. It is not the sort of thing fathers speak of to daughters who are not heirs.' Nacoya's voice implied reprimand.

Though it was now too late for recriminations, Mara said, 'I begin to see what you meant about needing to discuss many things right away.' Expecting to be led away, Mara began to turn toward her quarters. But the old woman held her; too shaken to question, Mara obeyed the cue to remain.

Papewaio stepped away from the others, then dropped to one

knee in the grass. The shadow of the ceremonial gate darkened his face, utterly hiding his expression as he drew his sword and reversed it, offering the weapon hilt first to Mara. 'Mistress, I beg leave to take my life with the blade.'

For a long moment Mara stared uncomprehendingly. 'What are you asking?'

'I have trespassed into the Acoma contemplation glade, my Lady.'

Overshadowed by the assassination attempt, the enormity of Papewaio's act had not registered upon Mara until this instant. He had entered the glade to save her, despite the knowledge that such a transgression would earn him a death sentence without appeal.

As Mara seemed unable to respond, Keyoke tried delicately to elaborate on Pape's appeal. 'You ordered Jican, Nacoya, and myself not to accompany you to the glade, Lady. Papewaio was not mentioned. He hid himself near the ceremonial gate; at the sound of a struggle he sent the gardener to fetch us, then entered.'

The Acoma Force Commander granted his companion a rare display of affection; for an instant the corners of his mouth turned up, as if he acknowledged victory after a difficult battle. Then his hint of a smile vanished. 'Each one of us knew such an attempt upon you was only a matter of time. It is unfortunate that the assassin chose this place; Pape knew the price of entering the glade.'

Keyoke's message to Mara was clear: Papewaio had affronted Mara's ancestors by entering the glade, earning himself a death sentence. But not to enter would have entailed a fate far worse. Had the last Acoma died, every man and woman Papewaio counted a friend would have become houseless persons, little better than slaves or outlaws. No warrior could do other than Papewaio had done; his life was pledged to Acoma honour. Keyoke was telling Mara that Pape had earned a warrior's death, upon the blade, for choosing life for his mistress and all those he loved at the cost of his own life. But the thought of the staunch warrior dying as a result of her own naïveté was too much for Mara. Reflexively she said, 'No.'

Assuming this to mean he was denied the right to die without shame, Papewaio bent his head. Black hair veiled his eyes as he flipped his sword, neatly, with no tremor in his hands, and drove the blade into the earth at his Lady's feet. Openly regretful, the gardener signalled his two assistants. Carrying rope, they hurried forward to Papewaio's side. One began to bind Papewaio's hands behind him while the other tossed a long coil of rope over a stout tree branch.

For a moment Mara was without comprehension, then understanding struck her: Papewaio was being readied for the meanest death, hanging, a form of execution reserved for criminals and slaves. Mara shook her head and raised her voice. 'Stop!'

Everyone ceased moving. The assistant gardeners paused with their hands half-raised, looking first to the head gardener, then to Nacoya and Keyoke, then to their mistress. They were clearly reluctant to carry out this duty, and confusion over their Lady's wishes greatly increased their discomfort.

Nacoya said, 'Child, it is the law.'

Gripped by an urge to scream at them all, Mara shut her eyes. The stress, her mourning, the assault, and now this rush to execute Papewaio for an act caused by her irresponsible behaviour came close to overwhelming her. Careful not to burst into tears, Mara answered firmly. 'No . . . I haven't decided.' She looked from face to impassive face and added, 'You will all wait until I do. Pape, take up your sword.'

Her command was a blatant flouting of tradition; Papewaio obeyed in silence. To the gardener, who stood fidgeting uneasily, she said, 'Remove the assassin's body from the glade.' With a sudden vicious urge to strike at something, she added, 'Strip it and hang it from a tree beside the road as a warning to any spies who may be near. Then cleanse the natami and drain the pool; both have been defiled. When all is returned to order, send word to the priests of Chochocan to come and reconsecrate the grove.'

Though all watched with unsettled eyes, Mara turned her back. Nacoya roused first. With a sharp click of her tongue, she escorted her young mistress into the cool quiet of the house. Papewaio and Keyoke looked on with troubled thoughts, while the gardener hurried off to obey his mistress's commands.

The two assistant gardeners coiled the ropes, exchanging glances. The ill luck of the Acoma had not ended with the father and the son, so it seemed. Mara's reign as Lady of the Acoma might indeed prove brief, for her enemies would not rest while she learned the complex subtleties of the Game of the Council. Still, the assistant gardeners seemed to silently agree, such matters were in the hands of the gods, and the humble in life were always carried along in the currents of the mighty as they rose and fell. None could say such a fate was cruel or unjust. It simply was.

The moment the Lady of the Acoma reached the solitude of her quarters, Nacoya took charge. She directed servants who bustled with subdued efficiency to make their mistress comfortable. They prepared a scented bath while Mara rested on cushions, absently fingering the finely embroidered shatra birds that symbolized her house. One who did not know her would have thought her stillness the result of trauma and grief; but Nacoya observed the focused intensity of the girl's dark eyes and was not fooled. Tense, angry, and determined, Mara already strove to assess the far-reaching political implications of the attack upon her person. She endured the ministrations of her maids without her usual restlessness, silent while the servants bathed her and dressed her wounds. A compress of herbs was bound around her bruised and lacerated right hand. Nacoya hovered anxiously by while Mara received a vigorous rub by two elderly women who had ministered to Lord Sezu in the same manner. Their old fingers were surprisingly strong; knots of muscular tension were sought out and gradually kneaded away. Afterward, clothed in clean robes, Mara still felt tired, but the attentions of the old women had eased away nervous exhaustion.

Nacoya brought chocha, steaming in a fine porcelain cup. Mara sat before a low stone table and sipped the bitter drink, wincing slightly as the liquid aggravated her bruised throat. In the grove she had been too shocked by the attack to feel much beyond a short burst of panic and fear. Now she was surprised to discover herself too wrung out to register any sort of reaction. The slanting light of afternoon brightened the paper screens over the windows, as it had throughout her girlhood. Far off, she could hear the whistles of the herdsmen in the needra meadows, and near at hand, Jican's voice reprimanding a house slave for clumsiness. Mara closed her eyes, almost able to imagine the soft scratch of the quill pen her father had used to draft instructions to distant subordinates; but Minwanabi treachery had ended such memories forever. Reluctantly Mara acknowledged the staid presence of Nacoya.

The old nurse seated herself on the other side of the table. Her movements were slow, her features careworn. The delicate seashell ornaments that pinned her braided hair were fastened slightly crooked, as reaching upwards to fix the pin correctly became more difficult with age. Although only a servant, Nacoya was well versed in the arts and subtlety of the Game of the Council. She had served at the right hand of Lord Sezu's lady for years, then raised his daughter after the wife's death in childbirth. The old nurse had been like a mother to Mara. Sharply aware that the old nurse was waiting for some comment, the girl said, 'I have made some grave errors, Nacoya.'

The nurse returned a curt nod. 'Yes, child. Had you granted time for preparation, the gardener would have inspected the grove immediately before you entered. He might have discovered the assassin, or been killed, but his disappearance would have alerted Keyoke, who could have had warriors surround the glade. The assassin would have been forced to come out or starve to death. Had the Hamoi murderer fled the gardener's approach and been lurking outside, your soldiers would have found his hiding place.' The nurse's hands tightened in her lap, and her tone turned harsh. 'Indeed, your enemy expected you to make mistakes . . . as you did.'

Mara accepted the reproof, her eyes following the lazy curls of steam that rose from her cup of chocha. 'But the one who sent the killer erred as much as I.'

'True.' Nacoya squinted, forcing farsighted vision to focus more clearly upon her mistress. 'He chose to deal the Acoma a triple dishonour by killing you in your family's sacred grove, and not honourably with the blade, but by strangulation, as if you were a criminal or slave to die in shame!'

Mara said, 'But as a woman –'

'You are Ruling Lady,' snapped Nacoya. Lacquered bracelets clashed as she thumped fists on her knee in a timeworn gesture of disapproval. 'From the moment you assumed supremacy in this house, child, you became as a man, with every right and privilege of rulership. You wield the powers your father did as Lord of the Acoma. And for this reason, your death by the strangler's cord would have visited as much shame on your family as if your father or brother had died in such fashion.'

Mara bit her lip, nodded, and dared another sip of her chocha. 'The third shame?'

'The Hamoi dog certainly intended to steal the Acoma natami, forever ending your family's name. Without clan or honour, your soldiers would have become grey warriors, outcasts living in the wilds. All of your servants would have finished their lives as slaves.' Nacoya ended in bitterness. 'Our Lord of the Minwanabi is arrogant.'

Mara placed her chocha cup neatly in the centre of the table. 'So you think Jingu responsible?'

'The man is drunk with his own power. He stands second only to the Warlord in the High Council now. Should fate remove Almecho from his throne of white and gold, a Minwanabi successor would assuredly follow. The only other enemy of your father's who would wish your ruin is the Lord of the Anasati. But he is far too clever to attempt such a shameful assault – so badly done. Had he sent the Hamoi murderer, his instructions would have been simple: your death by any means. A poison dart would have struck from hiding, or a quick blade between the ribs, then quickly away to carry word of your certain death.'

Nacoya nodded with finality, as if discussion had confirmed her convictions. 'No, our Lord of the Minwanabi may be the most powerful man in the High Council, but he is like an enraged harulth, smashing down trees to trample a gazen.' She raised spread fingers, framing the size of the timid little animal she had named. 'He inherited his position from a powerful father, and he has strong allies. The Lord of the Minwanabi is cunning, not intelligent.

'The Lord of the Anasati is both cunning and intelligent, one to be feared.' Nacoya made a weaving motion with her hand. 'He slithers like the relli in the swamp, silent, stealthy, and he strikes without warning. This murder was marked as if the Minwanabi lord had handed the assassin a warrant for your death with his own family chop affixed to the bottom.' Nacoya's eyes narrowed in thought. 'That he knows you're back this quickly speaks well of his spies. We assumed he would not find out you were Ruling Lady for a few more days. For the Hamoi to have been sent so soon shows he knew you had not taken vows from the instant Keyoke led you from the temple.' She shook her head in self-reproach. 'We should have assumed as much.'

Mara considered Nacoya's counsel, while her cup of chocha cooled slowly on the table. Aware of her new responsibilities as never before, she accepted that unpleasant subjects could no longer be put off. Though dark hair curled girlishly around her cheeks, and the robe with its ornate collar seemed too big for her, she straightened with the resolve of a ruler. 'I may seem like a gazen to the Lord of the Minwanabi, but now he has taught this eater of flowers to grow teeth for meat. Send for Keyoke and Papewaio.'

Her command roused the runner, a small, sandal-clad slave boy chosen for his fleetness; he sprang from his post by her doorway to carry word. The warriors arrived with little delay; both had anticipated her summons. Keyoke wore his ceremonial helm, the feather plumes denoting his office brushing the lintel of the doorway as he entered. Bare-headed, but nearly as tall, Papewaio followed his commander inside. He moved with the same grace and strength that had enabled him to strike down a killer only hours before; his manner betrayed not a single hint of concern over his unresolved fate. Struck by his proud carriage, and his more than usually impassive face, Mara felt the judgment she must complete was suddenly beyond her resources.

Her distress was in no way evident as the warriors knelt formally before her table. The green plumes of Keyoke's helm trembled in the air, close enough for Mara to touch. She repressed a shiver and gestured for the men to sit. Her maidservant offered hot chocha from the pot, but only Keyoke accepted. Papewaio shook his head once, as though he trusted his bearing better than his voice.

Mara said, 'I have erred. I will seek to avoid such error again –' She paused sharply, frowned, and made a nervous gesture that the sisters of Lashima had strived to eliminate. 'No,' said Mara, 'I must do better than that, for at the temple I learned that my impatience sometimes undoes my judgment. Keyoke, between us there must be a hand signal, to be used in times when my life, or the Acoma existence, may be threatened in ways I may not understand. Then perhaps the folly of this day's events may never be repeated.'

Keyoke nodded, his scarred face impassive, but his manner suggesting approval. After a moment of thought, he ran the knuckle of his index finger along an old scar that creased his jaw. 'Lady, would you recognize this gesure as such a warning, even in a crowded or public place?'

Mara nearly smiled. Keyoke had chosen a nervous habit of Papewaio's, his only outward sign of tension. Keyoke never fidgeted; through danger or stress, and even in battle, she supposed, her Force Commander never lost control. If he scratched a scar in her presence, she would notice, and hopefully take heed. 'Very good. So be it, Keyoke.'

A strained silence developed as Mara shifted her regard to the other warrior before her. 'My brave Pape, had I not erred in one instance, I would now be dead and all our holdings and retainers left without a mistress.' Wishing the moment of judgment could be delayed, the girl added, 'Had I but said let none follow me to the grove . . .' Her sentence trailed off, unfinished. All knew that her command would have been obeyed to the letter; duty would have compelled Papewaio to remain in the manor, leaving his mistress to fate's choices.

Mara said, 'Now one of my most valued retainers must forfeit his life for loyal and honourable service to his house.'

'Such is the law,' Keyoke observed, revealing no hint of sorrow or anger. Relieved that Mara had the strength to do her duty, his plumes of office stilled above his immobile features.

Mara sighed. 'I expect there is no other way.'

'None, child,' said Nacoya. 'You must specify the manner and time of Pape's death. You may allow him to fall upon his own sword, though, granting him a warrior's honour, to die by the blade. He deserves that, at least, mistress.'

Mara's dark eyes flashed; angry at having to waste such a stalwart servant, she knitted her brows in thought. Nothing was said for a time, then, abruptly, she announced, 'I think not.'

Keyoke seemed on the verge of speaking, then simply nodded, while Papewaio rubbed his jaw with one thumb, his familiar sign of distress. Shaken by the gesture, Mara continued quickly. 'My sentence is this: loyal Pape, that you will die is certain. But I shall decide the place and circumstance of that death in my own time. Until then you shall serve as you always have. Around your head wear the black rag of the condemned, that all may know I have pronounced death upon you.'

Papewaio nodded once. 'Your will, mistress.'

Mara added, 'And should fate cause my death before yours, you may fall upon your own blade . . . or seek to visit revenge upon my murderer, as you see fit.' She was certain which course Pape would choose. Now, until she selected the time and manner of execution, Papewaio would remain in her service.

Mara regarded her three most loyal followers, half-fearful her unorthodox judgment might be challenged. But duty and custom demanded unquestioned obedience, and no one met her glance. Hoping she had acted with honour, Mara said, 'Go now, and freely attend your duties.'

Keyoke and Papewaio rose at once. They bowed with stiff-backed formality, turned, and departed. Old and slow of movement, Nacoya performed her obeisance with less grace. She straightened, a hint of approval on her wizened face. 'That was well done, daughter of Sezu,' she whispered. 'You save Pape's honour and preserve a most loyal servant. He will wear the black rag of shame as if it were a badge of honour.' Then, as if embarrassed by her boldness, the old nurse left hastily.

The house servant who hovered by the door had to speak twice before Mara noticed her. 'As my mistress needs?'

Wrung out by the emotions and tensions of the afternoon, the Lady of the Acoma looked up. By the expectant look on the servant's face, she realized the afternoon had passed. Blue shadows dappled the door screens, lending a moody, sombre air to the decorative paintings of huntsmen. Longing for the simplicity of her girlhood, Mara decided to forego the formality of the evening meal. Tomorrow was soon enough to face the fact that she must sit in her father's place at the head of the table. She said to the maidservant, 'Let the evening breezes in, then withdraw.'

The servant hastened to obey her wishes and slid open the large outer screens that faced the west. The orange sun hung low, kissing the purple edge of the horizon. Red-gold light burnished the marshes where the shatra birds flocked at eventide. Even as Mara watched, the ungainly creatures exploded into flight. Within minutes the sky was covered with silhouettes of grace and elegance, whirling across clouds fired with scarlet and pink, and indigo before the approach of night. No man understood the reason for this splendid group dance upon the wing, but the sight was majestic. Though Mara had watched the display a thousand times through girlhood, the birds still took her breath away. She did not notice the tiptoe departure of the maidservant but for the better part of an hour sat absorbed as flocks numbering in the thousands gathered to wheel and turn, bank and glide, while the light slowly faded. The birds landed as the sun vanished. In the silvery twilight they gathered in the marshes, clustered tightly to baffle predators while they slept.

House servants returned in the warm, sweet hour of nightfall, bringing oil for the lamps and hot herb tea. But exhaustion had overtaken Mara at last. They found her asleep amid her cushions, lulled by the familiar sounds of herders driving the needra into shelter. In the distance the sad song of a kitchen slave kneading thyza bread for the morning meal was a soft counterpoint to the faint calls of Keyoke's sentries as they patrolled the grounds to ensure the safety of Acoma's newest Lady.

Accustomed to temple discipline, Mara awoke early. She blinked, at first confused by her surroundings; then the rich coverlet thrown over her sleeping mat reminded her: she lay in her father's chamber as Ruling Lady of the Acoma. Rested, but still aching from the bruises left by the Minwanabi assassin, she rolled on her side. Luxuriant strands of hair caught in her lashes; impatiently she pushed them away.

Dawn brightened the screens that faced east. The whistle of a herder driving needra to pasture cut through daybreak's chorus of bird calls. Made restless by memories, Mara arose.

Her maids did not hear her stir. Barefoot, and appreciative of the solitude, the girl crossed the chamber and slipped the catch on the screen. She slid it aside with the barest of squeaks. Cool air caressed her skin between the loose folds of her robe. Mara drew in the scent of dew, and moist earth, and the delicate perfume of akasi flowers. Mist rose off the marshlands, rendering the trees and hedges in tones of charcoal, and there the lone silhouette of a herdsman driving the slow-moving needra.

The soldier at his post in the dooryard turned about on his beat, and realized the girl who stood in the white shift and sleep-tangled hair was his ruling mistress. He bowed gravely. Mara nodded absently as he returned to his duty. The girl regarded the wide expanse of her family estates, in a morning as yet unmarred by the noise and bustle of the day. Shortly all who worked upon the estate would be busy about their tasks, and for only a few minutes longer would Mara have this serene glimpse of what was now hers to protect. Her brows knitted in concern as she realized how much she had to learn to manage these holdings. At present she didn't even know the extent of her inheritance. She knew vaguely that she had properties in other provinces, but she had no knowledge of their disposition and worth. Her father had disliked the details of farming and stock breeding, and while he had overseen his assets and his people's well-being with wisdom, his conversations with Mara had always been turned to matters of his liking, and of a lighter nature.

When the maid called softly from the doorway of the chamber, Mara shut the screen. 'I shall dress and breakfast at once,' she instructed. 'Then I will see this new hadonra, Jican, in the study.'

The maid bowed and hastened to the wardrobe, while Mara shook the tangles from her hair. Denied the comfort of servants in the temple, Mara reached automatically for her brush.

'My Lady, don't I please you?' The young maid's bearing revealed distress.

Mara frowned, annoyed by her thoughtless lapse. 'You please me well enough.' She surrendered the hairbrush and sat still as the serving girl began to tend her hair. As the maid worked, Mara conceded to herself that her decision to see Jican was as much to avoid Nacoya as to learn more of her estates. The old nurse had a natural tendency to be grumpy in the early morning. And beyond her normal ill temper, Nacoya would have volumes to say to the young girl on her responsibilities as Ruling Lady.

Mara sighed, and the maid paused, waiting for some indication from her Lady if there was a problem. When Mara said nothing, the girl continued, tentatively, as if fearing her Lady's disapproval. Mara mulled over questions for Jican, knowing that eventually she would have to contend with Nacoya's scolding manner. Again she sighed, much as she had when facing one of Nacoya's punishments for some girlish prank, and again the maid halted to see if her mistress was displeased. After a momentary pause, the girl resumed arranging her mistress's hair, and Mara became caught up in the questions of estate management.

Later, dressed and groomed, Mara sat with her elbow propped in a mound of cushions. Her lip was pinched between her teeth in concentration as she reviewed the latest of a sizeable heap of scrolls. Small, sun-bronzed, and nervous as a thyza bird, the hadonra,

Jican, looked over her shoulder. Presently he extended a tentative finger.

'The profits are listed there, my Lady. As you note, they are respectable.'

'I see that, Jican.' Mara laid the scroll on her knees as Nacoya ducked her head around the door. 'I am busy, Nacoya. I will see you shortly, perhaps at noon.'

The old nurse shook her head, her hairpins as crooked as ever. 'By my lady's leave, it is now an hour past noon.'

Mara raised her brows in surprise. She sympathized with her father's impatience with the management of his far-flung holdings. The task was more involved than she had suspected. Yet, unlike her father, she found the intricacies of finance fascinating. With a rueful smile at Nacoya's impatience, the Lady of the Acoma said, 'I lost track of time. But Jican is nearly finished. You may wait if you wish.'

Nacoya jerked her head in the negative. 'Too much to do, Lady. Send your runner for me when you are ready. But do not delay much longer. Decisions must be made, and tomorrow is too late to consider them.'

The nurse departed. Mara heard her pause to mutter to Keyoke, standing guard in the hallway beyond. Then, drawn back to Jican and her lesson in commerce, Mara reached for another scroll. This time she commented on the balance, without the hadonra's needing to prompt. 'We may lack warriors, Jican, but we are strong in property, perhaps even prosperous.'

'It is not difficult, mistress. Sotamu left clear records of the years he served your father. I but follow his example. Thyza crops have been bountiful for three years, while the hwaet blight in the plains provinces has driven high the prices of all grain – thyza, ryge, maza, even milat. With hwaet scarce, only a lazy manager carts his thyza to Sulan-Qu and sells it there. It takes only a little more effort to deal with a factor from a consortium of grain shippers in the City of the Plains.' The small man sighed in discomfort. 'My Lady, I mean no disrespect to any of your lofty class, but I have known many powerful lords to dislike the details of business. Yet at the same time they refuse their hadonras and factors the authority to act independently. Therefore we have traded with large houses and avoided the merchants of the city whenever we might. This has left us large profits more often than not.'

The hadonra paused, hands spread diffidently before him. Then, encouraged by the fact that Mara did not interrupt, he went on. 'And the breeders . . . they are a mystery. Again I mean no disrespect, but the lords of the north seem especially shortsighted concerning choice of breeding bulls.' More at ease, the little man shrugged in perplexity. 'A bull that is ill-tempered and difficult to manage, but that is heavily muscled and paws the ground in fierce display, or with a large' – he lowered his eyes in embarrassment – 'ah, male member sells better than a fat one that will breed good meat animals, or a docile one that begets solid draught stock. So animals a cannier man might have castrated or slaughtered bring prime prices, while the best remain here, and people wonder at the quality of our herds. They say "How can the Acoma meat taste so good, when they keep such weak bulls?" I do not understand such thinking.'

Mara smiled slightly, the first relaxed expression she had shown since leaving the temple. 'Those noble lords seek animals that reflect upon their own virility. I have no such need. And as I have no desire to be mistaken for any of my breeding stock, you may continue to select which cows and bulls to sell without regard for how their traits match up to mine.' Jican's eyes opened wide for an instant before he realized the girl was making a joke. He laughed slightly with her. Mara added, 'You have done well.'

The man smiled his thanks, as if a great weight had been lifted from him. Plainly he enjoyed the responsibilities of his new office and had feared his new mistress might remove him. He was doubly pleased to discover not only that he would continue as hadonra, but that Lady Mara recognized his worth.

But Mara had inherited her father's instinct for governance, even if it was only just beginning to emerge, and knew she had a competent, perhaps even gifted, estate manager beside her. 'Your diligence in business brings honour to the Acoma as much as our soldiers' bravery,' she finished. 'You may leave now, and attend your duties.'

The hadonra bowed from a kneeling position until his forehead touched the floor, an obeisance more abject than required from a man in his position. 'I bask in the sunlight of my mistress's praise.'

Jican rose and departed as a house servant came forward to gather the scrolls from the floor. Nacoya hurried through the doorway as the hadonra passed by. More servants followed at her heels with trays of refreshments, and with a sigh, Mara wished her overly abundant domestic staff could be transformed into soldiers.

Nacoya bowed, then sat before Mara had a chance to grant her leave. Over the soft clink of the serving ware and the bustle of servants setting down trays, she said, 'Does my Lady think she should work all morning and take no meals?' Her old, dark eyes turned critical. 'You've lost weight since you left for the temple. Some men might think you scrawny.'

Still preoccupied with her discussion with Jican, Mara spoke as though she had not heard. 'I have undertaken to learn of my estates and properties. You chose with care in selecting this Jican, Nacoya. Though I remember Sotamu with affection, this man seems a master of commerce.'

Nacoya's manner softened. 'I presumed much, mistress, but decisiveness was necessary at the time.'

'You did well.' Mara regarded the array of food, the odour of fresh thyza bread wakening her awareness of hunger. She reached for a slice, frowned, then added, 'And I'm not scrawny. Our meals at the temple were not so plain as you think.' She took a bite, chewing thoughtfully. She regarded her indomitable nurse. 'Now, what must we do?'

Nacoya pursed her lips, a sure sign that she broached what she guessed to be a difficult subject. 'We must move quickly to strengthen your house, Lady. Without blood family, you make a tempting target for many. Even those with no prior cause for strife with the Acoma might look upon your holdings with an envious and ambitious eye. Land and herds might not tempt a minor lord to move against your father, but against a young girl with no training? "There is a hand behind every curtain," ' she quoted.

' "And a knife in every hand," ' finished Mara. She set her bread aside. 'I understand, Nacoya. I have thought that we must send for recruits.'

Nacoya shook her head with such sharpness that her precariously pinned hair threatened to come loose. 'That is a difficult and dangerous proposition to attempt at this time.'

'Why?' Mara had forgotten the food in her annoyance. 'I just reviewed assets with Jican. The Acoma have more than enough wealth to support twenty-five hundred soldiers. We even have enough to pay recruiting fees.'

But Nacoya had not been referring to the fact a new master must indemnify the former master for each recruit's training. Gently she reminded, 'Too many have died, Mara-anni. The family ties that remain are too few to matter.' Tsurani tradition required that only a relative of a soldier already serving could join a household's garrison. As eldest sons tended to assume the same loyalties as their fathers, such recruits were further limited to second or later sons. Bearing these facts in mind, Nacoya added, 'With the heavy recruiting your father undertook prior to the invasion of the barbarian world, most of the able men have already been called. Any you found now would be young and unseasoned. The Lord of the Minwanabi will act before such as those would prove any benefit.'

'I have given that some thought.' Mara reached under the writing table before her and removed a case, delicately carved of costly hardwoods. 'I sent to the Guild of Porters this morning. The representative who arrives will be told to give this into the hand of the Lord of the Minwanabi, under bond and without message.' Grim now, Mara handed the box to Nacoya.

Nacoya opened the finely crafted catch and raised an eyebrow at what rested within. A single red cord, darkened with blood from Mara's hand, lay coiled next to a shatra feather. Closing the box as though it contained a scarlet dhast, the most venomous of serpents, Nacoya said, 'You openly announce blood feud with House Minwanabi.'

'I only acknowledge a feud begun ages ago!' Mara shot back, the murder of her father and brother too near yet for temperance. 'I am only telling Jingu that another generation of Acoma stands ready to oppose him.' Embarrassed suddenly by her emotions, the girl stared at the food tray. 'Mother of my heart, I am inexperienced in the Game of the Council, but I remember many nights when father discussed with Lano those things he plotted, teaching a son each move, and the reason for it. His daughter listened as well.'

Nacoya set the box aside and nodded. Mara looked up, sweating lightly in the heat, but composed. 'Our enemy the Minwanabi will think this represents something more subtle than it does. He will seek to parry whatever move he thinks we plot, giving us the chance to plan. All I can do now is hope to gain us time.'

Nacoya was silent, then said, 'Daughter of my heart, your boldness is admirable, yet while this gesture may gain you a day, a week, even more, in the end the Lord of the Minwanabi will move to obliterate all things Acoma.' The old nurse leaned forward, insistent. 'You must find allies, and for that, only one course remains open to you. You must marry. Quickly.'

Mara shot erect so abruptly that her knee banged the leg of the writing table. 'No!' A strained silence developed, while a dislodged parchment floated in her soup dish.

Nacoya brusquely disregarded her mistress's temper. 'You have no other choice, child. As Ruling Lady you must seek out a consort from among the younger sons of certain houses in the Empire. A marriage with a son of the Shinzawai, the Tukareg, or the Chochapan would gain an alliance with a house able to protect us.' She fell silent a moment, then said, 'For as long as any could. Still, time might tip the balance.'

Mara's cheeks flushed, and her eyes widened. 'I've never seen any of the boys you have named. I will not wed a stranger!'

Nacoya stood. 'You speak now from anger, and your heart rules your mind. Had you never entered the temple, your husband would have been selected from those found acceptable by your father or your brother after him. As Lady of the Acoma, you must do as much for the sake of your house. I leave you to think upon this.'

The nurse wrapped old fingers around the box to be delivered by the Porters' Guild to the Lord of the Minwanabi. She bowed stiffly and left.

Mara sat in silent rage, eyes fixed unseeing upon the soaked parchment, which slowly sank in the depths of the soup bowl. The thought of marriage evoked nameless fears, rooted somehow in her grief. She shivered, though the day was hot, and snapped her fingers for servants to remove the food trays. She would rest, and contemplate alone upon what her aged nurse had instructed.

Upon Keyoke's recommendation, Mara remained within the estate house throughout the afternoon. Although she would have preferred to continue her review of the Acoma holdings by litter, her warriors were too depleted; a retinue would be needed to ensure her safety in the open, leaving fewer guards available for routine patrols. Too conscientious to remain idle, the girl studied documents, to acquire further familiarity with the more distant assets of her family. She called for a light meal. The shadows lengthened, and the heat of the afternoon settled into stillness.

In the course of her reading, the Lady of the Acoma had come to understand a subtle but important fact of Tsurani life, one emphasized often by her father but only now appreciated: honour and tradition were but two walls of a great house; power and wealth comprised the other two. And of the four, it was the latter pair that kept the roof from collapsing. Mara clenched her fist against the handle of the scroll. If somehow she could keep those enemies who sought her death at bay, until she could muster the strength to enter the Game of the Council, then . . . She abandoned the thought unfinished. Keeping the Lords of the Minwanabi and Anasati at bay was the problem at hand. Vengeance was a useless dream unless she could secure her family's survival.

Deep in thought, Mara did not hear Nacoya call softly from the doorway. 'Mistress?' the nurse repeated.

Mara glanced up, startled, and motioned the old nurse inside. She waited, preoccupied and aloof, while the old woman bowed, then knelt before her.

'Lady, I have thought upon our talk this afternoon, and I beg your tolerance as I advise.'

Mara's eyes narrowed. She had no desire to resume their earlier discussion of marriage, but the lingering ache of the assassin's bruises reminded her of the need for prudence. She laid her scrolls aside and gestured for Nacoya to continue. 'As Ruling Lady of the Acoma, your status would not change with marriage. A husband might sit at your right hand, but he would have no voice in house matters, save that which you permit. He –'

Mara waved her hand. 'These things I know.'

The old nurse settled more comfortably upon the mat before her mistress. 'Your forgiveness, Lady. When I spoke earlier, I had forgotten that to a maiden of Lashima the concerns of the world beyond the temple walls would fade from mind. Matters between boys and girls, the meetings with the sons of noble houses, the kissing and the touching games – these things were denied you the past year and more. The thought of men . . .' Unnerved by the growing intensity of Mara's stillness, Nacoya faltered, but forcibly finished. 'Forgive an old woman's rambling. You were a maiden – and still are.'

That statement caused Mara to blush. During her time at the temple, she had been instructed to put things of the flesh aside. Nacoya's concern that the girl might be unable to deal with this question was unfounded, for within Mara the struggle to forget had been difficult. She had often caught herself daydreaming of boys she had known during childhood.

Mara rubbed nervously at the bandage that covered her injured palm. 'Mother of my heart, I am still a maiden. But I understand what is between a man and a woman.' Abruptly, as if piqued, she formed a circle with thumb and forefinger of her left hand and inserted her right forefinger with a thrusting motion. Herdsmen, farmers, and soldiers used such a mime to indicate fornication. While not obscene – sex was an unselfconscious fact of Tsurani life – her gesture was common and ill became the Lady of a great house.

Too wise to rise to such provocation, Nacoya said, 'Mistress, I know you played with your brother among soldiers and herdsmen. I know you have seen the bulls mount the cows. And more.' Given the close proximity of Tsurani living, many times over the years Mara and her brother had been within earshot of passion, or occasionally had blundered upon an encounter between slaves or servants.

She shrugged, as if the matter were of little account.

'Child, you understand what passes between men and women, here.' The nurse raised a forefinger to her own head. Then she pointed to her heart. 'But you do not understand here,' and she pointed toward her groin, 'or here. I may be old, but I remember.

'Mara-anni, a Ruling Lady is also a warrior. You must master your body. Pain must be conquered.' The nurse grew reflective with remembrance. 'And at times passion is more pain than any sword wound.' Low sunlight through the screen underscored the firmness of her features as she focused once more upon Mara. 'Until you learn your own body, and master its every need, you are vulnerable. Your strengths, or your weaknesses, are those of House Acoma. A handsome man who whispers sweetly in your ears, whose touch rouses fire in your loins, might destroy you as easily as the Hamoi tong.'

Mara flushed deeply, her eyes ablaze. 'What are you suggesting?'

'A Ruling Lady must be free of doubt,' Nacoya said. 'After your mother's death, Lord Sezu took steps to ensure that the desires of the flesh would not tempt him to act foolishly. Lust for the daughter of the wrong house could have destroyed the Acoma as surely as if he had lost a battle.

'While you were at the temple, he had women of the Reed Life brought to this house –'

'Nacoya, he had such women stay here when I was younger. I remember.' Mara drew breath impatiently and, by the heavy scent of akasi, realized that slaves were trimming the gardens beyond the screens.

But the cloying air seemingly had no effect upon Nacoya. 'Lord Sezu did not always act for himself, Mara-anni. Sometimes the women came for Lanokota, that he might learn the ways of man and woman, and not fall prey to the ambitions of wily daughters and their fathers' plots.'

The idea of her brother with such women unexpectedly offended Mara; yet the proximity of slaves forced her to maintain propriety. 'So, again I say what do you suggest?'

'I will send for a man of the Reed Life, one skilled in –'

'No!' Mara cut her off. 'I will not hear this!'

Nacoya ignored her mistress. '– ways of pleasure. He can teach –'

'I said no, Nacoya!'

'– all you need to know, that soft touches and sweet words whispered in the dark will not beguile you.'

Mara verged upon outright rage. 'I command you: say no more!'

Nacoya bit back her next words. The two women locked eyes and for a long, silent minute neither moved. At last the old nurse bowed her head until her forehead touched the mats upon which she knelt, a slave's sign of supplication. 'I am ashamed. I have given offence to my mistress.'

'Go! Leave me!'

The old woman rose, the rustle of her clothing and her stiff old back reflecting disapproval as she departed. Mara waved away the servant who appeared to inquire after her needs. Alone, surrounded by the mannered and beautifully calligraphed scrolls that honourably masked what actually constituted a cruel and deadly mesh of intrigue, Mara attempted to sort out the confusion created by Nacoya's suggestion. She could put no name to the fear that rose up to engulf her.

Holding herself, Mara sobbed silently. Bereft of her brother's comfort, surrounded by conspiracy, threat, and the unseen presence of enemies, the Lady of the Acoma bent her head, while tears soaked the bandage on her hand, stinging the scabs underneath.

A bell chimed faintly. Mara recognized the signal for the slaves to gather at their quarters for the evening meal. The workers who attended the akasi gardens rose and set aside their tools, while behind thin paper screens their mistress pushed aside her scrolls. She daubed at tear-swollen eyes, and softly called for servants to open the study and let in the outdoor air.

She rose then, feeling empty and wrung out; but the firm set had returned to her mouth. Thoughtfully biting her lip, the girl rested against the polished frame of the screen. Another solution besides marriage must exist. She pondered, but saw no answer, while the sun lowered, heavy and gold, in the western sky. Heat haze hung over the distant fields, and overhead the green-blue bowl of the sky was empty of birds. Akasi leaves pruned by the workers wilted upon the white stone walk, adding fragrance to the sleepy silence around the estate house. Mara yawned, worn out from grief and worry.

Suddenly she heard shouts. Shocked alert, she straightened. Running figures sped along the road towards the guards' barracks. Aware such disturbance must bode bad tidings, the girl turned from the screen, just as a serving girl rushed into the study.

A warrior strode at her heels, dusty, sweating, and breathing hard from what amounted to a long run in battle armour. He bowed his head in respect. 'Mistress, by your leave.'

Mara felt a knot of cold tighten her stomach. Already it begins, she thought to herself. Yet her tearstained face showed poise as she said, 'Speak.'

The soldier slapped his fist over his heart in salute. 'Mistress, the Force Commander sends word: outlaws have raided the herd.'

'Send for my litter. Quickly!'

'Your will, mistress.' The maidservant who had preceded the soldier ducked through the doorway at a run.

To the warrior, Mara said, 'Assemble an escort.'

The man bowed and departed. Mara unwrapped the light, short

robe Tsurani noblewomen preferred to wear in the privacy of their homes. She tossed the garment into the waiting hands of one attendant, while another rushed forward with a travelling robe, longer and more modest in cut. Adding a light scarf to hide the unhealed marks on her neck, Mara stepped outside.

Her litter bearers waited silently, stripped to loincloths and sweating in the heat. Four warriors waited with them, hastily fastening helmets and adjusting weapons at their belts. The soldier sent to inform Mara deferentially offered his hand and aided his mistress into the cushioned seat. Then he signalled bearers and escort. The litter swayed and jolted forward as the bearers complied with the need for haste and hurried towards the outer pastures.

The journey ended far sooner than Mara expected, miles inside the borders of the estate. This was a discouraging sign, since bandits would never dare to raid the inner fields if the patrols had been up to strength. With a motion made brisk by outrage, the girl whisked aside gauze curtains. 'What has passed here?'

Keyoke turned away from two soldiers who were studying the ground for tracks that might indicate the numbers and strength of the renegades. If he noticed her tearstained face, his own leathery features showed no reaction. Imposing in his lacquer armour, his plumed helm dangling by its strap from his belt, he gestured towards a line of broken fencing, which slaves in loincloths laboured to repair. 'Outlaws, my Lady. Ten, or perhaps a dozen. They killed a herd boy, smashed through the fence, and drove off some needra.'

'How many?' Mara gestured, and the Force Commander helped her from the litter. Grass felt strange under her sandals after temple confinement and months of echoing stone floors; also unexpected were the smells of rich earth and khala vines, which twined the fence rows. Mara pushed aside her momentary distraction and greeted Jican's presence with a frown the image of her father's when domestic affairs went amiss.

Though the hadonra had had little contact with the former Lord of the Acoma, that look was legend. Sweating, fingers clenched nervously to his tally slate, he bowed. 'Lady, at most you have lost three or four cows. I can report for certain when the strays are rounded up.'

Mara raised her voice over the bawl of agitated animals as

herders whistled, their long steering sticks and hide whips singing through the air as they drove their charges to a secure corral. 'Strays?'

Cross with Jican's diffidence, Keyoke answered, his tone better suited to the battlefield on the barbarian world than the trampled earth of a needra meadow. 'The beasts in this pasture were due for breeding. The smell of blood startled them into stampede, which alerted the herders.' He paused, eyes raking the distant line of the woods.

The tautness in his manner sharpened Mara's concern. 'What troubles you, Keyoke? Surely not the loss of a few cows, or one murdered slave?'

'No, Lady.' Eyes still on the woods, the old soldier shook his head. 'I regret the ruin of good property, but no, the cows and the boy are the lesser problem.' He paused while an overseer shouted; the team of slaves bent to raise a new post, while the Force Commander related the worst. 'We have been vigilant since the Hamoi dog sought your life, mistress. These were no petty thieves. They struck, and departed, during daylight, which speaks of advance planning and a thorough knowledge of patrols.'

Mara felt fear like a sliver of ice. Carefully steady, she said, 'Spies?' The Lord of the Anasati would not be above staging a false raid by 'bandits' if he wished to gauge the strength of the Acoma forces.

Keyoke fingered his sword. 'I think not, mistress.' He qualified this with his usual almost uncanny perception. 'Minwanabi is never so subtle, and the Anasati have no outposts far enough south to have organized an attack so swiftly. No, this seems the work of soldiers, masterless ones surely.'

'Grey warriors?' Mara's frown deepened as she considered the rough, clanless men who often banded together in the mountains. With the Acoma so severely undermanned, such as these under the guidance of a shrewd commander might prove as menacing as any plot by enemies.

Keyoke slapped dust from his cuffs and again regarded the hills, deepening now under shadow of dusk. 'With my Lady's permission, I would send out scouts. If grey warriors were responsible for this raid, they sought only to fill their bellies. There will be smoke, and cook fires; or if there are not, we know that word of our weakness travels swiftly to enemy ears.'

He did not mention counterattack. As guardedly subtle as Nacoya was not, his silence on the subject informed Mara that an open show of force might precipitate disaster. Acoma warriors were too few, even to drive out an enclave of needra thieves. How far the Acoma have fallen, Mara thought; but she gave the formal gesture of acquiescence. Keyoke hastened to command his soldiers. The litter bearers straightened in readiness, anxious for a swift return to the dinners they had left cooling on the tables at quarters; but the Lady was not ready to depart. While she knew Nacoya would have scolded her for lingering where her presence was not required, the urgent need for new fighting men seemed the root of immediate threat. Still resisting the idea of marriage as the only solution, she waved Keyoke back to her side.

He bowed, his face shadowed in twilight. 'Night comes, mistress. If you wish counsel, let me walk as your escort, for your safety might be in jeopardy after dark.'

Warmed by the same qualities Lord Sezu had prized in his Force Commander, Mara smiled. She permitted the old warrior to settle her into the litter, then addressed the problem at hand. 'Have you begun recruiting more warriors?'

Keyoke ordered the litter bearers forward, then matched his pace with theirs. 'My Lady, two of the men have contacted cousins in distant cities, asking for younger sons to be sent to your service. In a week or two, I will permit one or two more to do the same. Much more than that and every barracks from Ambolina to Dustari will know the Acoma lack strength.'

Lights bloomed in the shadows as the workers at the fence lit lanterns to continue their labour. As the Lady's litter turned towards the estate house, one man, then another, then more began tentatively to sing. Mindful that their security relied upon her judgment, Mara said, 'Should we buy contracts?'

Keyoke halted. 'Mercenaries? Common caravan guards?' In a stride he closed the distance the bearers had opened. 'Impossible. They wouldn't be dependable. Men who have no blood vows to the Acoma natami would be worse than useless. They owe you no honour. Against the enemies of your father, you need warriors who will obey without hesitation, even die at your order. Show me a man who will die for pay, and I'll swear to service. No, Lady, a house hires mercenaries only for simple tasks, like guarding warehouses, or patrolling against common thieves. And that is done only to free warriors for more honourable duty.'

'Then we need mercenaries,' Mara said. 'If only to keep grey warriors from growing fat on our needra.'

Keyoke unhooked his helm, fingering the plumes in the growing dark. 'My Lady, in better times, yes. But not now. Half the men you hired would likely be spies. Though I am loath to yield honour to masterless men, we must wait, and replenish our ranks slowly.'

'And die.' Unreconciled to the fact that Nacoya's suggestion of marriage seemed more and more inevitable, Mara set her teeth in bitterness.

Startled by her mood, one he had never known in the girl before, Keyoke stopped the litter bearers. 'My Lady?'

'How long before my Lord of the Minwanabi learns of the extent of the damage done us by his treachery?' Mara lifted her head, her face a pale oval between the white fall of the curtains. 'Sooner or later one of his spies will discover the heart of our house is weak, my own estates stripped of all but a handful of healthy warriors as we maintain the illusion of sufficiency. Our distant holdings are stripped bare, held by a ruse – old men and untrained boys parading in armour. We live like gazen, holding our breath and hoping the harulth will not trample us! But that hope is false. Any day now our act will be discovered. Then the Lords who seek our ruin will strike with brute force.'

Keyoke set his helm on his head, fingers slowly and deliberately fastening the strap beneath his chin. 'Your soldiers will die defending you, my Lady.'

'My point, Keyoke.' Once started, Mara could not stifle the hopeless, trapped feelings that welled up within her. 'They will all die. As will you and Pape, and even old Nacoya. Then the enemies who murdered my father and brother will take my head and the Acoma natami to the Lord of the Minwanabi and . . . the Acoma will be no more.'

The old soldier lowered his hands in silence. He could not refute his mistress's word or offer her any sort of comfort. Gently he ordered the bearers forward, towards the estate house, and lights, and the solace of beauty and art that was the heart of Acoma heritage.

The litter rocked as the slaves stepped from the rough meadow onto the raked gravel path. Shamed by her outburst, Mara loosed the ties, and gauze curtains fluttered down, enclosing her from view. Sensitive to the possibility she might be weeping, Keyoke walked with his head turned correctly forward. Survival with honour seemed an unattainable hope since the death of Lord Sezu and his son. Yet for the sake of the mistress whose life he guarded, he resisted the belief held by the warriors who still lived: that the gods' displeasure rested upon this house, and the Acoma fortune was irretrievably on the wane.

Mara spoke, jarring the Force Commander from thought with an unexpected tone of resolve. 'Keyoke, were I to die, and you survive me, what then?'

Keyoke gestured backward, towards the hills where the raiders had retired with their booty. 'Without your leave to take my own life, I would be as those, mistress. A wanderer, masterless and alone, without purpose and identity, a grey warrior with no house colour to wear.'

Mara pushed a hand through the curtain, forming a small crack to peer through. 'The bandits are all like this?'

'Some. Others are petty criminals, some thieves and robbers, a few murderers, but many are soldiers who have lived longer than their masters.'

The litter drew near the dooryard of the estate house, where Nacoya awaited with a small flock of servants. Mara pressed on quickly. 'Honourable men, Keyoke?'

The Force Commander regarded his mistress with no hint of reproof. 'A soldier without a house can have no honour, mistress. Before their masters fell? I assume grey warriors were good men once, but to outlive one's master is a mark of the gods' displeasure.'

The litter swept into the dooryard, and the bearers settled it to the ground with a barely perceptible bump. Mara pushed aside the curtains and accepted Keyoke's assistance. 'Force Commander, come to my quarters tonight, after your scouts return from the hills. I have a plan to discuss while the rest of the household sleeps.'

'As you will, mistress.' Keyoke bowed, fist pressed to his heart in formal salute. But as servants rushed forward with lanterns, Mara thought she caught a hint of approval on the warrior's scarred face.

Mara's meeting with Keyoke extended deep into the night. The stars glinted like ice. Kelewan's moon showed a notched, copper-gold profile at the zenith by the time the old warrior gathered up the helmet that rested by his knee. 'My Lady, your plan is dangerously bold. But, as a man does not expect aggression from the gazen, it may work.'

'It must work!' Mara straightened in the darkness. 'Else our pride will be much diminished. Asking security in exchange for marriage gains no honour, but only rewards those who plotted treachery against us. Our house would no longer be a major player in the Game of the Council, and the spirits of my ancestors would be unsettled. No, on this I think my father would say, "Safe is not always best." '

Keyoke buckled his helm with the care he might have used preparing for battle. 'As my Lady wills. But I don't envy the task of explaining what you propose to Nacoya.' He bowed, rose, and strode to the outer screen.

He slipped the catch and stepped out. Moonlight drenched the flower beds in gilt. Silhouetted against their brightness, the Force Commander's shoulders seemed straighter, his carriage the slightest bit less strained. With relief, Mara perceived that Keyoke welcomed a warrior's solution to Acoma troubles. He had agreed to risk her plan rather than see her bind the family through marriage to the mercy of a stronger house. She unlinked sweating fingers, afraid and exhilarated at the same time.

'I'll marry on my terms, or not at all,' she murmured to the night. Then she lay back on her cushions. Sleep came reluctantly. Memories of Lano tangled with thoughts of young, boastful sons of great houses, one of whom she must eventually choose as suitor.

Morning dawned hot. With a dry wind blowing from the south, moisture from the rainy season remained only in sheltered hollows, and the herders drove needra to pasture amid ochre clouds of dust. Mara broke her fast in the inner courtyard garden, beneath the generous shade of the trees. The trickle of water from an ornamental fountain soothed her where she sat, dressed in a high-collared robe of saffron. She seemed even younger than her seventeen years, her eyes too bright and her face shadowed with sleeplessness. Yet her voice, when she summoned Nacoya, was crisp with authority.

The old nurse arrived grouchy, as was usual for her in the morning. Mara's summons had reached her while dressing, for her hair was hastily bound back, and her lips pressed thin with annoyance. She bowed briskly and said, 'As my mistress wishes?'

The Lady of the Acoma gestured permission to sit. Nacoya declined; her knees pained her, and the hour was too early to argue with a headstrong girl whose stubbornness might lead the honour of her ancestors to ruin.

Mara smiled sweetly at her former nurse. 'Nacoya, I have reconsidered your advice and seen wisdom in marriage to thwart our enemies' plots. I ask that you prepare me a list of suitors whom you consider eligible, for I shall need guidance to choose a proper mate. Go now. I shall speak with you on the matter in due time.'

Nacoya blinked, obviously startled by this change of heart. Then her eyes narrowed. Surely such compliance masked some other intent, yet Tsurani ethics forbade a servant the right to question. Suspicious in the extreme, but unable to evade her dimissal, the old nurse bowed. 'Your will, mistress, and may Lashima's wisdom guide you.'

She shuffled out, muttering under her breath. Mara sipped chocha, the image of the titled Lady. Then, after an appropriate interval, she called softly to her runner. 'Send for Keyoke, Papewaio, and Jican.'

The two warriors arrived before her cup was empty, Keyoke in his battle armour, resplendently polished; Papewaio also was armed for action, the black headband of the condemned tied as neatly as the sash from which hung his sword. As Nacoya had guessed, he carried himself like a man awarded an honour token for bravery. His expression was otherwise unchanged. In her entire life there were few things as constant as Papewaio, thought Mara.

She nodded to the servant with the chocha pot, and this time Pape accepted a mug of the steaming drink.

Keyoke sipped his chocha without removing his helm, sure sign he was pondering strategy. 'All is ready, mistress. Pape oversaw dispensation of weapons and armour, and Strike Leader Tasido oversees the drill. So long as no fighting occurs, your warriors should give a convincing appearance.'

'Well enough.' Too nervous to finish her chocha, Mara laid sweating hands in her lap. 'All we need now is Jican, that the bait may be prepared.'

The hadonra reached the garden at that moment. He bowed, breathless and sweating, as he had come in haste. His clothing was dusty, and he still carried the needra tally he had been marking as the herds were driven to pasture. 'My apologies, mistress, for my soiled appearance. By your own command, the herders and slaves –'

'I know, Jican,' Mara cut in. 'Your honour is no less, and your devotion to duty is admirable. Now, have we crops and goods in the store sheds to mount a trading caravan?'

Startled by the praise and a wholly unexpected shift of topic, the hadonra squared his shoulders. 'We have six wagonloads of thyza of poor quality that were held back to fatten the needra, though the ones not bearing can do well enough without. The last calves were weaned two days ago. We have some hides suitable to be sold to the harness makers.' Jican shifted his weight, careful to hide his puzzlement. 'The caravan would be very small. Neither the grain nor the goods would realize significant profit.' He bowed deferentially. 'My mistress would do better to wait until the marketable produce comes in season.'

Mara ignored the suggestion. 'I want a small caravan prepared.'

'Yes, mistress.' The hadonra's fingers whitened on the edge of the tally slate. 'I shall send word to our agent in Sulan-Qu –'

'No, Jican.' Turning brusquely, Mara rose and crossed to the rim of the fountain. She extended her hand, letting water spill like jewels through her fingers. 'I wish this caravan to travel to Holan-Qu.'

Jican directed a startled glance at Keyoke, but saw no hint of disapproval on the Force Commander's lined face. Nervous, nearly pleading, he urged, 'Mistress, I obey your desire, but your goods should still be sent to Sulan-Qu, then downriver and on from Jamar by ship.'

'No.' Droplets dashed across marble tile as Mara closed her fist. 'I wish the wagons to travel overland.'

Again Jican glanced at Keyoke; but the Force Commander and his bodyguard stood like sun-cured ulo wood, facing correctly forward. Struggling to master his agitation, the hadonra of the Acoma appealed to his mistress. 'Lady, the mountain road is dangerous. Bandits lurk in the woods in good number, and we lack enough warriors to drive them out. To guard such a caravan would leave this estate unprotected. I must advise against it.'

With a girlish smile, Mara swung away from the fountain. 'But the caravan shall not strip our defences. Papewaio will head a company of hand-picked men. A dozen of our better soldiers should be sufficient to keep the bandits away. They've raided our herds and will not need food, and wagons without large numbers of guards obviously carry goods of little value.'

Jican bowed, his narrow face immobile. 'Then we would be wise to send no guards at all.' His manner concealed sharp disbelief; he dared the dishonour of his mistress's displeasure to dissuade her from folly.

'No.' Mara wrapped dripping fingers in the rich folds of her robe. 'I require an honour guard.'

Jican's face twisted with shock that vanished almost instantly. That his mistress intended to go along on this venture indicated that sorrow had stripped her of wits.

'Go now, Jican,' said Mara. 'Attend to my commands.'

The hadonra peered sideways at Keyoke, as if certain the Lady's demand would provoke protest. But the old Force Commander only shrugged slightly, as if to say, what is to be done?

Jican lingered, though honour forbade him to object. A stern look from Mara restored his humility. He bowed swiftly and departed, his shoulders drooping. Yesterday the Lady of the Acoma had deemed his judgment worthy of praise; now she seemed bereft of the instincts Lashima gave to a needra.

The servants in attendance kept proper silence, and Keyoke moved no muscle beneath the nodding plumes of his helm. Only Papewaio met his mistress's eye. The creases at the corners of his mouth deepened slightly. For a moment he seemed about to smile, though all else about his manner remained formal and unchanged.

3

Innovations

Dust swirled.

The brisk breeze did nothing to cut the heat, and stinging grit made the needra snort. Wooden wheels squealed as the three wagons comprising Mara's caravan grated over the gravel road. Slowly they climbed into the foothills, leaving behind the flatlands . . . and the borders of the Acoma estates. Brightly lacquered green spokes caught the sunlight, seeming to wink as they turned, then slowed as rocks impeded their progress. The drovers yipped encouragement to the needra, who rolled shaggy-lashed eyes and tried to balk as pasture and shed fell behind. The slaves carrying Mara's litter moved steadily, until rougher terrain forced them to slow to avoid jostling their mistress. For reasons the slaves could not imagine, their usually considerate Lady was ordering a man-killing pace, determined to see the caravan through the high passes before nightfall.

Mara sat stiffly. The trees that shaded the edges of the trail offered ready concealment, thick boles and tangled brush casting shadows, deep enough to hide soldiers. And the wagons were a severe disadvantage. The keenest ear could hear no rustle of foliage over the needra's bawl and the grinding creak of wheels, and the sharpest eye became hampered by the ever present dust. Even the battle-hardened soldiers appeared on edge.

The sun climbed slowly towards noon. Heat shimmer danced over the valley left behind, and scaly, long-tailed ketso scurried into hiding as the caravan rumbled past the rocks where they basked. The lead wagons, then the litter, breasted the crest of a rise. Keyoke signalled a halt. The bearers lowered the litter in the shade of an outcrop, giving silent prayers of thanks, but the drovers and the warriors maintained position under Papewaio's vigilant eyes.

Ahead, a steep-sided ravine cut the east-facing slopes of the Kyamaka Mountains. The road plunged steeply downward, folded into switchback curves, then straightened to slice across a hollow with a spring.

Keyoke bowed before Mara's litter and indicated a dell to one side of the hollow, where no trees grew and the earth was beaten and hard. 'Mistress, the scouts sent out after the raid found warm ashes and the remains of a butchered needra in that place. They report tracks, and evidence of habitation, but the thieves themselves have moved on. No doubt they keep moving their base.'

Mara regarded the ravine, shading her eyes against the afternoon glare with her hand. She wore robes of exceptional richness, with embroidered birds on the cuffs, and a waistband woven of iridescent plumes. A scarf of spun silk covered the welts on her neck, and her wrists clinked with bracelets of jade, polished by the nonhuman cho-ja to transparent thinness. While her dress was frivolous and girlish, her manner was intently serious. 'Do you expect an attack?'

'I don't know.' Keyoke's gaze swept the ravine again, as if by force of concentration he could discern any bandits lying hidden. 'But we must prepare ourselves for any turn of fate. And we must act as if enemies observe every movement.'

'Continue on, then,' said Mara. 'Have the foot slave broach a water flask. The soldiers and litter bearers may refresh themselves as we march. Then, when we reach the spring, we can make a show of stopping for drink and so seem more vulnerable than we are.'

Keyoke saluted. 'Your will, mistress. I will wait here for those who follow. Papewaio will assume command of the caravan.' Then with a surprising show of concern in his eyes, he added softly, 'Be wary, my Lady. The risks to your person are great.'

Mara held steady under his gaze. 'No more than my father would take. I am his daughter.'

The Force Commander returned one of his rare and brief smiles and turned from the litter. With a minimum of disruption, he saw Mara's orders carried out. The water-bearer hustled through the ranks with his flasks clanking from the harness he wore, dispensing drinks to the soldiers with a speed gained only by years of compaigning. Then Keyoke signalled, and Papewaio gave the command to move out. Needra drivers shouted, wheels creaked, and dust rose in clouds. The wagons rolled forward to the crest, then over to begin their ponderous descent to the ravine. Only a trained scout would have noted that one less soldier left the camp than had entered.

Mara appeared dignified and serene, but her small painted fan trembled between nervous fingers. She started almost imperceptibly each time the litter moved as one of her bearers shifted grip to sip from the flask carried by the water-bearer. Mara closed her eyes, inwardly pleading Lashima's favour.

The road beyond the crest was rutted and treacherous with loose stone. Men and animals were forced to step with care, eyes upon the path. Time and again the gravel would turn underfoot and pebbles would bounce and rattle downslope, to slash with a clatter through the treetops. Jostled as her slaves fought the uncertain terrain, Mara caught herself holding her breath. She bit her lip and forced herself not to look back or show any sign that her caravan was not upon an ordinary journey. Keyoke had not mentioned that the Acoma soldiers who followed could not cross this ridge without being observed; they would have to circle round by way of the wood. Until they regained their position a short distance behind, Mara's caravan was as vulnerable as a jigahen in the courtyard as the cook approaches with his chopping knife.

At the floor of the ravine the wood seemed denser: damp soil covered with blackferns spread between huge boles of pynon trees, their shaggy aromatic bark interlaced with vines. The slaves who carried the litter breathed deeply, grateful for the cooler forest. Yet to Mara the air seemed dead after the capricious breezes of the heights. Or perhaps it was simply tension that made the stillness oppressive? The click as she flicked open her fan caused several warriors to turn sharply.

Here even bare rock was mantled with leaf mould, and footfalls became deadened to silence. Creaking wagon sounds were smothered by walls of vines and tree trunks; this forest gave back nothing.

Papewaio faced forward, his eyes continually scanning the darkness on either side. His hand never strayed from the intricate hide lacings that bound the hilt of his sword. Watching him, Mara thought upon her father, who had died knowing allies had betrayed him. She wondered what had become of his sword, a work of art with its carved hilts and jewelled sheath. The shatra bird of the Acoma had been worked in enamel on the pommel, and the blade fashioned in the jessami method, three hundred needra hide strips, each scraped to paper thinness, then cleverly and painstakingly laminated – for even a needle-point bubble of air would render it useless – to a metal hardness with an edge unmatched save for the legendary steel swords of the ancients. Perhaps some barbarian warlord wore the sword as a trophy now . . . perhaps he would be an honourable man, if a barbarian was capable of being such. Mara forced away such morbid thoughts. Feeling smothered by the oppressive stillness and the dark foliage overhead, she clenched her hands until her delicate wood fan threatened to snap.

'Lady, I ask leave to permit the men a chance to rest and replenish the flasks,' said Papewaio.

Mara started, nodded, and raked back the damp hair that clung to her temples. The caravan had reached the spring without incident. Ponderous wheels ground to a halt; warriors arrayed themselves in defensive positions, while the foot slave and several of the drovers hastened to them with moist cloths and a meal of thyza biscuit and dried fruit. Other men attended to the needra, while the bearers lowered Mara's litter with stifled grunts of relief. They then stood patiently awaiting their turn to rinse their faces at the spring.

Papewaio returned from the lines of warriors and knelt before his mistress. 'Would my Lady care to leave the litter and walk about?'

Mara extended her hand, her full sleeve trailing nearly to the ground. The dagger concealed by the garment dragged at her wrist, an unfamiliar lump she carried awkwardly. She had wrestled with Lanokota as a child, to Nacoya's continual dismay, but weapons had never attracted her. Keyoke had insisted she bring the knife, though the hastily shortened straps had been fashioned for a larger arm and the hilt felt clumsy in her hand. Overheated, and suddenly uncertain, she permitted Papewaio to help her to her feet.

The ground before the spring was pocked by the prints of men and animals that had baked hard in the sun after the rainy season. While Papewaio drew a dipper of water, his mistress jabbed the earth with her sandal and wondered how many of the marks had been made by stock stolen from Acoma pastures. Once she had overheard a trader describe how certain clans in the north notched the hooves of their livestock, to assist trackers in recovering stolen beasts. But until now the Acoma had commanded the loyalty of enough warriors to make such precautions unnecessary.

Papewaio raised a dripping container of water. 'My Lady?'

Roused from reflection, Mara sipped, then wet her fingers and sprinkled water upon her cheeks and neck. Noon was well past, and slanting sunlight carved the soldiers into forms of glare and shadow. The wood beyond lay still, as if every living thing slept through the afternoon heat. Mara shivered, suddenly chilled as the water cooled her skin. If bandits had lain waiting in ambush, surely they should have attacked by now; an unpleasant alternative caused her to look at her Strike Leader in alarm.

'Pape, what if the grey warriors have circled behind us and attacked the Acoma estates while we travelled upon the road?'

The warrior set the crockery dipper on a nearby stone. The fastenings of his armour squeaked as he shrugged, palms turned skywards to indicate that plans succeeded only at the whim of fate. 'If bandits attack your estates, all honour is lost, Lady, for the best of your warriors have been committed here.' He glanced at the woods, while his hand fell casually to the hilt of his sword. 'But I think it unlikely. I have told the men to be ready. The day's heat lessens, but no leafhoppers sing within the wood.' Suddenly a bird hooted loudly overhead. 'And when the karkak cries, danger is near.'

A shout erupted from the trees at the clearing's edge. Mara felt strong hands thrust her backwards into the litter. Her bracelets snagged the silken hangings as she flung out a hand to break her fall. Awkwardly tumbled against the cushions, she jerked the material aside and saw Papewaio whirl to defend her, his sword gliding from its scabbard. Overturned by his foot, the dipper spun and shattered against a stone. Fragments pelted Mara's ankles as the swords of her warriors hissed from their sheaths to meet the attack of the outlaws who charged from cover.

Through the closing ranks of her defenders, Mara glimpsed a band of men with drawn weapons running towards the wagons. Despite being dirty, thin, and raggedly clad, the raiders advanced in well-organized ranks. The ravine echoed with shouts as they strove to break the line of defenders. Fine cloth crumpled between Mara's hands. Her warriors were many times outnumbered. Aware that her father and brother had faced worse battles than this on the barbarian world, she strove not to flinch at the crack of sword upon sword. Papewaio's voice prevailed over the confusion, his officer's plume readily visible through the press; at his signal, the battle-hardened warriors of the Acoma gave way with almost mechanical discipline.

The attack faltered. With no honour to be gained from retreat, the usual Tsurani tactic was to charge, not assume a defensive posture; the sight of wagons being abandoned warned the ruffians to caution. Enclosed by the green-armoured backs of her escort, Mara heard a high-pitched shout. Feet slapped earth as the attackers checked. Except for the unarmed drivers, and the cringing presence of the water-bearer, the wagons had been abandoned without dispute; seemingly the warriors had withdrawn to defend the more valuable treasure.

Slowly, warily, the bandits approached. Between the bodies of her defenders, Mara saw lacquered wagons gleam as an enemy force numbering five times greater than her escort closed in a half circle around the spring.

The trickle of water was overlaid by the creak of armour and the fast, nervous breathing of tense men. Papewaio held position by Mara's litter, a chiselled statue with drawn sword. For a long, tense minute, movement seemed suspended. Then a man behind enemy lines barked an order; two bandits advanced and sliced the ties binding the cloth that covered the wagons. Mara felt sweat spring along her spine as eager hands bared Acoma goods to the sunlight. Now came the most difficult moment, since for a time her warriors must hold their line regardless of insult or provocation. Only if the outlaws threatened Mara would the Acoma soldiers answer.

The bandits quickly realized then that no counterattack would be forthcoming. With shouts of exultation, they hefted bags of thyza from the wagon; others edged closer to the Acoma guard, curious to see what treasure would merit such protection. As they neared, Mara caught glimpses of grimy knuckles, tattered cloth, and a crude and mismatched accumulation of weapons. Yet the manner in which the blades were held indicated training and skill, and ruthless need. These were men desperate enough to kill and die for a wagon weight of poor quality thyza.

A shout of unmistakable authority cut through the jubilation of the men beside the wagon. 'Wait! Let that be!' Falling silent, the bandits turned from their booty, some with sacks of grain still clutched to their breast.

'Let us see what else fortune has brought us this day.' A slender, bearded man who was obviously the commander of the band broke through the ranks of his underlings and strode boldly towards the warriors guarding Mara. He paused midway between the lines, sword at the ready and a cocky sureness to his manner that caused Papewaio to draw himself up.

'Steady, Pape,' Mara whispered, more to reassure herself than to restrain her Strike Leader. Stifled in the confines of her litter, she watched the bandit make a disparaging gesture with his sword.

'What's this? Why should men with swords and armour and the honour of a great house not fight?' The bandit commander shifted his weight, betraying underlying uneasiness. No Tsurani warrior he had known had ever hesitated to attack, even die, since the highest accolade a fighter could earn was to perish in battle. Another step brought him near enough to catch sight of Mara's litter. No longer puzzled, he craned his neck, then cried, 'A woman!'

Mara's hands tightened in her lap. Head high, her pale face expressionless, she watched the bandit leader break into a wide grin. As if a dozen warriors standing ready to dispute his conquest were no deterrent, he spun to face his companions. 'A fine day, men. A caravan, and a captive, and not a man's blood spilled to the Red God!'

Interested, the nearer outlaws dropped sacks of thyza and crowded together, weapons aggressively angled towards the Acoma lines. Their commander turned in Mara's direction and shouted, 'Lady, I trust your father or husband is loving and rich, or if not loving, then at least rich. For you are now our hostage.'

Mara jerked aside the curtain of the litter. She accepted Papewaio's hand and rose, saying, 'Your conclusion may be premature, bandit.'

Her poise caused the outlaw leader a stab of uncertainty; he stepped back, daunted by her confidence. But the armed company at his back lost none of their eagerness, and more men drifted from the woods to observe the exchange.

Looking past the shoulders of her guards at the slender man, Mara demanded, 'What is your name?'

Regaining his bantering manner, the bandit leader leaned on his sword, 'Lujan, Lady.' He still showed deference to one obviously noble. 'Since I am destined to be your host for a time, may I enquire whom I have the honour of addressing?'

Several outlaws laughed at their leader's mock display of manners. Mara's escort stiffened with affront, but the girl herself remained calm. 'I am Mara, Lady of the Acoma.'

Conflicting expressions played across Lujan's face: surprise, amusement, concern, then at last consideration; he lifted his sword and gestured delicately with the point. 'Then you are without husband or father, Lady of the Acoma. You must negotiate your own ransom.' Even as he spoke, his eyes played across the woodlands behind Papewaio and Mara, for her confident stance and the smallness of her retinue suggested something out of place. Ruling Ladies of great houses did not place themselves at risk without reason. Something in his posture caused alarm in his men, nearly a hundred and fifty of them, as well as Mara could estimate. Their nervousness grew as she watched; some cast about for signs of trouble, while others seemed on the point of charging Papewaio's position without order.

As if the situation were not about to turn from dangerous to deadly, Mara smiled and fingered her bracelets. 'My Force Commander said I might be annoyed by an unkempt lot like you.' Her voice became peevish. 'I despise him when he's right. Now I'll never hear the end of his nattering!' At this some of the outlaws burst into laughter.

Papewaio showed no reaction to this unlikely description of Keyoke. He relaxed slightly, aware that his mistress sought to lessen tension and avoid an imminent conflict.

Mara looked at the bandit chieftain, outwardly defiant but secretly attempting to gauge his mood. He insolently levelled his weapon in her direction. 'How convenient for us you failed to take your adviser's suggestion seriously. In future you would be well advised to heed such counsel . . . if you have the opportunity.'

Several of the Acoma soldiers tensed at the implied threat. Surreptitiously Mara touched Papewaio's back to reassure him, then said girlishly, 'Why would I not have the opportunity?'

With a display of mock regret, Lujan lowered his sword. 'Because, Lady, if our negotiations prove unsatisfactory, you will be in no position to hear your Force Commander again.' His eyes darted, seeking possible trouble; everything about this raid was askew.

'What do you mean!' Mara stamped her foot as she spoke, ignoring the dangerous attitude the bandit's threat roused in her escort.

'I mean that while I'm not certain how much value you place on your own freedom, I do know what price you'll fetch on the slave blocks at Migran.' Lujan jumped back a half step, sword poised, as Acoma guards barely restrained themselves from answering such insult with attack. Sure of retaliation, the bandits raised weapons and crouched.

Lujan scanned the clearing furiously as both sides stood on the brink of combat. Yet no change came. A gleam of understanding entered the outlaw's eyes. 'You plot something, pretty mistress?' The words were half question, half statement.

Unexpectedly amused by the man's impudence, Mara saw that the outlaw's brash and provocative comments were intended to test her mettle in turn. She realized how closely she had come to underestimating this Lujan. That such a clever man could go to waste! she thought. Striving to buy time, she shrugged like a spoiled child.

Lujan stepped boldly forward and, reaching through the line of her guards, fingered the scarf at her neck with a rough and dirty hand.

Reaction followed instantaneously. Lujan felt sudden pressure against his wrist. Looking down, he saw Papewaio's sword a hairsbreadth away from severing his hand. The outlaw's head jerked up so his eyes were level with the Strike Leader's. In flat tones Papewaio said, 'There is a limit.'

Lujan's fingers unclenched slowly, freeing Mara's scarf. He smiled nervously, adroitly withdrawing his hand, then stepped away from Mara's guard. His manner now turned suspicious and hostile, for under normal circumstances to touch a Lady in such a way would have cost his life. 'There is some deception here, Lady. What game is this?' He gripped his sword tightly, and his men shuffled forward, awaiting only his order to attack.

Suddenly aware that Mara and her officer were closely observing the rocks above the clearing, the bandit chieftain swore. 'No Ruling Lady would travel with so few warriors! Aie, I am a fool!'

He started forward, and his men tensed to charge, when Mara shouted, 'Keyoke!'

An arrow sped through the air to strike the ground between the outlaw leader's legs. He pulled up short, as if reaching the end of a tether. Teetering for an instant on his toes, he awkwardly stumbled back a pace. A voice rang out from above. 'One step closer to my mistress, and you're a dead man!' Lujan spun towards the voice, and high above Keyoke pointed a drawn sword at the bandit chieftain. The Force Commander nodded grimly, and an archer fired a signal arrow over the ridge of the ravine. It rose with a whistling scream, cutting through his shout as he called to his subcommanders. 'Ansami! Mesai!'

Other shouts answered from the woods. Flanked from the rear, outlaws whirled to catch glimpses of polished armour between the trees, the tall plumes of an officer's helm at the fore. Uncertain how large a force had been pitched against him, the bandit chieftain reacted instantaneously. In desperation, he whirled and yelled his command to charge the guard around Mara's litter.

A second shout from Keyoke jerked his offensive short. 'Dacoya! Hunzai! Advance! Prepare to fire!'

The skyline above the ridge suddenly became notched with the silhouettes of a hundred helms, punctuated by the curved horns of bows. A racket erupted, as if several hundred men advanced through the woods that surrounded the clearing.

The bandit chieftain gestured, and his men stumbled to a halt. Caught at an uncomfortable disadvantage, he scanned the sides of the ravine in a belated attempt to assess his odds of recovery. Only one senior officer stood in clear sight; he had called the names of four Strike Leaders. Eyes narrowed against sun glare, Lujan reviewed the deployment of his own men. The situation was next to impossible.

Mara had abandoned her girlish airs. Without even a glance at her bodyguard for direction, she said, 'Lujan, order your men to put their weapons down.'

'Has reason fled?' Soundly outflanked, and caught in a bottle-necked position, the outlaw leader straightened with a defiant smile. 'Lady, I salute your plan to rid your estates of pesky neighbours, but even now, I must point out, your person is still at risk. We are trapped, but you could still die with us.' Even in the face of overwhelming odds, this man sought to wrest circumstance to his advantage. 'Perhaps we could come to some sort of accommodation,' he quickly observed. His voice reflected a roguish banter and desperate bluff, but never a trace of fear. 'Perhaps if you let us depart in peace . . .'

Mara inclined her head. 'You misjudge us.' Her jade bracelets clinked in the stillness as she placed a hand on Papewaio's arm, moving him slightly aside. Then she stepped past him and her guards, confronting the bandit chief face to face. 'As Ruling Lady of the Acoma, I have placed myself at risk so that we might speak.'

Lujan glanced at the ridgetop. Perspiration glistened on his forehead, which he blotted on his tattered and dirty sleeve. 'I am listening, Lady.'

Her guards like statues at her back, Mara caught the ruffian's gaze and held it. 'First you must put down your weapons.'

The man returned a bitter laugh. 'I may not be a gifted commander, my Lady, but I am not an idiot. If I am to greet the Red God this day, still I will not surrender myself and my companions to be hung for stealing some cows and grain.'

'Though you have stolen from the Acoma, and killed a slave boy, I have not gone to this trouble simply to see you hang, Lujan.'

Though Mara's words rang sincere, the outlaws were reluctant to believe; weapons shifted among their ranks, and eyes darted from the threatening force on the ridge to the smaller band of soldiers who guarded the girl. As tension intensified, Lujan said, 'Lady, if you have a point to make, I suggest you speak quickly, else we may find a number of us dying, you and I first among them.'

Without orders, and with no deference for rank, Papewaio closed the distance between himself and his mistress. Gently but firmly he moved Mara back and interposed himself between the Ruling Lady and the bandit leader.

Mara allowed the familiarity without comment. 'I will guarantee you this: surrender to me and listen to my proposal. If you wish to leave when I have done speaking with you and your men, then you will be free to depart. So long as you never again raid Acoma lands, I will not trouble you. On this you have my word.'

Uncomfortably aware that archers even now trained their weapons upon his person, Lujan regarded his men. To the last, miserable rank, they were undernourished, some scrawny to the verge of ill health. Most carried only a single weapon, a badly made sword or knife; few wore adequate clothing, much less armour. It would be a poor contest if it came to a fight against Mara's impeccably turned-out guard. The bandit leader glanced from face to scruffy face, meeting the eyes of men who had been his companions through difficult times. Most indicated with a nod they would follow his lead.

Lujan turned back to Mara with a slight sigh and reversed his sword. 'Lady, I have no house to call upon, but what shred of personal honour I call my own is now in your hands.' He surrendered his blade to Papewaio. Weaponless and entirely dependent upon her goodwill, he bowed with stiff irony and commended his following to accept his example.

The sun beat down on the green lacquered armour of the Acoma and the ragged shoulders of the bandit company. Only birds broke the silence, and the trickle of the spring, as men studied the girl in her fine robes and jewellery. At last one bandit stepped forth and surrendered his knife; he was followed by another with a scarred leg, and another, until in a wave the company gave over their weapons. Blades tumbled from loosened fingers, to fall with a clatter at the feet of the Acoma warriors. Shortly not an outlaw remained who carried arms.

When the men of her retinue had collected the swords, Mara stepped forward. The bandits parted to let her past, wary of her, and of the bared blade Papewaio still carried at her shoulder. While on duty, the First Strike Leader of the Acoma had a manner even the bravest man would not lightly challenge. The most reckless of the outlaws maintained their distance, even when the warrior turned his back to lift Mara to the tailboard of the nearest wagon.

Looking down on the ragged company, the Lady of the Acoma said, 'Is this all of your men, Lujan?'

The fact that she had issued no order to relax the stance of her archers caused the bandit leader to reply with honesty. 'Most are here. Fifty more maintain our camp in the forest or forage nearby. Another dozen keep watch on the various roads.'

Perched atop the thyza sacks, Mara hastily calculated. 'You command perhaps twelve dozen here. How many of these were soldiers? Let them answer for themselves.'

Of the band clustered around the rear of the wagon, close to sixty raised their hands. Mara smiled encouragement and said, 'From what houses?'

Proud to be asked of their former heritage, they shouted, 'Saydano!' 'Almach!' 'Raimara!' and other houses known to Mara, most of which had been destroyed in Almecho's rise to the office of Warlord, just before Ichindar's succession to the throne of the Empire. As the clamour died down, Lujan added, 'I was once Strike Leader of the Kotai, Lady.'

Mara arranged her sleeves and sat; her frown grew pensive. 'What of the rest of you?'

A man stepped forward. Burly despite the evident ravages of hunger, he bowed. 'Mistress, I was a farmer from the Kotai estates to the west of Migran. When my master died, I fled, and followed this man.' He pointed respectfully to Lujan. 'He has cared well for his own over the years, though ours has been a life of wandering and hardship.'

Mara gestured to the fringes of the company. 'Criminals?'

Lujan answered for the rest. 'Men without masters, Lady. Some were free farmers who lost their land for taxes. Others were guilty of misdemeanour. Many are grey warriors. But murderers, thieves, and men without principle are given no welcome in my camp.' He indicated the surrounding woods. 'Oh, there are murderers around, have no doubt. Your patrols have grown lax over the last few months, and the wilds provide safe haven. But in my band we have only honest outlaws.' He laughed weakly at his own jest, adding, 'If there be such.' He sobered and regarded Mara keenly. 'Now, will the Lady tell us why she concerns herself with the fate of such unfortunates as we?'

Mara gave him a smile that hinted at irony, and signalled to Keyoke. The Force Commander called for his troops to relax their battle-ready stance. As the archers on the ridge arose from cover, not even the sun's glare could hide the fact that they were not warriors at all, but boys and old farmhands and slaves, deceptively clad in bits of armour or green-dyed cloth. What had seemed an army was now revealed for what it was: a single company of soldiers who numbered less than half as many as the outlaws, accompanied by workers and children from the Acoma estates.

A mutter of chagrin arose from the outlaws, and Lujan shook his head with a look of surprise and awe. 'Mistress, what have you wrought?'

'A possibility, Lujan . . . for all of us.'

Afternoon cast long shadows across the grass by the spring where the needra grazed, their tails switching insects. Perched atop the wagon, Mara regarded the ragged band of outlaws who sat on the ground at the fringes of the forest eagerly finishing the meat, fruit, and thyza bread her cooks had distributed among them. Although the meal was better than many had seen in months, the Lady of the Acoma observed a pervasive discomfort among the men. To be taken in battle was to become a slave, that was an incontrovertible way of life. The fact that Acoma honour guaranteed their status as free men, and the generous hospitality that had fed them, earned a guarded if tenuous trust. Yet this strange young Ruling Lady had not spoken of why she had contrived this odd meeting, and the outlaws remained suspicious.

Mara studied the men and found them much like the soldiers, workers, and slaves of her estate. Yet one quality seemed absent; had these men stood dressed in nobles' robes, still she would have known them for outcasts. As the last crumbs of the meal were consumed, she knew the time had come to speak her offer.

With Papewaio and Keyoke stationed by the wagon at her side, the girl drew a resolute breath and raised her voice. 'You outlaws, I am Mara, Lady of the Acoma. You have stolen from me, and for that are in my debt. To discharge that obligation honourably, I ask that you listen to my words.'

Seated in the front ranks, Lujan set aside his wine cup and answered. 'The Lady of the Acoma is gracious to concern herself with the honour of outlaws. All in my company are pleased to agree to this.'

Mara searched the face of the bandit chief, seeking any sign of mockery; instead she found interest, curiosity, and sly humour. She found herself liking this man. 'You here are counted outcasts for many reasons, so I have been told. All are considered marked unkindly by fate.' The man with the scarred leg called out in agreement, and others shifted position, leaning raptly forward. Satisfied she had their attention, Mara added, 'For some of you, misfortune came because you outlived the masters you served.'

A man with bark wristbands shouted, 'And so we are dishonoured!'

Another echoed him. 'And so we have no honour!'

Mara raised her hand for silence. 'Honour is in doing one's duty. If a man is sent to guard a distant holding and his master dies beyond his capacity to defend him, is he without honour? If a warrior is wounded in battle and lies unconscious while his master dies, is it his fault that he lives and his master does not?' Mara lowered her arm with a brisk clash of bracelets, her tone changed to command. 'All who were servants, farmers, and workers, raise your hand.'

A dozen or so men complied without hesitation. The others shifted uncertainly, eyes flicking from the Lady to their comrades as they waited to see what she proposed.

'I have need of workers.' Mara made an encompassing gesture and smiled. 'I will allow you to take service with my hadonra.'

Order vanished. All the bandits began speaking at once, from mutters to shouts, for the Lady's offer was one unprecedented within the Empire. Keyoke waved his sword for silence, even as an emboldened farmer leaped to his feet. 'When the Lord of the Minwanabi slew my master, I ran away. But the law says I am slave to the conquering Lord.'

Mara's voice cut clearly over the confusion. 'The law says no such thing!' Stillness fell, and all eyes turned towards her. Poised, angry, yet seeming beautiful in her rich robes to men who had known months or even years of deprivation in the wilderness, she resumed with firm encouragement. '*Tradition* says a worker is a spoil of war. The conqueror decides who is more valued as a free man, and who is to be a slave. The Minwanabi are my enemies, so if you are a spoil of war, then I will decide your status. You are free.'

The silence at this point became oppressive, charged like the shimmer of heat waves above sun-baked rock. Men shifted restlessly, troubled by the upset of order as they knew it, for social subtleties dictated every walk of Tsurani life. To change the fundamental was to sanction dishonour and risk the unbinding of a civilization that had continued unbroken for centuries.

Mara sensed the confusion among the men; glancing first to the farmers, whose faces wore transparent expressions of hope, then to the most sceptical and hardened of the grey warriors, she borrowed from the philosophies learned at Lashima's temple. 'The tradition we live by is like the river that springs from the mountain lands and flows always to the sea. No man may turn that current uphill. To try would defy natural law. Like the Acoma, many of you have known misfortune. Like the Acoma, I ask you to join in turning the course of tradition, even as storms sometimes cause a river to carve a new bed.'

The girl paused, eyes veiled by her lashes as she stared down at her hands. This moment was critical, for if even one outlaw cried out in opposition to what she had said, she would lose control. The silence weighed upon her unbearably. Then, without a word, Papewaio calmly removed his helm; the black scarf of the condemned upon his brow lay bare for all to see.

Lujan exclaimed in astonishment, startled as the rest to find a man condemned to death standing in a position of honour in the retinue of a great Lady. Proud of Pape's loyalty, and the gesture he had made to show that shame could be other than tradition dictated, Mara smiled and laid light fingers on the shoulder of her Strike Leader. 'This man serves me with pride. Will others among you not do the same?' To the farmer displaced by the Minwanabi she said, 'If the Lord who vanquished your master wishes another farmer, then let him come for you.' With a nod towards Keyoke and her warriors, she added, 'The Minwanabi will have to fight to take you. And upon my estate you shall be a free man.'

The farmer sprang forward with wild cry of joy. 'You offer your honour?'

'You have my honour,' answered Mara, and Keyoke bowed to affirm his loyalty to her command.

The farmer knelt where he stood, and offered crossed wrists to Mara in the time-honoured gesture of fealty. 'Lady, I am your man. Your honour is my honour.' With those words the farmer announced to all that he would die as readily as any of her warriors to defend the Acoma name.

Mara nodded formally, and Papewaio left her side. He wended his way through the bandit company until he stood before the farmer. By ancient ritual, he placed a cord about the man's wrists, then removed the mock bonds, showing that the man who might have been kept as slave was instead accepted as a free man. Excited talk broke out as a dozen other men crowded around. They knelt in a circle around Papewaio, eager to accept Mara's offer and the hope of a new life.

Keyoke detailed a warrior to gather the newly sworn workers together; Acoma guards would accompany them back to the estate, where they would be assigned housing and field work by Jican.

The remaining company of bandits watched with the hope of the desperate as Mara spoke again. 'You who were outlawed, what were your crimes?'

A short man, pale with sickness, called hoarsely. 'I spoke ill of a priest, Lady.'

'I kept grain back from the tax collector for my hungry children,' cried another.

The list of petty misdemeanours continued until Mara had ascertained the truth of Lujan's claim that thieves and murderers found no sanctuary within his company. To the condemned she said, 'Leave as you will, or take service as free men. As Ruling Lady of the Acoma, I offer you pardon within the borders of my lands.' Although imperial amnesty was beyond the authority of any Ruling Lord or Lady, Mara knew no minister of the imperial government would likely raise objections over the fate of a lowly, next-to-nameless field hand – especially if he had never heard of such an amnesty.

The pardoned men grinned at the cleverness of the Lady and hurried to Papewaio to swear service. They knelt gladly. As Acoma workers they might face threat from Mara's enemies, but danger in service to a great house was preferable to their bitter existence as outlaws.

The shadows of afternoon lengthened beneath the trees; golden light scattered through where the branches were thinnest. Mara looked at the depleted ranks of the outlaw band, and her gaze settled at last upon Lujan. 'You soldiers without masters, listen carefully.' She paused, waiting while the jubilant talk of the newly sworn workers dwindled down the road. Delicate next to Papewaio's muscled fitness, Mara challenged the gaze of the roughest and most unkempt among Lujan's followers. 'I offer a thing no warrior in the history of the Empire has known: a second beginning. Who among you will return to my estate, to shape anew his honour . . . by kneeling outside the sacred grove and offering oath to the natami of the Acoma?'

Silence descended upon the glade, and for a moment it seemed that no man dared to breathe. Then pandemonium erupted. Men shouted questions and were shouted down in turn by others who claimed to know answers. Dirty hands jabbed the air to emphasize points of law, and feet stamped earth as excited men jumped to their feet and surged towards Mara's wagon.

Papewaio stopped the rush with drawn sword, and, hurrying from the wagons, Keyoke shouted a command.

Silence fell; slowly the bandits settled. Quiet once more, they waited for their leader to speak.

Respectful of Papewaio's vigilance, Lujan bowed carefully before the girl who threatened to upset the life he had known past recovery. 'Lady, your words are . . . astonishing . . . generous beyond imagining. But we have no masters to free us of our former service.' Something akin to defiance flickered in his eyes.

Mara noticed and strove to understand. Though roguish, even handsome beneath his grime, the outlaw bore himself in the manner of a man threatened; and suddenly the girl knew why. These men simply owned no sense of purpose, living from day to day, without hope. If she could make them take fate back into their own hands and swear loyalty to the Acoma, she would gain warriors of inestimable value. But she had to make them believe once more.

'You *have* no service,' she said gently to Lujan.

'But we gave oath . . .' His voice fell to barely above a whisper. 'No offer like this has been made before. We . . . Who among us can know what is honourable?' Lujan seemed half pleading, as if he wished Mara to dictate what was right; and the rest of the company looked to their chieftain for guidance.

Suddenly feeling every inch the unseasoned seventeen-year-old novice of Lashima, Mara turned to Keyoke for support. The old warrior did not fail her. Though he was as discomforted as Lujan by this abuse of tradition, his voice remained calm. 'A soldier must die in the service of his master, or be dishonoured, so it is held. Yet, as my Lady points out, if fate decrees otherwise, no man is fit to argue with the gods. If the gods do not wish you to serve the Acoma, their displeasure will certainly be visited upon that house. My Lady assumes that risk, in her own behalf, and yours. With or without the favour of heaven, all of us will die. But the bold among you will chance misfortune,' and he paused for a long moment before adding, 'and die as soldiers.'

Lujan rubbed his wrists, unconvinced. To anger the gods was to invite utter ruination. At least as an outlaw the miserable existence he would endure for life might expiate his failure to die with his master, perhaps earning his soul a higher station when it was next bound to the Wheel of Life.

As the bandits reflected the nervousness of their leader, each plainly divided within himself, Papewaio scratched his scar and said thoughtfully, 'I am Papewaio, First Strike Leader of the Acoma. I was born to service with this house, but my father and grandfather counted kin with cousins serving the Shinzawai, the Wedewayo, the Anasati . . .' He paused and, when no man spoke, added the names of several more houses.

Lujan stood frozen, his eyes half-closed, as behind him a man called out. 'My father served the house of Wedewayo, where I lived before I took service with the Lord of the Serak. His name was Almaki.'

Papewaio nodded, thinking quickly. 'Was this the Almaki who was cousin to Papendaio, who was my father?'

The man shook his head in disappointment. 'No, but I knew him. He was called Little Almaki, as my father was Big Almaki. I had other cousins of my father serving there, though.'

Papewaio beckoned the man from the ranks, and out of Mara's hearing, they spoke quietly for several minutes. After an animated interval the bandit broke into a broad grin, and the Strike Leader turned to his mistress with a deferential bow. 'My Lady, this is Toram. His uncle was cousin to a man who married a woman who was sister to the woman who married my father's nephew. He is my cousin, and worthy of service to the Acoma.'

Mara hid a smile behind her sleeve. Pape and the obviously clever Toram had seized upon a simple fact of Tsurani culture. Second and third sons of soldiers by tradition were free to take service with houses other than those in which they were born. By treating this grey warrior as if he were a youth, Papewaio had circumvented Lujan's question of honour entirely. When Mara had recovered her decorum, she said simply, 'Pape, call your cousin into our service, if he is willing.'

Papewaio caught Toram's shoulder in brotherly fashion. 'Cousin, you are called to serve the Acoma.'

The man raised his chin with newfound pride and crisply announced his acceptance. 'I will come!'

His words touched off a rush among the outlaws, as men crowded around the dozen Acoma soldiers and began exchanging the names of relations. Again Mara fought down a smile. Any Tsurani of noble birth, or any soldier, knew his bloodlines back several generations, as well as cousins, aunts, and uncles, most of whom he knew by name only. When two Tsurani met for the first time, an elaborate inquiry after the health of relatives began, until histories were exchanged and the two strangers knew who stood higher upon the social ladder. It was almost impossible that, after sufficient conversation, some tenuous relationship would not be discovered, allowing the grey warriors to be called to service.

Mara allowed Papewaio to offer his hand so she might step down from the wagon. Bandits gathered in knots around different soldiers, happy voices shouting out questions and answers as relationships were determined. Lujan shook his head in wonder and faced Mara, his eyes alight with poorly masked emotions. 'My Lady, your ruse to capture us was masterful and . . . alone would have made me proud to serve you. This . . .' His hand waved at the milling, excited men. 'This is beyond understanding.' Nearly overcome by his feelings, he turned away a moment, swallowed hard, then looked back at Mara, his face again a proper Tsurani mask, though his eyes were shining. 'I do not know if . . . it is right, but I will take service gladly, and I will make Acoma honour mine. My life will be yours as you will, my Lady. And should my life be short, it will be a good life, to again wear house colour.' He straightened, all trace of his rakishness put aside. He studied Mara for a long moment, his eyes locked with hers. The words he spoke then impressed her ever afterward with their sincerity. 'I hope fate spares me death for many years, mistress, that I may stay near your side. For I think you play the Game of the Council.' Then with a near loss of self-control, moisture gleamed in his eyes and his face split in a grin. 'And I think the Empire will never be the same for it.'

Mara stood silent, while Lujan bowed and moved away to compare relations with the Acoma soldiers and find common kin, no matter how distant the tie. Then, with Keyoke's permission, he sent runners to camp to call the rest of his following to the spring. The latecomers arrived in varying states of disbelief. But when they saw the lady seated upon the thyza wagon as though she held court in the pillared shade of her estate hall, their scepticism lost impetus.

Convinced in the end by the exuberance of comrades already sworn to Acoma service, they recited lists of cousins and in-laws until they, too, had regained the honour of house service.

Afternoon passed, the trees above the rim of the ravine striping the clearing with lengthened shadows. The heat lessened and the late breezes bore a woodsy scent, as the branches above the caravan rustled restlessly. Satisfied with the events of the day, Mara watched a flock of gaguin birds swoop down to feed upon insects blown along by the breeze. As they finished their meal and sped raucously off to the south, she realized how tired and hungry she was.

As though thinking in concert with her, Keyoke paused by Mara's side. 'Lady, we must leave directly if we are to reach your estate by nightfall.'

Mara nodded, longing now for soft cushions in place of rough bags of thyza. Weary as she was of the stares of hungry men, the privacy of her litter seemed suddenly inviting. Loudly enough for the men to hear, she called, 'Let us be away, then, Force Commander. There are Acoma soldiers here who would like a bath, a hot meal, and rest in a barracks where the fog won't dampen their blankets.'

Even Mara could not keep her eyes free of moisture at the shout of unalloyed joy that sprang from the lips of the bandits. Men who so recently had stood ready to fight against her now were eager to defend her. Silently the girl gave thanks to Lashima. This first victory had come easily; but against the strength of the Minwanabi, and the scheming cleverness of the Anasati, in the future her success would come with difficulty, if at all.

Jostled back against the cushions as her slaves raised her litter, Mara felt limp. She allowed herself a deep sigh of relief. All the doubt and fear suppressed through armed confrontation and negotiation with the bandits surfaced behind the privacy of her curtains. Until now she had not dared admit how frightened she had been. Her body quivered with unexpected chills. Aware that dampness would mar the fine silk of her gown, she sniffed and suppressed a maddening urge to weep. Lano had ridiculed her emotional outbursts as a child, teasing her about not being Tsurani – though women were not expected to hold themselves in check the way men did.

Remembering his laughing banter and the fact that she had never seen her father betray any uncertainty, any doubts or fears, she closed her eyes, immersing herself in an exercise to calm herself. The voice of the teaching sister who had schooled her at the temple of Lashima seemed to answer within her mind: learn the nature of self, accept all aspects of self, then the mastery can begin. Denial of self is denial of all.

Mara sniffed again. Now her nose dripped also. Pushing her sleeves out of harm's way, she silently admitted the truth. She had been terrified, most so at the moment she had thought the bandits might be attacking her estates while she futilely searched the hills for them.

Again Mara scolded herself: this is not how a Ruling Lady acts! Then she understood the root of her feelings: she didn't know how a Ruling Lady was expected to act. Lacking any schooling in governance, she was a temple girl thrust into the deadliest contest in the Empire.

Mara reviewed an early lesson from her father: doubts could only cripple one's ability to act decisively; and in the Game of the Council, to hesitate was to die.

To avoid dwelling on weakness, Mara peered through a crack in the curtains at the newly recruited Acoma retainers. Despite soiled clothing, haggard faces, arms like sticks, and eyes of frightened animals, these men were soldiers, yet now Mara recognized a quality in them she had failed to see before: these outlaws, even the roguish Lujan, had been just as frightened as she. Mara found that perplexing, until she reconsidered the ambush from their perspective. Despite being outnumbered, the Acoma warriors were all battle-tested soldiers, properly armed and fit. Some of these grey warriors hadn't seen a decent meal in a year. And their weapons were an odd assortment of discarded, stolen, or crudely fashioned swords and knives. Only a few had anything like a shield and none wore body armour. No, thought Mara, many of those sad, desperate men must have expected some of their unfortunate brotherhood to die this day. And each would have wondered if he'd be among that number.

The men marched unaware of their mistress's observation. Their faces revealed a play of other emotions, among them hope and the fear of false hope. Mara sank back upon the cushions, absently focusing on the colourful design of the litter's tapestry covering. How had she suddenly come to see all these things in these men's faces? Could her fear have triggered some perceptiveness she had not understood within herself? Then, as if her brother, Lanokota, sat beside her, memory of his presence filled her mind. If she closed her eyes she could hear him whisper, 'You are growing up, little sister.'

Suddenly Mara could no longer contain her tears. Now her weeping did not arise from sorrow but from a jubilant upwelling similar to the joy she had known when Lano had last won the summer games in Sulan-Qu. On that day Mara and her father had cheered like peasants from the stands, for a time unconcerned with the mores of social status and decorum; only now her emotions swept her tenfold more powerfully.

She had won. She had tasted her first victory in the Game of the Council, and the experience whetted her wits, left her yearning for something more and greater. For the first time in life she understood why the great Lords strove, and even died, for the chance to gain in honour.

Smiling through the tracks of tears, she allowed the motion of the litter to relax her body. No one she faced across the invisible gaming table of Tsurani politics would know of this move, at least not directly and not for some time. But where Minwanabi treachery had reduced the Acoma home garrison to fifty soldiers, she now commanded the loyalty of better than two hundred. Since grey warriors were scattered in hideouts the breadth of the Empire, she could employ these men to recruit more. Should she gain but another week from her sending the box with the feather and cord to the Lord of the Minwanabi, then she might have five hundred or more soldiers to offset his next threat. Mara felt joyous. She knew victory! And two voices arose from memory. On one hand the teaching sister said, 'Child, be wary of the lure of power and triumph, for all such things are transitory.' But Lano's impetuous voice urged her to appreciate her accomplishments. 'Enjoy victory while you can, Mara-anni. Enjoy it while you can.'

Mara lay back, tired enough to set her mind at rest. As her slaves bore her homeward through the deepening shadows of sundown, she smiled slightly in the privacy of her litter. While she knew that her situation was still almost hopeless, she was going to take Lano's advice. Life must be savoured while it lasted.

The wagon wheels creaked and turned and the needra snorted, while the dust of tramping men turned the air ochre and gold. Sunset faded slowly to twilight as Mara's unlikely caravan with its ill-assorted company of men-at-arms made its way down the road to the Acoma estate.

The torches by the main door of the estate house lit a courtyard thrown into confusion. The earlier arrival of the formerly masterless workers and farmers had busied Jican and his staff to the exclusion of all else, as meals and quarters and jobs were meted out to all. When Mara's caravan returned on the edge of nightfall with Lujan's ragged, underfed warriors, the hadonra threw his hands in the air and begged the gods for an end to an impossible day's work. Hungry himself, and by now resigned to a tongue-lashing from his wife for missing his children's bedtime, Jican dispatched word to the cooks to prepare yet another cauldron of thyza, and to cut cold meat and fruit. Then, shorter than most of his charges and having to make up the difference by being tirelessly energetic, the hadonra began the task of taking names and tallying which men needed clothing, and which sandals. While Keyoke began the task of sorting the newcomers into companies, Jican and his assistants assembled a team of slaves to sweep out an empty barracks and fetch blankets for sleeping mats. Without formal instructions from anyone, Lujan took on the role of officer, reassuring or bullying where necessary to help get his company settled.

Into this chaos of milling men and needra wagons sailed Nacoya, her hairpins askew in her agitation. She gave Lujan's raffish company a brisk glance and homed in at once on Mara's litter. Weaving a determined path through the press, she arrived just as Papewaio assisted his Lady from the cushions to her feet. Stiff from sitting and dazzled by the torchlight, Mara observed that silent moment when her Strike Leader surrendered her care to Nacoya. The invisible line between the domains of bodyguard and nurse lay approximately where the stone walk from the main doors of the house touched the roadway.

Nacoya accompanied her mistress back to her quarters, one step behind her shoulder as was proper. Once through the door, the old nurse gestured for the maids to withdraw. Then, her expression obscured by the wavering shadows cast by the oil lamps, she slid the screen firmly closed.

As Mara paused to remove the layers of bracelets and jewellery she had worn to seem frivolous throughout her ruse, the nurse addressed her with flint in her voice. 'What is this sudden return? And who are all those ragged men?'

Mara tossed a brooch and jade necklace into a coffer with a rattle. After tension, and danger, and the intoxicating euphoria of success, the nurse's peremptory manner set her teeth on edge; keeping firm rein on herself, she twisted off her rings one by one and related in detail the plan she had executed to replenish the Acoma garrison.

As the last ornament fell with a click into the pile, Nacoya's voice rose. 'You dared stake the future of the Acoma on so ill-conceived a plan? Girl, do you know what you risked?' Mara turned to face Nacoya and found the nurse's face reddened and her hands clenched. 'Had one of those bandits struck a blow, your men would have died defending you! And for what? So that a scant dozen warriors would remain to defend the empty shell of this house when the Minwanabi came? Who would have defended the natami? Not Keyoke or Papewaio. They would have died!' Near-hysterical with anger, the old woman shook. 'You could have been used by every one of them! You could have been killed!'

Nacoya's voice rose in pitch as if she was unable to contain her anger. 'Instead of this . . . reckless adventure . . . you . . . you should have been deciding upon an appropriate marriage.' Reaching out, Nacoya grabbed Mara's arms and began to shake her, as if she were still a child. 'If you continue in your headstrong foolishness, you'll find your prospects limited to the son of some wealthy fertilizer merchant looking to buy a name for his family, while cut-throats and needra thieves guard your estate!'

'Enough!' Startled by the hardness of her own voice, Mara pushed the old woman away; and the sharpness of her manner cut through Nacoya's tirade as a scythe cuts through grass. The old woman bit off her protests. Then, as she seemed on the verge of speaking again, Mara said, 'Enough, Nacoya.' Her tone was low and deadly, barely masking her anger.

Mara faced her old nurse. She stepped forward until scant inches separated them and said, '*I* am the Lady of the Acoma.' The statement reflected little of the ire of the moment before; softening faintly, Mara studied the face of the woman who had raised her from childhood. Earnestly she said, 'Mother of my heart, of all who serve me, you are most loved.' Then her eyes narrowed and fire returned to her words. 'But *never* forget for an instant you serve me. Touch me like that, address me in such a manner again, Nacoya – ever – and I will have you beaten like a kitchen slave. Do you understand?'

Nacoya wavered an instant and slowly bowed her ancient head. Wisps of loosened hair fluttered at the nape of her neck as she stiffly knelt before Mara until both old knees rested upon the floor. 'I beg my mistress's forgiveness.'

After an instant, Mara bent forward and put her arms around Nacoya's shoulders. 'Oldest and dearest companion, fate has changed our roles. Only days ago I was a novitiate in the temple and you were my teacher and mother. Now I must rule over you, even as my father did. You serve me best by sharing your great wisdom. But in the end I alone must choose which path to follow.'

Hugging the trembling old woman close, Mara added, 'And should you doubt, remember that I was not captured by bandits. Pape and Keyoke didn't die. I chose well. My plans succeeded, and now we gain back some of what was lost.'

Nacoya was silent, then whispered, 'You were right.'

Mara released the old woman and clapped her hands twice. Maids hurried in to tend their mistress while the old nurse rose from the floor. Shaking still from her reprimand, Nacoya said, 'Lady, have I permission to withdraw?'

Mara lifted her chin as a maidservant began unfastening the collar of her robe. 'Yes, old one, but attend me after I bathe. We have much to discuss. I have given much thought to what you've advised. The time has come for me to make arrangements for marriage.'

Nacoya's dark eyes opened wide. On the heels of Mara's sudden wilfulness, this concession came as a total surprise. 'Your will, my Lady,' she said. She bowed and departed, leaving the maids to their work. In the dimness of the corridor the old woman straightened her spine with relief. At last Mara had come to accept her role as Ruling Lady. And while the vehemence of Mara's rebuke had stung sharply, the release of responsibility for a child who must manage the honour of her ancestors brought a sense of profound satisfaction. The old nurse nodded to herself. If prudence was not among Mara's virtues, the girl at least had inherited her father's astonishing boldness and courage.

An hour later the Lady of the Acoma rose from her bathing tub. Two maids wrapped her glistening body in towels while another restored the screens that partitioned the wooden tub from the rest of the sleeping quarters. Like all Tsurani great houses, the number and size of rooms were strictly a function of where and how screens and doors were placed. By sliding another screen door, Mara's sleeping chamber could be reached from the study without leaving the central apartments.

The air was still hot. Mara chose the lightest of her silk robes, barely covering mid-thigh and almost transparent, with no heavy embroidery. The day had tired her greatly, and she wished for simplicity and relaxation. Later, in the cooler hours of late evening, she would don a longer, heavier outer robe. But in the presence of her maids, and Nacoya, Mara could enjoy the immodest but comfortable lounging robe.

At her Lady's command a maid pulled aside a screen that opened onto a small section of the inner court garden, always available to Mara for reflection and contemplation. While a dozen servants could hurry on errands through the central courtyard of the house, the clever placement of screening shrubs and dwarf trees provided a cranny of green where their passing would not intrude.

Nacoya appeared as Mara seated herself before the opening. Silent, and showing signs of nervous exhaustion, the girl motioned for the nurse to sit opposite her. Then she waited.

'Mistress, I have brought a list of suitable alliances,' Nacoya opened.

Mara continued to stare out the door, her only movement a slight turning of her head as the maidservant in attendance combed out her long, damp hair. Presuming permission to continue, Nacoya unrolled the parchment between her wrinkled hands. 'Mistress, if we are to survive the plots of the Minwanabi and the Anasati, we must choose our alliance with care. We have three choices, I think. We can ally ourselves with an old and honoured name whose influence has gone into decline. Or we can choose a husband from a family newly powerful and wealthy, but seeking honour, tradition, and political alliance. Or we might seek a family that would ally because your family's name would add to some ambition of their own in the Great Game.'

Nacoya paused to allow Mara the chance to reply. But the young woman continued to stare into the gloom of the garden, the faintest of frowns creasing her brow. The maid finished with the combing; she bundled Mara's hair into a neat knot, bowed, and withdrew.

Nacoya waited. When Mara still made no move, she cleared her throat, then opened the scroll with well-concealed exasperation and said, 'I have ruled out those families who are powerful but lack tradition. You would be better served by a marriage to a son of a house that in turn has powerful allies. As this means possible entanglements with the allies of the Minwanabi and, especially, the Anasati, there are few truly acceptable houses.' She looked again at Mara, but the Lady of the Acoma seemed to be listening solely to the calls of the insects that wakened into song after sundown.

As servants made rounds to trim the lamps, Nacoya saw that the frown had deepened upon Mara's face.The old nurse straightened the parchment with a purposeful motion. 'Of all those likely to be interested, the best choices would be . . .'

Mara suddenly spoke. 'Nacoya. If the Minwanabi are the single most powerful house in the Empire, which house is the most powerfully politically connected?'

Nacoya pushed her list into her lap. 'The Anasati, without question. If the Lord of the Anasati did not exist, this list would be five times as long. That man has forged alliances with more than half the powerful Lords in the Empire.'

Mara nodded, her eyes fixed upon the air as if it held something only she could see. 'I have decided.'

Nacoya leaned expectantly forward, suddenly afraid. Mara had not even taken the list, let alone looked at the names Nacoya had dictated to the scribe. Mara turned and focused her gaze keenly upon Nacoya's face. 'I shall marry a son of the Lord of the Anasati.'

4

Gambits

The gong was struck.

The harmonics of its sound reverberated through the breadth of the great hall of the Anasati. Hung with ancient war banners, the room was thick with the smell of old waxed wood and generations of intrigue. The vaulted tiled roof hid shadows so deep the place was sombre even with candles lit. The hall itself swallowed echoes, to the point where the assembled courtiers and retainers, seated and waiting, seemed barely moving statues who made no sound.

At the head of a long, carpeted centre aisle, upon an imposing dais, sat the Lord of the Anasati in his formal robes of office. Beneath the tiered weight of his ceremonial headdress, perspiration glossed his forehead; his bone-thin features showed no trace of discomfort, though his attire was stifling in the heat of midday. A dozen sashes of scarlet and yellow restricted his breathing, while the bows that flared out like starched wings behind him bound his shoulders; each time he moved, servants were obliged to rush to his side and adjust them. In one hand he held a large carved wand, its origins lost in time, sign of his supremacy as Ruling Lord. Across his knees rested the ancient steel sword of the Anasati – a relic second in importance only to the family natami – handed down from father to son since the days of the golden bridge and the Escape, when the nations first come to Kelewan. Now its weight bore down cruelly on old knees, an inconvenience he must endure along with all the other trappings of office while waiting for the upstart Acoma girl to arrive. The room was a veritable oven, for tradition dictated that all the screens must remain closed until the formal entry of the suitor.

Tecuma, Lord of the Anasati, inclined his head slightly, and his First Adviser, Chumaka, hurried to his side. 'How long?' the Lord whispered impatiently.

'Quite soon, master.' The loyal counsellor bobbed like a nervous rodent and elaborated. 'The gong has rung thrice, as Mara's litter reached the outer gate, while it entered the main house, and now as it passes through the gate to the courtyard. The fourth chime will sound when she is admitted to your august presence, Lord.'

Irked by stillness when he longed for music, the Lord of the Anasati said, 'Have you given thought to what I asked?'

'Of course, my Lord. Your wish is my desire. I have conceived of several appropriate insults to answer the Acoma bitch's presumption.' The adviser licked his lips and added, 'To ask for your son Jiro as consort . . . well, that would be brilliant' – the Lord of the Anasati shot his adviser a curious look, which caused his ritual gown to list left. Servants flocked to him and fussed until it was properly adjusted once again. Chumaka continued his comment – 'Brilliant, if it had even the remotest hope of success. A marriage with any of your sons would bind you to the Acoma in an alliance. Not only would that deplete your resources to protect them, but then the witch could turn her full attentions to the Lord of the Minwanabi.'

The Lord of the Anasati curled his lips with thinly disguised distaste for the man just named. 'I'd marry her myself if I thought she had even the remotest possibility of defeating that jaguna in the Game of the Council.' He frowned at mention of the foul-smelling carrion eater; then his knuckles tightened on his wand as he thought aloud, 'But what does she hope to gain? She must know I would never allow her to take Jiro as consort. The Acoma is the only family older than mine, after the Five Great Families. If it falls, and by some chance one of the Five Greats falls . . .'

Chumaka finished the often repeated wish of his Lord. '. . . then the Anasati becomes one of the Five Greats.'

Tecuma nodded. 'And someday one of my descendants might rise to be Warlord.' He cast a glance to the left, where his three sons waited upon a slightly lower dais.

Closest to his father sat Halesko, heir to the Anasati mantle. Beside him was Jiro, the most clever and able of the three, already likely to marry any one of a dozen great Lords' daughters, perhaps even a child of the Emperor's, bringing the Anasati another powerful political tie. Next to him slouched Buntokapi, intently picking dirt from under his thumbnail.

Studying the lumpish visage of his youngest, the Lord of the Anasati whispered to Chumaka, 'You don't suppose by some act of providence she'd take Bunto, do you?'

The counsellor's thin eyebrows rose. 'Our intelligence indicates she may be a bright girl, if unseasoned, but for her to ask for Bunto as consort would . . . show a little more cleverness than I'd expect, Lord.'

'Cleverness? In asking for Bunto as consort?' Tecuma twisted around in disbelief, causing his bows to droop and a second flurry of fussing from his servants. 'Are you bereft of your senses?'

Regarding the stolid third son, the counsellor said, 'You might be tempted to say yes.'

With a look close to open regret, the Lord of the Anasati sighed. 'I would have to say no, I suppose, wouldn't I?'

The First Adviser clicked his tongue through his teeth. 'Even Bunto would bring her too much political power. Consider, if the Minwanabi dog accidentally killed Bunto while obliterating the Acoma . . . don't forget the mess he made by sending that Hamoi assassin.'

The Lord of the Anasati nodded. 'Yes, I'd be forced to see his family suffer vengeance. It's a shame Minwanabi bungled Mara's assassination, but I guess that was to be expected: the man's worse than a jaguna; he has the subtlety of a needra bull in a breeding pen.' Tecuma shifted in an attempt to find a more comfortable position, and his bows teetered. As servants began their approach, he froze, keeping his costume in place. 'I didn't mind humbling her father – Sezu was certainly eager to get the best of me whenever he could. But that was certainly within the rules of the game. This business of blood feuds . . .' He shook his head, and the heavy headdress slipped almost beyond his ability to prevent its fall. Chumaka reached out and gently steadied it while Tecuma continued. 'And going to all this trouble to humiliate his brat seems a waste of time.' Looking around the hot chamber, he said, 'Gods, all these musicians, and not one note of entertainment.'

Fussy with detail to the point of being pedantic, Chumaka said, 'They must remain ready to play the formal entrance music, Lord.'

The Lord of the Anasati sighed in exasperation, his frustration only partly due to the droning of his counsellor. 'I was enjoying that series of new compositions the musicians had prepared this month.

Now the entire day is wasted. Perhaps they could play something until Mara arrives?'

Chumaka shook his head slightly as perspiration rolled over the bulb of his nose. 'Lord, any breach of etiquette and the Lady of the Acoma gains from the insult.' Though by nature more patient than his master, even he wondered why the girl's retinue was taking so long to cross the central court. To the nearest servant he whispered, 'Find out what's causing the delay.'

The man bowed and slipped unobtrusively through a side door. He returned to the First Adviser within moments with his report. 'The Lady of the Acoma sits before the doors, master.'

Short-tempered at last, Chumaka whispered, 'Then why doesn't someone ring the gong and admit her?'

The servant glanced uncomfortably at the main entrance, guarded still by the costumed forms of the ceremonial door openers. With a helpless gesture he whispered 'She complained of the heat and ordered scented damp towels and cool drinks brought for herself and her retinue so they could all refresh themselves before their appearance, master.'

Chumaka considered the Anasati court, all of whom had been sitting for over an hour in the sweltering heat of midday in a closed room. Inwardly he reconsidered his estimation of Mara. Her tardiness could be a clever manipulation, calculated to goad an opponent to petty anger, gaining her an advantage.

Tecuma said, 'Well, how long can it take to drink a cup of water?'

The servant said, 'My Lord, the Lady's request caught us by surprise. It's taken time to fetch drink for so large a retinue.'

The Lord of the Anasati exchanged glances with his First Adviser. 'Just how large *is* her retinue?' asked Chumaka.

The servant reddened; uneducated, he could not count reliably past twenty. Still, he did his best to answer. 'She brought five personal maids, and an old woman of some rank. I saw two officers with plumed helms.'

'Which means no fewer than fifty warriors.' Tecuma leaned towards his First Adviser and spoke so low and quickly he almost hissed. 'I thought you had informed me that her *entire home garrison* had been reduced to fewer than fifty warriors.'

Chumaka blinked. 'My Lord, our spy in the Minwanabi household indicated that the battle which killed Sezu and his son also obliterated the main strength of the Acoma.'

The servant looked uncomfortable at being within earshot of this conversation, but Chumaka ignored that fact. Louder he said, 'Then would the Lady of the Acoma dare bring her entire remaining force with her?'

Obviously wishing to be elsewhere, the servant answered, 'Sir, the hadonra said she brought more. To our shame' – seeing the Lord of the Anasati tense at the suggestion that this lack of preparation threw dishonour on his house, the servant quickly amended his report – 'the shame of your poor servants, of course, my Lord – she was obliged to leave another one hundred warriors in camp outside the gates of my Lord's estates, as we had no ready accommodations for them.'

To the servant's profound relief, Chumaka waved him away, while the Lord of the Anasati's mood shifted from umbrage at a servant's possible slight of honour to alarm at the implication of what he had just been told. 'The Acoma Force Commander' – his hand moved in a slight circle as he searched his memory for the name – 'Keyoke, is a seasoned campaigner, and no fool. If Mara brings a hundred and fifty warriors with her, we must assume that twice that number remain to guard her main estates. Sezu's reserve garrison must have been far larger than we judged.' His eyes reflected growing irritation, then narrowed with a hint of suspicion. 'Our spy is either in the employ of the Minwanabi or incompetent. Since you were the one who convinced me to accept one not born of this house into so sensitive a position of trust, I charge you with responsibility for making enquiries. If we are betrayed, we must know at once.' The heat and the discomfort were bad enough, but Tecuma recalled the expense and difficulty he had endured to place that spy in the Minwanabi lord's house. His eyes fixed on his First Adviser. 'Clearly I see you may have steered us to a bad course.'

Chumaka cleared his throat. He made a show of cooling himself with a decorative fan, to hide his lips from any who might read them. 'My Lord, please don't judge hastily. That agent has served us dependably in the past and is *remarkably* well placed.' He paused obsequiously and licked his teeth. 'Far more likely our Lady Mara has found a way to mislead the Minwanabi lord, which would explain why our agent provided bad intelligence. I will dispatch another agent. He will return with verification of what I have surmised, or news that a traitor is dead.'

Tecuma subsided, like an irritable killwing slowly allowing ruffled feathers to return to quiescence. At that moment the fourth gong rang at last. Servants stationed inside the hall slowly opened the doors to the court, while Chumaka intoned the ancient ritual of greeting a suitor. 'We welcome one to our house, like light and wind, warmth and rain, a bringer of life into our hall.' The words were an ancient formality, reflecting nothing of the true Anasati feelings towards the Acoma. In the Game of the Council the forms must always be observed. A light breeze stirred the hangings. The Lord of the Anasati almost audibly sighed in relief. Chumaka spoke louder, so his master's slight lapse of manners would be masked. 'Enter, suitor, and tell us your desire. We offer drink and food, warmth and comfort.' Chumaka smiled inwardly at the last. No one needed or desired additional warmth this day, and Mara would certainly find little comfort before the Anasati lord. He turned his attention to those entering the hall.

Timed to the beat of a single drum, grey-robed bearers entered through the door furthest from the Lord's dais. The flat, open litter they carried was piled high with cushions; upon these Mara sat motionless. The musicians struck up the entrance song of the suitor. While the irritatingly simple melody repeated itself, the Anasati court studied this slight girl carried at the head of an impressively garbed retinue, a girl who wore the mantle of one of the proudest names in the Empire. Like the Lord who was her host, she was dressed in a fashion dictated by tradition, dark hair bound up high and held with shell- and gem-decorated pins, her face seemingly perched on a stiff, beaded collar. Her formal gown beneath was starched into pleats, with large bows of Acoma green, and floor-length sleeves. Yet for all her makeup and heavy, embroidered clothing, the girl looked unruffled by the pomp or the heat.

On Mara's left, but one pace behind, walked Nacoya, now wearing the mantle of Acoma First Adviser. On Mara's right marched three officers, armour gleaming brightly from new lacquer and fresh polish. Their helms were bedecked with magnificent new plumes. With them came a command of fifty warriors. Equally splendid in newly polished armour, they marched on either side of Mara's litter.

The soldiers paused in neat array at the foot of the dais, a splash of green amid the scarlet and yellow of the Anasati. One officer remained with the soldiers while the other two accompanied Mara's litter up three steps to the dais. There the slaves set their burden down, and two rulers confronted each other, one a cord-thin, irritated man and the other a slight girl who bargained for her very survival.

Chumaka continued his formal greetings. 'The Anasati bid welcome to our most exalted guest, the Lady of the Acoma.'

Nacoya replied as tradition dictated. 'The Acoma give thanks to our most excellent host, the Lord of the Anasati.' Despite her age, the old woman bore up well under the weight of the formal costume and the heat. Her voice was clear, as if she had been born to the role of First Adviser rather than nurse.

Now that formal greetings were exchanged, Tecuma pressed on to the point of the meeting. 'We have your petition before us, Lady of the Acoma.' A hush fell over the waiting courtiers, for Tecuma's words offered a slight insult; to name the marriage proposal a petition implied that Mara's social rank was inferior, and she within his power to reward or punish.

But the girl upon the ceremonial litter answered without a moment's hesitation. She chose a tone and phrase commonly employed when filling an order with a merchant. 'I am pleased you have no difficulty in meeting our requirements, Lord Tecuma.'

The Lord of the Anasati straightened slightly. This girl had wits and was unfazed by her welcome. Still, the day was long and hot, and the sooner this ridiculous matter was put behind, the sooner he could take to a cool pool, perhaps with some music while he bathed. Yet even with an avowed enemy the amenities must be observed. He motioned impatiently with his wand of office.

Chumaka responded with an unctuous smile and a barely perceptible bow. 'What, then, does the Lady of the Acoma propose?' Had Mara's father lived, Sezu would have conducted negotiations for his son's or daughter's hand. But as Ruling Lady, she must contract all marriages within her house, even her own, from employing the marriage brokers who initiated the contact, to the formal meeting with the Lord of the Anasati.

Nacoya bowed, so shallow a movement that the returned insult was apparent. 'The Lady of the Acoma seeks –'

'A husband,' interrupted Mara.

A stir rippled across the room, quickly stilled to a state of keen attention. All had expected to hear this presumptuous Acoma ruler request a consort, one who by law would not share in her rule.

'A husband?' Chumaka raised his brows, openly curious at this turn of events. Evidently this proposal surprised the Acoma First Adviser as well, for the old woman shot a glance of astonishment at the girl for an instant before regaining her formal composure. Chumaka could almost see where this unexpected turn might lead, but not quite, causing him the discomfort of an unreachable itch.

Mara responded in her own behalf, her voice sounding small in the spacious hall of the Anasati. 'I am too young for this weighty responsibility, my Lord. I was to have been a sister of Lashima scant moments before this terrible honour was thrust upon me. My ignorance must not become a danger to the Acoma. With full knowledge of what I do, I seek a son of the Anasati to return with me. When we are wed, he shall be Ruling Lord of the Acoma.'

The Lord of the Anasati was caught speechless. Of all possible requests, this one had not been anticipated. For in one breath this girl not only had removed herself from power, but had also effectively given over control of her family to the Anasati, who numbered among her father's oldest political enemies. So unexpected was this request, a chorus of whispers broke out among those assembled in the hall. Quickly recovering his poise, the Lord of the Anasati silenced his courtiers with a sharp glance and the barest wave of his ceremonial wand.

He stared hard at the face of this girl who had come to seek the hand of one of his sons, then said bluntly, 'You seek to cast your honour to my house, Lady. May I know why?'

The Anasati courtiers waited motionless for the reply. The only movement in the room was a sudden, sparkling reflection as sunlight through the doorway caught on gem-decorated costumes. Ignoring the dazzle, Mara lowered her eyes as if ashamed. 'My position is weak, Lord Tecuma. The Acoma lands are still strong and rich, but I am only a girl, with few resources. If my house is to become a lesser power, then at least I may choose allies. My father's greatest enemy was the Lord of the Minwanabi. This is no secret. That he and you are presently at peace is only a matter of the moment. Sooner or later you must clash.' Her small hands clenched in her lap, and her voice rose with resolve. 'I would ally with anyone who might one day crush the man responsible for my father's death!'

The First Adviser to the Lord of the Anasati turned so none in the hall could see his face – it was a given that at least one of the Acoma guards would prove to be a spy who could read lips. He whispered into the ear of the Lord Tecuma, 'I don't believe a word of this, my Lord.'

Lord Tecuma inclined his head and answered through clenched teeth. 'I don't either. Yet if this girl takes Jiro as Lord of the Acoma, I gain a great house as a lifetime ally, my son rises to a rank above any I could hope for, and she's right: sooner or later we shall have to have a final accounting with Jingu of the Minwanabi. And if we destroy the Minwanabi, a son of mine will be Lord of one of the Five Great Families.'

Chumaka shook his head in the barest motion of resignation. His Lord would be thinking that someday descendants of his in two houses might contend for the office of the Warlord. Tecuma continued his reasoning. 'Besides, she will be but the wife of the Ruling Lord. Her husband will dictate Acoma policy. No, Chumaka, whatever Mara may plot, this is too good an opportunity to pass by. I do not think this girl clever enough to outwit us once Jiro rules the Acoma.'

Tecuma glanced at his three sons and found Jiro studying Mara with interest. By the intensity of his expression, the second son found both the rank and the girl intriguing; a sensible youngster, he should welcome the marriage. Presently the boy sought his father's gaze and nodded yes. Jiro's expression was a little too avid and his nod too emphatic for Tecuma's liking. The boy knew power was a hairsbreadth from his grasp and was openly coveting it. Tecuma almost sighed; Jiro was young and would learn. Still, there was a discordant note in all this the old man didn't like. For an instant he considered sending the girl away, leaving her to the not too tender mercies of the Minwanabi. Ambition prevented him. For his son to reach a heretofore unreachable rank, combined with the pleasure of seeing the daughter of an old enemy brought firmly, and finally, to heel, overturned his last vestige of doubt. Motioning his hovering counsellor aside, the Lord of the Anasati turned to face Mara and said, 'You have chosen wisely, daughter.' By naming her 'daughter,' he irrevocably sealed his acceptance of her offer of marriage before witnesses. 'Whom do you seek to wed?'

Nacoya barely concealed her outrage, the vigorous twitch of her fan being less to cool her face than to hide the angry shaking of her hand at this betrayal. Mara smiled. Looking nothing so much as a child whose parents had banished dreams of demons in the night, she allowed two officers to aid her in rising. According to tradition, she must now pick the bridegroom. Tecuma of the Anasati had no misgivings as his future daughter-in-law stepped from her litter. He disregarded the sudden agitation of his First Adviser as the girl moved towards Jiro, mincing steps being all her voluminous ceremonial costume would allow. Light caught in her jewelled headdress as she passed before cushions upon which the three sons sat in full court raiment. Halesko and Buntokapi watched their brother Jiro with different expressions, Halesko's being something close to pride, while the youngest showed open indifference.

Mara completed the formal bow of a girl to her betrothed and stepped forward. Without hesitation her hand fell upon the shoulder of the Anasati's third son and she said, 'Buntokapi of the Anasati, will you come and be Lord of the Acoma?'

Chumaka muttered, 'I knew it! Just as she stepped from the litter, I knew it would be Bunto.' He turned his attention to Nacoya, who still hid behind her fan, but whose eyes had changed from showing rage to showing nothing. Chumaka felt a sudden stab of uncertainty. Could they all have so grossly underestimated this girl? Recovering his poise, he returned his attention to his Lord.

In the Lord's place of honour, perched above the silent, stunned ranks of the Anasati court, Tecuma sat at a loss. His bullnecked third son rose and stepped awkwardly to Mara's side, a smile of smug self-congratulation on his face. The Lord of the Anasati urgently motioned for Chumaka to attend him and, as the First Adviser did so, whispered into his ear. 'What is this? Why Bunto, of all my sons?'

Chumaka kept his voice low. 'She seeks a husband she can control.'

Tecuma frowned with stormy displeasure. 'I must stop her.'

'Lord, you cannot. The ritual has gone too far. If you recant your formal acceptance, you must kill the Lady and all her warriors here and now. I must remind you,' he added, looking as though his collar had suddenly grown too tight as he surveyed the fifty Acoma guards only a half-dozen steps away, 'your own soldiers stand *outside* this building. Even if you survived such a bloodletting – which seems unlikely – you will forfeit all honour.'

The last remark stung, for Tecuma recognized the truth. Even if he ended Mara's existence now, he would have no moral position left; his word within the council would be meaningless, and his considerable power wasted to nothing. Flushed with ire, he whispered waspishly, 'If only that idiot Minwanabi had killed the bitch last month!' Then, as Mara glanced with apparent innocence in his direction, he forced himself to regroup. 'We must turn her cleverness against her and seize the advantage, Chumaka. Jiro is still free to make a strong alliance, and Bunto . . .' His voice fell silently. 'I have never thought he would amount to much. Now he will be Lord of a great house. A malleable husband this girl may have gained, but she is an inexperienced virgin from Lashima's order. Buntokapi shall become her overlord, the Ruler of the Acoma, and he is *my* son. For the honour of the Anasati, he will do as I require.'

Chumaka watched the unlikely couple return across the dais. He did his utmost to mask his own displeasure as Buntokapi bent his bandy legs and settled awkwardly beside Mara on the Acoma litter. Already his blunt and bored expression had changed to one none present in the hall had ever seen; the boy's lips curled with a pride that bordered upon arrogance. Something long dormant in Buntokapi was now awake, that same desire for power which Jiro had shown but a moment before. Only for Buntokapi this was no dream but a thing now in his grasp. From the set of his eyes and the sudden self-assurance in his smile, he would clearly die before he let that power escape him. To Tecuma the First Adviser whispered, 'I hope you are right, my Lord.'

Looking rumpled under the elaborate layers of his costume, the Ruling Lord of the Anasati did not acknowledge the comment. Yet all through the formalities, as Mara's retainers completed the betrothal ritual and left the hall, Chumaka watched the bows on the back of his master's elaborate robes quiver with outrage. The Anasati First Adviser knew that even if the killwing was wrapped in stifling cloth, it was no less deadly.

Nacoya fought against fatigue. Age and tension had made the day impossibly long. The lengthy, strenuous journey, added to the heat of the great hall and the shock of Mara's unexpected behaviour, had brought the old nurse to the limit of her strength. Yet she was Tsurani, and Acoma, as well as acting First Adviser; she would be carried from this hall unconscious before she would shame her house by asking permission to retire.

The traditional betrothal feast was sumptuous, as befitted a celebration for an Anasati son. Yet this occasion was oddly restrained, with no one quite sure what was really being celebrated. Mara had been quiet through the early part of the feast, saying nothing of consequence to anyone. Her officers, Keyoke, Papewaio, and Tasido, sat stiffly formal, imbibing little or no sā wine. At least, thought Nacoya, the evening breeze had come up. Now the great hall was only warm, not roasting as it had been throughout the day.

Attention centred upon the table where the Acoma sat. Every guest in the house was an Anasati retainer or ally, and all attempted to discern the implications of Mara's choice of husband. To all outward appearances the Acoma girl had traded control of her house for guarantees of security, a move none would applaud, but one not entirely lacking in honour. While the Acoma would be Anasati clients for many years to come, in the future a young Acoma lord might arise and seize his own part in the Game of the Council, forging new alliances; meanwhile, the Acoma name gained the protection it needed to continue. But for this generation of Acoma retainers, Mara's betrothal was a bitter admission of weakness. Chilly despite the summer heat, Nacoya pulled a fringed shawl over her shoulders.

She glanced to the head table and studied Tecuma. The Lord of the Anasati also showed reserve throughout the feast, his conversation sombre for a man who had just achieved an undreamed-of coup over an old rival. Though gaining the Acoma lordship for Buntokapi represented great advancement in the Game of the Council, he seemed as concerned as Nacoya about this marriage, but for different reasons. His son was an unknown.

Nacoya shifted her attention. Buntokapi seemed the only celebrant who truly enjoyed himself; after a drunken hour of repeatedly telling his brothers that they were no better than he, he had shouted across the table to Jiro that now a second son would have to bow to a third son whenever they met. From the pained and frozen smile on his older sibling's face, those occasions would clearly be few. As evening wore on, Buntokapi had subsided to loud muttering into his plate, nearly immobile from drinking sā wine during dinner and acamel brandy after.

Nacoya shook her head slightly. Jiro had looked long and hard at Mara after his brother's first pronouncement of superiority; as dinner progressed, it was clear the girl had acquired another enemy. That afternoon, Jiro might have thought he was to be Lord of the Acoma for only a moment, but that brief presumption had been enough for him to feel betrayed, to feel that Buntokapi wore a mantle rightfully his. That Jiro was frustrated by nothing more than unrealized expectations of his own making meant nothing. He blamed Mara. When Tecuma had sent servants to bring the ceremonial sā wine to the guests, Jiro had barely touched his cup to his lips. He had left the first moment he could without insult. Nacoya wearily forced her attentions back to the head table.

Tecuma looked at Buntokapi a long, hard moment, then spoke quietly to Mara, who glanced at her future husband and nodded her agreement. Buntokapi blinked, trying hard to follow the exchange, but obviously too drunk to comprehend. Tecuma spoke to Chumaka, who motioned towards a pair of servants. As the cooling evening air allowed Nacoya to catch her breath, two stout servants carried the future Lord of the Acoma off to bed. Mara waited an appropriate moment, then begged her leave. Tecuma nodded brusquely and the entire company rose in salute to the bride-to-be.

The musicians who had played throughout the evening struck up the appropriate tune while Mara bade the guests good night. As she stood with the rest of the Acoma retainers, Nacoya found Chumaka approaching.

'You're leaving soon?' he inquired.

Nacoya nodded. 'Tomorrow. My Lady wishes to return at once to our estates so that she may begin preparations for the wedding and the arrival of the new Lord.'

Chumaka spread his hands as if to indicate this was no problem. 'I shall have a scribe work throughout the night. The betrothal documents will be ready to sign before you depart.' He made as if to turn away, then said something unusually frank. 'I hope for the sake of all of us this young Lady of yours hasn't made a mistake.'

Taken off guard by this, Nacoya chose not to comment directly. Instead she said, 'I can only hope the gods see fit to bless this union.'

Chumaka smiled. 'Of course, as do we all. Until the morning, then?'

Nacoya nodded and departed, signalling for the two remaining

Acoma retainers to accompany her. As an Anasati servant guided her to her quarters, she thought upon Chumaka's unexpected words and wondered if he wasn't right.

Dust rolled under the feet of marching warriors as the Acoma retinue moved slowly to rejoin the balance of their soldiers, who waited in the camp by the bridge that marked the border of the Anasati estates. Nacoya had been quiet since she joined Mara on the cushions of the large palanquin. Whatever the Ruling Lady planned, she kept her own counsel, and Nacoya chose not to ask any questions. Even though she was acting as First Adviser, she could not guide unless asked; but an old nurse could let her doubts be heard. Conjuring up images of Buntokapi's crudities at the feast the night before, Nacoya spoke sourly to her charge. 'I hope you can control him, mistress.'

Roused from deep thought, Mara's eyes focused. 'What? Oh, Bunto. He's like a needra bull smelling the cows in season, Nacoya. All his brains are between his legs. I think he is exactly the man to gain us what we need.'

Nacoya muttered under her breath. Once the shock of Mara's choice of Buntokapi had worn off, the old nurse had come to sense a larger plan. Mara was not simply giving up her family's control to the Anasati in exchange for preserving the Acoma name. Since the ruse with the bandits in the hills, the girl confided only those things she felt Nacoya needed to know. Almost overnight, it seemed, the sheltered temple innocent had shown she was no longer a child. While Nacoya had doubts, even fears, concerning the girl's stubborn naïveté about men, Mara had forcefully demonstrated she was an aggressive player of the Game of the Council.

Nacoya reviewed the strengths and weaknesses, patterns and powers of the players in the light of her mistress's new commitment. And what she had observed in Buntokapi made her convinced that her beloved Mara might have underestimated him. There was something about the Anasati's third son, something dangerous that Nacoya could put no name to. Dreading how her well-ordered house would fare under such a Ruling Lord, she was drawn from her musing by Mara's voice. 'I wonder what's amiss?'

Nacoya parted the curtains. Squinting against the brilliance of the afternoon sunlight, she saw Acoma soldiers arrayed along the road where they had camped. But none stood ready to march; instead they faced each other in two groups, with some distance between. Softly Nacoya said, 'Trouble, I'm afraid.'

Mara ordered her own escort to halt. Pulling aside the gauzy hanging cloth, she approved Keyoke's request to investigate.

With a speed that belied his age, the Force Commander left the head of the procession and hurried into the midst of milling Acoma soldiers. Both groups descended upon him, several men trying to speak simultaneously. Keyoke ordered silence, and instantly all voices ceased. After two orderly questions he called back to Mara, 'Some difficulty arose while we were gone, mistress. I'll have the story for you in a moment.'

Heat shimmers danced in the air above the roadway. Keyoke asked questions, received quick replies, and soon had three men stand out. He briskly marched these before their mistress's palanquin. Even beneath dirt, and shining runnels of sweat, Mara could see the marks of a fight upon their faces.

'This is Selmon, my Lady.' Keyoke pointed to a man with a torn tunic and knuckles that still bled.

'I know.' Mara's expression was obscured by the deep shade of the curtains. 'One of the newcomers.' She used the term 'newcomers' for all who had recently been grey warriors. 'With only three officers, you left him in command as acting Patrol Leader.'

Keyoke appeared pleased that Mara was conversant with his management of the soldiers, but his attention never strayed from the three soldiers. 'Selmon seemed able enough, but perhaps I was wrong.'

Mara studied the other two men. One, Zataki, she had known for years; as a boy, he had played with Lanokota and herself. Mara remembered he had a temper, and ventured a guess as to what the problem was. 'Zataki, Selmon gave you an order and you refused.'

Zataki lifted his chin. 'My Lady, this Selmon ordered us to stand the first watch while he and his companions rested and ate after the long day's march.'

Mara regarded the third combatant. 'You are . . . Kartachaltaka, another newcomer. You took exception to Zataki's refusal to obey.'

Now Kartachaltaka stiffened his spine. 'My Lady, he and the

others act superior to us and put the least desirable duties upon us whenever they may.'

Mara returned her attention to Selmon. 'You took this one's side?'

Keyoke hastened to answer. 'No, my Lady. He simply sought to intervene and stop the scuffle. He acted appropriately.'

Mara rose from her cushions. Without awaiting Keyoke's help, she stepped from her palanquin and faced the two men who had fought. 'On your knees!' she commanded. Though a full head shorter than either man, the slight girl in pale yellow robes and sandals left no doubt she was the ultimate authority of the Acoma.

Armour rattled as both men instantly fell into postures of submission. 'Attend me!' Mara cried to the other soldiers. 'All of you.'

Keyoke shouted, 'Form ranks!' The entire retinue lined up facing Mara within seconds, the two soldiers on their knees with their backs towards the comrades.

To Keyoke, Mara said, 'What is fit punishment for such as these?'

Keyoke spoke without regret. 'Mistress, these men must be hanged, now.' Mara's head jerked as she met Keyoke's eyes. She had not expected the judgment to be so harsh. The Force Commander deliberately scratched his jaw with his thumb.

Warned by Keyoke's gesture that serious consequences could come of her decision, Mara regarded Papewaio, who looked on, his face an unreadable mask. Then, almost imperceptibly, he nodded once, indicating his full agreement with Keyoke's verdict.

Mara felt something go cold inside. She knew that if she did not act at once and without equivocation a breach might be fashioned between those who had served for years and those newly come to Acoma service. Steeling herself, Mara addressed the soldiers. Her voice held barely controlled anger. 'There are no favoured men in this garrison! There are no longer any "newcomers". There are no longer any "old guard". There is no one wearing Acoma green but Acoma soldiers. Each of you swore an oath to obey and to give your lives in service to House Acoma.'

She walked purposefully along the ranks, looked into one rough face after another, until she had locked eyes with each man. 'Some of you I have known since childhood. Others have been with us only a matter of weeks, but each of you bears equal responsibility to wear Acoma green with honour. I have just promised to give that name to another, to ensure that the Acoma will continue to live, and more than live . . . someday flourish!' Now her voice rose to a shout, her fury clearly revealed to each soldier present. 'Whoever dishonours himself while wearing Acoma green dishonours the Acoma' – her voice dropped to a soft, deadly sound – 'dishonours me.' While the men held their formations, their eyes shifted uneasily as they saw Mara turn suddenly to confront the two combatants. Looking down, she spoke to Zataki. 'You were given a lawful order by an officer placed over you by your Force Commander. You had no other choice but to obey!'

The man fell forward, pushing his forehead into the acrid dust of the road. He uttered no words in his own defence as his mistress turned to Kartachaltaka and said, 'And you struck a brother soldier while on duty!' He duplicated Zataki's gesture of abject obedience to his mistress. Bracelets chimed on her wrists; wrought of costly metal, these were the betrothal gift of the Lord of the Anasati, and that such wealth should be worn as personal adornment reminded the kneeling men of their station. They grovelled in the sun, sweating, as their mistress addressed their Force Commander. 'These two men are guilty of betraying Acoma honour. Hang them.'

Keyoke instantly detailed soldiers to carry out the execution. For just an instant, Mara could read something in the two condemned men's eyes: a flicker of fear. Not a fear of death, for either warrior would have gladly embraced death without hesitation; it was fear of being condemned to the shameful death of a slave: hanging. With the loss of a warrior's honour, each knew his next turn of the Wheel of Life would be at a lower station, a servant, perhaps even a slave. Then the proper Tsurani mask was returned. Only by bearing up properly in the face of this meanest of all deaths could either man hope for any mercy when next his spirit was tied to the Wheel.

Mara stood motionless before her litter, a statue of iron self-control, as soldiers marched the condemned to a large tree with massive branches. The two men were quickly stripped of their armour and their hands were tied behind their backs. Without ceremony or final prayer, ropes were fashioned into nooses and thrown over the tree limbs. The nooses were placed around the two men's necks and the signal given. A half-dozen soldiers pulled hard upon each rope, seeking to snap the men's necks and give them a mercifully quick death. Zataki's neck broke with an audible crack and he kicked once, quivered a moment, then hung motionless. Kartachaltaka's death was more painful, as he strangled slowly, kicking and swinging, but in the end he, too, hung motionless like bitter fruit from the tree.

Mara's voice was flat as she said, 'Keyoke, home.'

Abruptly, the sun seemed too bright. Overcome by the killing she had commanded to be done, Mara caught the edge of the palanquin canopy, steadying herself without betraying weakness to her soldiers. She motioned one of her slave boys, who brought her a fruit-sweetened drink of water. She sipped it slowly, striving to regain her composure, while Keyoke ordered the men formed into ranks for the march home.

Nacoya had kept her own counsel in the shelter of the litter, but as Mara stood motionless, she said, 'Mistress?'

Mara handed her empty cup to the slave. 'I'm coming, Nacoya. We must be off. There is a great deal to be done in the month before the wedding.' Without further words she climbed back into the litter. As her bearers reached down to resume their burden, she settled into the cushions beside Nacoya and her pensive silence returned. Keyoke gave the order to march, and her soldiers fell into ranks before, after, and on both sides of the palanquin, to outward appearances a single group once again.

Mara began to tremble, her eyes wide and distant. Without words Nacoya slipped her arm around the girl's shoulders. The tremors continued as the Acoma retinue began its march, until Mara quivered so violently Nacoya had to gather the shaking girl in her arms. Silently the very young Lady of the Acoma turned her face into her nurse's shoulder and smothered her sobs.

As they approached the borders of her estate, Mara considered the difficulties she faced. She had only spoken in passing to Keyoke and Nacoya since ordering the execution of the two soldiers. Mara knew that the conflict between the former grey warriors and the survivors of her father's garrison should have been anticipated.

Blaming herself for failing to do so, Mara pulled aside her litter curtain and called for her Force Commander. As he arrived at her side she said, 'Keyoke, why did Selmon order the older soldiers to stand first watch, rather than a mix of old and new?'

If he was surprised by his mistress's question, he showed no sign. 'Lady, Selmon erred by trying not to antagonize the older soldiers. He thought that by serving first duty they'd have an uninterrupted rest from meal to morning watch, and they'd appreciate it. Zataki was a young hothead, and had any of us been here' – he motioned to himself, Papewaio, and Tasido, the three officers who had accompanied Mara into the Anasati estate house – 'none of that would have occurred.' He paused as he considered his next statement. 'But Selmon did not do poorly. The conflict bordered upon open fighting between factions, yet he managed to restrain all but the two who were punished.'

Mara nodded. 'When we are home, promote Selmon to Patrol Leader. Our forces have grown to the point where we need more officers.'

Then Mara made one of the swift, unhesitating decisions that were earning her the respect of those who served her. 'Promote two of our best men in our old guard as well. Choose the very best of our family's oldest soldiers, perhaps Miaka, and make him a Strike Leader. Bring one of the new men up as well. That rascal Lujan was a Strike Leader with the Kotai. If you can't think of anyone more able, give the rank to him.'

Keyoke shrugged, offering no better candidate among the newcomers. Mara conceded her satisfaction at this, then added, 'I'll have these cadres and alliances quickly broken; there will be no favourites.' Keyoke nodded slightly, his leathery face showing the barest suggestion of a smile, as close as he ever came to openly expressing approval. Almost to herself, Mara added, 'Soon I'll need men at my side who will obey without hesitation. I cannot afford anything that interferes with my plans.'

Clearly she was occupied with the responsibilities of rulership. Keyoke hurried his pace back to the head of the column, considering how much like her father the girl was becoming.

As Mara's litter moved through the Acoma needra meadows, she felt optimistic for the first time since leaving Lashima's temple. Her thoughts churned. She would discuss her ideas with no one, not even Nacoya or Keyoke. For those notions were turning into plots, the beginnings of a master plan that led beyond simple survival into an ambition that turned her mind giddy.

Over time, Mara expected that her planning would have to be amended to deal with change: unanticipated shifts of power and alliances within the Game of the Council. In many ways, resolve came before means and method; she had years of learning before what she inwardly called her grand scheme could reach fruition. But marriage to Buntokapi was the first small step. Since leaving the Anasati lands, she had discovered hope, and the powerful allure of new dreams.

By the time the palanquin swayed up the walk towards the great house, practical matters eclipsed her dreaming. Lights blazed in the gloom of twilight, more than ordinary events might warrant. In their glow, Mara saw perhaps eighty men gathered outside the kitchen, many eating from bowls. Lujan walked among them, speaking and making expansive gestures with his hands. As her duty retinue approached, a few of the strangers set their meal aside and stood. The rest continued eating, though all looked nervous.

Mara glanced to see Nacoya, but the old woman was asleep, lulled by the heat and the rocking of the litter through the afternoon. As the palanquin settled to the ground, Lujan hurried over, bowing politely as Keyoke assisted Mara out. Before she could ask, the former bandit chieftain said, 'Mistress, these are all worthy men, at least worthy as I am likely to measure such things. All would gladly enter your service.'

'Soldiers?' Instantly interested, Keyoke released his hold upon Mara's hand.

Lujan doffed his helmet, the reflection of the lanterns like sparks in his deepset eyes. 'Only a few, unfortunately, Force Commander. But the others are armourers, fowlers, cordwainers, wheelwrights, and other skilled craftsmen, as well as two farmers.'

Mara said, 'Good, I'm running low on land to assign to new farmers. Now, how many soldiers?'

'Thirty-three.' Lujan stepped aside with a grace more suited to a dancer than a warrior. He assisted the newly awakened Nacoya from the palanquin. But his attention remained focused on his mistress.

Mara calculated. 'That will swell our main garrison to over three hundred. Our position is no longer helpless, only desperate.'

'We need more soldiers,' Nacoya concluded tartly. She shuffled past to enter the great house, sleepiness making her more cross than usual.

Lujan tossed his helm lightly from his right hand to his left. 'Mistress, getting more men will prove difficult. We have called in every grey warrior within reasonable distance of your borders. For more, we shall have to leave these lands and travel.'

'But you know where to look for such,' stated Mara, her eyes locked upon the hands that toyed still with the helmet.

Lujan returned a rakish smile. 'Mistress, I suffer from a shortage of humility, I know, but I have lived in every bandits' stand from here to Ambolina since the fall of the House of Kotai. I know where to look.'

'How much time do you need?'

A wicked gleam lit his eye. 'How many men do you wish to recruit, Lady?'

'One thousand; two would be better.'

'Aie, mistress, a thousand would take three, four months.' The helmet stilled as Lujan grew thoughtful. 'If I could take some trusted men with me, perhaps I could shorten that to six weeks. Two thousand . . . ?'

Mara's bracelets chimed as she gestured impatiently. 'You will have three weeks. The recruits must be returned here, sworn to oath, and integrated into our force inside a month.'

Lujan's smile turned to a grimace. 'My Lady, for you I would face a horde of Thūn raiders without weapons, but what you demand is a miracle.'

Evening shadow hid Mara's flush, but she showed uncharacteristic animation as she signalled for Papewaio. The moment her Strike Leader completed his bow, she said, 'Find some good men for Lujan.' Then she regarded the former outlaw appraisingly. 'Choose from both old and new soldiers. Perhaps some time on the trail together will convince them they have more in common than not.' Then she added, 'Any you think might become troublemakers.'

Lujan seemed unruffled by the proposition. 'Troublemakers are nothing new to me, my Lady.' His grin broadened. 'Before I rose to become an officer, I dare say I was something of a troublemaker myself.'

'I daresay you were,' commented Keyoke. Motionless in the darkness, he had all but been forgotten. The former bandit leader started slightly and immediately became more restrained.

'You must travel as fast and as far as possible for twelve days,

Lujan,' instructed Mara.' Gather as many reliable men as you can. Then return here. If you can't find me two thousand, find me two hundred, and if you can't find two hundred, find me twenty, but make them good warriors.' Lujan nodded, then bowed with a faultless propriety that earned a return smile from Mara. 'Now show me the ones you've found for me tonight.'

Lujan escorted Mara and Keyoke to where the poorly dressed men were sitting. All stood as soon as the Lady of the Acoma approached, and several knelt. To those who had known the hardships of outlawry, she seemed an imperial princess in her jewels and fine clothes. The roughest among them listened respectfully as Mara repeated the offer she had made to Lujan and his followers upon the trail in the mountains; and like three other bands since then, almost sixty skilled workmen rose to accept quarters and assignments from Jican. Mara smiled to see the light in her hadonra's eyes as he contemplated how he could turn their handiwork to a rich profit; and armourers would be needed if Lujan successfully recruited her hoped-for new warriors. The crowd thinned, and some of the confusion abated as the workers followed Jican.

Of the others who remained, Lujan said, 'My Lady, these are thirty-three well-seasoned warriors who would swear before the Acoma natami.'

'You've explained everything to them?'

'I daresay as well as anyone could, except yourself, of course.' As Keyoke snorted disapproval, Mara looked to see if the former outlaw chieftain was mocking; he wasn't, at least not openly. Aware, suddenly, of the strange pull this man seemed to exert on her, she recognized in him the same sly wit she had loved in her brother, Lanokota. His teasing caused her to flush slightly. Quickly she wiped her forehead as if the heat were making her perspire. This man was not her kin, or even a Lord equal in rank to her; unsure how to respond after months of isolation in the temple, she turned firmly to the task at hand. All the men were fit if undernourished, and they seemed eager, except for two who sat slightly apart. One of those exchanged glances with Lujan.

'You know this man?' asked Mara.

Lujan laughed. 'Indeed, mistress. This is Saric, my cousin, who served with the Lord of the Tuscai. Before he left the Kotai estates, he was my closest companion.'

Looking to nettle Lujan in return for her earlier embarrassment, Mara said, 'Is he an able soldier?'

Lujan grinned and his cousin returned a nearly identical broad smile. 'My Lady, he is as able a soldier as I.'

'Well then, that solves a problem.' Mara tapped the helm that still dangled from Lujan's wrist, called a soldier's pot, for its utter lack of unadornment. 'I was going to ask you to give that to him and assume one with an officer's plume. Keyoke had orders to promote you to Strike Leader, but as you are going to be away for three weeks, he might as well promote your cousin in your stead.'

His grin still in place, Lujan said, 'Well, almost as able as I, Lady.' Slightly more serious, he added, 'With your consent, I'll take him with me. I mean no disrespect for any other soldier here, but there is no man I would rather have at my side with a sword.' Then his tone turned light again. 'Besides, we might as well keep the party composed exclusively of troublemakers.'

Mara couldn't resist. For the first time since Lano's death the frown eased entirely from her face, lantern light revealing a surprisingly lovely smile. 'Then you had best collect your plume from Keyoke, Strike Leader.' To the newcomer she said, 'Welcome, Saric.'

The man bowed his head. 'Mistress, your honour is my honour. With the gods' favour I shall die a warrior – not too soon, I hope – and in the service of beauty such as yours, a happy one.'

With a lift of her brows, Mara glanced at both men. 'It seems flattery runs in your family, as well as a certain casual attitude towards rank.' Then she indicated the other man who had been sitting with Saric. He wore plain clothes and simple hide sandals. His hair was trimmed in nondescript fashion, not the close cut of a warrior, the fashionable ringlets of a merchant, or the ragged shag of a worker. 'Who is this?'

The man arose while Saric said, 'This is Arakasi, Lady. He also was in my Lord's employ, though he was not a soldier.'

The man was of medium build and regular features. But his manner had neither the proud bearing of a warrior nor the deference of a worker. Suddenly uncertain, Mara said, 'Then why did you not stand forward with the craftsmen and workers?'

Arakasi's dark eyes flickered slightly, perhaps in amusement, but his face remained expressionless. Then he changed. Though he hardly moved, his demeanour changed; suddenly he seemed the aloof, self-possesssed scholar. With that, Mara noticed what she should have seen at once: his skin was in no way weathered as a field worker's would have been. His hands had some toughness, but no thick pads of callus left by toil with tools or weapons. 'Lady, I am not a farmer.'

Something put Keyoke on his guard, for he moved without thought to interpose himself between his mistress and the stranger. 'If you are not a farmer or soldier, what are you, a merchant, sailor, a tradesman, a priest?'

Barely acknowledging Keyoke's intervention, Arakasi said, 'Lady, in my time I have been all of those. Once I guested with your father in the guise of a priest of Hantukama. I have taken the identities of a soldier, a merchant, a slave master, a whoremonger, a riverman, even a sailor and a beggar.'

Which explained some things, thought Mara, but not all. 'To whom were you loyal?'

Arakasi bowed startlingly, with the grace and practised ease of a noble born. 'I was servant to the Lord of the Tuscai, before the Minwanabi dogs killed him in battle. I was his Spy Master.'

Mara's eyes widened despite her attempt at self-control. 'His Spy Master?'

The man straightened, his smile devoid of humour. 'Yes, mistress. For one reason above all should you wish me in your service: my late Lord of the Tuscai spent the best part of his fortune building a network of informants, a network I oversaw, with agents in every city in the Empire and spies within many great houses.' His voice dropped, a strange mix of reluctance and pride. 'That network is still in place.'

Suddenly, sharply, Keyoke scratched his chin with his thumb.

Mara cleared her throat, with a keen look at Arakasi, whose aspect seemed to shift from moment to moment. 'Such things are best not discussed in the open.' She glanced about. 'I still have the dust of travel upon me, and have had no pause for refreshment since midday. Attend me in my chambers in an hour's time. Until then Papewaio will see to your needs.'

Arakasi bowed and joined Papewaio, who gestured for the Spy Master to follow him to the bathhouse near the barracks.

Left with Keyoke and the presence of thirty-three masterless warriors, Mara remained caught up in thought. After a silent interval she mused softly, 'The Spy Master of the Tuscai.' To Keyoke she said, 'Father always said the Lord of the Tuscai knew more than was righteous in the eyes of the gods. Men joked that he had a magician with a crystal locked away in a vault under his study. Do you suppose this Arakasi was the reason?'

Keyoke offered no direct opinion but said, 'Be cautious of him, mistress. A man who spies uses honesty least of all. You were right to send him away with Pape.'

'Loyal Keyoke,' said Mara with affection in her voice. She tilted her head in the torchlight, indicating the ragged group of men who awaited her command. 'Do you suppose you can swear this lot to service by the natami, and still have time for a bath and dinner?'

'I must.' The Force Commander returned a rare, wry shrug. 'Though how I've lived to be this old while burdened with so much work, only the gods know.' Before Mara could respond, he shouted a command, and like the trained soldiers they were, the scruffy men crowding the courtyard mustered at the voice of authority.

5

Bargain

Evening gave way to night.

Soft lights burned in Mara's chamber. The outer screens had been opened to admit the breeze and the lamplight flickered and danced. The Lady of the Acoma sent away her servants, ordering one to have chocha brought. Alone with Nacoya a moment before the others appeared, Mara stripped off the ostentatious bracelets given her by the Anasati lord. She peeled off her dirty travelling robe and dabbed a damp cloth over her body; a full bath would have to wait until after her meeting with Arakasi.

Nacoya remained silent while Mara refreshed herself, but her eyes never left her young mistress. Neither of them spoke. The reproach Mara saw in those old eyes told all: the girl was inexperienced and foolish, perhaps even dangerously so, in matching herself with Buntokapi. He might appear slow-witted, but he was a powerful warrior, and though barely two years older than she, he had been reared in the Game of the Council while Mara had sheltered in the temple of Lashima.

As Mara wrapped a delicate saffron-coloured robe about herself, the servant returned with the chocha. She motioned permission, and the slave placed his large tray in the centre of the low table, then departed. Mara nodded to Nacoya, indicating that the old woman should prepare cups and napkins.

Her two officers and the stranger arrived punctually upon the hour. Mara studied the newcomer keenly as he bowed and seated himself between Keyoke and Papewaio. Arakasi's style was impeccably correct, his manner a match for the clothing he now wore in place of his beggar's rags. Mara suddenly realized she had seen his tasselled scarlet shirt before; the garment was Papewaio's, his favourite, worn on feast days only. Mara considered the significance of his loan to Arakasi. In the hour that had passed since their meeting in the courtyard, the former Spy Master of the Tuscai must have impressed the Acoma First Strike Leader very favourably. That was a strong recommendation, for, like her father before her, Mara placed strong trust in Papewaio's instincts about people.

Bolstered by that confidence, she asked, 'Has Lujan spoken of what we do here?'

Arakasi nodded. 'He's off to find more grey warriors to take service.' He paused, then added, 'But each time you recruit, you greatly increase the chance spies might infiltrate. Soon you cannot trust any who come here.'

'You might be such an agent,' interrupted Nacoya.

'Old mother, I have nothing to gain by lying.' Arakasi took charge of the chocha pot, usurping Nacoya's role as server with flawless ease. Deferentially he filled Mara's cup, then Nacoya's, Keyoke's, and Papewaio's before his own. 'Were I a spy for another house, I would simply have enlisted and sent word of your desperate situation back to my master. Then the assassins would come, probably in the next band of recruits. Your suspicions then would become entirely academic, as you would be murdered along with your mistress.' He put down the pot. 'And if I didn't see an opportunity here for myself and my agents, I would have played a farmer, slipped away in the dark, and never troubled any of you again.'

Mara nodded. 'Your logic is difficult to fault. Now tell us what we need to know of you.'

The stranger answered frankly. 'I have been employed for over twenty years, to establish and oversee a network of spies spanning the Empire. It now rivals any in the land, including the Warlord's. I even have agents working for other Spy Masters, one who is dormant, never having been employed, harboured against a day of great need –'

At this, Keyoke leaned forward. 'The obliteration of your house was not a great enough need?'

Arakasi took Keyoke's rudeness in stride. 'No agent of mine could have aided my master, or prevented his final fate. Especially not the one I mentioned. He works within the Imperial Chancellery, on the staff of the Warlord.'

Even Keyoke couldn't hide his astonishment. The Spy Master

continued. 'My master was a man of vision but limited wealth. So extensive was his commitment to gathering intelligence, he was unable to use it to good effect. Perhaps if I had not been so ambitious in my requirements . . . ' Arakasi set down his chocha cup with barely a click. 'Had the Minwanabi not grown fearful of my Lord's ability to anticipate their every move, today the Tuscai might have been among the most powerful families in the Empire.' He sighed in regret. 'But "might have been is but ashes upon the wind", as they say. The attack was simple and straightforward. My lord's warriors were overwhelmed by brute strength. I have since learned that my agents do little good if their information cannot be acted upon.'

Keyoke had barely touched his cup of chocha. His eyes glinted through rising steam as he said, 'So where are your agents today?'

Without hesitation, Arakasi faced Mara. 'Lady, I will not reveal who they are. If I offend, I ask pardon. I still owe much to those who once served my master, and will not expose them to additional danger. If you take us into service, we shall require the same concessions that were made by my Lord of the Tuscai.'

Mara acknowledged Keyoke's warning glance with a half nod. 'Those being?' she prompted, and waited keenly for Arakasi's reply.

'I will oversee my couriers and contacts, and I alone will know the names of the agents, and how to reach them; you will be told only where they serve.'

Keyoke set his chocha cup down forcefully, as near as he had ever come to displaying anger. 'These are unreasonable requirements!'

'Force Commander,' said Arakasi, 'I do not wish to be difficult. I may not have served my master as well as I wished, but I protect those who worked so diligently on his behalf – in ways as dangerous to them as battle to a soldier. A spy dies in shame by the rope. My people risk both life and honour for a master they will not betray. I ensure that no matter what may happen, their master cannot betray them.'

Confronted by uncertain expressions, he nodded and qualified his statement. 'When the Minwanabi crushed the Tuscai, they interrogated my master . . . ' Shifting dark eyes to Mara, he softened his voice. 'There is no reason to relate details. I know of these things only because one of my people was left for dead and managed to observe for a while before escaping. Jingu's torturer was efficient. My master could not have withheld any information, despite being a courageous man. Lady, judge fairly: if you wish my services, and the services of those who worked for me, then you will have to take us on faith.'

'And if I don't?'

Arakasi stilled, his hands in plain view to banish any impression of threat. Slowly he turned his palms upward, a sign of resignation. 'Then I shall return to the hills.'

Mara cocked her head slightly. Here, at last, the man showed a moment of genuine feeling. To wear house colours again was more important to him than he cared to admit. Concerned lest she cause him embarrassment, Mara asked simply, 'Then what?'

Arakasi shrugged. 'My lady, I have worked in many guises to protect my identity. I can fix a wagon, play the flute, scribe, and do sums. I am also a talented beggar, if the truth be known. I will manage, have no doubt.'

Keyoke fixed him with a penetrating look. 'I think you could gain a position and live comfortably at will. So then what were you doing in the woods with outlaws?'

Arakasi shrugged, as if distrust of his motives was of no consequence. 'I keep in touch with Saric and others of the Tuscai. I often traded in the cities on their behalf, using my wits and talents. And through them I met Lujan and his band. I had just reached Saric's camp when Lujan's call came. I thought I'd come along and see what this odd business was.' With his head inclined towards Mara, he added, 'I must say I admire the way you bend tradition to suit your needs, Lady.'

Mara answered, 'Only as needed, Arakasi, and never broken.' She looked at the man for a moment. 'Still, you've not said why you haven't abandoned your network. I would think it safer if you all simply faded into the roles you portrayed when your master died and lived out your lives.'

Arakasi smiled. 'Safer, undoubtedly; even the infrequent contacts I've maintained over the last four years put some of my people at risk. But for our honour, we keep the network alive.' He paused, then said, 'Our reasons are part of my requirements to take service with you. And you shall hear them only if you choose to reach an agreement.'

About to speak, Keyoke then gave a simple shake of his head; no one should presume to bargain with the Ruler of the Acoma in this fashion. Mara glanced at Nacoya, who was thoughtfully following the conversation, then at Papewaio, who nodded once, lending Arakasi his silent endorsement.

Mara took a breath. 'I think I see the wisdom in your requirements, Spy Master. But what would become of your network should mishap befall you?'

'My agents have means of routinely checking upon one another. Should a needra pause to sit upon the spot where I nap, thus ending my career, another agent would make himself known to you within one month's time.' Arakasi sobered. 'He would give you proof that could not be counterfeited, and you could trust him as you would me.'

Mara nodded. 'Trust, though, that is the difficulty. Either of us would be a fool to relinquish caution too quickly.'

'Of course.'

A slight breeze caused the flames to gutter in the lamps, and for an instant the chamber swam with shadows. Nacoya made an unthinking gesture against disaster and the gods' displeasure. But Mara was too absorbed to worry over superstition. 'If I agree to your terms, will you take service?'

Arakasi bowed slightly from the waist, a gesture he accomplished with grace. 'I wish to serve a house as much as any soldier, mistress, but there is one thing more. We keep the network intact for reasons of honour. After the House of Tuscai fell, I and those who worked with me made a vow. We will not take service if we must break that vow.'

'What is the vow?'

Arakasi looked directly at Mara, and his eyes reflected fanatic passion, unmasked by any attempt at guile. In even tones he said, 'Vengeance upon the Lord of the Minwanabi.'

'I see.' Mara settled back against her cushions, hoping the passion in her own heart was not so easily read. 'We share an enemy, it seems.'

Arakasi nodded. 'For now. I know the Acoma and the Minwanabi are in contention, but the tides of politics often change –'

Mara held up her hand, silencing him. 'The Acoma have a blood feud with the Minwanabi.'

Arakasi stilled and regarded the worn heel of the sandal tucked under his knee. So profound was his silence that all in the chamber felt chilled. Here was a man of seemingly limitless patience, like the tree-lord serpent, who would blend with a branch, unseen, tirelessly waiting for prey to pass by, then strike with unexpected fury. When at last Arakasi stirred, Mara observed that the strain of this interview had begun to wear at his control. Despite his talents and training, the Spy Master had the same conflicting emotions as those ragged soldiers and servants who had come to her: he might gain a second beginning, only to become masterless once again. Yet his voice reflected no turmoil as he said, 'If you will have us, I and mine will swear loyalty to the Acoma.'

Mara nodded.

Arakasi's face suddenly became animated. 'Then, my mistress, let us begin, for an advantage may be gained if you act quickly. Before coming to the hills, I spent time in the north, with a friend in the House of Inrodaka. It is common gossip among the workers there that to the west, near the woodland borders of their Lord's estates, a cho-ja hive has spawned a new queen.'

'No word has been sent?' asked Mara, instantly interested.

Arakasi gestured in the negative. 'The Lord of the Inrodaka is a quiet man with few guests and even fewer sojourns abroad. But time is short. The fruit harvesters soon will carry word to the river. The news will then race the breadth of the Empire, but for now you are the only Ruling Lady or Lord to know that a new queen of the cho-ja will soon be seeking a home. She will have at least three hundred warriors to serve her,' and with a glint of humour he added, 'and if you win her loyalty, you can be certain none of them will be spies.'

Mara stood. 'If this is true, we must leave before morning.' Gaining a cho-ja hive for her estates would be a gift from the gods. Alien the cho-ja might be, but they made fierce and loyal allies. The new queen might begin her nest with three hundred soldiers, each easily the match for two Tsurani, but over the years the number might grow to several thousand; and as Arakasi pointed out, none of them could be agents for enemy houses. To Keyoke, Mara said, 'Have trailbreakers ready within the hour. We will start our journey to this hive at dawn.' As the Force Commander departed, she returned her attention to Arakasi. 'You will accompany us. Papewaio will arrange for servants and see that your needs are met.'

Mara signalled an end to the meeting. As her advisers rose to depart, Nacoya touched Arakasi's sleeve. 'The girl knows nothing of the cho-ja. How will she negotiate?'

Effortlessly courteous, Arakasi took the old woman's hand and ushered her to the doorway as if she were some treasured great-aunt. 'The sending of a new queen occurs so rarely, no one can be prepared to negotiate. The Lady of the Acoma must simply accommodate to whatever the new queen requests.'

As the pair disappeared into the corridor, Mara could barely contain her excitement. All thoughts of her forthcoming wedding were eclipsed by this news; to have a hive upon one's estate was more than an honour and a source of military power. For beyond being superior warriors, cho-ja were miners, able to find precious metals and gems buried deep within the earth, from which their artisans wrought jewellery of surpassing delicacy. The insectoid aliens also held the secret of making silk, the cool, soft fabric most prized by those who lived in the ever present heat of the Empire. Wars had been fought to control the silk trade, until imperial edict allowed for neither guild nor noble to monopolize it. Now any lord who could gain silk could trade it.

Cho-ja products were valuable, and their requirements simple: grain and items fashioned of hide; for these reasons families would kill to gain a hive upon their estates. And among all the hives known in the Empire, the cho-ja sent forth a new queen less often than once in a human lifetime.

But Mara would need to convince the new queen to migrate to Acoma lands. If she failed, representatives of other houses would follow, until the queen received an offer that pleased her. And as Arakasi had observed, what would strike the fancy of a creature as alien as a cho-ja remained a mystery.

Lujan and his company left for the hills to search for recruits, all but unnoticed amid the bustle of servants gathering supplies for the escort who would depart to bargain for the new cho-ja queen.

Mara left her quarters well before dawn. The herders had not yet stirred to drive the needra to the meadows, and the mists hung still over grasses shiny with dew. Cloaked in dark cloth against the damp, she waited before an unadorned litter with Jican at her side. His tally slate was written over with notes, and he held his stylus poised while Mara dictated last-minute instructions.

Suddenly she bit her lip in agitation. 'Gods, the excitement almost made me forget!'

Jican raised his brows. 'Mistress?'

'Wedding invitations.' Mara shook her head in frustration. 'Nacoya will direct you to the proper ritual verses. She will know even better than I who must be invited and who may be ignored. Be sure to ask her on my behalf to oversee all requirements I have forgotten.'

Jican questioned as he jotted hurried notes. 'What about the summer stock sale, mistress? Animals to be auctioned must be registered with the Breeders' Guild in advance.'

'You've chosen well so far,' Mara said, aware she had run out of time. 'I trust your judgment.' Keyoke arrived with a chosen troop of warriors, and Papewaio and Arakasi already waited, talking, a short distance away.

The men assembled with the silent efficiency of veterans, and soon the last one took his place. Keyoke approached, wearing the dark, serviceable armour suitable for unobtrusive travel in the wilds. His officer's helm carried only a single short plume, and his ornate ceremonial sword had been replaced with the one he preferred to use in battle.

Stopping before Mara, Keyoke bowed. 'Mistress, the men are ready. Your bearers stand with the supplies, and the trailbreakers are already on their way. We may depart at your word.'

Mara dismissed Jican with a wish for prosperity and fair trading. Then she entered her litter and reclined upon the cushions. 'Tell the men to march,' she ordered.

As the half-naked bearers bent to shoulder her weight, she knew the swift thrill of fear. This was no formal state visit to another Lord but a bold move to steal an advantage on every other player in the Game of the Council; that boldness carried risks. As the party swung around a small hillock, Mara watched her estate house fall behind. She wondered if she would return to see it again.

Guided by Arakasi, the Acoma retinue hurried secretly along backcountry trails. Each day Mara observed growing signs of strain in the soldiers' behaviour. Tsurani soldiers would never lose discipline in the presence of their Ruling Lord or Lady, but on previous marches she had listened to quiet conversation, banter and jokes about the campfires. Now the men kept strict silence, broken only at need and then in whispers. Their usually animated faces were now set in the expressionless masks of Tsurani warriors.

On the third day they waited in hiding until nightfall, then moved out in darkness, munching thyza bread and needra jerky as they hurried to avoid detection. The next daybreak they marched deep into the territory of a neighbouring lord, several times coming close to patrols of soldiers from the estate. Keyoke kept his men close by and avoided all contact. Even a minor lord might seize the chance to strike at trespassers if he thought his men could obliterate Mara and her fifty guards. If any other lord knew of the queen-spawning, there was not just a chance of attack along the way, but certainty.

Mara rode in a state of fatigue, unable to rest, not only because of the constant travelling and fear, but from the thrill of anticipation as well. Gaining this new hive would do more to preserve Acoma survival than any dozen clever plots in the High Council.

Four more days passed, in exhausting succession. The company snatched sleep at odd hours, for nights were spent avoiding patrols, or wading through exposed expanses of meadow or thyza paddies along the banks of the many tributaries to the river Gagajin. At such times slaves brought up the rear, setting the disturbed seedlings straight to hide all traces of their passage. At dawn on the ninth day, Mara sat upon bare earth like a soldier and ate cheese and journey biscuit. She called Keyoke and Arakasi to come sit with her.

Both declined to share her food, as they had eaten the same cold rations earlier. She studied their faces, one lined, leathery, familiar, and as constant as the sunrise, and the other seeming little more than an illusion, a mask to fit whatever persona the moment required. 'We have crossed three estates, each one of them well guarded. Yet no patrol has sounded the alarm. Am I to believe in the extraordinary skills of my guide and my Force Commander, or is it always this easy for armed soldiers to invade the estates of the Empire?'

'A pertinent question, mistress.' Arakasi regarded her with what seemed the beginning of respect. 'One does not need a network of spies to know Keyoke is accounted a superior officer. His experience is respected throughout the Empire.'

Keyoke inclined his head towards the Spy Master at the compliment. 'We could not have managed so well without the guidance Arakasi has given us. His knowledge of the backcountry is impressive, a thing the Acoma will value in times to come.'

Mara acknowledged this tacit acceptance of Arakasi. The Spy Master sat with the keen expression of a soldier, an attitude that now seemed his natural manner. The man's ability to appear what he wished slightly unnerved Mara. 'Tell me honestly,' she said, 'would you find it this easy to lead an armed company across the lands of the Acoma?'

Arakasi laughed, an unexpected sound in a humourless camp. 'Mistress, assuredly not. Keyoke is widely admired for his knowledge of warcraft. He knows the dangers of regularly scheduled, unvarying patrols. He is prudent, and cunning, even when his command is small.' With a look of respect at the Force Commander, he added, '*Especially* when his command is small. It is difficult for one man to trespass upon Acoma lands, let alone a force in strength.'

Keyoke seized upon a discrepancy. 'You said "difficult", not "impossible".'

Arakasi inclined his head in agreement. 'True.'

Mara said, 'Lujan's grey warriors seemed to take our needra with small difficulty.'

Arakasi couldn't avoid a grin. 'Again true, but he had an advantage: I told him when and where to strike.'

Keyoke became dangerously still. 'It seems we have something to discuss.' He gestured, indicating his desire to withdraw. 'My Lady?'

Mara withheld her consent. 'Is there any estate in the Empire so well guarded that no stranger or outlaw could slip through?'

'Only one,' said Arakasi, apparently unconcerned with Keyoke's ire. 'The estate of the Lord of the Dachindo, far to the east.'

Mara smiled, as if she had won a small victory. 'Now indeed, Keyoke, you and Arakasi have something to discuss.' She watched as the two men rose and moved apart, conferring quietly, heads close together in the misty grey dawn. As much as Keyoke might take umbrage at the implied shortcomings in his defence of the estate, Mara knew wisdom would prevail. He would relish any information the Spy Master could offer to better his protection of his mistress. Confident that by the time of her wedding the Dachindo would no longer be the only estate impenetrable to trespassers, she sent a slave for her comb. In the last minutes before the company started off down the trail, she applied herself to the ongoing frustration of trying to work the knots from her long hair without benefit of a maid.

The day grew hot. The soldiers marched uncomplaining, through a gradually changing landscape. The lowland plains with their patchwork of paddies and meadows gave way to forested hills crowned with rocks. The trees became old and wild, veiled in flowering vines and thorn. Yet the more difficult the terrain, the more the spirits of the men rose. They had made good time, and as sunlight fell slanting across the trail, the travellers reached the far border of the Inrodaka estates. Arakasi asked for a halt. While the soldiers changed from field armour to lacquered and polished dress armour, he said, 'We must leave this trail and cut across this ridge to another over there.' He waved at a notch in the woodlands, barely more than a path, that led upward into denser forest.

Keyoke paused in his changing, his plumed helm half unpacked. 'I thought cho-ja built hives in meadows or valleys.'

Arakasi wiped sweat from his forehead. The light was fading quickly and he seemed concerned that they reach their destination before nightfall. 'Mostly that's true; at least, I've never heard of a hive that's not situated in the open.' He pointed up the trail. 'Further on, the woods thin. There's a meadowed valley about a thousand feet higher up. That's the place we seek.'

Mara overheard. 'So this old hive is not on Inrodaka lands?'

'No, but there is some sort of treaty nevertheless.' Arakasi gestured to the north, where the forest grew wild and thick. 'These lands were once part of a larger estate, who knows how many years ago. When that Lord, whoever he was, fell, his holdings were divided among the conquerors, the Inrodaka among them. This area was left unclaimed. It's not very good land. The timber's rich, but too difficult to log out, and there are only two or three meadows for herds, all without trails to lowland pastures. Still, the cho-ja accept the Inrodaka as their landlords without making an issue of it. Who knows how they think.' Directing the lead soldiers up the trail, he said, 'From here we must be cautious but restrained. We may be challenged by cho-ja soldiers. We must not fight. With a new queen in the hive, even the seasoned warriors will be very tense and aggressive. They may feint attack, so let no man draw sword, else we'll all be slaughtered.'

Mara consulted Keyoke, then approved the Spy Master's order. Arrayed in brilliant Acoma green, they began their climb. The trail cut sharply upward, angling between jagged outcrops of rock. Travel by litter became impossible, and even on foot Keyoke had to help Mara with the more difficult ascents. These were no switchback trails cut for humans, but paths fit only for kumi, the six-legged mountain goat of Kelewan; and for the agile cho-ja. The bearers fared worst of all, sweating and grunting under their loads, while others hauled the empty litter along by main force.

The sun shone hot on the backs of the soldiers. Strange mountain birds took flight from the trees at their approach, and thickets teemed with game. Fascinated by sights utterly new and strange, Mara never thought to complain of sore feet.

Just after midday, a shout arose from the lead patrol. Keyoke caught Mara's arm and hurried her to the head of the trail, where a dozen cho-ja soldiers stood with spears across their upper torsos, at the ready but not menacing. Shiny black, with six jointed limbs and bodies segmented like those of insects, they all looked identical to Mara, as if struck from the mould of a guild craftsman. She regarded the aliens and felt utterly at a loss.

'These are old hive warriors,' Keyoke observed. 'They will not attack us unless we give them cause.'

Keyoke's words helped steady her. She waited, tense as her escort, while her Force Commander advanced and saluted, his upraised arm bent at the elbow, palm forward. 'Honour to your hive.'

The nearest cho-ja spoke in a surprisingly intelligible voice. 'Honour to your house, men of the Acoma. Who speaks? The hive must be informed of your presence.'

'I am Keyoke, Force Commander of the Acoma.'

The lead cho-ja returned the salute. As he moved, Mara saw how his body was segmented, a larger rear thorax with four three-jointed legs and a smaller upper thorax, roughly comparable to a man's torso, with two almost human arms. His flesh was encased in chitin, and each forearm possessed a natural ridge that appeared as sharp as a sword edge. Upon his head he wore a helm of obvious Tsurani manufacture. The face within was oval, with large multifaceted eyes above two slits where a nose should be. The cho-ja's jaw and mouth were surprisingly human in appearance, though his voice was singsong and high-pitched. 'I am Ixal't, Force Leader of the Second Command of hive Kait'lk.'

'Now I remember.' Keyoke relaxed fractionally, as if in the presence of an old acquaintance. 'You served during the invasion of the Thuril Highlands.' That explained how this cho-ja recognized Acoma colours. He motioned Mara to his side. 'This is our Lady of the Acoma. She has come to negotiate with your new queen.'

Eyes like faceted metal flickered briefly over the girl at Keyoke's side. Then the cho-ja executed a fair imitation of a human bow. 'Welcome, Lady. Your arrival is timely. The new warriors are restless. This hatching is abundant and we are crowded. You may pass, and may your gods bless this bargaining.'

The cho-ja moved nimbly aside and allowed the Tsurani party to continue up the trail. Mara was curious about the unexpected expertise of her Force Commander. 'Keyoke, I didn't know you understood the cho-ja.'

'I know their soldiers, as much as any man can. I served with some, many years ago – when your grandfather led many houses in battle against the Eastern Confederation.' If the old campaigner felt his years, he did not show them, ascending the difficult trail with hardly a sign of exertion.

'The cho-ja seemed to welcome us with good grace.'

'Mistress, those were old, disciplined soldiers upon the ridge,' Arakasi cautioned. 'Keyoke was correct in addressing their officer. But from now until we reach the hive we must be wary. Many young warriors have been hatched to protect the new queen as she travels. These will be undisciplined and aggressive – quick to provoke to violence until the young queen is safely within the earth of her new hive.'

Keyoke cleared a thorn branch from the path. 'You speak as one who knows the cho-ja, Arakasi,' he said.

The Spy Master avoided the branch as it swung. 'No man knows the cho-ja. But I once hid from Minwanabi assassins for a week in a cho-ja hive. I learned something of them. It is my nature to ask many questions about things I do not understand when the opportunity presents itself.'

Mara was intrigued. Even when the ground became suitable for travel by litter once again, she remained afoot. 'Tell me of the cho-ja, then, Arakasi. What are they like?'

'The older ones are as ordered as the seasons, Lady. The young are unpredictable. They are hatched in a crèche. A dozen lesser females, called rirari, do nothing but lay eggs.' The term was archaic Tsurani, meaning a second-level queen, or duchess. 'But the eggs are infertile. The queen swallows them whole and passes them through a chamber in her body which fertilizes them, and more.'

'More?' asked Mara.

'By some cho-ja means, as the queen is being serviced by a breeding male, she determines the sex and function of each egg, or leaves it sterile. At least, this is what I have been told.'

'They can choose these things?' wondered Mara. 'Tell me more.'

'Male cho-ja are roughly divided into three groups: the breeders, the workers, and soldiers. The workers are either clever or strong, artisans or beasts of burden, depending on what the hive needs. The soldiers are both strong and clever. The breeders are stupid, but they have only one task, to mate with the queen.'

Arakasi glanced aside and saw that Mara still listened raptly. A few of the nearest soldiers paid heed to the Spy Master as well. 'Once the queen takes residence in the royal chamber, she never moves. Workers constantly feed her, while she is passed eggs by the rirari and serviced by the breeding males. Each one mates with her for hours at a time, until near exhaustion, when he is replaced by another. You will see when we are presented to the old queen.'

'Fascinating.' Mara paused, a little breathless, for the trail had grown steep once again. 'What of the young?'

'There is much I do not know of the females,' Arakasi admitted. 'But as immature cho-ja, all males are free to play and grow, much like human children – except that one day these young cho-ja are sporting about like needra calves and the next they awake, knowing their time to serve has begun. Only when a new queen is born are the soldiers hatched and hastened to maturity. This makes for an aggressive, unpredictable warrior, I'm afraid. They are quick to anger, and only the new queen can command them to instant obedience.'

Arakasi fell silent, for the trail crested a small rise, to cut sharply downwards into a valley tucked like a fold between hills. Through the arched boughs of a matched pair of ulo trees, they saw a sun-warmed meadow. The grass grew emerald, too meticulously clipped to be natural.

Arakasi pointed. 'The hive lies ahead, beyond those trees.'

Keyoke commanded the soldiers to smarten up their columns. The company started forward in battle-ready array, with their Lady protected in their midst.

As her escort reached the edge of the ulo trees, Mara's heart quickened with excitement. Through the raised shafts of the warriors' spears she glimpsed the far end of the meadow, where a vast mound rose, ancient in that small trees had taken root and flourished upon it. An entrance was visible on one side, arches shored up with delicately carved stonework. On the beaten path that led inward, hundreds of cho-ja hurried to and from the hive, upon what errands only they knew.

Mara paused and commanded slaves to bring her litter. She might have been too excited to ride upon the ridge, but she would meet the cho-ja queens as Lady of a great house. As the bearers shouldered the litter poles once more, Keyoke and Arakasi marched at her side. Then all stood at readiness. One of the soldiers raised a battle horn to his lips and blew an announcement call. Then the Force Commander of the Acoma ordered Mara's escort to step briskly from the shadow of the woods into sunlight.

Nothing changed at first. The cho-ja workers hustled about their tasks much as before, until the humans reached the valley floor. Then suddenly a dozen figures emerged from behind the right side of the hive. They raced forward like a herd of needra panicked by lightning, feet pounding upon the sod. 'Warriors,' Arakasi said. 'Hold the men steady: this rush is probably a feint.' Sweating slightly under his armour, Keyoke signalled the men. None readied weapons, though many might have questioned the prudence of the order, for the cho-ja bore down at a furious gallop. Closer they came, until the Acoma soldiers could see the sunlight gleam on the razor-sharp edges of their fore-arms. Then, when they were close enough to strike, the cho-ja veered off at the last second. With a sound like human laughter they ran off towards the hive.

Mara watched them go with a shuddering sigh of relief. 'They are so swift. How did we ever manage to subdue them?'

Arakasi wiped his brow and returned an indulgent smile. 'We never did, Lady. Humans settled land the cho-ja never wanted, until the queens found their hives surrounded. By then it was easier for both sides to make treaties than to fight. It takes skilled soldiers to face a force of cho-ja and survive. When aroused, they are efficient killers.'

As the retinue continued steadily towards the mound, more and more cho-ja appeared. Soon hundreds passed on every side, some with baskets strapped to their thoraxes, others wearing belts slung with tools. Aroused to curiosity by such industry, Mara peered through the curtain of her litter. 'Arakasi, is this hive of normal size?'

'A little larger than most, mistress, but not remarkably so.'

'How many cho-ja live within?'

Without hesitation, Arakasi replied, 'Twenty, twenty-five thousand.'

Mara was stunned. Before her lay a city in the wilderness. 'How many will travel with the new queen?'

'I don't know. In the past, I think the hives would split when population pressure became too much.' Arakasi shrugged. 'Now there is little apparent logic in the decision to birth a new queen. For, despite their breeding continuously, the cho-ja control the hive's numbers. Perhaps the old queen must reproduce herself each generation. Perhaps it is chance that brings a new queen. I do not know.'

Close at hand the mound seemed a symmetrical, steep-sided hill. The soldiers tightened formation, for the roadway became crowded. Here the grass had worn away to fine dust continually stirred by busy feet. Several times Mara's party was approached by bands of young cho-ja. They pointed and stared with metallic eyes and chirped lively phrases in their own tongue, but the adults paid the visitors little heed. A band of workers scuttled past, carrying bundles of wood large enough to require five humans to lift, yet one cho-ja worker was sufficient for the task.

Then a band of young warriors came racing towards Mara's party. Workers scattered from their path, bundles swaying, and jaws clacking a strange signal of dismay. Within a matter of moments the Tsurani found themselves surrounded. Keyoke called a halt. Dust swirled, and spear butts struck the earth in the formal stance of soldiers at rest, though the cho-ja appeared ready to fight. None was armed or helmeted in the manner of the guards upon the ridge. But with their powerful, naturally armoured bodies and razor-sharp forearm ridges, they would still make fearsome opponents.

Arakasi remained in position by the litter as Keyoke hastened forward. The Force Commander had barely reached the head of the column when a cho-ja charged. With the uncanny ability of his race to go from frenetic movement to absolute stillness, he halted scant inches before Keyoke, then stood there trembling, as if eager to fight. Yet when the cho-ja made no further provocative moves, Keyoke bowed with cautious courtesy. 'We are of the Acoma,' he announced. 'My Lady of the Acoma wishes to speak with your queen.'

The cho-ja warrior remained motionless while the constant traffic of workers flowed by on either side. Tense and silent, the Acoma soldiers awaited any hint of threat to their mistress, while Arakasi advised Keyoke. 'I don't think these warriors understand Tsurani. This one here is barely mature. We may be forced to defend ourselves.' Controlled but urgent, the Spy Master lowered his voice. 'If the one in front attacks, the others may come to aid him. If we provoke him, they certainly will. Strike only at those who attack first, for some who come may be seeking to aid us.'

Keyoke returned a fractional nod. His hand lightly gripped his sword hilt, Mara saw. Yet he made no move to draw, even when the creature twitched his head to get a better view of the brightly armoured fighter. Long, tense moments dragged by; then another, larger, cho-ja arrived. Mara waited, edgy as her escort, as the newcomer pushed through the press of young warriors. It paused at the side of the one who confronted Keyoke, and shouted what might have been a command in a high-pitched clicking language. Several of the surrounding youngsters dipped their forelimbs and hurried away, but more stayed, including the one who blocked the trail. Without warning, the larger cho-ja reached out and seized the youngster around the middle of the upper body. He locked his limbs in an immovable grip, and for a moment the two cho-ja strained against each other, grunting with effort as their chitin grated together. The first cho-ja tottered; pulled off balance, he fell to the ground, where he thrashed for an instant in panic. The elder placed a leg atop the younger cho-ja, holding him down for a moment, then stepped back, allowing the younger to scramble to his knees. The instant he regained his footing, he spun and ran away, and the last of the young warriors fled with him.

The remaining cho-ja clicked apologetically and saluted. 'Honours to your house, humans.' Keyoke returned the salute as the cho-ja said. 'That young one was unused to the sight of humans. He was ready to attack, and the others would have followed him had I not thrown him down.'

Softly, but so that all could hear, Arakasi said, 'Cho-ja are most vulnerable when on the ground. They are extraordinarily agile, and terrified of losing their footing.'

'That is true,' agreed the cho-ja. 'When I pulled the youngster over and held him down, he knew I was his better and he would not stand against me. I am Ratark'l, a soldier of the Kait'lk.' He bowed in a very human fashion, then motioned for them to follow. 'I do not know your colours, humans, but I can see you are not of the Inrodaka. His men wear the colour that can't be seen, which you humans call red.'

'We are of the Acoma.' Keyoke indicated Mara's litter and added, 'This is my mistress, the Lady of the Acoma. She has travelled far to meet with your queen.'

The cho-ja spun around and seemed agitated. 'My knowledge of your language seems now to be inadequate. I know of your Lords. What is a Lady?'

Keyoke responded with an imitation of a cho-ja gesture of respect. 'She is our ruler.'

The cho-ja almost reared. His eyes glittered as, with a deference not shown before, he bent his head towards the litter where Mara rode hidden from sight. 'Ruler! Never have we seen one of your queens, human. I shall hurry to my Queen and tell of your arrival.'

The cho-ja spun abruptly and darted between the press of commerce towards the hive entrance. Somewhat disoriented by the brevity of its manners, Keyoke turned to Arakasi. 'What do you make of that?'

Arakasi shrugged and indicated that the party should resume the approach to the hive. 'I suppose the home garrison has never seen a Tsurani woman before. Only traders and envoys of the Lord of the Inrodaka come here. It's quite possible that this may be the first time in memory that a Ruling Lady has come to deal with a hive queen. The novelty may prove interesting.'

Keyoke halted the march. 'Dangerous?'

Arakasi considered. 'Probably not, though with the young warriors as nervous to be moving to a new hive as they are, I can't say for certain. Still, I've never heard of a cho-ja harming a guest. For the moment I expect we are safe.'

Mara spoke from inside the litter. 'I don't care about the risk, Keyoke. If we don't gain an alliance with the new queen . . .'

Keyoke glanced at his mistress. Like Nacoya, he knew Mara plotted and planned and took counsel from no one. But unlike the nurse, he simply accepted the fact. The Force Commander nodded his plumed head and resumed the approach to the hive. When the soldiers reached the entrance, an honour guard stepped from the arched entrance to meet them, a pair of cho-ja warriors wearing plumed and crested helms styled after those of Tsurani officers. Although no order was spoke, instantly the stream of cho-ja bearing burdens and messages rerouted their comings and goings through smaller openings on either side of the main entrance. The Acoma retinue halted before the honour guard. As the dust swirled and settled, the cho-ja in the lead bowed from the joint of his two thoraxes. 'I am Lax'l, Force Commander of hive Kait'lk.'

Keyoke bowed also. 'I am Keyoke, Force Commander of the Acoma. Honours to your hive.'

'Honours to your house, Keyoke of the Acoma.'

Keyoke motioned towards the litter. 'Within rests Mara, Ruling Lady of the Acoma.'

At once attentive, Lax'l said, 'One of our warriors announced a human queen has come to call. Is she the one?'

Before Keyoke could answer, Arakasi said, 'She is young but will be mother to Acoma lords.'

All the cho-ja in the honour guard made a sudden keening cry. All activity around the entrance halted. For a moment no one moved, human or cho-ja. Then the cho-ja Force Commander bowed low, like a needra kneeling; moments later, all the other cho-ja in sight, even the ones bearing burdens, did likewise. Over the shuffling sound as they rose and continued with their errands, Lax'l said, 'We welcome the human queen to hive Kait'lk. Our Queen shall be informed of your arrival without delay. We would also tell her the reason for your coming, if you will permit.'

'I permit,' said Mara promptly. Since delay seemed inevitable she allowed the bearers to lower her litter to the ground, though she remained hidden behind the gauze curtains. 'Inform your queen that we come requesting the honour of bargaining for the new queen's hive to be built upon Acoma land.'

At this the cho-ja cocked his head; one forelimb lifted in astonishment. 'News travels swiftly through the Empire. The young Queen is barely more than a hatchling, not ready as yet to venture above ground.'

Mara bit her lip; time now was critical, with the wedding date set and her estate left vulnerable by her absence. Nacoya and Jican were competent, but they could not prevent the inevitable reports by enemy spies that she was off on a secret errand. Each day she was absent increased the risk of attack against a garrison still dangerously undermanned. Prompted by impulse and a driving, intuitive ambition, Mara whipped aside the curtains. 'Force Commander of the cho-ja,' she said, before Arakasi or Keyoke could counsel otherwise. 'If the new queen cannot meet with me outside, I will come to her, should your ruler permit.'

Arakasi stiffened, startled, and Keyoke froze with his hand half-raised to rub his chin. The request was presumptuous; neither man guessed how the cho-ja might react. For a moment each warrior held his breath, while the cho-ja stood trembling in the same manner as the young warrior who had been poised to attack them only a short while before.

But Lax'l proved uncertain rather than angry. 'Lady Queen, no human has asked such a thing in our memory. Wait here, and I shall enquire.' He whirled and scuttled into the hive.

Slowly Keyoke lowered his arm. 'That was a dangerous move, mistress. If the queen should receive your request with displeasure, your warriors are outnumbered two hundred to one.'

'And yet the cho-ja officer did not act affronted,' Arakasi pointed out, 'merely astonished.' He shook his head with what might have been admiration.

Nevertheless, Keyoke kept his soldiers on guard. With weapons near to hand, all waited for the cho-ja commander's return.

Lax'l scuttled abruptly from the dark beyond the entrance. He bowed low, the polished dome of his head segment almost brushing the dust. 'Our Queen is honoured that you are willing to visit the heart of the hive to see her daughter. She will allow you to enter with one officer, five soldiers, and as many workers as you need. Lady of the Acoma, come at once, for my Queen waits to greet you within the great chamber.'

Mara signalled through the hangings and a somewhat bemused Keyoke chose Arakasi and four others to follow Lax'l. Then the Force Commander ordered the remaining guards to take their ease while their mistress was absent. In short order, Mara, her picked attendants, and her guards entered the hillside, immediately engulfed by the gloom of the tunnel.

Mara's first impression was of moist, earth odours, and of another scent intermingled, a nutty, spicy smell that could only be the cho-ja. The large arch they passed under was faced with carvings of surpassing delicacy, decorated with precious inlays of metal and gems. Mara imagined Jican's exclamations of delight should the Acoma estate gain craftsmen capable of such work. Then the shadows deepened as the tunnel sloped downwards, out of the direct light of the entrance. Behind gauzy curtains, Mara was virtually blind until her eyes adjusted to the darkness. The cho-ja Force Commander scuttled ahead with the quickness characteristic of his race. The humans walked briskly to keep up, the panting of the slaves strangely amplified as they bore the litter down a mazelike array of ramps. The tunnels had been hewed out of the ground, then braced with some strange compound that set into the hardness of stone. Sounds echoed easily off this substance, lending an eerie quality to the creak of armour and weaponry. Deeper the party marched, through curves that undulated apparently without pattern. Odd globes of light had been placed at junctions, causing intersections to be islands of illumination between long stretches of gloom. Mara studied the globes, amazed to find they contained neither oil nor flame. She wondered how such a glow might be fashioned, even as her litter was jostled by a constant press of cho-ja intent upon hive business. Most turned to regard the humans a moment before continuing on.

As the third intersection disappeared behind, Mara pondered the different cho-ja in her view. Warriors seemed uniformly powerful, with huge lower thorax, broad shoulders on the upper body, and a height half again as tall as the tallest Tsurani. The workers were noticeably shorter and stockier, more placid in their demeanour. But she had seen others, more agile than the workers, yet less formidable than the warriors. When she asked Arakasi about these, he answered, 'Artisans, mistress.'

The way steepened as they descended into the hive. Intersections became more frequent and the cho-ja scent thickened in the air. In time the passage widened, opening out into a large cavern hung with many light globes. Mara pushed the curtains of her litter wide and stared in surprise and wonder. Clinging to the ceiling of each tunnel into the chamber were small cho-ja, about the size of a human child of five. Transparent wings upon their backs beat furiously, the movement a blur in the dim light. Each creature seemed to rest for a minute or two, then resume the beating for an equal amount of time. The constant changing caused the air to hum with almost musical shifts in rhythm. Arakasi noticed Mara's amazement and explained. 'These must be worker females.'

'I thought you said you knew only of the males,' commented Mara.

'I've never seen these before,' he acknowledged. 'But only the females have wings.'

Lax'l revealed unexpectedly keen hearing as he glanced back at Mara and her escort. 'Your adviser is correct, Lady Queen. These you see above are sterile females; they are nearly mindless and live only to move the air through the deep tunnels and chambers. It would grow difficult to breathe down here if not for their labour.' He guided the Acoma party swiftly across the cavern, turned a bend, and entered a low passage, which quickly became a ramp heading downward. The slaves carrying Mara's litter struggled for breath. Mara considered calling an early shift change; but the tunnel suddenly opened out into what could only be the Queen's chamber.

The cho-ja Queen was immense, at least thirty feet long from her head to the end of her second thorax. Dark, almost polished black, she lay upon a raised mound of earth, and from the withered appearance of her legs Mara realized she never moved from that location. Fine hangings draped portions of her anatomy, and between them her workers darted, preening her enormous body, attending diligently to her every comfort and need. High above her, and mounted back upon her thorax, a stocky male perched, his soldierlike body surmounted by the small head of a worker. He rocked over the Queen with a rhythmic motion. Arakasi inclined his head and said, 'A breeding male, my Lady. One is always with the Queen.' A dozen cho-ja males were arrayed before her, some with crested helms and others without visible ornament; all awaited the arrival of the Acoma party in polite silence. On either side of the chamber, smaller versions of the Queen lay upon their stomachs, and attendants bustled about each of them. Arakasi pointed these out to Mara and murmured, 'Rirari, I expect, the lesser queens who lay the eggs.'

Lax'l indicated that they should wait, then scuttled forward with a loud series of clicks. A hush fell over the chamber, though the workers still attended to their tasks. The bearers placed Mara's litter upon the earth, and with Keyoke's assistance she stepped forth. No longer hidden by gauze hangings, she felt small, almost lost, in a chamber at least four times the size of the grand hall of the Anasati; up close, the size of the Queen was overpowering. Maintaining her poise with an effort of will, Mara stood while a slave from her retinue slipped a jewelled overrobe over her shoulders. She strove not to quail as the alien Queen stared intently at her. The dark, faceted eyes reflected no expression. Mara endured with an outward show of calm, though her knees began to tremble as her attendant stepped back. Then the cho-ja Queen spoke in a voice surprisingly slight and delicate to be issuing from so enormous a form. 'You are the human Queen?'

Mara bowed slightly, the jewels on her sleeves flashing in the dim light. 'I am Mara, Ruling Lady of the Acoma. We have no queens as you do, but I rule my house in the same manner as you would your hive.'

The Queen made a sound. Her chitin features remained immobile, but her manner suggested amusement, and her outburst seemed akin to human laughter.

'I didn't expect your kind to breed like us, Mara of the Acoma. I have been told of your odd matings. I am very old. But among humans I have heard only of Ruling Lords. How is it that you hold command, and the men who accompany you do not?'

Mara explained that only when no male heirs remained within a noble family did a female come to power. The Queen listened, and when Mara finished, said, 'You humans are so alien. We often wonder what makes you strive so. But I distract myself. The new Queen, my daughter, is anxious to meet a human queen, particularly one who ventures below ground in deference to the customs of our kind.'

Now the old Queen sang out in a loud, piping whistle, and a pair of cho-ja workers came forward. Between them they ushered a cho-ja smaller than any the human party had encountered so far. Mara looked a long moment before she understood. 'This is the new Queen?'

'Such was I once, long ago. She will grow and within a matter of weeks she will be big enough to rule; a few months after, she will start reproduction.'

The young Queen regarded Mara, circling her to get a better look. She seemed to move with a grace not seen in any cho-ja before, her steps fluid, even lithe; she showed none of the rapid movement Mara had observed in the workers and soldiers. But even as she spoke in the clicking tongue of her kind, bright, faceted eyes never left Mara. The cho-ja matriarch said, 'Our young are born knowing our language, as they are taught while they grow within the egg sac. Your tongue they must learn after they hatch. My daughter will be unable to speak with you for some time yet to come.'

The young Queen's scrutiny made Mara's skin prickle self-consciously; yet she held still and waited. Presently the young Queen finished her inspection and fell silent. The old Queen answered rapidly and then translated in Tsurani. 'She said you are all alien-looking – frightening.' To Mara she added, 'Though you are less frightening than the males.'

Mara bowed slightly to the new Queen. 'Please tell her I think she is lovely.' The remark was not empty flattery; although the young Queen would someday grow to be the monstrous equal of her mother, at present she was delicately formed and pleasing to observe. Unlike the blue-tinged males, she was a deep maroon in colour and possessed a quality that Mara could only call feminine.

The old Queen interpreted and the new Queen trilled, seemingly in pleasure. Mara went on, 'We come seeking a treaty. We would welcome this new Queen and her followers to build a hive on our land. We would like to begin negotiations as soon as possible.'

The old Queen answered, 'I do not understand. The negotiations have begun.'

Mara felt a stab of concern. The finality of the event came too suddenly for her to cope, for she had banked upon the counsel of

Arakasi. She strove politely to buy time. 'I am weary from days of travel. Might I have leave to rest a day before we speak of these matters?'

The old Queen repeated the request and followed with the young Queen's answer. 'My daughter Queen says she will hear what you bid, now.'

Mara looked at Arakasi, who whispered, 'If you leave, you may offend her and lose any chance to speak to her again.'

Suddenly Mara felt worn. The excitement of reaching the hive had buoyed her for the last hour, but now she felt ready to collapse. The stress of dealing with the young Queen combined with the killing pace of the last week made her mind seem fog-clouded. Still, there seemed no choice but to go on. Mara signalled for a cushion from her litter to be placed upon the floor. She seated herself as formally as she could manage and opened negotiations. 'What would your daughter wish to come live upon Acoma lands?'

The young Queen crouched cho-ja fashion, by lowering her four legs in a squat while maintaining an erect upper torso, arms crossed in very human fashion. She fixed large eyes upon Mara and spoke. The old Queen translated. 'My daughter wishes to know if the earth of your estates is wet or dry.'

Mara answered without hesitation. 'Both. The Acoma lands are wide and rich, from water-flooded thyza paddies to high forests. We have meadowlands which rise up into hills not unlike those that surround this hive.'

The young Queen listened to her mother's interpretation, then responded. 'My daughter Queen would settle her following near clean water, but not where the ground is too wet. She asks also that the place be away from the forest, as the old root systems make digging the upper tunnels difficult. The first chamber must be dug quickly, for she would not risk staying above ground any longer than necessary.'

Mara conferred with Keyoke. 'We could give her the lower needra meadow to the west of the river. Slaves can then clear new land for the herd to the east.' When the Force Commander nodded agreement, Mara said, 'Tell your daughter that we offer a low hill of land, surrounded by open meadow, within a short march to fresh, clear water. But the land is located above the higher of the two banks of the river and stays dry, even during the heavy rains.'

The old Queen and the young engaged in discussion. The cho-ja language of clicks and whistles seemed more efficient than human words; or else the aliens exchanged information in ways that supplemented language. Mara waited, inwardly nervous.

Suddenly a strident whistle echoed through the hive's great chamber. Mara's retinue stiffened in alarm, and the old Queen's conversation with her daughter ceased abruptly. Fearful the disturbance might herald alarm, Keyoke gripped his sword hilt.

But Arakasi seized the Force Commander's upper arm and whispered urgently, 'Pull steel this close to two queens and we all die instantly.' The older Queen showed no sign of alarm, but the males near her had all risen to a half crouch, a battle posture that readied them to explode into a charge. Half-raised forearms quivered slightly as razor-sharp chitin ridges were angled towards Keyoke. The old Force Commander had seen cho-ja at war; these were a hairsbreadth away from attack. He released his sword and at once the warriors before the old Queen subsided into their squatting position. The old Queen made no comment. Arakasi released a pent-up breath and offered slight reassurance. 'Should danger arise, those warriors will protect us as well as their Queen.' Keyoke nodded at the logic of this, but he still stepped closer to his Lady.

On the dais, the old Queen clicked and twitched a forelimb; and in response to her command, Lax'l rose from his place at her feet and scuttled off.

Watching him, Mara wondered whether she could ever adjust to the speed at which the cho-ja moved at need. As messengers, they would be unparalleled, and that prompted remembrance of a childhood rhyme recited by Nacoya that ended, '. . . the cho-ja are the first with news and early-season fruit.' Phrased as nonsense, and treated by humans as entertainment for youngsters, Mara pondered now whether the jingle held some element of truth.

Lax'l returned before she could pursue the idea with inquiry. He exchanged rapid whistles and clicks with his matriarch; and the old Queen's next words banished all musings upon nursery tales from Mara's thoughts.

'Lady Queen of the Acoma,' the ruling cho-ja said, 'word arrives that a Lord of your kind has travelled to the hive to bargain against you for the new Queen's favour.'

6

Ceremony

Mara stiffened.

Dismay, disappointment, and anger welled up within her all at once; then fear prevailed over all else. Somehow, someone had relayed word of the cho-ja Queen's hatching.

If the news had spread indiscriminately across the countryside, more than one family might be travelling to the hive in the hill. The one waiting above would be only the first of many. Yet this boded ill even if the news had not been widely dispersed, for then the Lord of the Inrodaka might have invited some special friend to be first to seek the new Queen's hive. He would most certainly not be pleased to discover trespassers upon his land to steal a march upon his ally. With or without the young Queen's approval, Mara now faced returning across the lands of a hostile Lord aware of her presence. Even more frightening, some agent of the Minwanabi might have learned of Mara's errand and sent an informant back to his master. Perhaps Jingu himself waited above to communicate with the young Queen.

Careful to hide her distress from the Queens, Mara took a deep breath. Her throat felt as dry as sand, even as she reminded herself of a teaching mother's lesson: 'Fear is the little death, daughter. It kills in tiny pieces.'

With the appearance of calm, Mara looked to the old Queen. 'Honoured ruler,' she said, 'be advised that I am most determined to win the loyalty of this new hive. Acoma lands are rich and wide, and another Lord of the Empire is unlikely to better the terms I can offer.'

On the dais, the old Queen huffed through her nose slits, the cho-ja equivalent of laughter. 'Loyalty? Lady Ruler of the Acoma, that is a concept not shared by my kind. Workers, warriors, rirari, all do as is their nature, for without the hive there is nothing. A queen is the sole arbiter of a hive, and we make our trade contracts for the best terms we may. Always we serve the highest bidder.'

Mara sat speechless at this revelation. By chance the Queen had disclosed a thing no Tsurani in the Empire had guessed. Tsurani society had always believed the cho-ja were above certain human failings. Now what was believed to be an unassailable sense of honour was revealed as the crassest sort of service mongering. These cho-ja were nothing more than a race of merchants. Their legendary loyalty was open to sale to the highest bidder, and perhaps subject to renegotiation should the cho-ja receive a better offer from a rival Lord. One of the underpinnings of the Empire's power structure was far more vulnerable than anyone knew, for never before had anyone thought to test cho-ja loyalty by contacting the hive upon another lord's lands. Through her dismay, Mara saw advantage: so long as no other ruler in the Empire guessed the truth, she might use such knowledge for her own gain – provided she survived the next hour.

'Keyoke.' Mara leaned across her cushions and motioned the Force Commander closer. 'These warriors who came with us must be sworn to absolute silence.' With her face kept carefully blank, she added, 'The slaves must not be permitted to reveal what we have just heard.' Nothing more would be said, but the old warrior knew she had just pronounced death sentence upon eight men. He in turn whispered something to Arakasi and, his expression unreadable, the Spy Master nodded once, indicating he affirmed the decision.

Mara straightened. To the old Queen she said, 'Then we shall bargain.'

Excited by the prospect, the old Queen trilled her pleasure. 'I shall inform the other human Lord that he has a competing offer.'

The Queen then issued commands to waiting cho-ja workers. These were of the smaller, more intelligent artisan class. Mara waited with the appearance of patience as they scuttled away. Other workers entered the chamber, clearly establishing a relay of messengers, since the newly arrived Lord preferred to negotiate from the surface, in the traditional Tsurani manner. Mara resolved to extract what advantage she could from that circumstance.

The first message arrived from above, and after clicking communication with the courier and the young Queen, the hive matriarch inclined her head towards Mara. 'Your rival Lord also possesses fine meadowlands that are dry year round, near to good water, and free of tree roots. He says as well that his soil is sandy and easy to tunnel.' She paused and conferred with her daughter Queen, then added, 'Lady of the Acoma, my hatchling wishes to know if you care to improve your offer.'

Mara resisted an impulse to twist her fingers in the fringes of her cushion. 'Kindly relate to your daughter that sandy soil may be easy to dig, but it also leaches water and tends to collapse easily.'

Enjoying herself, the old Queen responded with her odd laugh. 'We know, Lady of the Acoma. We find it entertaining that a human would presume to know more of tunnelling than a cho-ja. Still, sandy soil presents no difficult problem for us.'

Mara thought quickly. 'You are the finest miners in the world, yet I will provide slaves to help with the digging so that your daughter's wait upon the surface is short. One hundred of my warriors will safeguard the site, and my own pavilion will shade her from the sun until her chambers are ready underground.' Mara swallowed hard. 'In addition, each day she remains above ground she shall have twenty baskets of fruits and thyza harvested from my fields, that her workers may remain full of industry with no need to forage.'

The old Queen clicked her translation and the young Queen replied. A moment later a messenger scuttled up the passage towards the surface. Perspiring lightly in the spicy warmth, Mara managed not to fidget. Negotiations might proceed very slowly, she thought, but the messenger returned unexpectedly fast.

When the new terms had been related to her daughter, the old Queen translated for Mara. 'Should any tunnels collapse, your rival says he offers a suite of rooms in his estate house to the Queen and her chosen attendants, until her own quarters may be rebuilt.'

Something in the Queen's voice lent Mara an insight. Despite her fluent Tsurani, the Queen was an alien being with alien needs. Few common values overlapped; by repeating the rival offer, the cho-ja ruler might not be indicating her preference but instead inciting the human rulers to bid each other up as high as possible. Mara strove to be as shrewd as possible. 'That is silly. What reason would your daughter have to wish to reside in a Tsurani house? My pavilion would be more comfortable.'

The old Queen answered without hesitation. 'This is true. But he also offers a hundredweight in jade and an equal weight in fine metal to endow my daughter's craft workers.'

Mara shivered slightly under her thin robes. The items just named amounted to a fortune. Her rival above was most determined, to raise his stakes so high this soon. Cleverness alone would not suffice, and Mara imagined Jican wringing his hands as she debated the wealth the Acoma would pledge as a counter-offer.

Mara's voice was unsteady as she spoke. 'Honourable Queen, tell your daughter that Tsurani estate houses are suitable to workers and soldiers only, not queens. Far better, tunnels that never collapse. Say also that metals and jade are useless without tools to work them; so then, what would the cho-ja wish: gems and metals which they can find more easily than any human miner, or tools which can work such into things of beauty and value, to be traded to humans for whatever the cho-ja truly wish to possess? I will match the other Lord's offer in value, but with things cho-ja do not fashion for themselves: tools, and needra hide of equal worth, and resin-worked woods.' She paused, then added, 'Also weapons and armour for her warriors.'

'A generous offer,' observed the old Queen. Her eyes glittered brightly while she translated, as if she enjoyed the striving between human rulers. The exchange was punctuated by excited trills.

Strained and tired, Mara closed her eyes. The Acoma resources stood in danger of depletion, and the pledge she had just made relied heavily on the craftsmen brought in by Lujan, armourers and weapons makers whose work had yet to be evaluated. And the cho-ja would be insulted by inferior work, perhaps even moved to wrath.

The messenger returned quickly. He exchanged rapid clicks with the Queen matriarch, and the daughter Queen broke into a series of loud trills.

Mara dreaded the translation; surely the outburst from the daughter Queen signified a magnanimous concession from the rival Lord.

The old Queen finished with the messenger. Still as a statue of obsidian, she said, 'Lady Ruler, the Lord above ground has informed us that he recognizes Acoma colours upon the warriors who wait by the hive entrance. He says he knows of your resources and claims further that you cannot possibly meet the terms you have just named.'

Mara's eyes narrowed before the glittering gaze of the Queen. 'His words are untrue.' She paused, contained a sharp, dangerous anger, and arose from her cushion. 'This Lord speaks from ignorance.'

Indifferent to Mara's ire, the Queen said, 'I do not understand.'

Mara strove to control her fury. 'Do the cho-ja know the details of every hive, the workings, the goings-on?'

The Queen flicked her forearms in perplexity. 'Whatever transpires in a hive is known to all queens.' She paused a long minute, then chittered softly to the young Queen. To Mara she added, 'Clearly your human ways differ from ours.'

Mara licked her lips and tasted sweat. Strain must not drive her to act rashly. Deep below ground, with only six warriors standing between herself and the most rigorous of hive defences, a single mistimed gesture might prove fatal. 'I am Ruling Lady of the Acoma,' Mara said carefully. 'I say that no house in the Empire dares to presume to know the extent of my resources! This rival Lord bargains without honour and his charge is an insult to my house.' She stepped forward, fear masked by the proud bearing of her ancestors, and faced the young Queen directly. 'Lady of the cho-ja, I negotiate in good faith. Know that, as an Acoma, I hold my word more important than my life.'

The wait as her words were translated threatened to break her, yet Mara endured, hands clenched hard together. The young Queen studied the human visitor with keen curiosity, while the old Queen gave instructions to her messengers. Mara's challenge to her unseen rival above ground broached matters of honour, and a bloodletting might result that could carry even into the hive. Fighting an onset of panic, Mara cursed inwardly. Not knowing the identity of her rival placed her at a severe disadvantage.

A faint scrape sounded in the passage as the next messenger whisked into view. The old Queen heard him, then spoke. 'Lady Ruler, the Lord above concedes his words were spoken in anger. Perhaps you might have armourers who can fulfil the obligation you have promised, but he says all the Empire knows that his wealth is greater than that of the Acoma. For the young Queen he will better any and all offers the Lady Mara cares to make, if my daughter will choose his land for her new hive.'

Jade bracelets clashed against silence as Mara stiffened. 'Who boasts his wealth is superior to mine?'

'The Lord of the Ekamchi,' answered the Queen.

Mara looked askance at Arakasi, for the name was only vaguely familiar. The Spy Master left his place among her retinue and whispered swiftly, 'Inrodaka's closest friend. He has some wealth, a little more than your own, I think. His army is small, though he probably has an escort with him that outnumbers us. I remember him as a fat man, with no personal history of warcraft and most likely little courage.'

Mara nodded. The speed with which the Lord of the Ekamchi had retracted his claim to know Acoma resources seemed to indicate the hesitancy of a man unsure of himself. Relying on Arakasi's implicit advice, Mara said, 'Advantage shifts away from us the longer we wait. I think I need to be bold.'

The Spy Master flashed a quick smile as he bowed and returned to his place. Making her voice ring with a confidence she did not feel, Mara addressed the young Queen. 'Daughter Queen of the cho-ja, I say now the Acoma will match any bid set forth by this arrogant braggart who stands above us. All material goods he offers I will equal in kind for your hive. I also promise that sweet-smelling blossoms will be delivered each day of the spring, that those pleasures of life above ground will not be forgotten by you as you care for your subjects. I will have hangings of pretty colours made by our finest weavers, so your quarters will always be pleasant, and these hangings shall be replaced each season, that you not tire of your surroundings. And I will come, and sit, and discuss with you the affairs of the Empire, so you may grow in understanding of human affairs. I beg that you now choose which estate you will have as home for your new hive.'

Silence fell. The attendant workers seemed to tense slightly as the Queen matriarch began her translation, each click and whistle starkly emphasized. Mara listened with the breath stopped in her throat, while at her sides Keyoke and Arakasi exchanged grim signals of readiness. Their mistress had made a bold request, and no man knew how the alien cho-ja might respond.

The two queens conferred. Tense, aching with pressure, Mara felt the minutes stretched like the strings of a gikoto tightened past pitch by an overanxious musician. Every shred of self-control she had learned at the temple came into play as she endured cruel suspense. The faces of her retainers surrounded her, from the familiar, lined visage of Keyoke, to each of her soldiers, to the enigmatic countenance of Arakasi. Chills pricked her skin as she wondered what fate would befall should the cho-ja Queen decide against the Acoma; if the bargain went to the Lord of the Ekamchi, she would have enemies waiting above. Any advantage she had gained by entering the hive would be lost; her boldness ultimately might bring her death, since no man knew what guest customs the alien race observed.

Then, without warning, the old Queen's faceted eyes swivelled towards the humans. Mara stood motionless as judgment was pronounced. 'The Queen daughter has chosen. She says she will bring her hive to the estate of Mara of the Acoma.'

Lax'l gestured. The messenger sped off up the passage for the last time, with word of defeat for the Lord of the Ekamchi. Keyoke and Arakasi exchanged small smiles of relief, while Mara briefly covered her face with both hands to smother a laugh of triumph. Her instinct had proven correct. Now the Acoma would gain a rare and precious advantage for years to come.

With her fatigue swept away by excitement and curiosity, Mara said, 'If I may ask, why did your daughter finally choose Acoma lands, when the offers were so close?'

The queens exchanged remarks, then the elder said, 'My daughter likes you. You called her pretty.'

'That's something most men would never have thought,' Arakasi mused, 'that even queens of the cho-ja are not immune to flattery.'

'Indeed,' observed Keyoke.

The old Queen inclined the polished dome of her head towards Mara. 'And we both count it a great courtesy that you would come below ground to negotiate rather than use messengers, for you are the first of your race to do so.'

Arakasi almost chuckled aloud. He said to Keyoke, 'Simply because most lords would not set foot within another's house without first being *invited to enter*. It seems Tsurani civility is cho-ja rudeness.'

The Force Commander seemed less amused. 'Swords may yet

determine the outcome of this encounter,' he reminded the Spy Master, with a jerk of his thumb indicating the less than friendly forces waiting above.

Mara did not comment on her retainer's remarks, but instead looked up at the old Queen. 'I have been led to understand that the young Queen's retinue will be scant.'

The old Queen motioned with a forelimb. 'This is true, patron of my daughter's hive. I have birthed three hundred warriors, two hundred of which have been matured at fast rate to accompany her, the other hundred to follow when they have grown. I will allow her two rirari, two breeding males, and seven hundred workers.'

Mara pondered this. The presence of the cho-ja on the Acoma estate would prove a hindrance to any but the boldest enemy, for no one else was likely to know the cho-ja warriors were young and difficult to control. 'In the normal course of things, how long do you judge before a new hive is able to begin commerce?'

The old Queen twitched her jaws, as if divining Mara's intent. 'In the normal course of things, two to three years.'

Fatigue returned in numbing waves. Mara's mind drifted, and she forced herself to apply something said earlier by the old Queen. 'I would like to bid for additional workers and warriors to be sent with your daughter.' Careful to conceal her exhaustion, Mara stepped steadily back to her litter. She entered, and motioned to a slave to hold the curtains back to keep an unobstructed view of the two queens. Settled upon her cushions – and hoping she didn't appear too wilted – Mara said, 'I would talk terms.'

'That is wise,' answered the Queen. 'The young warriors are fractious; older, more experienced soldiers will be needed to bring them quickly to order at the new hive.'

Mara's heart leaped in pleasure; she had understood the old Queen's comments on the nature of the cho-ja. Behind her, Keyoke murmured his astonishment. 'They barter their own!'

The old Queen showed keener hearing than expected by saying, 'Only the hive matters, Force Commander. And I am the hive. Those I sell will serve your Lady as they would me. She will be their new Queen.'

Mara said, 'I wish only that your daughter have a stronger hive, as soon as possible. I buy workers and warriors as a gift for her.'

The old Queen nodded. 'That is generous. I will keep that in mind as I set my price.'

Mara took a moment to consult her advisers. Then, making sure her shoulders didn't droop, she spoke to the Queen. 'I have need for twenty of your warriors, Majesty. I would also ask for artisans.'

Keyoke straightened in surprise. 'I thought we came for warriors, my Lady?'

Mara assumed a faraway look, as she often had lately; as the Acoma position stabilized, she strove to plan for the future; more and more, she kept her own counsel. But an old and valued adviser deserved an explanation. 'Since my betrothal to the Anasati son, our position is safe for the present. This young Queen can breed more warriors, in time. But their most valued skill is not inborn, I think. What I want is silk makers.'

The Queen matriarch reared up as high as her immobile rear segment allowed. 'For the makers of silk to be given over to you would cost greatly.'

Mara returned a half bow, that her boldness might not offend. 'What price?'

The Queen waved her forelegs for a long moment. 'A hundred bags of thyza for each worker.'

'Agreed,' said Mara without hesitation. 'I require five such workers.'

But the old Queen clicked scoldingly at Mara's haste. 'You must also give one thousand swords, one thousand helmets, and one thousand shields, to be shipped upon your arrival home.'

Mara frowned. Since Jican was a competent manager, she had finances to buy what was not on hand in the warehouse. 'Agreed.' The bargain was hard, but fair; in time a flourishing silk trade would repay the expenditure many times over. Anxious now to deliver her news to Jican and Nacoya, Mara said, 'When will the Queen depart?'

The matriarch conferred with her daughter, then answered, 'Not until the autumn.'

Mara inclined her head in a gesture of respect. 'Then I will leave at dawn and set about fulfilling our obligation to you. My workers will see that the needra are moved and the meadow is clipped and made ready, that the Queen your daughter will be welcome upon her arrival.'

The Queen matriarch signalled dismissal. 'Go, then, Mara of the

Acoma. May your gods grant you prosperity and honour, for you have dealt graciously with our kind.'

Mara spoke through a profound feeling of relief. 'And may your hive continue to grow in prosperity and honour.'

Lax'l stepped forward to guide the humans to the surface, and the Queen's bright eyes turned away, absorbed once more with hive matters and the complex decisions of breeding. Able to give in to exhaustion, and shaking slightly from hours of sustained stress, Mara sank back into the cushions of her litter. She gestured, and her company moved to depart. During her ride towards the surface, she felt like laughing aloud, then like crying. Seeds now sown might someday bring forth rich fruit, for she had won the means to expand upon Jican's already impressive financial base. The silk trade in the south was not yet an established industry. Northern silk varied in quality and availability. Mara did not know how to convince this young Queen to turn silk production into the major speciality of her hive, but she would endeavour to find a means. Produced near the major southern markets, Acoma silk might someday come to dominate the trade.

Then, as her bearers bore her along the dark, richly scented tunnels of the cho-ja hive, her euphoria dimmed. Barely two weeks remained for the elaborate preparations that a wedding of two great houses entailed. Although the past night's efforts might add to the Acoma wealth, soon that wealth must be turned over to another, the son of one of her most bitter enemies. Mara brooded in the privacy of her litter; of her acts since the death of her father and brother, her marriage to Buntokapi posed the greatest risk of all.

The last intersection fell behind, yet the tunnel did not darken. Through the thin curtains of her litter, Mara saw the arches of the entrance of the hive, with daylight shining brightly between. Negotiations with the cho-ja queens had lasted throughout the night. The girl's eyes ached as they adjusted to the increased light, and her head swam with weariness. Content to lie back and doze while Keyoke marshalled his escort and readied the slaves and warriors for the long march home, she did not recognize trouble until her litter shuddered to a halt, followed by the hiss of weapons being drawn.

Alarmed, Mara sat up. She reached to draw open the curtains, just as a stranger's voice rang out in anger.

'You! Thief! Prepare to answer for your crimes!'

Chilled awake by fear and anger, Mara whipped the gauze aside. Keyoke and the Acoma warriors waited with drawn swords, ready to defend. Beyond them stood the white-haired Lord of the Inrodaka, red-faced, tousled, and furious from a night spent in the open. Swiftly Mara took stock of his retinue. She counted a full company of soldiers, two hundred at the least, and not all of them wore Inrodaka red. Fully half were armoured in the purple and yellow of the Ekamchi.

The old Lord thrust his jaw forward and pointed his decorative family sword. 'Lady of the Acoma! How dare you trespass upon Inrodaka lands! Your audacity oversteps your strength, to the grief and shame of your name. For stealing the daughter Queen's hive you shall be made to pay dearly.'

Mara met the accusation with a cool look of contempt. 'Your words are without much thought, and of less honour.' She glanced at the fat man at Inrodaka's side, assuming him to be the Lord of the Ekamchi. 'The lands surrounding this hive are unclaimed – have your hadonra check the archives in Kentosani, if you doubt me. And the cho-ja are no man's slaves. They choose with whom they bargain. And to call one who bargains in good faith a thief is an insult demanding apology!'

Both Lords regarded the Acoma ruler. She might seem a young girl taken by a fit of pique, but in the face of the armed and able company waiting on her word to extract such apology, both men lost some of their fury. Still, they remained uncowed by Mara's unexpected boldness. The Lord of the Inrodaka spluttered in indignation and his companion shook a pudgy fist. The unmannerly displays might have been comic except for the glowering rows of warriors and weapons behind them.

'You have slighted me, caused me to break faith with a trusted ally,' Inrodaka raged. Yet he seemed more inclined to speak than fight. 'I had promised the Ekamchi exclusive rights to bargain with the daughter Queen, and by treachery you Acoma became privy to my secrets!'

Now Mara understood. The man suspected the Acoma of having an agent in his household. Arakasi had spent several weeks as a guest of the Inrodaka; if anyone recognized him, a fight might result. Mara chanced a surreptitious glance that ended in a blink of confusion. The Spy Master had disappeared. Another searching glance, a little more careful, revealed his presence among the soldiers, but even there she had trouble picking him out. At one with the others in Acoma ranks, he stood poised for trouble, but his helm hung slightly lower over the bridge of his nose, and his chin was thrust forward, making his jaw seem squarer than usual. Very likely he would remain unnoticed. Relieved by this, Mara sought to avoid conflict. 'My Lord, I take no responsibility for causing a break in a pledge beyond your right to promise. The cho-ja keep their own counsel. As for being privy to your secrets, "the cho-ja are the first with news and early-season fruit." If you but ask, they'll tell you that one hive knows the affairs of all others. Whether or not your workers, servants, or slaves set foot off your land, the news was accessible in all parts of the Empire. I was simply the first to act. You could not prevent me, my Lord. And in the last, since when must the Acoma nursemaid the honour of the Inrodaka?'

The Lord of the Inrodaka bristled. His ally, the Lord of the Ekamchi, looked as if he would just as soon be done with the whole affair and go elsewhere. Yet honour prevented his withdrawal as Inrodaka said, 'For that, you presumptuous girl, you will not leave my lands alive.'

Mara met this threat in proud and stony silence. She must not capitulate, for such cowardice would shame the bones of her ancestors. Though her heart leaped in fear, she saw her men were ready, showing no sign of concern for the odds against them. She nodded once to Keyoke.

The Force Commander signalled the warriors of the Acoma to raise weapons while, like imperfect reflections in a mirror, Inrodaka and Ekamchi commanders ordered their own men to the ready.

Through the rattle of blades and the creak of armour, Mara felt her pulsebeat quicken. She tried one last time to negotiate. 'We have no desire for strife, especially as we have done nothing for which we need to defend ourselves.'

Inrodaka's reply rang crisp on the morning air. 'You will not leave without a fight.'

A heartbeat away from precipitating bloodshed, Mara held the irate old man's gaze, while whispering furiously to Keyoke. 'Dare we count on our alliance with the young Queen?'

Keyoke kept his eyes upon the opposing forces. 'Lady, the old Queen rules this hive, and her alliance is with the Inrodaka. Who knows how her warriors will react if the young Queen's ally is threatened?' Gripping his sword tightly, he said, 'I doubt there has ever been such a confrontation in the long history of the Empire.'

As he spoke, a full hundred old, experienced cho-ja warriors marched from the hive entrance. Black carapaces and razor forelimbs gleamed in the sunlight as they interposed themselves between the opposing lines of humans. Dozens more scurried from the earth, even as Lax'l moved a half-dozen paces closer to the two fuming lords and said, 'The Acoma and their ruler are our Queen's guests and the Inrodaka lord her ally. None shall bring strife to her hive. If both armies quit the field, no blood need be shed.'

Incensed, the Lord of the Inrodaka jerked his chin upward. 'But your hive has been in service to my house for three generations!'

'Allied,' repeated Lax'l. His eyes glinted with something Mara thought might be anger, though his voice was calm. 'As the Lady of the Acoma said, the cho-ja are no man's slaves. Leave at once.' As if to drive home the point, another command of cho-ja scurried around from behind the hive to take position behind the forces of the Inrodaka and the Ekamchi. A similar force was appearing behind Mara's soldiers.

Inrodaka glanced to either side, where another two hundred cho-ja warriors approached with their limbs angled forward to charge. His rage faltered, even before he turned to discover Lord Ekamchi already signalling his forces to retire. Mara observed that Inrodaka was as relieved as not to be forced to depart. His reputation had long been that of a man who avoided conflict, and his display had probably been for the benefit of his ally rather than from any true sense of outrage.

Weakness overwhelmed the Lady of the Acoma as sleepless nights and tension overcame her staunch will. She allowed herself to fall back into her pillows as Lax'l span to face Keyoke. 'Force Commander, my company will escort you to the limit of the Inrodaka boundaries with a full hundred warriors.'

Keyoke signalled and, over the sound of men returning swords to sheaths, said, 'Are you among the twenty who will join the new hive?'

'I am.' Lax'l made an odd facial expression, perhaps the cho-ja equivalent of a smile. 'Since you undertook great expense to ensure the safety of her daughter, the old Queen has given you the best of her soldiers. Another will assume my post here, and I will be the new hive's Force Commander.'

Then as if in afterthought, he said, 'I believe the Lady of the Acoma has won what you Tsurani would call the old Queen's affection.'

Tired to the core of her bones, Mara still managed a half bow of appreciation. 'You are not needed by the young Queen?'

The cho-ja Force Commander gestured in the negative with his forelimbs. 'The young Queen is most vulnerable when growing, so even our presence would not mitigate the young warriors' aggression – as it should not. Once within our new hive, we shall teach them what they must know to become good warriors.'

As the Inrodaka and Ekamchi forces retreated over a rise and vanished from sight, Keyoke mustered the men for the long march home. When the last soldier was in place, he looked at his mistress. 'My Lady?'

Mara indicated they should depart, but requested Arakasi walk beside her litter. He arrived looking drawn and dusty, like the rest of the men, except for the glint of victory in his eyes. Warmed by his pride of accomplishment, Mara spoke softly as the column moved out. 'You have been better than your word, Arakasi. Not only have you shown the value of your advice, but your wisdom has benefited the Acoma well. How long will you need to reactivate your network?'

The Spy Master's satisfaction spread across his face until he showed a genuine smile. He bowed slightly to his new mistress. 'A year, Lady, if I encounter no difficulties.'

'If there are difficulties?'

'A year, a year and a half.' The Spy Master paused significantly, then added, 'More, if you require.'

Mara glanced to either side, assuring herself that no men marched close enough to overhear. 'When we make camp tonight, I want you to leave and begin seeking out your agents. Return to our estates in a year. Should you have need to reach me, our signal will be the phrase "the young Queen's silk makers." Do you understand?'

Arakasi returned the hint of a nod, the gesture concealed behind an adjustment to the strap of his helm. 'If I do not return and swear upon the Acoma natami, I am not bound to the bidding of the Lady of the Acoma until I am ready to do so.' Then he added pointedly, 'Or the bidding of the Lord of the Acoma.'

'You understand.' Mara closed her eyes and reined back strong emotion. The gods were kind that this man should be perceptive enough to divine her intentions regarding her husband-to-be.

Arakasi qualified softly. 'Buntokapi might not share our enthusiasm for our vow, Lady.'

Mara nodded, chilled by relief that this man was an ally and not an enemy. If Jingu of the Minwanabi should ever secure the talents of a man like Arakasi . . . but fatigue could not be permitted to fan the embers of unfounded fears. With an effort, the Lady focused on the present. 'When you have returned, we shall see how things are. If all has progressed as I hope, we may then moved forward with our plans for Jingu of the Minwanabi.'

Arakasi inclined his head slightly towards Mara's litter. 'In my heart I have sworn loyalty to you, my Lady. I pray the gods grant me the opportunity to make a more formal oath before the Acoma contemplation glade someday.' He glanced around at the heavy matted greenery of the forest. 'This seems as good a place as any to leave. May the gods protect you, Lady of the Acoma.'

Mara thanked him and fell silent as Arakasi turned and faded away into the woods. Keyoke glanced back and saw him go. If the Force Commander wondered at this sudden departure, he said nothing, but simply returned his attention to his warriors and the dangers of the march home. Mara lay back, Arakasi's last words turning over and over in her mind. She added a prayer that his wish would come to pass; for if he lived and did not swear before the natami, either she would be dead, or Buntokapi would be firmly in place as Lord of the Acoma, and beyond her power to control.

The maids waited upon their mistress. Seated upon cushions in the chamber she still considered her father's, Mara opened her eyes and said. 'I am ready.'

But in her heart she knew she was not prepared for her marriage to the third son of the Anasati, and never would be. With her hands clenched nervously together, she endured as her maids began the torturous process of combing out her hair and binding it with threads and ribbons into the traditional bride's headdress. The hands of the women worked gently, but Mara could not settle. The twist and the tug as each lock was secured made her want to squirm like a child.

As always, Nacoya seemed to read her mind. 'Mistress, the eye of every guest will be upon you this day, and your person must embody the pride of Acoma heritage.'

Mara closed her eyes as if to hide. Confusion arose like an ache in the pit of her stomach. The pride of Acoma heritage had enmeshed her in circumstances that carried her deeper and deeper into nightmare; each time she countered a threat, another took its place. She wondered again whether she had acted wisely in selecting Buntokapi as husband. He might be influenced more easily than his well-regarded brother Jiro, but he also might prove more stubborn. If he could not be controlled, her plans for the resurgence of Acoma pre-eminence could never be achieved. Not for the first time, Mara stilled such idle speculations: the choice was made. Buntokapi would be Lord of the Acoma. Then she silently amended that: for a time.

'Will the Lady turn her head?' Mara obeyed, startled by the warmth of the maid's hand upon her cheek. Her own fingers were icy as she considered Buntokapi and how she would deal with him. The man who would take her father's place as Lord of the Acoma had none of Lord Sezu's wisdom or intelligence, nor had he any of Lano's grace, or charm, or irresistible humour. In the few formal occasions Mara had observed Buntokapi since his arrival for the wedding, he had seemed a brute of a man, slow to understand subtlety and obvious in his passions. Her breath caught, and she forestalled a shudder. He was only a man, she reminded herself; and though her preparation for temple service had caused her to know less of men than most girls her age, she must use her wits and body to control him. For the great Game of the Council, she would manage the part of wife without love, even as had countless women of great houses before her.

Tense with her own resolve, Mara endured the ministrations of the hairdressers while the bustle and shouts through the thin paper of the screens indicated that servants prepared the great hall for the ceremony. Outside, needra bawled, and wagons rolled, laden with bunting and streamers. The garrison troops stood arrayed in brightly polished full armour, their weapons wrapped with strips of white cloth to signify the joy of their mistress's coming union. Guests and their retinues crowded the roadway, their litters and liveried servants a sea of colour against the baked grass of the fields. Slaves and workers had been granted the day off for the festivities, and their laughter and singing reached Mara where she sat, chilled and alone with her dread.

The maids smoothed the last ribbon and patted the last gleaming tresses into place. Beneath coiled loops of black hair, Mara seemed a figure of porcelain, her lashes and brows as fine as a temple painter's masterpiece. 'Daughter of my heart, you have never looked so lovely,' observed Nacoya.

Mara smiled mechanically and rose, while dressers slipped the simple white robe from her body and dusted her lightly with a powder to keep her dry during the long ceremony. Others readied the heavy embroidered silk gown reserved for Acoma brides. As the wrinkled old hands of the women smoothed the undergarment over her hips and flat stomach, Mara bit her lip; come nightfall, the hands of Buntokapi would touch her body anywhere he pleased. Without volition she broke into a light sweat.

'The day grows warm,' muttered Nacoya. A knowing gleam lit her eye as she added a little extra powder where Mara would need it. 'Kasra, fetch your mistress a cool drink of sā wine. She looks pale, and the excitement of the wedding is not yet begun.'

Mara drew an angry breath. 'Nacoya, I am able to manage well enough without wine.' She paused, frustrated, as her women hooked the laces at her waist and lower chest, temporarily constricting her breath. 'Besides, I'm sure Bunto will drink enough for both of us.'

Nacoya bowed with irritating formality. 'A slight flush to your face becomes you, Lady. But husbands don't care for perspiration.' Mara chose to ignore Nacoya's cross words. She knew the old nurse was worried for the child she loved above all others.

Outside, the busy sounds told Mara that her household scrambled to finish the last-minute tasks. The august of the Empire and a nearly overwhelming list of invited guests would gather in the great hall, seated according to rank. Since those of highest rank would be shown to their cushions last, the arrangement of the guests became a complex and lengthy affair that began well before dawn. Tsurani weddings occurred during the morning, for to complete so important a union in the waning part of the day was believed to bring ill luck to the couple. This required guests of modest rank to present themselves at the Acoma estate before dawn, some as early as four hours before sunrise. Musicians and servants with refreshments would entertain those seated first, while the priests of Chochocan sanctified the Acoma house. By now they would be donning their high robes of office, while out of sight a red priest of Turakamu would slaughter the needra calf.

The maids lifted the overrobe, with its sleeves sewn with shatra birds worked in rare gold. Mara gratefully turned her back. As attendants arranged her bows, she was spared the sight of Nacoya checking each last detail of the costume. The old nurse had been on edge since Mara chose to grant Buntokapi power over the Acoma. That Mara had done so with long-range hopes in mind did nothing to comfort Nacoya, what with Anasati warriors encamped in the barracks, and one of the Acoma's most vigorous enemies living in style in the best guest chambers in the house. And with his brassy voice and artless manners, Buntokapi offered no reassurance to a servant who would shortly be subject to his every whim. And she herself would also, Mara remembered with discomfort. She tried to imagine being in bed with the bullnecked boy without shuddering, but could not.

Cued by a servant's touch, Mara sat while the jewelled ceremonial sandals were laced onto her feet. Other maids pressed shell combs set with emeralds into her headdress. Restive as the needra calf being perfumed for sacrifice – so that Turakamu would turn his attentions away from those at the wedding – the girl called for a minstrel to play in her chambers. If she must endure through the tedium of dressing, at least music might keep her from exhausting herself with thought. If fate brought her trouble through this marriage to Buntokapi, she would find out soon enough. The musician was led in blindfolded; no man might look upon the bride until she began her procession to the wedding. He sat and picked out a soothing melody on his gikoto, the five-string instrument that was the mainstay of Tsurani composition.

When the last laces and buttons had been fastened, and the final string of pearls looped to her cuffs, Mara arose from her cushions. Blindfolded slaves bearing her ceremonial litter were led into the chamber, and Mara climbed into the open palanquin crafted solely for Acoma weddings. The frame was wound with flowers and koi vines for luck, and the bearers wore garlands in their hair. As they lifted the litter to their shoulders, Nacoya stepped between them and lightly kissed Mara on the forehead. 'You look lovely, my Lady – as pretty as your own mother on the morning she wed Lord Sezu. I know she would have been proud to see you, were she alive this day. May you find the same joy in marriage as she, and be blessed with children to carry on the Acoma name.'

Mara nodded absently. As serving women stepped forward to lead her bearers through the screen, the minstrel she had summoned faltered in his singing and awkwardly fell silent. With a frown, the girl berated herself for carelessness. She had done the musician a discourtesy by leaving him without praise. As the litter moved from the chamber into the first empty connecting hall, Mara quickly dispatched Nacoya to give the man a token, some small gift to restore his pride. Then, wrapping her fingers tightly together to hide their shaking, she resolved to be more alert. A great house did not thrive if its mistress concerned herself with large matters only. Most often the ability to handle the petty details of life comprised an attitude that allowed one to discover the path to greatness; or so Lord Sezu had admonished when Lano had neglected his artisans for extra drill with the warriors.

Mara felt a strange detachment. The distant bustle of preparations and the arrival of guests lent a ghostly aspect to the corridors emptied for the passage of her litter. Wherever she looked she saw no one, yet the presence of people filled the air. In isolation she reached the main corridor and moved out of the estate house, into the small garden set aside for meditation. There Mara would pass an hour alone in contemplation, as she prepared to leave her girlhood and accept the role of woman and wife. Acoma guards in elaborate ceremonial armour stood watch around the garden, to protect, and to ensure the Lady would suffer no interruption. Unlike the bearers, they wore no blindfolds, but rather stood facing the walls, straining their hearing to the limit, alert, but not tempting ill luck by gazing upon the bride.

Mara turned her mind away from the coming ceremony, seeking instead to find a moment of calm, some hint of the serenity she had known in the temple. She settled gracefully to the ground, adjusting her gown as she settled on the cushions left for her. Bathed in the pale gold of early morning, she watched the play of water over the rim of the fountain. Droplets formed and fell, each separate in its beauty until it shattered with a splash into the pool beneath. I am like those droplets, thought the girl. Her efforts throughout life would, in the end, blend with the lasting honour of the Acoma; and whether she knew happiness or misery as the wife of Buntokapi would not matter at all when her days ended, so long as the sacred natami remained in the glade. And so long as the Acoma were accorded their rightful place in the sun, unshadowed by any other house.

Bending her head in the dew-bright stillness, Mara prayed earnestly to Lashima, not for the lost days of her girlhood, or for the peace she had desired in temple service. She asked instead for the strength to accept the enemy of her father as husband, that the name Acoma might rise once again in the Game of the Council.

7

Wedding

Nacoya bowed deeply.

'My Lady, it is time.'

Mara opened her eyes, feeling too warm for the hour. The cool of early morning had barely begun to fade, and already her robes constricted her body. She looked to where Nacoya stood, just before the flower-bedecked litter. Only a moment longer, Mara thought. Yet she dared not delay. This marriage would be difficult enough without risking the bad omen of having the wedding incomplete by noon. Mara rose without aid and re-entered the litter. She gestured readiness, and Nacoya voiced a command. The slaves removed their blindfolds, for now the bridal procession would begin. The guards surrounding the garden turned as one and saluted their mistress as the bearers lifted her litter and began their journey to the ceremonial dais.

The slaves' bare feet made no sound as they carried Mara into the tiled hall of the estate house. Keyoke and Papewaio waited at the entrance and let the litter pass before they fell in behind, following at a watchful distance. Servants lined the doorways along the hall, strewing flowers to bring their mistress joy and health in child-bearing. Between the doorways stood her warriors, an added fervour in each man as they saluted her passage. Several could not keep moisture from their eyes. This woman was more to them than their Lady; to those who had been grey warriors, she was the giver of a new life, against any expectation. Mara might give over their loyalty to Buntokapi, but she would always have their love.

The bearers halted outside the closed doors of the ceremonial hall while two maidens dedicated to the service of Chochocan pinned coloured veils to Mara's headdress. Into her hands they pressed a wreath wound of ribbons, shatra feathers, and thyza reed, to signify the interdependence of spirit and flesh, of earth and sky, and the sacred union of husband and wife. Mara held the circlet lightly, afraid her damp palms might mar the silk ribbons. The brown-and-white-barred plumes of the shatra betrayed her trembling as four elegantly garbed maidens closed around her litter. They were all daughters of Acoma allies, friends Mara had known in girlhood. While their fathers might keep their distance politically, for this one day they were again her dear friends. Their warm smiles as the nuptial procession formed could not ease Mara's apprehension. She might enter the great hall as the Ruling Lady of the Acoma, but she would leave as the wife of Buntokapi, a woman like all other women who were not heirs, an adornment to further the honour and comfort of her Lord. After a short ceremony before the natami in the sacred glade, she would own no rank, except through the grace of her husband.

Keyoke and Papewaio grasped the wooden door rings and pulled, and silently the painted panels slid wide. A gong sounded. Musicians played reed pipes and flutes, and her bearers started forward. Mara blinked, fighting tears. She held her head high beneath her veils as she was carried before the eyes of the greatest dignitaries and families in the Empire. The ceremony which would join her fate to that of Buntokapi of the Anasati was now beyond the power of any man to prevent.

Through the coloured veils the assembled guests appeared as shadows to Mara. The wood walls and floors smelled of fresh wax and resins, blending with the fragrance of flowers as the slaves bore her up the stairs of a fringed dais built in two layers. They set her litter down upon the lower level and withdrew, leaving her at the feet of the High Priest of Chochocan and three acolytes, while her maiden attendants seated themselves on cushions beside the stair. Dizzied by the heat and the nearly overpowering smoke from the priest's censer, Mara fought to catch her breath. Though she could not see beyond the priests' dais, she knew that by tradition Buntokapi had entered the hall simultaneously from the opposite side, on a litter adorned with paper decorations that symbolized arms and armour. By now he sat level with her on the priests' right hand. His robes would be as rich and elaborate as her own and his face hidden by the massive plumed mask fashioned expressly for weddings by some long-distant Anasati forebear.

The High Priest raised his arms, palms turned towards the sky, and intoned the opening lines. 'In the beginning, there was nothing but power in the minds of the gods. In the beginning, they formed with their powers darkness and light, fire and air, land and sea, and lastly man and woman. In the beginning, the separate bodies of man and woman re-created the unity of the gods' thought from which they were created, and so were children begotten between them, to glorify the power of the gods. This day, as in the beginning, we are gathered to affirm the unity of the gods' will, through the earthly bodies of this young man and woman.'

The priest lowered his hands. A gong chimed, and boy chanters sang a phrase describing the dark and the light of creation. Then, with the squeak of sandals and the rustle of silks, brocades, beads, and jewelled feathers, the assembled guests rose to their feet.

The priest resumed his incantation, and Mara fought the urge to reach beneath her veils and scratch her nose. The pomp and the formality of the ceremony made her recall an incident from her early girlhood, when she and Lano had come home from a state wedding similar to the one she sat through now. As children, they had played bride and groom, Mara seated on the sun-baked boards of a thyza wagon, her hair decked out in akasi flowers. Lano had worn a marriage mask of mud-baked clay and feathers, and the 'priest' had been an aged slave the children had badgered into wearing a blanket for the occasion. Sadly Mara tightened her fingers; the ceremonial wreath in her hands was real this time, not a child's imitation braided of grasses and vines. Were Lanokota alive to be here, he would have teased and toasted her happiness. But Mara knew that inwardly he would have been weeping.

The priest intoned another passage, and the gong rang. The guests reseated themselves upon cushions, while the acolyte on the dais lit incense candles. Heavy scent filled the hall as the high Priest recited the virtues of the First Wife. As he finished each – chastity, obedience, mannerliness, cleanliness, and fecundity – Mara bowed and touched her forehead to the floor. And as she straightened, a purple-robed acolyte with dyed feet and hands removed one of her veils, white for chastity, blue for obedience, rose for mannerliness, until only a thin green veil for Acoma honour remained.

The gauzy fabric still itched, but at least Mara could see her surroundings. The Anasati sat to the groom's side of the dais, just as the Acoma retinue sat behind Mara's. Before the dais the guests were arrayed by rank. Brightest shone the white and gold raiment of the Warlord, who sat closest to the ceremony, his wife beside him in scarlet brocade sewn with turquoise plumes. In the midst of the riot of colours worn by the guests, two figures in stark black robes stood forth like nightwings resting in a flower garden. Two Great Ones from the Assembly of Magicians had accompanied Almecho to the wedding of his old friend's son.

Next in rank should have been the Minwanabi, but Jingu's presence was excused without insult to the Anasati because of the blood feud between Minwanabi and Acoma. Only at a state function, such as the Emperor's coronation or the Warlord's birthday, might both families be present without conflict.

Behind the Warlord's retinue, Mara recognized the Lords of the Keda, the Tonmargu, and the Xacatecas; along with Almecho's Oaxatucan and the Minwanabi, they constituted the Five Great Families, the most powerful in the Empire. In the next row sat the Shinzawai lord, Kamatsu, with the face of Hokanu, his second son, turned handsomely in profile. Like the Acoma and the Anasati, the Shinzawai were counted second in rank only to the Five Great Families.

Mara bit her lip, the leaves and feathers of her marriage wreath trembling. Above her the High Priest droned on, now describing the virtues of the First Husband while the acolytes draped necklaces of beads over the paper swords of Bunto's litter. Mara saw the red and white plumes of his marriage mask dip as he acknowledged each quality as it was named, being honour, strength, wisdom, virility, and kindness.

The gong chimed again. The priest led his acolytes in a prayer of blessing. More quickly than Mara had believed possible, her maiden attendants arose and helped her from her litter. Bunto arose also, and with the priest and acolytes between them they stepped down from the dais and bowed to the gathered guests. Then, in a small procession that included Buntokapi's father, the Lord of the Anasati, and Nacoya, as the Acoma First Adviser, the priest and his acolytes escorted bride and groom from the hall and across the courtyard to the entrance of the sacred grove.

There servants bent and removed the sandals of Mara and Buntokapi, that their feet might be in contact with the earth and the ancestors of the Acoma as the Lady ceded her inherited rights of rulership to her husband-to-be. By now the sun had risen high enough to warm the last dew from the ground. The baked warmth of the stone path felt unreal beneath Mara's soles, and the bright birdsong from the ulo tree seemed the detail of a childhood dream. Yet Nacoya's grip upon her arm was quite firm, no daydream. The priest chanted another prayer, and suddenly she was walking forward with Buntokapi, a jewelled doll beside the towering plumage of his marriage mask. The priest bowed to his god, and leaving his acolytes, and the Lord, and the Acoma Chief Adviser, he followed the couple into the glade.

Rigidly adhering to her role, Mara dared not look back; if the ritual had permitted, she would have seen Nacoya's tears.

The procession passed the old ulo's comfortable shade and in sunlight wended through the flowering shrubs, low gates, and curved bridges that led to the Acoma natami. Woodenly Mara retraced the steps she had taken not so many weeks earlier, when she had carried the relics to mourn her father and brother. She did not think of them now, lest their shades disapprove of her wedding to an enemy to secure their heritage. Neither did she look at the man at her side, whose shuffling step betrayed his unfamiliarity with the path, and whose breath wheezed faintly behind the bright red-and-gold-painted features of the marriage mask. The eyes of the caricature stared ahead in frozen solemnity, while the eyes of the man darted back and forth, taking in the details of what soon would be rightfully his as Lord of the Acoma.

A chime rang faintly, signalling the couple to meditate in silence. Mara and her bridegroom bowed to the godhead painted on the ceremonial gate, and stopped beneath at the edge of the pool. No trace of the assassin's presence remained to defile the grassy verge, but a canopy erected by the priests of Chochocan shaded the ancient face of the natami. After a session of prayer and meditation, the chime rang again. The priest stepped forward and placed his hands on the shoulders of the bride and groom. He blessed the couple, sprinkled them lightly with water drawn from the pool, then paused, silent, while the vows were spoken.

Mara forced herself to calm, though never had the exercise learned from the sisters of Lashima come with such difficulty. In a voice of hammered firmness, she spoke the words that renounced her inherited birthright of Ruling Lady of the Acoma. Sweating but steady, she held fast, while the priest tore away the green veil and burned it in the brazier by the pool. He wet his finger, touched the warm ash, and traced symbols upon Bunto's palms and feet. Then Mara knelt and kissed the natami. She remained with her head pressed to the earth that held the bones of her ancestors, while Buntokapi of the Anasati swore to dedicate his life, his honour, and his eternal spirit to the Name Acoma. Then he knelt beside Mara, who finalized the ritual in a voice that seemed to belong to a stranger.

'Here rest the spirits of Lanokota, my brother; Lord Sezu, my natural father; Lady Oskiro, my natural mother: may they stand as witness to my words. Here lies the dust of my grandfathers, Kasru and Bektomachan, and my grandmothers, Damaki and Chenio: may they stand as witness to my deed.' She drew breath and managed not to falter as she recited the long list of ancestors back to the Patriarch of the Acoma, Anchindiro, a common soldier who battled Lord Tiro of the Keda for five days in a duel before winning the hand of his daughter and the title of Lord for himself, thus placing his family second only to the Five Great Families of the Empire. Even Buntokapi nodded with respect, for despite his father's formidable power, the Anasati line did not go as far back in history as the Acoma. Sweat slid down Mara's collar. With fingers that miraculously did not shake, she plucked a flower from her wreath and laid it before the natami, symbolizing the return of her flesh to clay.

The chime sounded, a mournful note. The priest intoned another prayer, and Bunto spoke the ritual phrases that bound him irrevocably to the Name and the honour of the Acoma. Then Mara handed him the ceremonial knife, and he nicked his flesh so the blood flowed, beading in dusty drops upon the soil. In ties of honour more binding than flesh, of previous kinship, more binding than the memory of the gods themselves, Buntokapi assumed Lordship of the Acoma. The priest removed the red and gold marriage mask of the Anasati; and the third son of an Acoma enemy bowed and kissed the natami. Mara glanced sideways and saw her bridegroom's lips curl into an arrogant smile. Then his features were eclipsed as the High Priest of Chochocan slipped the green marriage mask of the Acoma onto the new Lord's shoulders.

Mara could not remember getting up. The procession back to the entrance of the glade passed in a blur, a dream set in time to birdsong. Servants awaited to wash her soiled feet and replace her jewelled sandals. She endured while the Anasati lord bowed formally to his host, the new Lord of the Acoma, and she did not cry as Nacoya took her place one pace behind Buntokapi's shoulder. Dazzled by the flash of sunlight on the priest's robe, she followed into the main hall, to complete the formal portion of the marriage ceremony.

The hall had grown warm. Great ladies fluttered fans of painted feathers, and the musicians who had entertained them wiped sweaty fingerprints from their instruments, as attendants helped bride and groom into their litters, then raised them to the level where the High Priest and his acolytes presided. Garbed now in an overrobe sewn with precious sequins of silver, gold and copper, the High Priest invoked the ever present eye of Chochocan, the Good God. The gong chimed as he crossed his arms over his chest, and a boy and girl mounted the dais, each carrying a cage woven of reeds. Within perched a male and a female kiri bird, their white-and-black-barred wingtips dyed the green of the Acoma.

The priest blessed the birds, and acolytes accepted the cages. Then, lifting the ivory ceremonial wand from the pocket in his sleeve, the priest invoked his god for a blessing upon the marriage of Buntokapi and Mara. The hall grew hushed and fans stilled in the hands of the ladies. From the lowliest of landed nobles, to the gem-crusted presence of the Warlord, all craned their necks to see as the priest tapped the cages with his wand.

Reeds parted under his ministrations, leaving the birds free to fly, together in joy as in well-omened unions, or separately, to the woe of the couple on the litters, for much stock was placed in Chochocan's favour.

Nacoya closed her eyes, her old hands clenched around an amulet she held under her chin. Bunto looked on with his expression hidden behind the luridly painted marriage mask; but his bride stared off, unseeing, into the distance, as if the ritual in the grove had drained her of interest.

The gong chimed, and servants slid wide the paper screens enclosing the hall. 'Let this marriage be blessed in the sight of heaven,' intoned the priest.

The acolytes tipped the cages, jostling the birds from their perches. The female chirped angrily and flapped her wings, while the male leaped to the air and circled above the assembly, then swooped down towards his mate. He attempted to land on the perch next to the female, but she puffed up and flapped her wings in fury, pecking him unmercifully. The male retreated, then approached, but the female shot into flight, her dyed wingtips a green blur across shadow. With a loud cry she sped for freedom, and vanished, a flash of pale feathers in sunlight. The male bird gripped tightly to the vacated perch. His feathers fluffed and he shook his beak in annoyance. As the chamber stilled with waiting silence, he preened his tail and hopped to the top of the cage, where he relieved himself. After a strained minute passed, the High Priest motioned with his finger, a small but noticeably irritated gesture. An embarrassed acolyte shooed the male bird off. All eyes watched as he circled lazily, then landed in the flower bed just beyond the open screen door and began to peck for grubs.

Brocades and feathers shifted like a wave across the assembly. The High Priest cleared his throat, his wand drooping in one wrinkled hand. At length, with a glance at the stiff-backed Bunto, he said, 'Praise the goodness of Chochocan, and heed his lesson. Under his guidance, may this couple find mercy, understanding, and forgiveness.' Again he cleared his throat. 'The omen shows us that marriage requires diplomacy, for as man and wife, this Lord and Lady must ever strive for unity. Such is the will of the gods.'

A stiff interval followed as acolytes and guests waited for the priest to continue. Eventually it became evident that he would not say more, and the gong chimed. An attendant removed Buntokapi's marriage mask. He faced Mara, who seemed dazed, except that her eyes were narrowed slightly and the faintest of frowns marred the line of her brows.

'Exchange the wreaths,' prompted the priest, as if he seemed worried the couple might forget.

Bunto bent his head, and Mara pressed the somewhat wilted ceremonial circlet over his dark hair. It slipped somewhat as he straightened, and she smelled wine on his breath as he leaned close to crown her in turn.

Mara's frown deepened; during her hour of contemplation, custom demanded that the groom share a ritual sip of wine with his bachelor friends, to bring them fortune, and wives of their own. Yet it seemed that Bunto and his companions had emptied the ceremonial flagon, and possibly one or two more. Annoyed at his indiscretion, Mara barely heard the priest pronounce them man and wife for the duration of their mortal lives. She did not even realize the formal portion of the ceremony had ended until the guests began loudly to cheer and throw luck charms of elaborately folded paper in a colourful blizzard over bride and groom.

Mara managed a mechanical smile. Now came the time when each guest presented the wedding tribute, in the form of a work of art, recitation, or musical composition. Some of these would be elaborate and expensive affairs patronized by the great Lords and politically powerful of the Empire. Rumour held that the Warlord had imported an entire theatrical company, complete with costumes and stage. But his presentation would not occur for days to come, since the lowest in rank would perform first.

Picking a paper charm out of his shirtfront, Buntokapi spared himself the tedium of the first acts, pleading the need to relieve himself and don more comfortable clothing. By tradition he could not bed his bride until the last of the guests had offered tribute; and the heavy marriage robes hid enough of her that staring at slave girls offered better pastime.

Mara nodded courteously at her Lord. 'I shall stay here, my husband, that the least of our guests may know of Acoma gratitude for their presentations.'

Buntokapi sniffed, believing she avoided him deliberately. He would see to her later; meantime a feast waited, with fine music and drink, and the chance to see his brothers bow to him for the first time, as he was now Lord of the Acoma. Smiling under his crooked marriage wreath, Buntokapi clapped his hands for his slaves to carry him from the hall.

Mara remained, despite the fact that most of her wedding guests followed her Lord's example. The sun climbed towards noon, and already heat haze shimmered over the distant acres of the needra fields. The highest-ranking guests retired to their quarters and sent servants for cool drinks and a change of clothes. Then, like brightly coloured birds, they emerged to feast on flavoured ices, chilled jomach fruit, and sā wine, until the cooler comfort of evening.

But in the airless confines of the hall the lowest-ranking stayed stiffly in their seats, while hired performers or a talented family member acted, sang or recited a tribute to the married Acoma couple. At smaller weddings the bride and groom might watch the first few performances out of courtesy; but at the greatest houses truly spectacular events occurred later in the roster, and couples most often left the first day's efforts for the amusement of their off-duty servants.

Yet Mara lingered through the first round of performers, a juggler more successful as a comedian, two singers, a stage conjurer – whose magic was all of the sleight-of-hand variety – and a poet whose own patron snored loudly throughout his recitation. She applauded each act politely, and if she did not offer the accolade of tossing one of the flowers from her litter, she remained politely attentive until the intermission. The performers to follow waited stiffly, certain she would leave for the feasting. Yet, instead of litter bearers, she called for maids to bring her a tray of light food and drink. The guests murmured in surprise.

The fat Sulan-Qu merchant in the first row blushed and hid behind the fan of his wife. Even in dreams he had never dared think the Lady of the Acoma would be present to watch his flute-playing son perform. The boy had a terrible ear, but his mother beamed with pride. Mara remained, sipping chilled jomach juice, upon the dais. She nodded graciously when the young flautist bowed and fled, nearly tripping in his haste to clear the way for the next act. Mara smiled at the embarrassed father and his wife, and realized that despite the tedium of enduring such music, should she ever need a favour from that merchant, it was hers for the asking.

Through mimes, a man with trained dogs, a singing liendi bird, and two more poets, the great lady showed no restlessness. She awarded the second of the poets a flower, deftly thrown into his hat. And the painter who followed made her laugh at his comical drawings of needra bulls charging a warrior. When in the second intermission she called maidservants to remove her outer robe, that she might be more comfortable in the noon heat, the lowliest guests murmured that this Lady was generously disposed beyond any they had known in the Empire. The performers sensed her interest and breathed new life into their offerings. And as servants dispatched by the Lady began to dispense refreshments, along with tokens of gratitude for those guests whose tribute had been heard, some of the stiffness melted from the gathering. As the wine took effect, the bolder tongues whispered that the Lady was very fine and deserving of the honour of her ancestors.

Mara overheard such remarks and smiled gently. As the third intermission began, she bade her maids unbind the constricting coils of her headdress and comb her long hair freely down her back. While the marriage wreath wilted by her knee, she sat back to hear the next round of performances, and the next, to the joy of all who acted for her pleasure. As afternoon wore on, the hall grew hotter; and other guests drifted in to see what held the Lady of the Acoma enthralled.

At sunset the groom put in an appearance, his step slightly unsteady and his voice too loud. Buntokapi mounted the dais, waving a flagon of sā wine, and demanded to know why his wife dallied so long in the hall; the Warlord and others of the Acoma guests were feasting, and wasn't she avoiding him by sitting gaping at common minstrels and officials of low rank?

Mara bowed her head in submissive silence, then looked up into her husband's eyes. He smelled of drink and sweat. She managed a smile anyway. 'My Lord, Camichiro, the poet, will read next, and while his work is too new for fame, his patron the Lord of the Teshiro has a reputation for recognizing genius. Why not stay, and celebrate the introduction of a coming talent?'

Bunto straightened, arms crossed, unmindful of the dribble from the flagon that marred his left cuff. Faced by the serene innocence of a wife whose clothing prevented any view of what lay underneath, and outflanked by the beaming pride of Camichiro and Lord Teshiro, he grunted. To contradict his wife's praise would be extremely bad form. Sober enough to disengage before compromising his obligations as host, Buntokapi bowed in return and snapped, 'I shall have time for poetry later. Others of your guests have begun a game of chiro, and I have placed bets on the winners.'

The Lord of the Acoma retired from the hall. His Lady called servants to bring another round of wine to the performers; and by remaining against the preference of her bridegroom, she earned the admiration of her least-important guests. Loudest in her praise were the merchant and his awkward flautist son, followed closely by the gushy, painted wife of the poet Camichiro. Among the commons of

Sulan-Qu, it was no secret that she was the lover of Lord Teshiro, and that her saucy charms alone had earned the family's patronage.

Sunset came, and the shatra birds flew. The gathering of the marriage tribute adjourned until the next day, while the cooks produced exotic dishes decorated with paper symbols for luck. Lanterns were lit, and musicians played, and at nightfall acrobats juggled sticks of fire. Mara sat at her husband's side until he clapped for slave girls to begin a veil dance. At that time, exhausted, the Lady of the Acoma retired to a special ceremonial hut of painted paper, where she undressed and bathed, and lay a long time without sleeping.

The morning dawned dusty and dry, with no hint of a breeze. Servants had laboured through the night to prepare for a fresh day's festivities, and the akasi flowers sparkled, freshly watered by gardeners who now wore smocks and cut vegetables for the cooks. Mara arose and, hearing her husband's groans through the thin screen that divided the wedding hut, presumed correctly that he had a hangover. She dispatched the prettiest of her slave girls to attend him; then she called for chocha for herself. While the cool of the morning still lingered, she took a walk about the grounds. Soon the cho-ja Queen and her hive mates would be arriving on Acoma lands. Defences would no longer be critical. That thought eased her somewhat; with Jican competent to manage the family assets, and the estate itself secure, she could pitch all her resources into dealing with the Lord she had married. Memory visited, of a woman's high-pitched laughter, and Bunto's voice, querulously demanding, before he drifted into snores near to dawn. Frowning, a firmer set to her mouth, Mara prayed to Lashima for strength.

She looked up from meditation in time to see a retainer with a banner leading a small procession into the great hall. The second day of the marriage tribute was about to begin, and against all precedent Mara dispatched servants to attend to her litter. She would watch the performers to the very last; and though no guest of equal or superior rank was scheduled to present tribute until late afternoon, she would see that no earlier performance went unrewarded. With Buntokapi a Ruling Lord, the Acoma would need all the goodwill she could inspire.

*

Wind came the afternoon of the following day; cloud shadows raced over the needra meadows, and the sky to the east threatened rain. Yet despite the risk of dampened finery, the Acoma guests sat in the open, watching the closing act.

To the astonishment of all in attendance, the Warlord had paid from his personal treasury for a performance by the Imperial Jojan Theatre. Jojan was the formal theatre enjoyed by the nobility, as the commoners preferred to watch the more raucous and ribald Segumi theatre troupes that toured the countryside. But the Imperial Jojan were the finest actors in the realm, being the training ground for the Imperial Shalo-tobaku troupe, who performed only for the Emperor and his immediate family. The performance was *Lord Tedero and the Sagunjan*, one of the ten classic sobatu, literally 'grand high style,' the ancient opera form.

Luxuriating in the coolness of the breeze, and enjoying every moment she could delay joining her husband in the marriage bed, Mara tried to concentrate on the coming finale. The actors were superlative, handling their lines with aplomb despite the breeze that twisted the plumes of their costumes awry. A shame that the script they performed was so overwritten, thought the Lady of the Acoma, whose taste did not run to sobatu, preferring as she did Grand Dō; and the trappings of the travelling stage were gaudy, even to Tsurani eyes.

Then, at the height of the opera, when Lord Tedero entered the cave to free ancient Neshka from the clutches of the dreaded sagunjan, two black-robed figures entered the hall. The presence of the Great Ones alone would have marked this a special occasion, but the two magicians cast illusions. Rather than the traditional paper sagunjan, inside of which a singer and several stagehands walked the stage, an illusion of startling appearance was cast. A sagunjan, twelve feet at the shoulder, all golden scales and breathing red flames, emerged from the doorway painted to resemble the cave. A wonderful baritone voice erupted from the terrible fangs, and though all in the hall knew the singer walked alone, none could see him. Even Mara was transported by the sight, all her worries banished. Then Tedero's sword fell, and the illusion of the sagunjan faded to a mist, then to nothing. Traditionally, the sobatu ended with a formal bow by the cast to polite applause; yet the climax of this opera raised a loud cheer and furious beating of hands, more common to street theatre. As all watched, the Warlord's expression melted into a rare smile as he basked in the reflected glory brought by his theatre troupe and his magician friends. Mara sighed faintly, sorry when the performers finished their final bow. As the sequined curtains swished closed, or tried to, for the breeze by then had stiffened into gusts, she resigned herself to the inevitable. 'Now, wife,' said Buntokapi in her ear. 'The time has come for us to retire.'

Mara stiffened reflexively, the appropriate smile frozen like paint on her face. 'Your will, my husband.'

But a blind man would have sensed her reluctance. Buntokapi laughed. With a shout of drunken triumph, he raised her into his arms.

The guests cheered. Mindful of the thoughtless strength in the arms that held her, Mara tried to calm her racing heart. She would endure, *had to endure*, for the continuance of the Acoma name. She nestled her face into the sweat-damp fabric of her husband's collar and permitted him to bear her from the dais. Paper fertility charms thrown by the crowd showered them both as he carried her from the crowd of well-wishers and down the path to the brightly painted structure of the marriage hut.

Keyoke and Papewaio stood as honour guards at the end of the path. Buntokapi passed them by like common servants and stepped across the threshold into the silvery half-light of sky shining through walls constructed of reed paper and lath. The servant and the maid in attendance within bowed low as their master and mistress appeared. Buntokapi set Mara upon her feet. At his half-grunted syllable, the maid rose and slid the screen entrance closed. The manservant settled motionless in a corner, awaiting his Lordship's pleasure.

The hut had been rearranged during the day; the screen dividing the quarters of husband and wife had been removed, replaced by a wide sleeping mat covered with sheets of fine silk against the east wall, for dawn symbolized beginnings. In the centre of the floor lay an array of sitting cushions, and a low, bare table. Mara took a shaky step forward and settled upon the cushions before the table. She kept her eyes downcast as Bunto sat across from her.

'Send for the priest of Chochocan,' demanded the Lord of the Acoma. His gaze fixed upon Mara, fevered and intense, as the servant leaped from the corner to obey.

The priest entered alone, carrying a tray upon which sat a decanter of golden tura wine, two goblets of crystal, and a candle in a jewelled ceramic stand. He raised the tray skyward, intoning a blessing, and set it on the table between husband and wife. With eyes that seemed to hold misgiving, he glanced at both, the Lady with hands that trembled beyond control, and the young Lord whose impatience was tangible. Then, with resignation, he lit the candle. 'Let Chochocan's wisdom enlighten you.' He traced a symbol in chalk around the candle stand and lifted the wine in blessing. He filled the two goblets and set them opposite bride and groom. 'May the blessing of Chochocan fill your hearts.' He scribed more symbols in chalk around each goblet and the half-empty decanter.

'Drink, children of the gods, and know each other as your masters in heaven have ordained.' The priest bowed in benediction and, with near to visible relief, left the marriage hut.

Buntokapi waved his hand, and the servants retired. The paper screen clicked shut, leaving him alone with his bride in a shelter that quivered in the gusts of rising wind.

He turned dark eyes to Mara. 'At last, my wife, you are mine.' He lifted his goblet too quickly, and wine splashed, obliterating one of the symbols. 'Look at me, my Lady. The priest would prefer if we drank together.'

A gust slammed the screens, rattling the paper against the frames. Mara started, then seemed to take hold of herself. She reached out and lifted her own goblet. 'To our marriage, Buntokapi.'

She took a small sip while her Lord drained his wine to the dregs. He then emptied the remains of the decanter into his glass and finished that also. The first drops of rain spattered heavily against the oiled-cloth ceiling of the marriage hut as he set glass and decanter down.

'Wife, fetch me more wine.'

Mara set her goblet on the table, within the chalk markings scribed by the priest. Thunder growled in the distance, and the wind ended, replaced by a tumultuous downpour. 'Your will, my husband,' she said softly, then lifted her head to call for a servant.

Bunto surged forward. The table rocked, spilling the wine with a splash of liquid and glass. Her call became a cry as the heavy fist of her husband slammed her face.

She fell back, dazed, among the cushions, and the falling rain drummed like the blood in her ears. Her head swam, and pain clouded her senses. Shocked unthinkingly to rage, still Mara retained her Acoma pride. She lay breathing heavily as her husband's shadow fell across her.

Leaning forward so his form obliterated the light behind him, he pointed at Mara. 'I said you do it.' His voice was low and filled with menace. 'Understand me, woman. If I ask you for wine, *you will fetch it. You will never again give that task, or any other, into the hands of a servant without my permission*. If I ask *anything* of you, Lady, you will do it.'

He sat back again, his brutish features emphasized in the half-light. 'You think I'm stupid.' His tone reflected long-hidden resentment. 'You all think I'm stupid, my brothers, my father, and now you. Well, I'm not. With Halesko and, especially, Jiro around, it was easy to look stupid.' With a dark and bitter laugh he added, 'But I don't have to look stupid anymore, heh! You have married into a new order. I am Lord of the Acoma. Never forget that, woman. Now fetch me more wine!'

Mara closed her eyes. In a voice forced to steadiness she said, 'Yes, my husband.'

'Get up!' Bunto nudged her with his toe.

Resisting the urge to touch her swollen, reddened cheek, Mara obeyed. Her head was bowed in the perfect image of wifely submission, but her dark eyes flashed with something very different as she bowed at Buntokapi's feet. Then, even more controlled than she had been when she renounced her rights as Ruler of the Acoma, she arose and fetched wine from a chest near the door.

Buntokapi watched her right the table, then retrieve and refill his glass. Young, and lost in his anticipation as he watched the rise and fall of Mara's breasts beneath the flimsy fabric of her day robe, he did not see the hate in her eyes as he drank. And by the time the wine was finished and his goblet thrown aside, he closed sweaty hands upon that maddening obstruction of silk. He pushed his new wife down into the cushions, too far gone in drink and lust to care.

Mara endured his hands upon her naked flesh. She did not fight him, and she did not cry out. With a courage equal to any her father and brother had shown on the barbarian battlefield on Midkemia, she accomplished what came after without tears, though Bunto's eagerness caused her pain. For long hours she lay upon crumpled, sweaty sheets, listening to the drumming rain and the rasp of her husband's snores. Young and aching and bruised, she thought upon her mother and her nurse, Nacoya; and she wondered if their first night with a man had been different. Then, turning on her side away from the enemy she had married, she closed her eyes. Sleep did not come. But if her pride had suffered sorely, her Acoma honour was intact. She had not cried out, even once.

Morning dawned strangely silent. The wedding guests had departed, the Lord of the Anasati and Nacoya bidding farewell on behalf of the newlyweds. Servants cracked the screens of the wedding hut, and fresh, rain-washed air wafted inside, carrying the calls of the herders driving the stock to the far meadows to graze. Mara inhaled the scent of wet earth and flowers and imagined the brightness of the gardens with the layer of summer dust washed off. By nature she was an early riser, but tradition dictated she must not be up before her husband on the morning after the marriage was consummated. Now, more than ever, the inactivity chafed, left her too much time to think, with no diversion from the various aches in her body. She fretted and fidgeted, while Bunto drowsed on, oblivious.

The sun rose, and the marriage hut grew stuffy. Mara called a servant to slide the screens all the way open, and as noon sunlight sliced across the coarse features of her husband, he groaned. Straight-faced, Mara watched him turn in to the pillows, muttering a sharp command to draw screens and curtains. Before the shadows of the drapes fell, she saw his complexion turn greenish and sweat bead the skin of his neck and wrists.

Sweetly, knowing he had the grandsire of all hangovers, she said, 'My husband, are you indisposed?'

Bunto moaned and sent her for chocha. Sweating herself from memory of his abuses, Mara rose and fetched a steaming pot. She pressed a hot cup into her Lord's shaking hand. As it had been brewing all morning, it was probably too strong to be considered drinkable, but Buntokapi sucked the cup dry. 'You're a small thing,' he observed, comparing his large-knuckled hand to her slight one. Then, sulky from his headache, he reached out and pinched her still-swollen nipple.

Mara managed not to flinch, barely. Shaking the hair over her shoulders so its loose warmth covered her breasts, she said, 'My Lord wishes?'

'More chocha, woman.' As if embarrassed by his clumsiness, he watched her fill his cup. 'Ah, I feel like a needra herd has stopped to deposit their night soil in my mouth.' He made a face and spat. 'You will attend me while I dress and then you will call servants to bring thyza bread and jomach.'

'Yes, husband,' said Mara. 'And after?' Longingly she thought of the cool shadows of her father's study, and Nacoya.

'Don't bother me, wife.' Bunto rose, tenderly nursing his head. He stretched, naked before her, the knobs of his knees only inches from her nose. 'You will oversee the affairs of the house, but only when I have done with your services.'

The shadows of the drapes hid Mara's shudder. Heartsick at the role she must live, she braced herself to endure; but drink and excessive feasting had blunted her husband's desire. He abandoned his empty cup on the bedclothes and called for his robe.

Mara brought the garment and helped to slip the silk sleeves over arms that were stocky and thick with hair. Then she sat at tedious length while servants brought water for her Lord's bath. After she had sponged his great back until the water cooled in the tub, he permitted his Lady to dress. Servants brought bread and fruit, but only she might serve him. Watching him shovel jomach into his mouth, juice dripping down his chin, she wondered how the shrewd Lord of the Anasati had come by such a son. Then, looking beyond his coarse manners into his secretive eyes, she realized with a chill of purest panic that he watched her as carefully in return; like a predator. Mara realized his insistence that he wasn't stupid might be no boast. A sinking feeling hit her. If Buntokapi was simply cunning, like the Lord of the Minwanabi, there would be ways to manage him. But if he was also intelligent . . . The thought left her cold.

'You are very clever,' Buntokapi said at last. He caressed her wrist with a sticky finger, almost dotingly possessive.

'My qualities pale beside my Lord's,' whispered Mara. She kissed his knuckles, to distract his thinking.

'You don't eat,' he observed. 'You only ponder. I dislike that in a woman.'

Mara cut a slice of thyza bread and cradled it in her palms. 'With my Lord's permission?'

Buntokapi grinned as she nibbled a bite; the bread seemed tasteless on her tongue, but she chewed and swallowed to spite him. Quickly bored with watching her discomfort, the son of the Lord of the Anasati called for musicians.

Mara closed her eyes. She needed Nacoya, so badly she ached inside. Yet as mistress of the Ruling Lord she could do nothing but await his pleasure as he called for ballads and argued with the singer over nuances in the fourth stanza. The day warmed, and with closed drapes the marriage hut became stifling. Mara endured, and fetched wine when her husband tired of the music. She combed his hair and laced his sandals. Then, at his bidding, she danced until the hair dampened at her temples and her bruised face stung with exertion. Just when it seemed her Lord would while away the entire day within the marriage hut, he rose and bellowed for the servants to prepare his litter. He would pass the time until evening in the barracks reviewing the numbers and training of the Acoma warriors, he announced.

Mara wished Lashima's patience upon Keyoke. Wilted from heat and strain, she followed her husband from the hut into the blinding sun of afternoon. In her discomfort she had forgotten the waiting honour guard, and so her bruised cheek was uncovered as she appeared before Papewaio and Keyoke. Years of the harshest training enabled them to see such a mark of shame without expression. But the stolid hand of Keyoke tightened upon his spear haft until the knuckles shone white, and Papewaio's toes clenched on the soles of his sandals. Had any man save the Ruling Lord put such marks upon their Mara-anni he would have died before he completed another step. Mara stepped into a day as bright and clean as the gods could make it; but as she walked past her former retainers, she felt their anger like black shadows at her back.

The marriage hut was burning before she reached the estate house. By tradition, the building was set aflame to honour the sacred passage of woman to wife and man to husband. After tossing the ritual torch over the threshold, Keyoke turned silently towards the guards' quarters, to await the orders of his Lord. Papewaio's expression remained like chipped stone. With an intensity fierce for its stillness, he watched the paper and lath, with its array of soiled cushions and tangled sheets, explode into flame. Never had he been happier to see something burn; for in watching the violence of the fire he could almost forget the bruise on Mara's face.

Nacoya was not in the study. With an unpleasant jolt, Mara remembered that here also marriage changed the order she had known. The master's study was now the province of Buntokapi, as Lord of the Acoma. Hereafter no aspect of the household she had known would be the same. Jican would tally his accounts in the wing assigned to the scribes, as before, but she could no longer receive him. Feeling weary despite her seventeen years, Mara retired to the shade beneath the ulo in her private garden. She did not sit but leaned against the smooth bark of the tree while the runner she had dispatched hastened to fetch Nacoya.

The wait seemed to last interminably, and the fall of water from the fountain did not soothe. When Nacoya appeared at last, breathless, her hair fallen crooked against its pins, Mara could only stare at her in a silence of pent-up misery.

'Mistress?' The nurse stepped hesitantly forward. Her breath caught as she saw the bruise on Mara's cheek. Without words the old woman raised her arms. The next instant the Lady of the Acoma was only a frightened girl weeping in her embrace.

Nacoya stroked Mara's shoulders as sob after sob convulsed her. 'Mara-anni, daughter of my heart,' she murmured. 'I see he was not gentle, this Lord you have married.'

For an interval the fountain's mournful fall filled the glade. Then, sooner than Nacoya expected, Mara straightened up. In a surprisingly steady voice she said, 'He is Lord, this man I have married. But the Acoma name will outlive him.' She sniffed, touched the bruise on her face, and directed a look of wounding appeal to her former nurse. 'And, mother of my heart, until I conceive, I must find strength to live with things my father and brother would weep to know.'

Nacoya patted the cushions beneath the ulo, encouraging Mara to sit. Her old hands made the girl comfortable, while a servant brought a basin of chilled water and soft cloths. While Mara lay back on the cushions, Nacoya bathed her face. Then she combed the tangles from her glossy black hair, as she had when the Lady had been a child; and as she worked, she spoke, very softly, into her mistress's ear.

'Mara-anni, last night brought you no joy, this I know. But understand in your heart that the man you have wed is young, as impetuous as a needra bull at the time of its third spring. Do not judge all men by the experience of only one.' She paused. Unspoken between them was the fact that Mara had disregarded advice, and rather than educating herself to awareness of men through a gentle encounter with one hired from the Reed Life, she had been headstrong. Nacoya dabbed chill water over her mistress's bruises. The price of that stubbornness had been cruelly extracted.

Mara sighed and opened swollen eyes. To her nurse she directed a look that held painful uncertainty but no regret. Nacoya laid cloth and basin aside and nodded with reflective approval. This girl might be young, and small, and battered, but she owned the toughness of her father, Lord Sezu, when it came to matters of family. She would endure, and the Acoma name would continue.

Mara tugged at her day robe and winced slightly as the cloth abraded sore nipples. 'Mother of my heart, the ways of men are strange to me. I am much in need of advice.'

Nacoya returned a smile that held more craft than pleasure. Her head cocked to one side, and after a moment of thought she pulled the pins from her hair and carefully began binding it afresh. Watching the ordinary, even familiar movements of the nurse's wrinkled hands, Mara relaxed slightly. Day always came after night, no matter how dark the clouds that covered the moon. She listened as Nacoya began to speak, quite softly, that only she could hear.

'Child, the Empire is vast, and many are the lords and masters whose ambitions turn their hearts hard with cruelty. Hapless servants often suffer beneath the rule of such men. But from such adversity wisdom springs. The servants have learned, as you shall, that the codes of honour can be two-edged as a weapon. Every word has two meanings, and every action, multiple consequences. Without compromising loyalty or honour, a servant can make the life of a cruel overlord a living hell.'

Mara regarded the leaves of the ulo, dark, serrated patterns notching small windows of sky. 'Like you and Keyoke and Jican, the day Papewaio rescued me from the Hamoi tong,' she murmured dreamily.

To answer would border upon treason. Stony-faced and silent,

Nacoya only bowed. Then she said, 'I will summon the midwife for you, Lady. She owns the wisdom of the earth and will tell you how to conceive with all possible speed. Then your Lord need not trouble your sleep with his lust, and the Acoma name will be secured by an heir.'

Mara straightened upon her cushions. 'Thank you, Nacoya.' She patted the old woman's hand and rose. But before she turned to go, the nurse looked deep into the girl's eyes. She saw there the same pain, and a measure of fear; but also she saw the bright spark of calculation she had come to know since Lord Sezu's death. She bowed then, swiftly, to hide an upwelling surge of emotion; and as she watched Mara walk with a straight back to her quarters, Nacoya blinked and wept.

The ashes of the marriage hut cooled and dispersed in the wind, and dust rose, for the weather turned hot and dry. The days lengthened, until the summer had passed its peak.

Needra were slaughtered for the feast of Chochocan, and the freemen dressed in their best for the ritual blessing of the fields, while priests burned paper effigies to symbolize sacrifice for bountiful harvests. Buntokapi remained sober for the ceremony, largely because Mara had the servants add water to his wine. If the company of her loud-voiced husband wore upon her, no strain showed in her bearing. Only her personal maids knew that the hollowness around her eyes was hidden by makeup, and that the clothing on her slender body sometimes concealed bruises.

The teachings of the sisters of Lashima sustained her spirit. She took comfort from the counsel of her midwife and learned to spare herself some of the discomfort when her husband called her to his bed. Sometime between the midsummer feast and the next full moon, Kelesha, goddess of brides, blessed her, for she conceived. Buntokapi's ignorance of women served well, as he accepted the news they could no longer join as man and wife until after the baby's birth. With a minimum of grumbling he let her move into the quarters that had once been her mother's. The rooms were quiet, and surrounded by gardens; Buntokapi's loud voice did not carry there, which was well, because she fell ill several hours each morning and slept odd times of the day.

The midwife smiled widely and rubbed sweet oil over Mara's

belly and breasts to soften the skin as she swelled with child. 'You carry a son, my Lady, I swear by the bones of my mother.'

Mara did not smile back. Denied a part in Buntokapi's decisions, and shamed by the way he treated some of the servants, the Lady of the house seemed to retreat within herself. But her resignation was only on the surface. Daily she spoke with Nacoya, who gathered the gossip of the servants. While out in her litter to enjoy the fresh early autumn air, Mara questioned Papewaio until he mockingly complained he had no air left to answer. But as she adjusted to the submissive role of wife, no detail of Acoma affairs missed her grasp.

Tired of the massage, Mara rose from the mat. A servant handed her a light robe, which Mara donned, fastening it about a belly beginning to round. She sighed as she considered the baby's father and the changes his rule had wrought in the estate. Buntokapi commanded the respect of the warriors through brutish displays of strength, and an occasional turn of cleverness that kept them wary to a man. By suddenly deciding to have battle practice or grabbing whichever soldiers were in sight to accompany him to the city without regard to what duty they had previously been assigned, he reduced the garrison to shambles on a regular basis. His habit of rearranging standing orders had Keyoke running ragged to compensate. Jican spent increasingly long hours in the outermost needra fields with his tally slate. Mara knew the hadonra well enough to interpret his growing dislike of the new Lord. Clearly, Buntokapi had little head for matters of commerce. Like many sons of powerful Lords, he thought wealth was inexhaustible, readily available for his every need.

At mid-autumn the needra herders took to the roads, and curtains of dust hung on the air as the previous year's calves were driven to feedlots, and thence to slaughter. The spring calves were gelded or set aside for brood or driven to the high meadows to grow. Mara felt the passing of time like a child awaiting her adulthood celebration, each day dragging interminably.

The inactivity lifted when the cho-ja arrived. The hive came without warning; one day the east meadow left open for them lay empty, and the next, workers bustled about in energetic enterprise. Dirt piles arose along the fence line. That the message from the Queen came addressed to Mara nettled Buntokapi. In the midst of his tirade he realized these cho-ja had come from the hive on the Lord of the Inrodaka's estate. He guessed Mara's bargain for their loyalty must have taken place between the petition for marriage and the wedding, for his eyes narrowed in a manner his Lady had learned to dread.

'You are more clever than even my father guessed, wife.' Then, with a glance at Mara's middle, he smiled without humour. 'But your days of travelling in haste and secrecy are over. Now I am ruling Lord, the cho-ja are mine to command.'

But as Mara had been primary negotiator for the Acoma, the Queen addressed only her until the new Lord would take time to renegotiate in his own behalf. But activities with the warriors seemed always to take precedence. If the young wife spent increasing time in the freshly dug chambers of the Queen drinking chocha and gossiping, Buntokapi barely noticed, engrossed as he was in betting on bouts of wrestling in Sulan-Qu. For this Mara was grateful, for her discussions with the young Queen offered relief from the boredom of home life. Gradually she was learning the ways of an alien race. In counterbalance to Buntokapi's blunders, the relationship she cemented now might add wealth to the Acoma for years to come.

Returning above ground, to holdings that now were Buntokapi's, Mara realized she had come to enjoy ruling. Reduced to the secondary role of woman and wife, she chafed, and counted the days until winter. After the spring rains fell, her child would be born, and the Acoma would have an heir. Until then she must wait; and the waiting came hard.

Mara touched her belly, feeling for the life within. If the child was male, and healthy, then would her husband have cause to beware, for in the Game of the Council even the most mighty could be vulnerable. Mara had made vows to the spirits of her father and brother, and she would not rest until vengeance was complete.

8

Heir

The baby kicked.

For a moment Mara's eyes opened wide. Then she relaxed, laid aside the parchments she had been reviewing, and patted her rounded middle, smiling slightly. Her child was nearly due. She felt as cumbersome as a needra cow, though Nacoya still insisted she had not gained the weight she should. Mara shifted upon her mat in a vain effort to find a more comfortable position. She prayed to the goddess of fertility that the old midwife's efforts before conception had ensured a son. Let it be a boy child, so that she would not have to encourage attention from her husband to gain an heir for the Acoma.

The baby kicked again, vigorously, and Mara gasped. She waved away the solicitous maid who hovered nearby, and reached for the parchments. Already this child within her seemed restless, as if he could force his way into life with his tiny feet and fists. *He*, Mara thought, and a smile touched her lips. He would indeed be a son, to kick so hard in the womb; and he would lead her house to greatness. He would be Lord of the Acoma.

A shout from outside broke Mara's reverie. She nodded, and the serving maid quickly opened the screen, letting in a hot breeze, strong with the dry smell of dust from the fields. Mara snatched, but too late, and the parchments listing Jican's success in marketing the first cho-ja goods scudded across the floor. She murmured a mild imprecation, but not for the reports, which her runner bent to gather. Across the clipped lawn beyond the screen marched a party of warriors, with Buntokapi boisterously leading. His hair was spiked with sweat and his tunic frayed, a casualty she could have expected from the rigours of a week-long hunt. And as usual he would visit her chambers after cleaning his weapons but before taking time to bathe. Mara sighed. The days had been quiet with her Lord gone. Now she prepared herself for confusion.

As the hunters drew nearer, Mara gestured. Two maidservants bent and helped her awkwardly to her feet. Misa, the prettier one, had damp palms already; Mara sympathized. Her husband's presence often made the girls jumpy, since he might drag any one of them off to his bedchamber. At least her pregnancy had freed her of that odious responsibility. With a flash of malice, Mara made a mental note to ask Jican to buy ugly slaves the next time Bunto sent him to the auctions for girls.

The hunters reached the gravel path. The jingle of their gear seemed louder as their manner and voices became more subdued in the presence of their mistress. Yet their excitement remained high, with Buntokapi not in the least restrained. He smelled of the woods. Mara saw dried bloodstains on his sleeves. He waved in her direction, then pointed over his shoulder, like an artist unveiling a masterpiece. The slaves who trailed him carried a long pole, from which hung a matted bundle of brindled orange-and-grey fur. Mara stepped away from the support of her maids as she recognized the white-masked eyes and fanged muzzle of a sarcat. The deadly nocturnal predator ranged in the rain forests southwest of the estate. Fearfully swift, the creature was a powerful killer, a terror to herders because domestic needra made easy prey and sarcats had no fear of humans. Then Mara noticed an arrow marked with the Lord's green stripes pierced through the creature's shoulder, just behind the massive jaws. By the shaft's position she guessed Buntokapi had stood in the path of the beast's charge, then dropped it with a single bowshot. The feat was impressive. Despite his other qualities, Buntokapi had displayed great courage and formidable skill with a bow.

Looking from his kill to his broadly smiling face, for a moment Mara could almost forget that the man was utterly lacking in sensitivity. He disliked poetry, unless it was ribald. His taste in music ran to the common – low minstrels and folk tunes – with no patience for the elegance of Grand Dō theatre or opera. His appreciation of art was nonexistent unless the subject was erotic. Yet in the hunt he excelled, and not for the first time Mara regretted that Tecuma had been too busy with Halesko and Jiro to train this, his third, son. As much as she despised Buntokapi upon occasion, he had much raw potential. Had he been instructed in the manners and propriety befitting one born to the Anasati name, he might have become a man of substance. But her regret lasted only until Buntokapi reached the estate house.

He swaggered mightily, a little drunk from tanlo berry wine imbibed along the route home. Stinking of campfires, sweat, and whatever he had eaten for breakfast, he leaned upon the doorpost to his quarters and waved to his slaves, who deposited the sarcat's corpse at Mara's feet. 'Leave us,' he commanded his guard.

As his warriors departed, he stood erect with his fists on his hips and shouted, 'There, what do you think, my wife, heh? That is some beast, is it not?'

Mara inclined her head, politely concealing revulsion. The kill stank as badly as the hunter, with buzzing insects clustered on the eyes and limp tongue, while carcass and pole dirtied the newly waxed floor. Anxious to be rid of it, and the man as well, she attempted flattery. 'My Lord shows great courage and skill in defeating such a beast. Herdsmen to the south will sing your praises, Bunto.'

Her husband grinned drunkenly. 'What do I care for the praise of stinking herdsmen, heh? I say to you the head will look splendid mounted over the writing desk where that faded banner hangs now.'

Mara bit back instinctive protest lest she invite Buntokapi's rage upon herself. Though that banner was one of the oldest Acoma victory relics and had graced the study of the Lord of the Acoma for centuries, Buntokapi had no care for tradition. He changed things as he liked, most often in perverse malice to establish beyond doubt that he was Ruling Lord. Mara felt an unexpected stab of sadness, that desperation should have driven her to such a marriage.

'Wife!' Buntokapi snapped, breaking Mara from reflection. She bowed submissively, though pregnancy made her awkward.

'I wish this sarcat's head stuffed and mounted over my desk in my study. See to it! I must go bathe.' Then, straightening as an afterthought struck him, he peered into the gloom of the room behind and stabbed a pointing finger at Misa. 'You, girl, come along. I need someone to wash my back, and my attendant is ill.'

The pretty maid left her mistress's side. All knew her duties would be more personal than merely soaping down her master's back. She departed in resignation as Buntokapi spun around and strode off, leaving his kill oozing upon the threshold, over a day dead and already turning putrid. Mara fought a moment of nausea. Then, with a poise as fragile as fine china, she called the small boy who served as runner away from the corner where he cowered. Buntokapi had a tendency to cuff him for simply being in the way. 'Kedo, fetch two slaves from the kitchens to carry this off to the butcher's shed. Tell the assistant who prepares trophies he must ready the head. When it is completed, have him deliver it to my Lord's study to hang where he indicated.' Here Mara quelled another of the little sorrows that seemed a daily part of life since her marriage. To her remaining maid she said, 'Juna, go and carefully fold the banner over the desk and bring it to me. I will ensure it is safely kept.'

The runner departed with a patter of sandals, and the maid followed. Mara pushed a trailing strand of hair behind one ear and returned to her documents. Let Buntokapi sport with the maids and hunt and play at being a warrior; his obsessions kept him occupied, and that was to the good. That, and the confinement of pregnancy, furthered her opportunity to study the documents of commerce that came each day. Within the limits Buntokapi allowed, Mara continued to manage the affairs of the Acoma. And she learned. Every day she understood more about what truly brought a house to greatness. Thinking aloud, she said, 'I wonder if we have recent maps?'

'Mistress?' said her remaining attendant.

Mara only stared fiercely at an indeterminate point between her parchments and the matted muzzle of the sarcat. The next time her Lord went hunting, or into Sulan-Qu to visit the gambling houses or the women of the Reed Life, she would search her father's cabinets for maps. Then, catching herself short, she reminded herself that the cabinets were not her father's anymore but the province of a husband who was her enemy.

Wine splashed, sticky red on the linens, as the horn flask thrown by Buntokapi bounced and clattered through the cutlery. He blinked once, as if amazed at his own strength, but his anger did not fade. 'Woman, cease plaguing me!'

The power of his voice made the flames in the lamps tremble.

Mara sat quietly before her husband, who had only moments before been singing clumsily along with a pair of minstrels. 'Can't you see I am enjoying this performance? Aren't you always after me to read poetry and listen to music? How can I listen if you constantly nag at me?'

Mara concealed a grimace. Buntokapi's uncritical appraisal stemmed from the fact that one of the musicians was the buxom daughter of the other; the tight-stretched fabric of her robe, and the expanse of flesh left bare by the short hem and open collar, undoubtedly seemed to add allure to their poor singing. But management of the estate must continue, and with acerbity Mara lifted the scroll she had brought out of the path of spilled wine.

'My Lord, these decisions cannot wait –'

'They will wait if I say they will wait!' Buntokapi's shout caused the servant who appeared with rags and basin to scurry about his cleanup. 'Now be silent, wife.'

Mara sat obediently at his side while the servant finished wiping up the spill and hurried away. Red-faced, Buntokapi waved at the musicians to resume and tried furiously to concentrate on the song the girl had been singing. But the soft, unmoving grace of Mara's presence unnerved him, as few things could. After a moment, nettled, he said, 'Oh, what is it?'

The musicians faltered and started uncertainly into the last stanza; Mara silently handed Buntokapi a scroll, and as her gown shifted, he saw that she carried six more. He quickly glanced at the first and said, 'These are household budgets and accounts. Why bother me with them?' He glared at his wife, unmindful that his musicians desperately wished his leave to fall silent. Lacking that, they straggled raggedly into a chorus.

'This is your estate, my husband,' said Mara flatly. 'None may spend a cinti of your wealth without your permission. Some of the merchants in Sulan-Qu send polite, but emphatic, requests for payment.'

Buntokapi scratched his groin while scowling over the tallies. 'Wife!' The musicians ended their lay, and he suddenly found himself shouting into stillness. 'We have funds to pay these?' He glanced about, as if startled by his own shouting.

'Of course, husband.'

Lowering his voice, he said, 'Then pay them.' His expression darkened. 'And why must you bring these to me? Where is Jican?'

Mara gestured to the scrolls. 'You ordered him not to address these things to you, husband. He obeys, but avoiding him cannot resolve these matters.'

Buntokapi's irritation turned to anger. 'So then my wife must pester me like a clerk! And I suppose I'll have to give my approval each time something needs to be done, heh?'

'It is your estate,' Mara repeated. She watched, coiled with tension, as she waited for an opening to suggest that he turn the management of the house over to her.

But instead he sighed with a mildness she had never seen. 'That is true. I must put up with these inconveniences, I expect.' His eyes strayed to the buxom vielle player, then swung back to focus upon Mara's thickened middle. The contrast inspired. 'Now, you must take care not to become overtired, wife. Go to bed. If I must study scrolls, I shall keep these musicians playing for my amusement until late.'

'Husband, I –' Mara stopped, abruptly aware she had made a misjudgment as Buntokapi surged to his feet. He caught her shoulders and dragged her roughly upright. Her hands dropped instinctively to cradle her middle, to protect the unborn life growing there. The gesture forestalled her husband's violence but did not stay his fury.

The musicians looked on in frozen discomfort as Buntokapi's fingers tightened, painfully twisting the flesh of her shoulders. 'Wife, I warned you. I am not stupid! These accounts shall be seen to, but at *my* pleasure.' His rage seemed to swell, to feed upon itself, until it became a tangible thing shadowing the atmosphere of the room. The moonlight seemed to darken beyond the screens, and the musicians set aside their instruments, cowering. Mara bit her lip, frozen in the grasp of her husband like the gazen before the relli. He shook her, that she should know the power of his strength. 'Hear me, wife. You shall go to bed. And if you ever think to cross my will, even once, I shall send you away!'

His fingers released, and Mara all but fell to her knees as a stab of fear shot through her. She hid the emotion behind a bow low enough to have been a slave girl's, and pressed her forehead to a floor still sticky with wine. 'I pray my husband's forgiveness.' The words were fervently sincere; if Buntokapi saw fit to exercise his rights as the Ruling Lord of a troublesome wife, and she were sent from the estates to an apartment with a pension and two maidservants, the affairs of the Acoma would pass forever from her influence. Her father's proud family would become what this coarse man chose, with no hope of escaping Anasati vassalage. Afraid to tremble, afraid even to breathe, Mara waited motionless, her face a mask to hide the terror in her heart. She had hoped to bore Buntokapi with expenditures he did not understand, encourage him to grant her control and freedom to put some plans in motion. Instead, she had nearly precipitated disaster.

Buntokapi regarded her bent back with distaste until the promise of what lay beneath the robes of the vielle player distracted him. Bored now in truth, and annoyed by the pile of scrolls awaiting his attention, he shoved his wife with his toe. 'To bed now, wife.'

Mara rose awkwardly, relief eclipsed by an anger at herself. Her pushing her husband had been partly due to pique, that she and the affairs of the Acoma could be of less consequence than the jiggling bust of a minstrel girl. But the results of her loss of control had almost set the future of the Acoma in the hands of a brute and an enemy. Hereafter caution would be necessary, extreme cleverness, and no small amount of luck. With a panicky feeling, she wished for the counsel of Nacoya; but the old woman was long asleep, and now as never before, Mara dared not disobey the direct orders of her Lord by sending a servant to waken her. Frustrated, and more uncertain than ever before in her life, Mara smoothed her wrinkled robe straight over her shoulders. She left the room with the beaten carriage of the chastised and subservient wife. But as the music began raucously behind her, and Buntokapi's eyes fastened once more on the cleft bosom of the vielle player, her mind turned and turned again. She would endure; somehow she would find a way to exploit her husband's weaknesses, even his overpowering lust. If she did not, all was lost.

'Wife?' Buntokapi scratched himself, frowning over a piece of parchment upon his writing desk.

'Yes, Bunto?' Mara concentrated on her needlework, partly because needle and thread took on a life of their own in her grasp – forever tangling into knots – but mostly because she must seem the image of meekness and obedience. Since the incident with the musicians and the household accounts, Buntokapi had watched her critically for the smallest sign of disobedience; and, as the slave girls whispered in corners, often he saw things as his mood of the moment demanded. Mara stabbed her needle through a robe for her unborn child, though the quality of the work at best could be called poor. No heir of the Acoma would wear such a rag. But if Buntokapi thought sewing an appropriate pastime for his pregnant wife, she must play along with at least a semblance of enthusiasm.

The Lord of the Acoma shifted knobby knees beneath the desk. 'I am answering my father's letter. Listen to this: "Dear Father: Are you well? I have won all my wrestling matches at the soldiers' bath at Sulan-Qu. I am well. Mara is well." ' He looked at her with a rare expression of concentration on his face. 'You are well, aren't you? What should I say next?'

Barely masking irritation, Mara said, 'Why don't you ask if your brothers are well?'

Oblivious to sarcasm, Buntokapi nodded, his expression showing approval.

'Master!'

The shout from outside almost caused Mara to prick her finger. She set the precious metal needle out of harm's way, while Buntokapi moved with startling speed to the door. The caller cried out again, urgently, and without waiting for servants Buntokapi pushed open the screen to reveal a sweating, dust-covered soldier.

'What is it?' demanded Buntokapi, instantly less irritated, for concerns of arms and war were easier for him than those matters of the pen.

The warrior bowed with extreme haste, and Mara noticed that his sandals were laced tight; he had run for some distance to deliver this message. Her posed role of submission forgotten, she listened as the soldier caught his wind and spoke. 'Strike Leader Lujan sends word of a large force of bandits moving over the road from Holan-Qu. He is holding at the small spring below the pass, to harass them if they attempt to push through, for he thinks they are staging to raid us.'

Buntokapi took brisk charge. 'How many are there?' And with a presence of mind and consideration he had never shown to his household staff, he gestured, allowing the tired runner to sit.

Mara murmured for a servant to bring the man water, while he sank to a crouch and qualified. 'A very large force, master. Perhaps as many as six companies. Almost certainly they are grey warriors.'

Bunto shook his head. 'So many? They could prove dangerous.' He turned to Mara. 'I must leave you now, my wife. Be fearless. I will return.'

'Chochocan guard your spirit,' Mara said in ritual, and bowed her head as a wife should before her Lord. But not even appearances could make her shrink from the dangers of the affair at hand. As Buntokapi strode briskly through the screen, she peeked through her lashes at the dust-covered messenger, who bowed in turn to his master. He was young, but scarred and experienced in battle. Mara remembered his name, Jigai, once a well-regarded member of Lujan's band. His eyes were hard, unreadable, as he raised his head to accept the water brought by the maidservant. Mara hid a stab of uncertainty. How would this man and his fellows feel about facing men who but for chance might have been comrades rather than foe? None of the newcomers had yet faced an Acoma enemy in battle; that their first encounter should pitch them against grey warriors raised anxieties dangerous to contemplate.

She watched in frustration as Acoma soldiers hurried past the great house to fall into formation, each commanded by a Patrol Leader, who in turn took orders from their Strike Leaders, all under the certain direction of Keyoke. To the right of his plumes stood Papewaio, who as First Strike Leader would take charge should the Force Commander fall in battle. Mara could not but admire, for the Acoma soldiers acted in every way like Tsurani warriors. Those who had been outlaws blended indistinguishably into those who had been born in service. Her doubts lessened slightly. Thanks to the security afforded by the cho-ja Queen's warriors, only Tasido's company need remain to guard the estate. Absently Mara considered the benefits of recruiting more cousins to the Acoma colours soon. With more warriors, the command could be split, with Papewaio and another elevated to the rank of Force Leader, giving the Acoma two garrisons . . . A loud shout killed her thoughts. Buntokapi strode into view, his trailing servants busily buckling his armour about his stolid body. As her Lord took his place at the head of the column, Mara reminded herself: this was not her army to order about. Not anymore. Her thoughts turned in upon themselves.

The last men fell into position, hurried by the voice of Buntokapi. Fully armoured, and bearing a tasselled scabbard with his favourite sword for battle, the usually lumbering Lord of the Acoma was a typical Tsurani warrior: stocky, tough, with legs able to carry him for miles at a steady run, and enough stamina remaining to fight an enemy. Sullen and brutish in peacetime, Buntokapi was trained for war. Briskly he relayed his orders.

Mara listened from the open door of her quarters, proud of the spectacle in the marshalling yard. Then the baby kicked. She winced at the force of his unborn feet. By the time his tantrum ceased, the Acoma garrison had dashed from the estate, four hundred individuals, green armour glinting in sunlight as they rushed towards that very same ravine where Mara had sprung the trap that had brought Lujan and his outlaws into service.

Silently she prayed that this confrontation by the quiet, rippling spring would resolve as favourably for the Acoma as that first one had.

Nacoya appeared unbidden to attend her mistress's comforts. Her old ears had not missed the commotion, and in typical fashion she brought scraps of gossip from the soldiers, things the young wife hankered to know but no longer had means to obtain. After she had sent a servant for chilled fruit and urged Mara back to her cushions, the two women settled in to wait. It was barely midmorning, thought Mara, glancing at the cho-ja timepiece upon the table her husband had been writing upon less than a quarter hour before. Swiftly she calculated. The early morning patrol must have spotted the bandits' advanced scouts and located their main body entering the high pass. Working out times and locations from the bits of news brought by Nacoya, Mara smiled slightly. The discussion she had precipitated between Arakasi and Keyoke on the journey to the cho-ja hive had yielded results. Among other items, the Spy Master had mentioned need for a predawn sweep of the area to the west of the estate, for ruffians could easily infiltrate the mountains, avoiding Acoma patrols under cover of darkness, then go to ground during the daylight hours. The midnight departure of Lujan's patrol ensured that men were high enough in the hills above the Acoma estates by dawn so that signs of outlaw activity were swiftly detected. And the wily former bandit knew every likely hiding place between the Acoma boundaries and Holan-Qu.

Tired, suddenly, for her pregnancy was trying, Mara nibbled sweet fruit slices, while the sound of Acoma soldiers marching in haste towards the hills carried through the morning air. The cho-ja clock ticked softly, and the tramping grew faint, then fainter, until Mara could barely tell if the sound was still heard or only imagined.

At noon Nacoya poured herb tea and ordered some toasted bread and sweet berry paste brought, with fruit and kaj sung – a steaming bowl of thyza with tiny pieces of river fish, vegetables, and nuts. Anxious to please, the head cook brought the dishes before her mistress, but Mara could only absently pick at her meal.

Aware now that Mara's preoccupation had little to do with lassitude, Nacoya said, 'Lady, do not fear. Your Lord Buntokapi will return unharmed.'

Mara frowned. 'He must.' And in an unguarded moment, Nacoya saw a hint of anger and determination behind her former charge's mask of calm. 'If he dies now, all goes for naught . . . .' Instincts aroused, Nacoya sought the girl's eyes; and Mara looked quickly away. Certain now that something was being considered here beyond her understanding, but shrewd enough to guess its bent, the old woman sat back upon her heels. Age lent her patience. If the young Lady of the Acoma chose to plot alone, then so be it. This most dangerous of plans might perish before fruition if shared, even with one loved and trusted. Nacoya observed, yet revealed nothing of the fear that twisted her old heart. She understood. She was Tsurani. And under the master's roof, the word of the master was as law.

Buntokapi motioned his company of soldiers to a halt and slitted his eyes against the glare as two Acoma soldiers approached at a run, their armour silhouetted against a sun sliced in half by the horizon. Winded, dusty, but proud despite fatigue, the men saluted, and the nearer one delivered his report. 'Lord, the bandits camp in the lower dell, beyond the crest where Strike Leader Lujan waits. He thinks they will move before dawn.'

Buntokapi turned without hesitation to Keyoke. 'We rest here. Send two fresh men to summon Lujan.'

The Force Commander relayed the Lord's order, then relaxed the columns from duty. The men fell out, removing helms and sitting at the roadside, but making no fires to reveal their presence to the raiders.

Buntokapi unbuckled his own helm with an audible sigh. While functional, it was also heavy, and ornamented after the Tsurani fashion of reflecting the deeds of a man's life. Recently added was the band of sarcat-hide trim around the edge, to complement the flowing tail of zarbi hair that hung from the crest. Such trophies looked grand on parade, but to the young Lord's chagrin he discovered every added ounce became onerous after a day-long march. He eased the armour from his head and raked his dark hair up into spikes with his knuckles.

Then he squatted, leaning back against a smooth outcropping by the side of the trail where his officers attended him. 'Keyoke, what is this dell the men speak of?'

The Force Commander crouched and scribed a crude map in the dust with his dagger point. 'Like this, Lord. The trail from Holan-Qu narrows at a small crest, enters a narrow clearing – the dell – next to a spring, just before rising to another crest, then falling to this trail, about six miles above here.' He gave facts without mentioning the ambush the Lady had sprung to bring Lujan and his men into Acoma service.

'Good place for a trap,' Buntokapi muttered. He scratched at an insect bite.

Keyoke said nothing. He waited, patient in a manner only Mara might have understood, while his master loosened his sword belt and stretched. 'Still, we must wait for Lujan's report. Wake me when he arrives.' Buntokapi folded his arms behind his head and closed his eyes.

With a look of veiled exasperation, Papewaio rose. Keyoke followed him saying, 'I will post sentries, Lord.'

Buntokapi grunted approval and the two officers left their Lord to slumber. Within the hour a shout from the sentry heralded Strike Leader Lujan's arrival in camp.

Buntokapi started awake without being called. He sat up, scratching a fresh collection of insect bites, as the dusty Lujan came before him and saluted. The former outlaw had run for six miles and yet showed little outward signs of exhaustion, other than being short of breath. Keyoke and Papewaio joined him as Buntokapi grabbed his helm, jammed it over his tangled head, and pointed cryptically at the scratches in the dirt. 'Show me.'

Lujan hunkered down and with his own dagger added details to the little map Keyoke had drawn. 'Six companies of fifty men have come over three different routes to this dell, my Lord. They marched here, here, and here.'

Buntokapi stopped with his hand poised over the reddening welts on his leg. 'They did not come up to the higher vale, the one with the small lake?'

'No, Lord.' Lujan hesitated.

Buntokapi gestured impatiently in the gathering dark. 'Well, what? Speak.'

'There is something here that . . . is not right.'

Buntokapi scratched his stomach, lifting his breastplate with his thumb. 'They don't move like bandits, heh?'

Lujan smiled slightly. 'No, more like trained soldiers, to my eye.'

'Grey warriors?' Buntokapi got heavily to his feet.

'Perhaps,' said Keyoke.

'Ha!' Buntokapi's tone turned bitter. 'Minwanabi, or my mother bore a stone-headed pup.' To the senior officers with him he said, 'Before I wed I knew of the feud between Jingu and the Acoma. And my father recently warned me to expect a sudden strike.' He frowned. 'I swear he knew this attack was coming.' Buntokapi paused significantly, but did not share whatever else he concluded upon the matter. His voice took on a sullen note. 'Lord Jingu thinks his men the best in the Empire and your Lord a stupid bull. And he seems to have grown cocky enough to risk my father's ire. Yet he is not so strong or so arrogant that he dares to show his true colours, heh? We shall show him he is wrong on the first two counts.' He barked a rude laugh. 'And right on the last.' He looked at Keyoke. 'I think you have a plan already, heh, Force Commander?'

Keyoke's lined face remained expressionless as he set his dagger to the lines representing the place where the trail narrowed this side of the vale. 'We could hold them here with little trouble, I judge, my Lord.'

Buntokapi fingered the tassels of his scabbard. 'Better we let them come into the vale, send a company behind them, and trap them there.'

In the rapidly falling light, Keyoke studied the drawing, recalling each detail of the land remembered from his last patrol. Quietly he ventured his opinion. 'If we sneak a company along the ridge above, we can have it in place by dawn. The bandits then could not retreat, and a quick sortie into the dell from this side might rout them.'

'Good, but I think we do not charge.' Frowning intently now, Buntokapi qualified. 'We sit quiet, like frightened little birds, heh? They will go past us, deep into the little clearing, and we will leap up and rain arrows and rocks upon them, until they break.'

Lujan nodded in appreciation. 'Still, they will break out.'

Buntokapi rubbed his jaw with a stubby thumb as he considered everything laid out before him. 'No, you see,' he said at last, 'we shall strike just before they reach the second crest, so they think that they have been engaged by our advance patrol. But most of our men will lie in wait to the rear.' He grinned with vicious anticipation. 'The bandits will think the bulk of the Acoma garrison in front of them, defending the borders of the estate. They will run back the way they came, through our arrows, onto our shields and swords.' He paused and added, 'Papewaio, you will go with Lujan to the other end of the vale, with' – he quickly calculated – 'all but fifty of the best archers. Keyoke will take twenty archers and station himself at the high ridge pass, just out of sight.' His anticipation grew ugly. 'Keyoke, when the bandits come, have the men yell war cries and strike their armour and dance to send up dust, so the enemy will think you an army. If they still advance, shoot them down.'

The matter decided, Buntokapi shouldered his bow. 'The archers will take cover on the rim above the bandits, the better to rain death down among them. It is wisest if I oversee this company.' Keyoke nodded agreement, recalling the practice bouts in the yard before the barracks. Buntokapi might be slow with a blade, but with a bow he was a demon. Excited now, Buntokapi delivered his last orders to Papewaio to ensure no bandit would slip through the line.

Grim beneath the shadow of his helm, Keyoke admired the audaciousness of the plan. Buntokapi expected a victory; and with the bold twists the young Lord of the Acoma had added, the bandit force might indeed be doomed.

Crouched upon the ridge, Buntokapi waved to the archer concealed across the dell. But the men moving below did not see his signal, for early morning mist whitened the dell like a blanket, obscuring anything more than a dozen yards away. The sun barely reddened the rocky rim of the eastern peaks, and the haze would not burn off for several hours. The invaders were only beginning to stir; here a man squatted in cover to relieve himself, while others washed at the spring, beat dust from their blankets, or gathered dry wood to make fires for tea. Few yet wore armour. If scouts were posted, they were indistinguishable from the warriors rubbing sleep from their eyes. Amused by the general lack of preparation, Buntokapi laughed quietly, picked his target – the squatting man – and let fly. His arrow thudded into flesh, and battle at last was joined.

The first victim fell with a strangled cry. Instantly every Acoma archer loosed their bows from the ridges. Thirty raiders were struck down before a man among them could react. Then the bandit company erupted like a hive. Blankets fluttered abandoned and cooking pots rolled into fires as the men under attack broke for cover. Buntokapi chuckled viciously and let fly another arrow. It struck his target in the groin, and he fell, writhing, and tripped a fleeing companion. Too many men were crowded together in too small an area, and their panic made the slaughter easy. Before their commanders could restore order, another twenty were struck down. Voices shouted commands in the clearing. Acoma archers picked their targets with increasing difficulty as the raiders went to ground, using fallen trees, large rocks, or even shallow depressions for cover. Yet still the arrows found targets.

An officer's shouted orders caused the raiders to break towards the Acoma borders. Buntokapi's exultation turned savage. Probably the ruffian in command thought he had encountered a patrol whose intent was to drive his men back into the hills. Those bandits who managed to regroup and obey reached the shadow of the second ridge, only to be stopped by shouts and the squeak of armour. Five men in the van fell with arrows bristling from them as Keyoke's archers entered the fray. The soldiers in the lead jostled to a disorganized halt. Another dozen went down before the rear guard understood their predicament and an officer ordered a retreat.

Sunlight touched the mist, dyeing the fringes red as the original thirty archers continued their murderous fire from the ridge. Hampered, and dying by the moment, the invaders pulled back through the narrow defile. An elated Buntokapi guessed a full third of their number lay dead or wounded. He kept up his rapid shooting, and calculated that another third would be down before his retreating victims encountered the Acoma soldiers who waited to their rear. Yet well before he ran short of targets, Buntokapi exhausted his supply of arrows. Frustrated at his inability to kill, he grabbed a large rock and sighted upon a man lying just behind an outcropping of stone. He reared back and hurled the stone, rewarded by a cry of pain from below. Heated with the lust of battle, he sought more rocks.

Other bowmen out of arrows soon joined in, and now a hail of stones descended upon the raiders. From the east, dust rose along the trail, accompanied by the sound of men shouting, Keyoke and his band lending the appearance that their 'army' charged to attack. Several of the raiders sprang to their feet in alarm, while the more panic-stricken spearheaded a general break to the west. Buntokapi sent his last stone whistling downwards. Afire with the anticipation of glory and victory, he drew his sword and shouted, 'Acoma!'

The men in his company followed his reckless charge down the steep sides of the dell. Stones loosened under their feet, rattling down with their hurtling bodies. Clammy mist enfolded them as they reached the floor of the clearing, and the rout was on. Nearly two hundred raiders lay dead or dying upon the ground, while to the west the survivors rushed upon the waiting shields, spears, and swords of the men under Papewaio and Lujan.

Buntokapi hurried along, his short legs pumping furiously as he raced to reach the battle before the last enemy was slain. He encountered a desperate-looking man in a simple robe. The sword and plain round shield he carried reminded Buntokapi of his own shield, abandoned somewhere in the rocks above in the excitement. He cursed himself for carelessness, but still charged the raider, crying, 'Acoma! Acoma!' in almost boyish glee.

The raider braced himself for swordplay, but Buntokapi beat the raised blade away. He hurled himself into the shield, depending upon strength and bulk rather than risking facing a swordsman who might have superior skill. The man stumbled, and Buntokapi raised his sword, bearing down in a two-handed slash that smashed the man's shield and broke the arm beneath. The raider fell back with a cry.

Buntokapi beat away a feeble attempt at a thrust. Grinning madly, he stabbed and his opponent died with a gurgling cry. The Lord of the Acoma cleared his blade and rushed after Acoma bowmen who had followed his impetuous charge into the dell.

From the west the sounds of battle raged. Winded, eager, and exulting in his strength and prowess, Buntokapi breasted the small pass through the rocks. The mist was thinning, a sheet of gold through which armour and bloody swords glinted against shadowy greenery. The flight of the raiders had broken upon a waiting mass of Acoma soldiers. Papewaio had stationed kneeling shield men, with bowmen behind and spearmen beside. Not one raider in twenty had reached their lines, and even as Buntokapi pounded down to join them, he saw those last enemies die on the points of the long spears. The surrounding wood fell suddenly, eerily still. As he picked his way around grotesquely sprawled corpses and heard, for the first time, the moans of the wounded and dying, Buntokapi's excitement did not fade. He glanced over the carnage his plan had wrought, and spied the plume of an officer.

Papewaio stood with folded arms, overseeing the binding of a soldier's wound.

Buntokapi shouldered his way through the bystanders. 'Well?'

'My Lord.' With barely a glance away from the injured man, Papewaio saluted with his sword. 'They hesitated when they saw our lines – that was their mistake. Had they continued their charge, our losses would have been worse.' The man on the ground groaned as the bandage tightened over his wound. 'Not so taut,' snapped Papewaio, seemingly forgetting the waiting presence of his Lord.

But Buntokapi was too elated from victory to mind the lapse. Leaning on his bloodied sword, he said, 'How many casualties?'

Papewaio looked up, his attention focused for the first time. 'I do not know yet, but few. Here, the Force Commander approaches.' He turned with swift instructions for the care of his wounded warrior, then fell into step with the Lord of the Acoma.

Lujan joined them as they met Keyoke, dusty from his efforts in the clearing, and his plumes beaded with mist. The officers consolidated their information with a minimum of words, and Buntokapi's heart swelled with pride. He struck a playful blow to Keyoke's shoulder. 'See, they broke and we slaughtered the dogs, just as I said. Ha!' He frowned, but not with displeasure. 'Any prisoners?'

'I think about thirty, my Lord,' Lujan said, his voice queerly flat after the animated tones of his master. 'Some will live long enough to become slaves. Who their officers were I cannot tell, since none wore helms of office.' He gave a thoughtful pause. 'Nor house colours.'

'Bah!' Buntokapi spat. 'These are Minwanabi's dogs.'

'At least one was.' Lujan pointed to a man who lay dead not twenty feet distant. 'That was a man I knew' – he caught himself just short of revealing his odd origin – 'before I first took house colours. He is the elder brother of a boyhood friend, and he took service with the Kehotara.'

'Minwanabi's favourite pet!' Buntokapi waved his fouled sword as if the presence of a soldier of Jingu's vassal proved his contention.

Lujan stepped out of range of the gesture, smiling slightly. 'He was a bad man. He might have turned outlaw.'

Buntokapi shook his blade in Lujan's face, any humour clearly beyond him. 'This was no outlaw raid! That dog lover Jingu thinks the Acoma soft, and ruled by a woman. Well, he now knows he faced a man.' He spun around, brandishing his weapon in the air. 'I will send a runner to Sulan-Qu to buy a few rounds in the taverns by the docks. Jingu will know within a day I have tweaked his nose.'

Buntokapi brought his sword whistling downward. He stared at the drying blood, and after a moment of deliberation thrust the weapon into its tasselled sheath. A slave could polish it later. With an enthusiasm not shared by his officers, he said, 'We shall sort this out at home. I am dirty and hungry. We leave now!' And he began abruptly to march, leaving Keyoke and Papewaio and Lujan to organize the men, fix litters for the wounded, and hustle the companies on the road to the estate. The Lord of the Acoma wished to be home before dinner, and his company of battle-fatigued soldiers concerned him little. They could rest once they were back in their barracks.

As men rushed to form ranks, Papewaio looked at his Force Commander. Eyes met for a moment and both men shared a thought. This bullish man, barely more than a boy, was dangerous. As they parted to attend their duties, both prayed silently for Lady Mara.

Hours passed, and the shadows shortened. The sun climbed to the zenith while the needra herders returned from the meadows for the noon meal, and servants and slaves went about their chores as if no disaster were possible. Mara rested, attempting to read, but her mind refused to concentrate on the convoluted organization of lands and businesses owned by the dozens of major Lords and hundreds of minor ones in the Empire. One night, a month before, she had thought she recognized a pattern in the way one estate's distant holdings were placed, then after hours of further study decided the perception had been an illusion. But such pursuits had given rise to another thought: where a family's holdings lay, even those that appeared insignificant, could prove as important as any other fact in the nuances of the Game of the Council.

Mara pondered this new angle through the heat of the afternoon. Sundown came and went, and in the cooler air of evening she sat to a long and silent meal. The servants were subdued, which was unusual in the absence of their Lord. Feeling her pregnancy like a weight, Mara retired early to sleep. Her dreams were troubled. Several times in the night she started awake, her heart pounding and her ears straining for sounds of returning men; but instead of marching feet and the creak of armour, the night stillness held only the soft lowing of needra cows and the chirp of night insects. She had no clue how her husband and Keyoke fared against the raiders in the mountains, except that the peace of the estate remained unbroken. Just before the dawn she fell into a deep and oppressive sleep.

She woke with sun on her face, having opened the screen in her restlessness during the night. Her morning maid had forgotten to close it, and the heat already made her sweat. Mara raised herself upon her pillows and suddenly felt ill. Without waiting to call for a servant, she hurried to the chamber for night soil and was sick to her stomach. The morning maid heard her distress and ran to attend her with cool cloths. Then she saw her mistress back to her mats and hastened to fetch Nacoya.

Mara stopped her at the door. 'Nacoya has worries enough without adding more,' she snapped and gestured grumpily at the open screen. The maid closed it hastily, but the shade did not help. Mara lay back, pale and sweating. Throughout the day she fretted, unable to concentrate upon the matters of commerce that had never before failed to hold her interest. Noon came, and the men did not return. Mara began to worry. Had Buntokapi fallen to a raider's sword? Had the battle been won? The wait exhausted her, cloaking her mind in shadows of doubt. Beyond the screen the sun crawled across the zenith, and Nacoya arrived with the midday meal. Grateful her illness had passed, Mara managed to eat a little fruit and some sweet cakes.

After her meal the Lady of the Acoma lay down to rest through the afternoon heat. Sleep eluded her. As the shadows of the leaves elongated slowly across the screens, she listened to the sounds outside diminish as the free workers retired to their huts. The slaves were not permitted this midday break, but whenever possible the work performed from midday to the fourth hour of the afternoon was the least strenuous of the day.

The waiting bore down like a thousand stones; even the cooks in the kitchen were cross. Distantly Mara heard a servant scolding a slave for some chore improperly done in the scullery. Impatient with the stillness, she rose, and when Nacoya appeared to inquire after her needs, Mara returned a snappish reply. The room fell silent. Later she refused the entertainment of musicians or poetry. Nacoya rose then and sought duties elsewhere.

Then, as the shadows slanted purple across the hills, the sound of the returning soldiers reached the estate house. Mara held her breath and recognized voices raised in song. Something inside her broke. Tears of relief wet her face, for if the enemy had triumphed they would have come with battle cries as they assaulted the remaining soldiers of the estate. Had Buntokapi been killed or the Acoma driven back from the attack, the warriors would have returned in silence. Instead, the lusty ring of voices through the late afternoon heat heralded a victory for the Acoma.

Mara rose and motioned for servants to open the door to the marshalling yard. Tired, but no longer tense, she waited with one hand on the doorframe while the Acoma companies marched into view, their bright green armour muted by a layer of dust. The officers' plumes drooped from fatigue, but the men marched in even step and their song filled the air. The words might be ragged, for to many the verses were new; still, this was an Acoma victory. Old soldiers and former bandits alike sang with joy, for battle had knit them solidly together. The accomplishment was sweet after the grief that had visited this house scarcely one year before.

Buntokapi came straight to his wife and bowed slightly, a formality Mara found surprising. 'My wife, we have been victorious.'

'I am so very pleased, my husband.' That her reply was genuine startled him in return. Her pregnancy seemed to be taxing her, for she did not look well.

Strangely abashed, Buntokapi qualified. 'Minwanabi and Kehotara dogs garbed as grey warriors sought to marshal along the trail above our lands. They intended to strike us at first light, as all lay asleep.'

Mara nodded. That was how she would have planned such a raid. 'Were there many, my Lord?'

Buntokapi dragged his helm off by one strap and tossed it to a waiting servant. He scratched vigorously at his wet, matted hair with both hands, his lips parted in satisfaction. 'Aie, it is good to get that off.' Peering up at his wife in the doorway, he said, 'What? Many?' His expression turned thoughtful. 'A great deal more than I would have expected . . .' He shouted over his shoulder to Lujan, who was attending to the dispersal of the men with Keyoke. 'Strike Leader, how many finally attacked?'

The reply floated cheerfully over the bedlam in the yard. 'Three hundred, my Lord.'

Mara repressed a shudder. She laid a hand on her middle, where the baby moved.

'Three hundred killed or captured,' Buntokapi reiterated proudly. Then, struck as if by an afterthought, he shouted again across the yard. 'Lujan, how many of our men?'

'Three dead, three dying, and another five seriously wounded.' The reply was only slightly less exuberant, by which Mara interpreted that Lujan's recruits had fought well.

Buntokapi grinned at his Lady. 'How do you like that, my wife? We waited in hiding above them, rained arrows and rocks upon their heads, then drove them against our shields and swords. Your father could not have done better, heh?'

'No, my husband.' The admission was grudging, but true. Buntokapi had not wasted the years he trained as a soldier. And for a fleeting instant her usual disdain and revulsion were replaced by pride for her husband's actions on behalf of the Acoma.

Lujan crossed the yard, accompanied by a soldier named Sheng. The rigours of the day had left the Strike Leader's jaunty gallantry undaunted, and he grinned a greeting to his Lady before bowing and interrupting the boasting of his master. 'Lord, this man has something important to say.'

Granted leave to speak, the soldier saluted. 'Master, one of the prisoners is a cousin of mine, well known to me. He is the son of my father's brother's wife's sister. He is not a grey warrior. He took service with the Minwanabi.'

Mara stiffened slightly, her indrawn breath overshadowed by Buntokapi's loud response. 'Ha! I told you. Bring the dog forth.'

Movement swirled through the yard, and a burly guard stepped into view. He pushed a man with both hands tied behind his back, and threw him down before Buntokapi's feet.

'You are of the Minwanabi?'

The prisoner refused to answer. Forgetting the presence of his wife, Buntokapi kicked him in the head. Despite her hatred of the Minwanabi, Mara winced. Again Buntokapi's studded sandal raked the man's face, and he rolled, splitting blood. 'You are of the Minwanabi?' repeated Buntokapi.

But the man would admit nothing. Loyal, Mara thought through her sickness; she expected as much. Jingu would hardly send weak men on such a risky venture, for all his standing and his honour rested on not being held responsible. Yet the truth could not entirely be concealed. Another Acoma soldier approached with a story similar to the first: several other grey warriors were recognizably Minwanabi, or members of the house of Jingu's vassals, the Kehotara. Buntokapi kicked the man on the ground several more times, but he gained no more than a glare of venomous hatred. Bored finally, Buntokapi said, 'This fool offends Acoma soil. Hang him.'

He raised bright eyes to Keyoke. 'Hang all of them. We have no need of slaves, and dogs make poor workers. String them up along the roadside and have a sign proclaim that this fate awaits any who trespass on Acoma lands. Then let the patrol leaders go to the city. Have them buy wine in the taverns and drink to the men of the Acoma who have bested the Minwanabi.'

Stiff-faced, Keyoke said nothing. Buntokapi visited a terrible insult upon the Minwanabi Lord by publicly hanging his soldiers. Prisoners of war were either killed honourably, with a sword, or kept as slaves. Only when the feuds grew old and bitter did a man affront a foe in this way. To boast of such a deed in public was to invite a more bitter retaliation, until the alliance with the Anasati would not be sufficient to shield them. Mara realized the stakes. If Jingu grew incensed enough, the next raid might be not three hundred men dressed as grey warriors, but three thousand armoured soldiers in Minwanabi orange and black descending like insects upon Acoma land. Mara saw Keyoke scrape his chin with his thumb and knew his concern matched her own. She must try to dissuade her husband.

'My Lord.' Mara touched Buntokapi's damp sleeve. 'These were only soldiers doing the duty of their master.'

A feral look entered Buntokapi's eyes, startling for its cleverness. 'These?' The calmness of his voice was new, the more chilling in that it was genuine. 'Why, these are but grey warriors, bandits and outlaws, my wife. You heard me ask this one if he was of the Minwanabi, didn't you? Had he answered, I would have killed him honourably with my own sword. But he is only a criminal, fit for hanging, heh!' He smiled then, widely, and shouted to the men in the yard, 'Let my orders stand.'

The Acoma soldiers hastened to bring rope, and the prisoners were herded down the gravel path that led to the trees at the side of the Imperial Highway. A craftsman would fashion the sign to make their shame public, and by sundown the last of them would hang.

Those soldiers not involved dispersed to the barracks. Buntokapi stepped into the estate house without removing his sandals, and his studded soles raised splinters from the fine wood as he spun and shouted for servants. Making a mental note to ask for a slave to resand and polish the floors, Mara returned to her cushions. Her husband did not dismiss her when his attendants arrived, so she was compelled to remain while servants removed his outer armour.

Stretching heavy shoulders as his breastplate was lifted from him, the Lord of the Acoma said, 'This Minwanabi lord is a fool. He thinks to outrage my father by killing me, then turning his attentions upon you, my wife, a simple woman. He did not know what a soldier he faced, heh! How fortunate that you chose me instead of Jiro. My brother is clever, but he is not a warrior.' Again that feral light entered Buntokapi's eyes, and Mara saw something beyond mere cunning. She was forced to agree with Buntokapi's remark on their wedding night. This man she had married was not stupid.

Quietly Mara tried to temper his bullish mood. 'The Acoma were indeed fortunate to be led by a soldier today, my Lord.'

Buntokapi puffed up at the praise. He turned away, handing the last piece of armour to his attendant. He regarded his stained knuckles and suddenly acknowledged the fatigue of the last two days. 'I will take a long bath, my wife, then I will join you for our evening meal. I will not go to the city. The gods do not love too much pride, and perhaps it is best not to mock Jingu more than I already have.'

He stepped to the screen, letting the soft breeze of evening dry his sweat. Mara regarded him, silent. His stocky body and bandy legs made a comic silhouette against the yellow sky of evening, but the sight only made her feel chilled. When Buntokapi departed, she stared at the filthy pile of clothing and sandals he had left in a heap on the floor. Her thoughts turned very dark, and she did not hear Nacoya enter and bow by her elbow. The old woman whispered, her voice a near-silent hiss. 'If you are going to kill him, do it soon, Lady. He is far more clever than you thought.'

Mara only nodded. Inwardly she counted the hours. Not until her baby was born. Not until then.

'Mara!'

The shout reverberated through the house. The Lady of the Acoma rose with the aid of her maids. She was halfway to the door of her quarters when the door slid open and Buntokapi entered, his face red with temper.

Her bow was immediate. 'Yes, Bunto.'

He lifted a meaty hand and shook a sheaf of papers, each sheet covered with tiny rows of numbers. 'What are these? I found them piled on my desk when I awoke.' Stamping past, he looked the image of an enraged needra bull, a likeness heightened by his bloodshot eyes, the legacy of entertaining some friends the night before.

Several young soldiers, second and third sons of families loyal to the Anasati, had stopped to visit on their way to the City of the Plains. They had talked for long hours, for their houses mustered garrisons for a spring campaign against the barbarians on the world of Midkemia, on the other side of the magical rift. The war was entering its third year, and tales of riches lured a number of politically neutral houses to join the Alliance for War. Such shifts caused the War Party and the conservative Imperial Party to be in contention for dominance of the High Council. The Lord of the Minwanabi was a stalwart in the War Party, headed by the Warlord, and the Lord of the Anasati was the central figure in the Imperial Party, a position of high prestige because it was limited to blood relations of the Emperor.

With none of the propriety of his imperial cousins, Buntokapi tossed the papers in a shower over his wife. 'What am I supposed to do with all these things?'

'Husband, they are the monthly tallies of the house, the quarterly budget and reports from your factors and inventories of far holdings' – she lowered her eyes to see what else lay scattered about her ankles – 'and a projection of needra hide demand for the next year.'

'But what am I supposed to do with them?' Buntokapi threw up his hands in exasperation. As third son he had been expected to become a career warrior, much like Keyoke and Papewaio, or marry the daughter of some rich merchant seeking alliance with a powerful house. Now that he had exceeded his father's most extreme ambitions, his preparation for ruling a great house was nonexistent.

Mara squatted, since pregnancy made bending impossible, and with perfect patience began to gather the scattered parchments. 'You are to read these reports. Approve, disapprove, or amend them, then send them back to the appropriate member of your household staff, Bunto.'

'What about Jican?'

'He'll advise you, husband.' Again she waited for an opportunity to take some responsibility off his shoulders, but he only said, 'Very well. After I've eaten, have the hadonra come to my study.' Without another word he snatched the papers from the hand of his wife and left.

Mara beckoned to her runner. 'Find Jican.'

The hadonra appeared breathless from his summons. He had ink-stains on his hands, and from that Mara knew her runner had found him in the scribes' wing, on the far side of the house. When he had completed his bow, Mara said, 'My Lord asks your counsel, Jican, on the many business issues facing the Acoma. Please attend him after he has bathed and eaten.'

The hadonra dabbed at a blackened knuckle, barely able to

contain his distaste for dealing with the plodding Buntokapi. 'I see, Lady.'

Mara watched him with bland humour. 'My Lord is new to matters of commerce, Jican. Perhaps it would be best if you dealt with each issue slowly and in detail.'

Jican's expression did not change, but his eyes seemed to light. 'Yes, mistress.'

Now Mara returned a veiled smile. 'Take as much time as you need. I think you'll find sufficient topics to discuss for the entire evening, and perhaps into the night.'

'Of course, mistress.' Jican's enthusiasm brightened. 'I will give orders not to be disturbed while Lord Buntokapi needs my aid.'

The hadonra had always been quick-witted. Mara rejoiced in his attributes, yet she showed no trace of her feelings. 'That is good, Jican. Since my Lord is showing an interest in household matters, take along any documents you think he might need to study.'

In a voice of smothered delight, Jican said, 'Yes, mistress.'

'That is all.' Mara waved in dismissal, then stood thoughtfully, racking her mind for other matters that needed to be called to her husband's attention. Yet as she plotted, she feared. The path she had chosen was perilous; no law and no person could protect her if she stepped wrongly. The sunlight upon the painted screen suddenly seemed very dear. Mara closed her eyes and recited the teachings of the sisters of Lashima to herself for what seemed a very long time.

Mara winced at the sound of Buntokapi's huge hand striking flesh. Another slave would sport a bruised cheek or black eye in the morning. Braced for the inevitable onslaught, she was unsurprised when the screen to her quarters slid open with no knock in warning. Even when he was was not angry, Buntokapi seldom employed the courtesy her rank normally entitled.

'Mara,' he began, his fury near the point of explosion; and Mara cursed inwardly as he strode in, his battle sandals carving up the floors for the second time that week. Fortunately, the slaves who repaired the damage lacked the right to complain.

Buntokapi stopped, sweating under his heavy armour. 'I have spent days with these important business matters Jican claims I must personally attend to! I go out to drill my soldiers for the first time in a week, and when I am tired from the sun, the first thing I find is more . . . of these!' He threw down a heavy sheaf of documents. 'I grow bored! Who oversaw all this before I came here?'

Modestly Mara lowered her eyes. 'I did, husband.'

Buntokapi's anger dissolved into astonishment. 'You did?'

'Before I asked for you in marriage, I was Ruling Lady.' Mara spoke lightly, as if the matter were of small importance. 'The running of the estate was my duty, as it is now yours.'

'Aie!' Buntokapi's frustration was palpable. 'Must I oversee every tiny detail?' He yanked off his helm and shouted for assistance. A servant appeared at the door. 'Bring a robe,' Buntokapi commanded. 'I'll not stand in this armour another moment. Mara, help me.'

Mara rose awkwardly and came to her husband, who stood with arms held out straight. Touching him as little as possible, for he was dirty, she unfastened the buckles that held the breast and back plates together. 'You may, if you choose, delegate some of these tasks. Jican is capable of taking care of the daily operations of the estates. I can give him the benefits of my opinion if you're too busy.'

Buntokapi shrugged the lacquered plates off over his head and sighed in relief. Unaccustomed to lifting, Mara struggled with the weight, until her husband reached one-handed and tossed the heavy armour to the floor. He tugged the light gambeson over his shoulders, and spoke through a muffling layer of cloth. 'No. I want you looking after our son.'

'Or daughter,' Mara shot back, nettled that a wife might do a body servant's chores but not tally accounts. She knelt and unbuckled the green leather greaves from her husband's hairy calves.

'Bah, it will be a boy. If not, we shall have to try again, heh?' He leered down at her.

Mara showed none of her revulsion, but untied the cross-gartered sandals, which were as crusted with filth as the broad feet they protected. 'As my Lord wills.'

Buntokapi peeled away his short robe. Nude except for a loincloth, he unselfconsciously reached under it to scratch his groin. 'Still, I will allow Jican to make decisions about the business matters he has been in charge of since your father's death.' The servant arrived with the clean robe, and the Lord of the Acoma quickly donned it without calling for a bath. 'The hadonra is competent. And he can still come to me for important decisions. Now I plan to spend some time in Sulan-Qu. Several of my friends are –'

He paused, puzzled, as Mara suddenly clutched at the cloth of her dayrobe. She had been having mild contractions all morning, but this was strong, and her face drained of colour. At last her time had come. 'Bunto!'

The usual violent-tempered man was suddenly both delighted and alarmed. 'Is it time!'

'I think so.' She smiled calmly. 'Send for the midwife.'

Solicitous for the first time in his life, Buntokapi was furiously patting Mara's hand to the point of inflicting bruises when the midwife came, followed in an instant by Nacoya. The two of them chased him away with a briskness no husband in the Empire could withstand. Buntokapi left like a whipped dog, looking over his shoulder as he disappeared through the screen.

The next hour he spent pacing in his study as he waited for his son to be born. As the second hour dragged on, he sent for wine and something to eat. Evening faded into night, still without word from the birth chamber. An impatient man who had no outlet for his concern, he drank and ate, then drank again. After the supper hour he sent for musicians, and when their playing failed to soothe his nerves, he called for the hot bath he had neglected that afternoon.

In a rare mood of respect, he decided to forgo the company of a girl. Bed play seemed inappropriate while his wife was giving birth to his heir, but a man could not be expected to sit waiting with no comforts. Buntokapi bellowed for the runner to fetch a large jug of acamel brandy. This he would not surrender, even when servants pulled the screens away and filled his tub with steaming water. They waited with soap and towels. Buntokapi stripped off his robes and patted his expanding girth. He grunted to himself about needing to practise with the sword and bow more, to keep fit, as he slid his bulk into the water. A weaker man would have winced, but Buntokapi simply sat down. He took a brandy cup from a servant's hand and drained it in one long pull.

The servants worked with diffident care. None of them wanted a beating for letting suds inadvertently spill in to the open cup and sour the brandy.

Bunto sloshed back in his bath. He absently hummed a tune while the servants soaped his body. As their hands kneaded his taut muscles and the heat drew him into a sleepy, amorous mood, he luxuriated in the bath, and soon he drifted into a doze.

Then the air was cut by a scream. Bunto bolted upright in the tub, overturning his brandy and splashing the servants with soapy water. Heart pounding, he groped about for a weapon, half expecting to see the servants running for safety while armoured men answered the alarm. Instead all was quiet. He looked to the musicians, who awaited his order to play, but as his mouth opened to speak, another scream rent the stillness.

Then he knew. Mara, slender, girlish Mara, was giving birth to his son. Another scream sounded, and the pain in it was like nothing Buntokapi had heard in his short life. Men wounded in battle made loud, angry cries, and the moans of the wounded were low and pitiable. But this sound . . . this reflected the agony of one tormented by the Red God himself.

Buntokapi reached for his brandy. Dark fury crossed his face when he found the cup missing. A servant retrieved it quickly from the door, filled it, and placed it in his master's hands. After Buntokapi drained it he said, 'Go see that nothing is amiss with my wife.'

The servant ran off and Buntokapi nodded to another servant for a refill. Long moments passed while the sounds of Mara's torment filled the night. Shortly the servant returned and said, 'Master, Nacoya says it is a difficult birth.'

Buntokapi nodded and drank again, feeling the numbing warmth of the brandy rise up from his stomach. The scream came again, followed by a low sob. Exasperated, the Lord of the Acoma shouted over the noise, 'Play something lively and loud.'

The musicians struck up a march tune. Buntokapi emptied the brandy. Irritated as Mara's cries cut through the music, he tossed away the cup and motioned for the jug. He set the jug to his lips and took a large gulp.

His head began to swim. The screams seemed to come at him like a swarming foe, unwilling to be blocked by a shield. Buntokapi drank until his senses grew muddled. A happy glow suffused his vision and he sat with a stupid smile on his face until the water began to cool. The master still showed no signs of arising, and worried servants scurried to heat more water.

More brandy was brought, and after a time Buntokapi, Lord of the Acoma, could barely hear the music, let alone the unrelenting screams of his tiny wife as she struggled to bear his child.

In time, dawn silvered the screens to his chamber. Exhausted from a sleepless night, Nacoya slid open the study door and peeked in. Her Lord lay back sleeping in the cool water of the tub, his great mouth open and snoring. An empty jug of brandy rolled on the floor below his flaccid hand. Three musicians slept over their instruments, and the bath servants stood like battle-beaten soldiers, the towels hanging crumpled from their hands. Nacoya snapped the screen shut, disgust on her wrinkled face. How grateful she was that Lord Sezu was not alive to know that the successor to his title, Buntokapi, Lord of the Acoma, lay in such condition when his wife had laboured long to bear him a healthy son and heir.

9

Snare

A shout rang out.

'Mara!'

Buntokapi's anger rent the morning quiet like the challenge of a needra bull. Mara winced. She glanced instinctively at the crib near her side. Little Ayaki still slept, undisturbed by his father's bellow. His eyes were tightly closed, and his stocky limbs half tangled in his covers. After two months of Buntokapi's roars, the infant could sleep through a thunderstorm. Mara sighed. The boy was his father's son, thick of body and with a big head that had made his mother wish for death when he had been born. The difficult labour had drained Mara in a way she would not have thought possible before. While but eighteen years of age, she felt like an old woman, tired all the time. And the first sight of her son had saddened her. She had secretly hoped for a lithe, handsome child, such as her brother Lano must have been as a baby. Instead Buntokapi had given her a red-faced, round-headed little brute, with a visage wrinkled like a tiny old man's. From the first moment he filled his lungs with air, he had a shout to rival his father's; already he affected the same scowl. Still, as Ayaki lay asleep, Mara could not feel other than love for him. He is my son as well, she thought, and the blood of his grandfather is in him. The traits he has inherited from his Anasati heritage will be trained out of him and those from the Acoma will be nurtured. He will not be like his father.

'Mara!' Buntokapi's irritable shout sounded very near at hand, and the next instant the screen to the boy's nursery slammed back. 'Here you are, woman. I've been all over the house looking for you.' Buntokapi entered with a frown like a storm cloud.

Mara bowed with serenity, only too glad to lay her embroidery aside. 'I have been with our son, husband.'

Buntokapi's expression eased. He went to the crib where the boy lay, restless now from his father's loud entrance. Buntokapi reached down, and for a moment Mara feared he would ruffle the boy's black hair, as he did his hounds'. But instead his meaty hand gently straightened the cover that lay twisted between the tiny legs. The gesture caused Mara an instant's affection towards Buntokapi, but she banished such sentiment at once. Though he wore the Acoma mantle, Buntokapi was a son of the Anasati, a house second only to the Minwanabi in despite for things Acoma. This Mara knew in her heart. And soon the time would come for change.

Exaggerating her whisper – Ayaki was a sound sleeper – she said, 'What do you desire, husband?'

'I must go to Sulan-Qu . . . ah, on business.' Buntokapi straightened from the crib with studied lack of enthusiasm. 'I will not be returning this night, and perhaps tomorrow as well.'

Mara bowed in acquiescence, not missing the haste in her husband's tread as he departed through the screen. She needed no incongruities to guess that there was no business for her husband to conduct in Sulan-Qu. During the past two months his interest in business had waned, until it bordered on open neglect.

As Jican resumed control of the Acoma management, he kept his Lady well informed. Buntokapi still played hob with Keyoke's administration of the warriors: which men were assigned and to what post. Having barely reached the point where she could influence a few small household matters, Mara could do nothing about that, at least not yet.

She stared at her embroidery in distaste, glad that in Buntokapi's absence she need not keep that up for the sake of appearances. More and more she needed time to think and plan for the future. Her husband's suspicious nature had partially played into her hands. Aware in his plodding way that Mara's talent for commerce overshadowed his, Buntokapi had confined himself to seeing that his wife did not gain control of his household. Never did he realize that she had managed the garrison as adroitly before their marriage. As a result, he never thought to question other strange practices around the estate, such as Papewaio's wearing a black headcloth. And despite his interests in warcraft, Buntokapi never became familiar with the men. Their heritage held no interest for him; otherwise he would have discovered that grey warriors had come to wear Acoma green. Certainly he lacked the imagination to embrace such changes in tradition, Mara thought, then caught herself, sharply. Even in thoughts she must not be careless. Too often he had shown he was more than a simple warrior.

Still, the man had no subtlety. Hearing his booming laugh in the mustering yard as he gathered the warriors for his escort, Mara wondered what prompted his clumsy effort at subversion. Boredom might be taking him to Sulan-Qu in the heat of high noon, to bathe with other soldiers and exchange stories, and perhaps to wrestle or gamble . . . or to sport with a woman of the Reed Life.

Buntokapi had returned to Mara's bed soon after childbirth, but now that the Acoma had a living heir, she had no reason to play the dutiful wife. Buntokapi's clutching, slobbering embrace revolted her, and she had lain still, sharing none of his passion. The first night he seemed not to notice, but on the second he became angry. The third night he complained bitterly of her lack of enthusiasm and the fourth night he beat her, then slept with one of her maids. Since then she had met his advances with no response at all, and at the last he had fallen to ignoring her.

But now Buntokapi set off for the city for the third time in ten days, and Mara was intrigued about the reason. She called Misa to open the screen, and the moment her husband's litter and his small escort of warriors jogged smartly down the lane to the Imperial Highway, she sent her runner for Nacoya.

The old woman answered her summons tardily, but there seemed no lack of respect in her bow. 'My mistress requires?'

'What takes our Lord Bunto into the city so much of late?' asked Mara. 'What gossip do the servants tell?'

Nacoya glanced significantly at Misa, who awaited her mistress's wishes by the screen. Warned that the nurse's answer might be best not shared with servants, Mara sent her maid to fetch the noon meal. As Misa hurried off, Nacoya sighed. 'As you would expect. Your husband has taken an apartment in the city so he may visit a woman.'

Mara sat back. 'Good. We must encourage him to stay in the city as much as possible.'

Nacoya brightened with curiosity. 'Daughter of my heart, I know some things have passed, never to be regained, but I am still the only mother you have known. Will you not tell me what you are planning?'

Mara was tempted. But her scheme to regain control of her house bordered on treason to her Lord. Although Nacoya had already deduced Mara's intent to dispose of Buntokapi, the plan was too risky to confide. 'That is all, old mother,' Mara said firmly.

The nurse hesitated, then nodded, bowed, and departed, leaving Mara staring at the baby, who had begun to stir in his crib. But Ayaki's well-being was far from her thoughts. That her Lord had a woman in the city might provide exactly the opportunity Mara required. Hoping the gods were looking after her at long last, she had begun to ponder the options of this new development when Ayaki's healthy wail spoiled thought. Mara lifted the fussy baby to her breast and winced as the little boy bit hard upon her nipple. 'Ow!' she said in surprise. 'You are your father's son, no doubt.' The baby quieted as he began to suck, and Misa returned with a tray. Mara ate the food without interest, her mind busy with a plan more risky than anything her old nurse might have guessed. The stakes were high. One misjudgment, and she would lose all chance of regaining the title of Ruling Lady; indeed, if she failed, the sacred honour of her ancestors might be shamed past hope of expiation.

Mara poured a cup of chocha and sat back upon her heels as Gijan, son of Lord Detsu of the Kamaiota, nodded politely. His gesture concealed biting impatience, but even his critical nature could not fault the young wife's hospitality. She had seen him comfortable in the finest cushions, brought him refreshment, and sent immediate word to her husband that an old friend had arrived unexpectedly and was waiting to greet him.

Gijan lounged back, admiring the rings on his hands. His nails were clean to the point of fussiness and his jewellery ostentatious, but the rest of his dress showed restraint. 'And where might Lord Buntokapi be?'

'On some matter of business in the city, I expect.' Mara displayed none of the pique a young, pretty wife might feel at a husband's absence. Aware that Buntokapi's guest held her under closest scrutiny, she fluttered one hand offhandedly. 'You know these things are beyond me, Gijan, though I must say he spends a great deal of time away from home.'

Gijan's eyes narrowed, his self-absorbed admiration of his jade now an obvious act. Mara sipped her chocha, certain now that this guest had come to spy for the Anasati. No doubt Lord Tecuma wished information on how his third son fared as Lord of the Acoma. He had sent a handsome messenger, perhaps hoping the contrast to Buntokapi would entice a young wife to speak freely. After the barest interval the young noble said, 'Is that rascal neglecting his affairs, then?'

'Oh no, Gijan.' To avoid giving her father-in-law an excuse to pry further into Acoma affairs, Mara qualified expansively. 'If anything, Lord Buntokapi is too rigorous in his attention to details. He spends long hours at his desk.'

Lord Gijan's polished façade broke before incredulity. 'Bunto?' Aware he might have betrayed his appraisal of the new Lord of the Acoma, he closed his gaping mouth and added, 'Of course. Bunto was always a diligent fellow.'

Mara smothered a smile. Both of them lied outrageously, and each knew it; but a guest might not question the word of a host without raising the thorniest implications of honour.

With the topic of Buntokapi's management effectively closed, the morning wore on in polite conversation. Mara sent for thyza bread and fish, which slowed Gijan's effort at interrogation until at last her runner returned from town. Stripped to his loincloth, and breathless from the road, he dropped to his knees before Mara. 'Mistress, I bring word from the Lord of the Acoma.'

Pleasantly Mara said, 'What does my husband wish?'

The slave had barely washed his feet clean of dust before presenting himself; gasping still from his journey, he said, 'My Lord Buntokapi says he is most apologetic for being absent when his dear friend Gijan of the Kamaiota calls. He is presently unable to return to the estate and wishes for Gijan to join him in Sulan-Qu.'

Gijan nodded to the exhausted slave boy. 'Tell my servant to have my litter prepared.' Then he smiled at Mara. 'If my Lady has no objection?' Mara returned the smile, as if his presumption in ordering her runner was only another right of a man in the presence of a mere wife. How different it had been when she had been Ruling Lady. And things would be different again, soon; this she vowed as she ordered her maid to remove the food tray. Then, all lightness and grace, she saw Gijan to the door of the estate house.

While waiting in the hallway for the visitor's escort to assemble, she dismissed her runner and inwardly acknowledged relief. She had feared that Buntokapi might be returning. Though the journey to the city from the estates took two hours on foot, a message runner could make it there and back in half that time. By litter, Gijan would not reach Sulan-Qu until nearly sundown. No doubt Gijan also loved gambling, so Buntokapi would hardly subject his boyhood friend to a return trip after dark. Dice and cards and betting would keep them both in the city for the night, which was a small blessing from the gods. Already Mara had begun to treasure his absence, but this was a freedom she dared not love too much lest impatience prove her downfall.

Gijan bowed formally in farewell. 'I shall give your husband compliments on your hospitality when I greet him, Lady Mara.' He smiled at her, suddenly charming, and Mara realized this young man was wondering if she was another neglected woman ready for a romance.

Formal and distant, she showed him briskly to the screen. She did not need to waste time fending off the advances of amorous younger sons. What Bunto had shown her of lovemaking had convinced her she needed little from men. If ever she came to desire the company of a lover, he would be nothing like this silly, vain nobleman who took his leave to join Bunto in a night of gambling, wine, and prostitutes. As the litter departed, Mara heard a loud wail from the nursery.

'Men,' she muttered under her breath, and hurried to attend her son. The boy needed changing. Preoccupied, Mara gave him over to Nacoya, who had not lost her knack for dealing with infants. As the old woman began a game with the child involving his fingers and toes, Mara considered what Buntokapi's reaction to Gijan's visit would likely be.

The following afternoon, it seemed she had read his mind. Wearing his wrestling cloth, and gleaming still with the oil and sweat of his exercise, Buntokapi scratched the mat of hair on his chest. 'When someone calls and I am in the city, do not waste so much time sending messages, wife. Simply send them along to my town house.'

Mara bounced Ayaki one more time on her knee, her eyebrows raised in inquiry. 'Town house?'

As if the matter were of small account, Buntokapi answered over his son's shriek of pleasure, 'I have moved to larger quarters in Sulan-Qu.' He gave no reason, but Mara knew he had established the apartment to meet with his mistress, a woman named Teani. As far back as Mara could remember, Lord Sezu had never felt the need to take a town house. Though the practice was common enough among other lords whose estates were remotely located, no matter how late business kept Sezu in the city he always returned home to sleep under the same roof as his family. If Mara was generous in her assessment, Buntokapi was barely more than a boy, only two years older than she, and with none of her level-headed nature. While she had sat next to her brother, hearing the lessons on governance her father gave, Bunto had been a neglected, lonely boy who had spent time off by himself brooding, or in the rough company of soldiers. Her own coldness did not upset him but encouraged a return to his former habits of finding the pleasures he understood. Still, Mara had not selected this husband because she wanted someone strong-minded and resolute, like her father. Now her plans demanded that she encourage his self-indulgent, bad-tempered nature, though the course would be dangerous in the extreme.

Ayaki gave a last, deafening squeal and grabbed her beads. Prying his grip from her throat, Mara pretended indifference to her husband's indulgence. 'Whatever my Lord requires.'

Bunto returned one of his rare smiles, and ducking a swipe of Ayaki's tiny fist, Mara wondered briefly on the mistress, Teani. What sort of woman would infatuate a brute like her husband? But Buntokapi's pleased expression vanished as, with faultless timing, Jican appeared with a dozen scrolls in hand. 'My Lord, by the grace of the gods, you are back fortuitously. I have some papers dealing with matters of your distant holdings that need your immediate approval.'

With a beleaguered cry, Bunto said, 'Fortuitous! I must return to the city tonight.' He stalked from Mara's presence without so much as a good-bye, but his wife seemed not to care. Her eyes were fixed on the rosy face of her son as, drooling, he tried with fierce concentration to stuff her amber beads in his mouth. 'Your appetites might kill you one day,' she warned mildly; but whether she referred to her husband or his offspring only the gods might guess. After rescuing her jewellery, Mara smiled. The mistress, Teani, had wrapped another twist into the fabric of ideas evolved since the day the grey warriors had sworn service. The hour had come to begin Buntokapi's education on what it really took to conduct the business of the Acoma.

Alone in the cool shadow of the nursery, Mara consulted the wax tally started in secret during the last month. No one would interrupt her. Nacoya was out with Ayaki, and the slave who changed the covers in the crib could not read. Reflectively Mara chewed the end of her stylus. Each day Buntokapi visited his town house, she had sent at least one servant or Jican with some minor document to sign. From their dozens of reports, she had patiently pieced together the fact that her husband lived a very patterned existence. When in Sulan-Qu, Buntokapi arose at midmorning, but never later than the third hour after sunrise. He would then walk to a public training arena where mercenary guards and warriors whose masters were staying in the city gathered to practise at arms. Buntokapi preferred wrestling and archery to sword work, but with a diligence that had surprised Gijan he now practised all three. His technique with the blade improved steadily, but he still chose the company of common soldiers over that of the other lords who occasionally availed themselves of the facilities. Midday saw him bathed and changed and on the way to his town house; for about two hours thereafter he remained receptive to any work sent from the estates by Mara. His mistress, Teani, was rarely out of bed before mid-afternoon, and his tolerance for business fled the instant she awoke. With a charm that even the oldest messenger had described with admiration, she would lure Buntokapi to her bed until barely enough time remained to rise and dress for dinner. Then the couple would attend the theatre to see comedies, the taverns to listen to minstrels, or the gambling houses, though Teani had no wealth except what came to her as gifts. She derived a perverse pleasure from encouraging her paramour to bet, and if he lost, rumour held that her eyes sparkled all the more brightly. Mara frowned. Many servants had been cursed and cuffed to glean this information – the last runner to carry a document to Lord Buntokapi had been severely beaten – but in this matter a slave boy was of little consequence. Worse might come if the man she had married continued to wear the Lord's mantle.

An enraged yell from Ayaki echoed down the corridor beyond the screen, followed by Nacoya's chiding voice. If the child had soiled himself, the nursery would shortly become the site of a minor commotion. Ayaki battled like a young harulth whenever anyone tried to change him. Sighing with indulgence mixed with exasperation, Mara concealed the wax slate beneath an old parchment map and resumed her study of the Empire. The border lines and the estates on this rendition were slightly out of date, having been drawn up when she was a little girl. But the dyes were still bright and most of the holdings of the major Lords of the Empire were clearly marked. Since Buntokapi detested everything to do with words on paper, he would never miss this one document from his study. The only use he had for a map was to find which lands were open for hunting.

As Ayaki's wails drew nearer, Mara noticed an interesting fact at the outset: the Lord of the Zalteca, a minor neighbour who had a very prosperous trade in pottery, used a strip of land between his own estates and the Imperial Highway that appeared to be the property of the Lord of the Kano, who lived far to the east near the city of Ontoset. Mara found this indefinably amusing. If other families exercised such usurpation of property rights, that knowledge might later prove useful. She would ask Arakasi about it when he returned, and that thought sparked realization: only a week remained before she and Buntokapi celebrated their first wedding anniversary. The Spy Master might return to the estate at any moment.

Apprehension gripped Mara, even as Nacoya entered with Ayaki screaming in her arms. 'Your son would make a fine substitute for a guli,' said the old woman, referring to the hairy, troll-like creatures of children's tales; they scared their victims to death with hideous screams.

Mara only nodded. Wondering whether her mistress had gone deaf, Nacoya called the slave away from freshening the crib to help manage the Acoma heir, who yelled until his face was red, and made everyone's ears sore. Eventually Mara arose. She bent over her baby and jingled her beads to amuse him. As Ayaki's wails changed to laughter in another of his mercurial shifts of mood, her thoughts continued.

Somehow she must prevent Arakasi from coming under Buntokapi's control. Her bull of a husband would only waste that information network or, worse, make it available for his father's use, which would place far too dangerous a power in the hands of the Lord of the Anasati. Necessity made Mara bold. She must prepare for Arakasi's arrival with no further delay, so that his loyalty should remain hers alone. Inwardly reviewing her husband's schedule of activities, Mara spoke briskly to the slave who laboured over the kicking, naked legs of her son. 'Call for Jican.'

Nacoya raised her eyebrows. 'To the nursery?' she said, startled, but her mistress ignored the liberty.

'The matter will not wait.' Without further fuss, Mara relieved the slave of the damp cloths and began to cleanse her infant's soiled bottom.

Jican arrived, any puzzlement he felt well concealed. He bowed deeply as his mistress tied a clean loincloth around her son. 'Have we some documents that would be appropriate for my Lord husband's review?'

Barely able to contain his distaste at the mention of the Lord of the Acoma, Jican said, 'My Lady, there are always documents that are appropriate for the Lord of the house to review.' He bowed, shamed at how close to insult his words came in their implication that Buntokapi neglected his responsibilities. Mara sensed her hadonra's discomfort as she lifted Ayaki onto her shoulder.

In a tone sweet as red-bee honey, she said, 'Then I think it would be fitting to send a scribe to my husband's town house at three hours after noon.'

Jican stifled open curiosity. 'If you think that is wise, mistress, then it shall be done.'

Mara dismissed him and saw that Nacoya, too, regarded her with a shrewd glint in her eyes. 'You are deaf, mother of my heart,' the Lady of the Acoma said softly. 'And business matters are never conducted in the nursery.'

The nurse bowed promptly, guessing something of her mistress's intentions; but the full extent of those plans would have terrified the old woman beyond measure. As I am terrified, Mara thought, and silently wondered whether the Goddess of Wisdom would hear the prayers of a wife who knowingly provoked a husband already renowned for his bad temper.

Buntokapi raised his head from rumpled, sweat-damp pillows. The screens were drawn closed, but even the decorations painted in scarlet, maroon, and ochre could not entirely block out the afternoon sun in the garden beyond. A golden glow suffused the chamber, lending warm highlights to tangled sheets and to the sleeping form of his mistress, Teani. The Lord of the Acoma regarded the rounded length of her thigh, his thick lips bent into a smile. This was a woman, he thought. Naked, she took his breath away, as Mara's slenderness never had. He had felt passion for his wife when he had first wed; but having tasted the delights of Teani's talents, he now realized that his feelings for Mara arose from desire to dominate the daughter of a great family – and to rectify his own limited experience with women prior to becoming a Lord. Once he had a son, he had tried to do a husband's duty, but Mara lay like a corpse, and what man could stay interested in a woman who offered no sport?

Mara's strange intellectual passions, her love of poetry, and her fascination with the cho-ja Queen's hive gave Buntokapi a general headache. His mistress was another matter. In silent appreciation, he studied Teani's long legs. A fold in the sheets hid her hips and back, but masses of red-gold hair, rare in the Empire, tumbled down shoulders like fine porcelain. Teani's face was turned away, but Buntokapi imagined her perfection: the full, sensuous mouth that could tease him until he was crazy, and the straight nose, high cheekbones, and eyes almost amber in colour that brought admiring stares from every man when she clung to his arm. Her powers of attraction lent force to the manhood of Buntokapi, and just watching her slow breathing aroused him. With a leer he pressed a hand beneath the sheets to seek her firm, round breast. Someone chose that instant to knock at the door.

Buntokapi's questing fingers balled into a fist. 'Who is it!' His irritable bellow caused Teani to half spin, half sit up, in sleepy disarray.

'Huh?' she said, blinking. A toss of her head dislodged a river of loosened hair and the light shone warm on her breasts. Buntokapi licked his lips.

A servant's muffled voice called from beyond the screen. 'Master, a messenger from your hadonra brings documents for you to see.'

Buntokapi considered rising for a moment, but Teani levered herself up on her elbows, and her nipples jutted across his line of sight. The ache in his groin intensified. His movement changed to a half-roll that placed his head between those inviting pillows of flesh.

The sheets fell away. He ran tickling fingers down Teani's exposed stomach and she giggled. That decided Buntokapi. Surrendering to lust, he shouted, 'Tell him to come back tomorrow!'

The servant hesitated from the other side of the screen door. Timidly he said, 'Master, you've told him to come back three days in a row now.'

Shifting expertly under his hands, Teani whispered in Buntokapi's ear and then nipped at the lobe. 'Tell him to come back in the morning!' shouted Buntokapi. Then he remembered he had to wrestle a Strike Leader of the Tuscalora in the morning. 'No, tell him to come at noon and bring his documents then. Now leave me!'

Buntokapi waited, stiff with annoyance, until he heard the servant hurry away. Sighing at the tremendous responsibilities of his office, he decided he was entitled to his pleasures; otherwise the work load would grind him to a nub. As the ultimate favourite of his pleasures had begun to bite his shoulder, he thought it time to be diverted. With a half laugh, half grunt, the Lord of the Acoma pulled his concubine to him.

Late the following morning, Buntokapi marched through the streets of Sulan-Qu, feeling full of himself. He had easily defeated the Tuscalora Strike Leader and had won a fair amount of money as well, thirty centuries, which, while trivial to him now that he was Ruling Lord, still was a nice amount to have clinking in one's purse. Accompanied by his escort, two young Acoma guards who shared his passion for wrestling, he left the congestion of the main streets and rounded the corner to his town house. His mood darkened at once, for his hadonra sat on the stoop, the two servants with him burdened with leather carriers stuffed to capacity with parchments.

Dust arose in small puffs as Buntokapi stamped to a stop. 'What now, Jican?'

The little hadonra scrambled to his feet and bowed with a deference that somehow always annoyed. 'You instructed my messenger to see you at noon, Lord. As I had other business in town, I thought I would personally bring these papers here.'

Buntokapi sucked air through his teeth and recalled somewhat belatedly the words he had uttered through the screen in the course of his afternoon frolic with Teani. He scowled at his patient hadonra, then waved to the slaves who carried the sheaves of documents. 'Very well, bring them inside.'

Soon the writing tables, two food trays, and nearly every available area of flooring were tiered with stacks of parchments. Buntokapi laboured through page after page until his eyes stung from squinting at tiny columns of figures, or lists and lists of inventory. His leg developed a cramp, which he kneaded with his knuckles. The cushions compressed and grew damp with his own sweat, and finally his foot went to sleep. Exasperated, Buntokapi heaved himself to his feet and noticed the sunlight had traversed the length of the garden. The afternoon had almost fled.

Indefatigable, Jican handed him another document. Buntokapi forced watering eyes to focus. 'What is this?'

'As it says, Lord.' Jican tapped gently on the title script with one finger.

'Estimates on needra droppings?' Buntokapi jabbed the paper angrily in the air. 'By all the gods of heaven, what foolishness is this!'

Jican remained unfazed by his Lord's wrath. 'No foolishness, master. Each season we must estimate the weight of the dung, to judge whether we have a shortage of fertilizer for the thyza paddies and need to import, or excess to sell to the farm broker.'

Buntokapi scratched his head. Just then the screen leading to the bedchamber slid open. Teani stood in the doorway, inadequately wrapped in a robe sewn with scarlet birds of passion. The tips of her breasts pressed clearly through the cloth, and her hair tumbled sensuously over a shoulder artfully left bare. 'Bunto, how much longer are you going to be? Should I dress for the theatre?'

The open seduction in her smile left a staring Jican scarlet to the roots of his hair. Teani blew him a teasing kiss, more in sarcasm than fun; and frustration pricked Buntokapi to jealous rage. 'No longer!' he roared to his hadonra. 'Take this list of needra dung, and your tallies of hides ruined by mould and mildew, and the estimates on repairing the aqueduct to the upper meadows, and reports listing damages from the warehouse fire in Yankora, and give every one of them to my wife. Henceforth you will not come here unless I call you. Is that clear?'

Jican's flush drained to a yellowed, trembling pallor. 'Yes, master, but –'

'There are no buts!' Buntokapi chopped the air with his hand. 'These matters can be discussed with my wife. When I ask you, give me a summation of what you have been doing. From now on, if any Acoma servant appears here with a document without my having asked to read it, I'll have his head over the door! Is that understood?'

The list of needra dung estimates pressed protectively to his chest, Jican bowed very low. 'Yes, master. All matters of the Acoma are to be given over to the Lady Mara and reports prepared at your request. No servant is to bring a document to your attention unless you ask for it.'

Buntokapi blinked, as if unsure that this was exactly what he intended. Exploiting his confusion, Teani picked that moment to open the front of her robe and fan cool air across her body. She wore nothing underneath. In the sweet rush of blood to his groin, Buntokapi lost all interest in clarifying his point. With an impatient wave of his hand he dismissed Jican, then trod across crackling piles of parchments to sweep his mistress into his arms.

Jican gathered the creased tallies with near-frantic haste. Still, as the couple in the doorway retired into the shadows of the bedchamber, he saw his parchments stacked straight and the carrying cases neatly tied before he turned their heavy burden over to his servants. As he walked out through the main door of the town house, where an escort of Acoma soldiers waited to accompany him home, he heard Buntokapi laugh. To the long-suffering servants it was unclear who, at that moment, was the happier man.

The estate settled sleepily into the routines of midsummer. The maids no longer sported bruises in the mornings; Keyoke's subordinates lost their harried look; and Jican's whistling as he returned from the needra meadows to take up his pens and parchment once again became a reliable way to tell time. Aware that this calm was an illusion, the temporary result of her husband's long absences, Mara fought the tendency to grow complacent. Though the arrangement was fortunate, the courtesan Teani could not be depended upon to divert Buntokapi indefinitely. Other steps must be taken, each more dangerous than the last. On her way to her chambers, Mara heard a squeal of baby laughter.

She smiled indulgently to herself. Ayaki was growing like a weed, strong and quick to smile now that he had begun to sit up. He kicked his stumpy legs as if impatient to be walking, and Mara wondered whether, when that time came, old Nacoya would be up to handling him. Mentally she made note to find the nurse a younger assistant, so that the boisterous child would not try her ancient bones too much. That thought in mind, Mara entered the doors to her chamber, then froze, her foot raised between one step and the next. Motionless in the shadow sat a man, his dusty, ragged tunic dyed with the symbols of a mendicant priest of the order of Sularmina, Shield of the Weak. But how he had eluded Keyoke's defences, and the comings and goings of the servants, to gain the privacy of her quarters, was utterly confounding. Mara drew breath to shout an alarm.

The priest forestalled her as, in a voice undeniably familiar, he said, 'Greetings, mistress. I have no wish to disturb your peace. Should I leave?'

'Arakasi!' The rapid beat of Mara's heart slowed, and she smiled. 'Stay, please, and welcome back. Your appearance, as always, surprised me. Have the gods favoured your endeavours?'

The Spy Master stretched, taking the liberty to unwind the cords that secured his head covering. As the cloth slid into his lap, he smiled back. 'I was successful, Lady. The entire network has been revived, and I have much information to convey to your husband.'

Mara blinked. Her joy deflated, and her hands tightened at her sides. 'My husband?'

Reading the small signs of tension in her stance, Arakasi spoke carefully. 'Yes. News of your wedding and the birth of your son reached me in my travels. I will swear fealty to the Acoma natami, if your agreement with me is honourable. Then I must reveal all to my Lord of the Acoma.'

Mara had anticipated this. Despite her planning on the matter, the reality of Arakasi's loyalties caused a prickle of deepest apprehension. All her hopes might come to nothing. If her husband did not blunder like a needra bull through the subtleties of the Game of the Council, and see the Acoma set upon by intrigue and power-hungry Lords whose secrets had been indiscreetly used, he might turn the Spy Master's talents over to his father. Then her enemies the Anasati would become strong enough that no family could stand safely against them. Mara tried desperately to act as if the matter were casual. Now that the time was upon her, the stakes seemed frighteningly high.

She glanced quickly at the cho-ja clock on the writing desk and saw the time was still early, only three hours since dawn. Her mind spun in calculation. 'I think you should rest,' she said to Arakasi. 'Take the time until noon to relax and bathe, and after the noon meal I will attend the ceremony to swear your fealty to the Acoma natami. Then you must go to Sulan-Qu and introduce yourself to my Lord Buntokapi.'

Arakasi regarded her shrewdly, his fingers creasing the priest's mantle over and over in his lap.

'You may dine with me here,' Mara added, and she smiled in the sweet way he remembered.

Marriage, then, had changed nothing of her spirit. Arakasi rose and bowed in a manner utterly at odds with his dress. 'Your will, Lady.' And on silent feet he departed for the baths and the barracks.

Events developed swiftly after that. Seated on cushions in the breeze from the screen, Arakasi sipped the hot tea, made from fragrant herbs and fruit tree blooms. Enjoying the quickness of Mara's wit, he talked of the state of the Empire. The Thuril war that had ended years before had caused a loss of prestige for the Warlord and his War Party. The Blue Wheel Party and the Party for Progress had combined to almost force a change in imperial policy, until discovery of the alien world of Midkemia, populated by barbarians and rich with metals beyond the dreams of the maddest poet. Scouts had found metal lying about, obviously fashioned by intelligent beings, then discarded, wealth enough to keep an estate running for a year. Few reports followed, for the Warlord's campaign against these barbarians had strangled all outgoing information. Since the death of her father and brother, Mara had lost all track of the wars beyond the rift. Of late, only those who served the new Alliance for War knew what was taking place in the barbarian world – or shared in the spoils.

Arakasi's well-placed agents had access to such secrets. The war progressed well for the Warlord, and even the most reluctant members of the Blue Wheel Party had now joined in the invasion of Midkemia. Animated as he rarely was in his disguises, Arakasi gave a general outline to Mara, but he seemed reluctant to discuss details with anyone but the Lord of the Acoma.

Mara for her part showed him nothing but the dutiful wife, until the tea was drunk to the dregs and even Arakasi's large appetite seemed satisfied. Her glance at the wall clock seemed casual enough as she said, 'The day passes. Shall we swear you to our service, that you may go to my husband in Sulan-Qu?'

Arakasi bowed and rose, his sharp eyes not missing the slight tremble in Mara's voice. He studied her eyes, reassured by the look of resolve in their dark depths. The incident with the cho-ja queens had instilled in him a deep respect for this woman. She had won his trust, and for that he stepped forward to swear his loyalty and his honour to an unknown Lord.

The ceremony was simple, and brief, the only oddity being that Arakasi swore on behalf of his agents also. Mara found it strange to consider the Acoma had loyal retainers whose names were unknown to her, yet who might willingly give their lives for the honour of a master and mistress they had never met. The greatness of Arakasi's gift, and the fear that his sacrifice and his labours might be wasted, threatened to bring tears to her eyes. Briskly Mara turned to the practical.

'Arakasi, when you visit my husband . . . go in the guise of a servant. Tell him you are there to discuss the shipment of the needra hides to be sold to the tentmakers in Jamar. He will then know if it is safe to talk. There are servants in the town house new to our service, so my Lord may be cautious. He will instruct you about what you shall do.'

Arakasi bowed and left her side. As the light slanted golden across the lane leading to the Imperial Highway, Mara bit her lip in earnest hope. If she had timed things right, Arakasi's arrival should coincide with the height of Buntokapi's passion in the arms of Teani. Very likely the Spy Master would find a reception far different from anything he expected – unless her husband was in an utterly uncharacteristic mood of tolerance. Worried, excited, and frightened at the frail odds that supported her hopes, Mara put off the poet she had called in to read. Instead she spent the afternoon in the ironclad disciplines of meditation, for the beauty of his words would be wasted in her present frame of mind.

Hours passed. The needra were driven in from their day pastures, and the shatra flew, heralding the approach of night. As the chief assistant gardener lit the lamps in the dooryard, Arakasi returned, dustier than he had been that morning, and visibly footsore. He entered Mara's presence as the maids laid out cushions for her comfort. Even in the unlit gloom of the chamber, the large red welt upon his cheek showed plainly. Silent, Mara dismissed her maids. She sent her runner after cold food, and a basin and cloth for light washing. Then she bade the Spy Master sit.

The tap of the runner's sandals diminished down the hall. Alone with his mistress, Arakasi bowed formally. 'My Lady, your Lord listened to my coded greeting, then erupted into a fury. He struck me and bellowed that any business I had was to be directed to Jican and you.' Mara endured his penetrating gaze without expression. She seemed coiled, waiting, and after an interval Arakasi continued. 'There was a woman there, and he seemed . . . preoccupied. In any event, your husband is a superb – actor. Or he wasn't acting at all.'

Mara's expression remained innocent. 'Many of the duties of this household my husband has given over to me. After all, I was Ruling Lady before he came here.'

Arakasi was not fooled. ' "When the Game of the Council enters the home, the wise servant does not play," ' he quoted. 'In honour, I must do exactly as my Lord bids, and I will assume things are as they seem until proven otherwise.' His stare turned cold then, even in the veiling of shadow of dusk. 'But I am loyal to the Acoma. My heart is with you, Mara of the Acoma, because you gave me colours to wear, but I am duty-bound to obey my lawful Lord. I will not betray him.'

'You say only what a loyal servant would be honour-bound to say, Arakasi. I expected no less.' Mara smiled, unexpectedly pleased by her Spy Master's warning. 'Do you have any doubts about my husband's wishes?'

The slave arrived with the food tray. Gratefully choosing a jigabird pastry, Arakasi answered. 'In truth, I would have, if I hadn't seen the woman he was . . . speaking with when I appeared.'

'What do you mean?' Mara waited, impatient, while he chewed and swallowed.

'Teani. I know her.' Arakasi qualified with no change in tone, 'She is an agent of the Lord of the Minwanabi.'

Mara felt a stab of cold pass through her. Still enough that Arakasi noticed her distress, she spoke after a long moment. 'Say nothing of this to anyone.'

'I hear, mistress.' Arakasi snatched the interval to eat in earnest. His travels had left him gaunt, and he had crossed many leagues since dawn. Guilty because he also bore the painful marks of Buntokapi's wrath, Mara allowed him to finish his meal before asking for his full report.

After that, excitement made her forget his tiredness. As Arakasi unfolded the intrigue and the complexities of Empire politics in spare words, and a sprinkling of amusing anecdotes, she listened with shining eye. For this she had been born! As the evening grew old and the moon rose beyond the screen, pictures and patterns began to form in her mind. She interrupted with questions of her own, and the quickness of her deductions made Arakasi visibly shed his weariness. At last he had a mistress who appreciated the nuances of his work; henceforward her enthusiasm would sharpen his skills. As the men in his network saw the Acoma rise in power, their part would engender a pride they had never known under the Lord of the Tuscai.

Slaves came to tend the lamps. As new light spilled across the planes of the Spy Master's face, Mara noticed the changes in Arakasi's manner. What a treasure this man was, his talents an honour to House Acoma. Mara listened to his information long into the night, torn inside by a frustration even his sharp perception did not discern. Now, at long last, she had the tools she needed to enter the game and find a way to earn her father and brother vengeance against the Minwanabi. But no move could be made, and no bit of information acted upon, with Buntokapi in place as Lord of the Acoma. When at last Arakasi departed, Mara sat with eyes fixed sightlessly on the stripped bones of jigabirds scattered upon the food tray. She brooded, and did not sleep until dawn.

The guests arrived late the next morning. Red-eyed from lack of sleep, Mara regarded the seven litters that wended their way towards the estate house. The colours of the escort's armour were known to her, and not a cause for joy. With a sigh of resignation, Mara bade her maid bring her a proper robe for the greeting of guests. That these were an intrusion to ruin a fine morning mattered not at all. The honour and hospitality of the Acoma must be maintained. When the first litter reached the dooryard, Mara was waiting to meet its occupant, three maids accompanying her. Nacoya came from another door and joined her lady as the first guest rose from his cushions.

Mara bowed formally. 'My Lord Chipaka, what an honour.'

The wizened old man blinked weak eyes and attempted to identify who spoke. Since he was also hard of hearing, Mara's words had escaped him as well. Edging closer to the young girl standing nearest, he squinted and bellowed, 'I am Lord Chipaka of the Jandawaio. My wife and my mother and my daughters have come to visit your master and mistress, girl.'

He had mistaken Mara for a servant. Barely able to contain her amusement, the Lady of the Acoma ignored the slight. Speaking directly into the elder's ear, she said, 'I am Mara, wife of Lord Buntokapi, my Lord. To what do we owe this honour?'

But the old man had shifted his attention to the frail and ancient woman, looking to be near a hundred, who was being assisted as delicately as a jewelled egg from the most ostentatious of the litters. Mara dispatched her maids to help, as a gesture of respect, for the bearers were filthy with dust from the road. The old woman returned no thanks. Wizened and beaked like a featherless bird, she simply squatted between the two servants who supported her. Three other women emerged from other litters behind, each a younger replica of her grandmother, but equally waspish in the calm of midmorning; they indulged in the most faddish of fashions. Gathering around the ancient woman, they at once began a nattering chatter. Mara reined in her distaste, for already this invasion of her home had become an exercise in tolerance.

The old man shuffled closer, smiling and patting her rump. Mara hopped forward, blinking in shock and disgust. But the old man seemed oblivious to her discomfort. 'I was unable to attend your mistress's wedding, girl. My estates near Yankora are far indeed, and Mother was ill.' He waved at the frail woman, who now stared blankly into space, while her granddaughters steadily cursed the inept handling of the servants who supported the ancient crone. Into this clutch of hen jigahens hobbled the woman from the last litter. She was gowned in embroidered sharsao cloth, and behind the affected fluttering of her fan she sported a face of the same vintage as Lord Chipaka's. Mara decided she must be the Lady of the Jandawaio.

The old man plucked insistently at the sleeve of the Lady of the Acoma. 'Since we happened to be passing north on our way to the Holy City, we had our barge put in at Sulan-Qu, and came to call upon your Lord . . . ah yes, that's his name. I'm an old friend of his father's, you know.' The old man winked knowingly at Mara. 'My wife's a sound sleeper, don't you know. Come by later tonight, girl.' He attempted to pat Mara's arm in what was intended to be a seductive manner, but his hand was so palsied, he missed her wrist.

A wicked gleam lit Mara's eyes. Though the Lord was tastelessly lascivious, and his breath stank of rotting teeth, she barely smothered her delight. 'You wish to see the Lord of the Acoma? Then, my Lord, I am afraid you must return to the city, for my Lord Buntokapi is now in residence at his town house.'

The old man blinked, blank-faced. Obligingly Mara repeated her message at a shout.

'Oh. Why certainly. His town house.' The old man leered again at Mara. Then he bobbed his head briskly and waved to his retinue.

The women, still chattering, remained oblivious as their slaves gathered by the litters. The bearers who had been carrying the tiny old woman did an abrupt about-turn and headed their confused-looking charge back towards her cushions. Over her mumble of complaint the old man cried, 'Go on. Go on now, Mother, we must go back to the city.'

The girls and their mother, uniformly plain and loud, protested bitterly at the idea of returning to their litters. They simpered and delayed, hoping to cadge an invitation for refreshments from the Lady of the Acoma, but the deaf Lord Chipaka paid no heed to their noise. As he seemed in haste to descend upon Lord Buntokapi, Mara decided not to impede his departure. When the matriarch and her brood were safely buttoned into their litters, she graciously offered a messenger slave to guide the way to the town house, that the courtesy visit to her Lord suffer no more unnecessary delays.

The Lord of the Jandawaio waved absently and shuffled to the litter he shared with his mother. One hand upon the curtains, he paused and said, 'And tell your mistress I am sorry to have missed her, girl.'

Shaking her head slightly, Mara said, 'I will, my Lord.'

The slaves bent, muscles shining with sweat as they hefted the litter poles. As the procession traipsed back down the lane, Nacoya said, 'My Lady, Lord Bunto will be furious.'

Mara watched the departing retinue with sharp calculation. If the ancient matriarch of the Jandawaio resented the jostling of anything but a slow walk, Buntokapi's visitors would arrive within an hour after he had returned to Teani's bed. Fervently Mara murmured, 'I certainly hope so, Nacoya.'

She returned to her quarters, where her maps and documents awaited further study. Nacoya stared after her in astonishment, wondering what possible motive would justify the young mistress's inviting the wrath of that brute she had married.

Three days later, ignoring the presence of Nacoya and the other servants, Buntokapi stamped into Mara's quarters unannounced. At the sight of his dusty sandals, Mara winced reflexively. But this pair was for walking only, lacking the studs used in battle or on the practice ground. 'You should never have allowed that old fool and his clutch of jigahens to come to my town house,' the Lord of the Acoma opened. The timbre of his voice caused the maids to shrink in the corners.

Mara lowered her eyes, as much to hide her amusement at Buntokapi's calling the Lord of the Jandawaio's women barnyard fowl as from any contrition. 'Is my husband displeased?'

Buntokapi lowered himself to the mat before her with a sigh of aggravation. 'Woman, that old fool was a friend of my grandfather's. He's damn near senile! Half the time he thinks my father is his old boyhood pal, and that I am Tecuma of the Anasati. And his mother is worse, a near corpse he drags along wherever he goes. Gods, wife, she must be close to a century of years. And all she does is stare, drool, and mess the mats upon which she's sitting. And Lord Chipaka talks to her all the time; all of them talk to her, the wife, the daughters, even the servants! She never answers, but they think she does!' His voice rose as his recounting of the visit inflamed his temper. 'Now, I want to know which brainless serving girl sent them along to my town house! All Chipaka could remember was she had large breasts!'

Mara stifled a smile, barely. The nearsighted Lord Chipaka might perhaps have thought Mara's breasts large, since his nose had hovered within inches of her chest as he spoke to her. Puzzled by his wife's blush, and the suspicion that she laughed at him, Buntokapi shouted until he shook the timbers of the doorframes. 'And he groped my . . . servant girl. Right before my eyes he reached out and he . . . pinched her!'

Too angry to contain himself, Buntokapi leaped to his feet. He shook his fists in the air, ranting himself into a sweat. 'And they stayed for two days! For two days I had to give my quarters to that old fool and his wife. My . . . servant girl, Teani, had to take quarters in a hostelry nearby. The old lecher wouldn't keep his hands off her.'

Mara sat up then and deliberately provoked him. 'Oh, Bunto, you should have let him bed the girl. She's only a servant, and if the old Lord was still capable after all these years, at least the diversion would have kept him occupied.'

Buntokapi's colour deepened. 'Not in my town house! If I can find that stupid cow who sent Jandawaio to me in Sulan-Qu, I'll personally strip the skin from her back.'

Mara's reply sounded meek in contrast to her husband's bellow. 'Bunto, you said, should anyone come to call, send them along to you at your town house, not keep them waiting here. I'm sure Jican informed all the servants and that any of them would have done the same.'

Buntokapi paused in his pacing, one foot half-raised like a shatra bird's. The pose would have been funny were he not so coiled for violence. 'Well, I made a mistake. From now onward, send no one to my town house without my prior consent!'

His thunderous shout roused Ayaki, who stirred in his pillows. Apparently preoccupied, Mara turned towards her baby. 'No one?'

The interruption of his son inflamed Buntokapi still further. He stormed about the room, his fist waving in the air. 'No one! If a member of the High Council calls, they can wait!'

The baby began to wail. Mara's brow knitted slightly as she said, 'But of course you don't mean your father?'

'Send that child off with a servant!' Buntokapi raged. He gestured furiously at Misa, who ran to take the infant from Mara's arms. Buntokapi kicked a pillow hard, sending it sailing into the fish pool in the garden beyond the screen. Then he resumed as if no interruption had occurred. 'My father thinks I am stupid, and that I'll do whatever he asks. He can go piss in the river! The Acoma are not his to command!' Buntokapi paused, his face dark purple. 'No, I don't want him soiling my fish. Tell him to go downstream off my lands, then he can piss in the river!'

Mara hid her hands in the fabric of her robe. 'But surely if the Warlord –'

Buntokapi cut her off. 'If the Warlord himself arrives here, do not send even him along to my town house! Is that understood!' Mara regarded her husband in shocked amazement. Bunto's rage redoubled. After being repressed for two days with the Lord of the Jandawaio, his tantrum was impressive. 'Even Almecho can damn well wait upon my pleasure. If he does not wish to wait here, he can sit in the needra pens, if he prefers. And if I don't get back the day he arrives, he can sleep in needra shit, for all I care, and you can tell him I said so.'

Mara pressed her forehead to the floor, almost in the bow of a slave. 'Yes, my Lord.'

The obeisance forestalled her husband, who longed to strike out with his fists now that his anger had found a focus. 'And another thing. All these messages you keep sending. I want them stopped. I come home enough to oversee the running of my holdings. I do not need servants disturbing me throughout the day. Is that understood?'

He bent swiftly, snatching his wife upright by the collar. She replied stiffly, her breathing hampered by his knuckles. 'You do not wish to be disturbed, and all messages are to stop.'

'Yes!' Bunto shouted into her face. 'When I am resting in town, I do not wish to be disturbed for any reason. If you send a servant to me, I will kill him before he can tell me what you say. Is that understood?' He shook her slightly.

'Yes, my Lord.' Mara struggled feebly, her slippers all but lifted clear of the floor. 'But there is this one matter here –'

Buntokapi pushed her roughly backward, and she tumbled into the cushions. 'Enough! I will hear nothing more.'

Mara raised herself valiantly. 'But, husband –'

Bunto lashed out with one foot, catching the hem of Mara's gown. Cloth ripped, and she cowered, her hands protecting her face. He shouted, 'I said enough! I will not listen to another word! Have Jican take care of any business. I am returning to town immediately. Do not disturb me for anything!' With a last kick in Mara's direction, he spun and stalked from her quarters. As his footsteps faded, distantly Ayaki could be heard crying.

After the barest of prudent intervals, Nacoya rushed to her

mistress's side. Helping her upright, and shaking with fright, she said, 'Mistress, you said nothing to your husband about the message from his father.'

Mara rubbed the reddening bruise on her thigh. 'You saw, Nacoya. My Lord husband granted me no chance to relay his father's message.'

Nacoya sat back on her heels. Grimly she nodded. 'Yes, that is true, my Lady. My Lord Buntokapi did indeed not give you the opportunity to speak.'

Mara straightened her torn robe, her eyes fixed significantly on the ornamented scroll that had arrived that morning, announcing the impending arrival of her father-in-law and his most august travelling companion, Almecho, the Warlord of Tsuranuanni. Then, her bruises forgotten beside the enormity of her husband's commands, she smiled.

10

Warlord

The servants hurried.

As anxious as the rest of the household staff in the face of the coming visit, Nacoya sought her mistress through hallways crowded with last-minute activity. Artists blotted brushes after refurbishing the screens, and slaves trooped to and from the kitchens with foods and drink especially imported to please the tastes of guests. Nacoya wove through the confusion, muttering. Her bones were too old to take kindly to haste. She dodged a bearer carrying an immense load of cushions and finally found her mistress in her private gardens. Mara sat beneath a jō fruit tree, her son asleep in a basket by her side, and her hands at rest in the fabric of a blanket she had been sewing with embroidered animals for Ayaki. By the work still left to be done, Nacoya judged the Lady had not minded her needlework for most of the afternoon. Not for the first time, the old nurse wondered what the girl might be planning; and as had become her habit since Buntokapi's assumption of the lordship, she bowed without asking.

'You bring word of our guests?' Mara stated softly.

'Yes, mistress.' Nacoya looked closely, but found no sign of nervousness in the young girl who reclined on the cushions. Her hair was brushed to a polished black sheen, tied neatly back, and pinned with jewels. Her dress was rich but not ostentatious, and the eyes she raised to Nacoya were shadowed obsidian, impossible to read.

The old nurse resumed with asperity. 'The Anasati retinue has reached the borders of Acoma lands. Your runner reports four litters, two dozen body servants, and two full companies of warriors, one under the Anasati banner, the other Imperial Whites. Six are officers worthy of private accommodations.'

Mara folded the half-completed blanket with fussy care and laid it aside. 'I trust that Jican has arranged everything?'

Nacoya gestured acquiescence. 'He is a fine hadonra, Lady. He loves his work and requires little supervision, a thing my Lord would do well to appreciate, since he is so often absorbed with his affairs in town.'

But Mara did not respond to the prompt. Instead of sharing, the Lady of the Acoma excused her closest confidante. Then she clapped briskly for her maidservant and asked that Ayaki be returned to the care of his day nurse. Another servant fetched the jewelled overrobe that was proper attire for greeting guests of High Council rank. Mara stood through the arranging and fastening, her face a secretive mask. By the time she was readied to meet the Warlord, Lord Almecho, and Tecuma, Lord of the Anasati, she seemed a girl in the trappings of a great Lady; except that her eyes stayed hard as flint.

Keyoke, Jican, and Nacoya were on hand to greet the entourage upon arrival. Keyoke wore ceremonial armour, decorated with fluted scrollwork entirely unsuitable for battle, but handsome in the extreme. His formal trappings were completed by a plumed helm and tasselled sword, and Papewaio, his adjutant, stood in armour as splendid. Every man in the garrison not on sentry duty was properly turned out to greet the guests, and the green lacquer of their armour shone in the late sunlight. To a man they held themselves proudly as the first of the Imperial Guard marched between fence rows newly painted and gardens planted afresh for the occasion. The litters in the centre of the cortege approached the house, and Mara joined the heads of her household. She had watched state visitors arrive at her father's household since she was a small child, and the routine was familiar; but never before had her palms sweated through the formalities.

The dooryard echoed with the tramp of feet as the first company of warriors marched in; the Warlord's Imperial Whites led, since his was the senior rank. Keyoke stepped forward and bowed to the plumed officer in command. Then, with Mara's leave, he directed the guest officers to quarters. An elite cadre of bodyguards remained behind to attend upon their master. With a dry feeling in her mouth, Mara noticed that Lord Almecho retained six soldiers, the full complement to which his rank entitled him. Clearer than words, the Warlord showed that his arrival was no honour to the Acoma but a favour to his ally the Anasati lord, Tecuma. With a slight motion of her hand, Mara signalled Papewaio to remain; his presence in ceremonial armour would return the impression that she acknowledged no weakness before those of superior rank; the Acoma would bear no slight.

'Mistress,' murmured Nacoya so that no other could hear, 'please, in the name of the gods, go cautiously; boldness is a dangerous choice for a lady in the absence of her Ruling Lord.'

'I'll remember,' whispered Mara, though her face showed no sign she had heard the warning at all.

Then the other litters arrived, sparkling with precious metal. The Warlord's bearers bore tasselled sashes, darkened with sweat and dust from the road. His servants wore beaded livery, and all were matched in height and colouring. Next came the scarlet and yellow of the Anasati standard, behind which marched Tecuma's honour guard; his servants also were decked out in costly array, for the Lord of the Anasati, like many Tsurani, sought to outshine his betters with ostentatious displays of wealth.

Mara considered the metal ornaments that tinkled and flashed on the Anasati palanquin; if his slaves slipped and dropped the lot in the river, her father-in-law's showy accoutrements would sink him like a stone, she thought with grim amusement. But her face remained impassive as her guests entered the dooryard, and the shade muted the splendour of jewelled trappings and red-and-yellow-lacquered trim.

The bearers set the litters down and stepped smartly aside, while body servants rushed to draw the curtains and help their masters to rise. Poised between her retainers, Mara observed the proper interval, allowing time for her guests to gain their feet, adjusting their clothing and dignity, before greeting her. Since the Warlord was a stocky man, and his attire included robes set about with sashes with elaborate battle decorations, his servants were kept occupied for a long minute. Mara glimpsed the Lord of the Anasati craning his neck to see around the confusion; and the absence of Buntokapi was met with an irritable frown before protocol smoothed over his expression. Behind the fan Tecuma fluttered before his chin, Mara guessed that he whispered furiously to his first Adviser, Chumaka. The hollow feeling in the pit of her stomach intensified.

'Mistress, pay attention!' snapped Nacoya under her breath.

Mara looked away from her late father's enemy and saw that Kaleska, the Warlord's First Adviser, had stepped forward to bow before her.

She bowed in return. 'Welcome to the house of the Acoma.' The Warlord stepped up behind him, surrounded by his soldiers and servants. Mechanically Mara recited the traditional greeting: 'Are you well?' She went on, wishing joy and comfort to her guests; but as she exchanged courtesies, she sensed the puzzlement of Lord Almecho, who also had noticed the absence of the Lord of the Acoma. Mara gestured for servants to open the doors to the estate house. The Warlord exchanged glances with the Anasati lord; then, as if echoing his master's disquiet, the Anasati First Adviser, Chumaka, plucked nervously at his clothing.

Mara bowed again and stepped back, permitting her guests to file into the comfort of her house. She stood meekly as they passed, except when Lord Tecuma whispered a furious query concerning Buntokapi's whereabouts. With caculated timing, she raised her wrist to adjust the brooch that pinned her robe; the jingle of her jade bracelets effectively foiled his question. And as the Warlord's booming voice demanded cold drinks from a waiting servant, no time could be snatched to ask again without causing notice. Looking hot, Tecuma followed his travelling companion into the wide hall. There Mara arranged for musicians to play while trays of sliced fruit were provided for the refreshment of her guests.

Once inside, Nacoya snagged Kaleska and Chumaka in an involved conversation concerning the state of disrepair in certain of the roads throughout the Empire, most notably those that caused difficulty for Acoma trading. Mara made a show of making certain her servants fussed over the Warlord's comfort, and then managed artfully to appeal to the man's vanity so that he would explain the origin of each decoration upon his sash. Since many had been won in battle by his ancestors, and the newest had been wrested away from a barbarian lord during a raid beyond the rift, the recounting took no small amount of time.

Reddened light fell through the screens. Finished with his first goblet of wine, Tecuma fumed in silence. The absence of his son clearly embarrassed him, for the purpose of his visit was to have his grandson presented, a ritual tradition appointed to the Lord of the house. Tecuma knew as well as Mara that the Warlord's conversation was merely a gracious way to buy time, postponing comment on Buntokapi's absence, perhaps to spare an important ally the shame of making excuses. Almecho needed the support of the Imperial Party in his Alliance for War, and anything that could cause difficulty between his interests and the Anasati's was to be politically avoided. Each minute that passed placed the Anasati more in the Warlord's debt for such kindness, as Chumaka was also aware. He masked irritation by eating, unmindful that the fruit had been soaked in fine spirits and the servants had replenished the tray of fruit by his elbow three times in an hour.

The Warlord's recitation lagged by sunset. Smiling, delivering compliments glib enough to make a fish blush, Mara clapped her hands. Servants rushed in and opened the screens, in time to display the splendour of the shatra birds' flight at the end of the day. Their clear, fluting calls temporarily defeated conversation, and when at last the phenomenon came to an end, more servants arrived to escort the guests to an elaborate ceremonial dinner. By now Mara's hospitality was plainly a desperate, stopgap diversion.

'Where is my son?' Tecuma demanded through clenched teeth. His lips assumed a frozen smile as the Warlord glanced his way.

Mara winked, as if to a conspirator. 'The main dish is Buntokapi's personal favourite, but it sours if it stands too long. The cooks have been at work all day for your pleasure, and the jigabirds and the needra are spiced with rare sauces. My most graceful maid, Merali, will show you your seat. She will bring a basin, if you need to wash.'

Sweating, and infuriated by what he saw as girlish prattle, the Lord of the Anasati permitted himself to be ushered in to dinner. He noticed, with narrowed eyes, that the Warlord showed signs of restlessness; at that point he was glad Mara had gone to the trouble of bringing in priests to bless the repast, and that her musicians played very well, if too loudly for protocol.

He barely tasted what had been touted as Buntokapi's favourite dish. When Chumaka snatched time to query how long he intended to be led on by such nonsense, he nearly choked on his meat. Mara set down her knife and signalled Nacoya, who in turn nodded to a servant in the doorway. The musicians struck up a wildly arythmic melody, and female dancers dressed in little but beads and gauze whirled into the space between the tables.

That their performance was brilliantly provocative could do nothing to hide the fact that Buntokapi of the Acoma was nowhere in evidence, though his father and the most august personage in the High Council presently bided their time at his dinner table.

Lord Tecuma seized the moment when the dancers spun about and finished their finale. He heaved himself to his feet, almost stepping on his hems in haste, and bellowed over the last notes of music, 'My Lady Mara, where is your husband, Buntokapi?'

The musicians stopped their strings, but for one laggard vielle, which scraped an abandoned solo before its owner stilled his bow. Silence fell, and all eyes turned to Mara, who stared in turn at the dainties which her cooks had laboured to prepare, but which she obviously had barely tasted. She said nothing; and the Warlord set down his spoon with a clink.

A hairsbreadth shy of discourtesy, she met her father-in-law's eyes. 'My Lord, forgive us both. I will explain everything, but such words will go more graciously after the servants have brought wine.'

'No!' Almecho spread heavy hands before him upon the table. 'Lady, this has gone on long enough! Your dinner is exquisitely prepared and your dancers are talented, but we who visit your house will not be treated as buffoons. You must send for your Lord and let him explain himself.'

Mara's expression revealed nothing, but she turned dramatically pale. Nacoya seemed openly shaken, and the Lord of the Anasati felt sweat spring beneath his collar. 'Well, girl? Send for my son, that my grandson may be presented!'

Mara's reply was phrased with perfect deference. 'Father of my husband, forgive me, but I cannot do as you ask. Let my servants bring wine, and in time my husband will explain himself.'

The Warlord turned a dark expression on Mara. At first he had treated the delay in Buntokapi's appearance as something of a joke, indulging an old ally. But as the day had passed, the waiting and the heat had plainly worn away what patience he possessed. Now Tecuma of the Anasati dared not take the girl's suggestion without severe loss of face, for clearly her efforts suggested something was amiss. To swallow her excuses would indicate weakness, a serious setback before the pre-eminent member of the Imperial Council. If Buntokapi was drunk, even to incapacity, that shame would be less than the one incurred should he slight his father and his guests by hiding the fact behind his wife.

Tecuma said, in deadly even tones, 'We are waiting.'

Overtly nervous, but still ingenuous, Mara answered, 'Yes, father of my husband, that is true.'

The silence that followed was ponderous.

The musicians set down their instruments, and the dancers filed from the room. When it became painfully evident that the Lady of the Acoma intended no explanation, the Anasati lord was forced once more to intervene.

As if he had to bite down to control his urge to shout, Tecuma demanded, 'What do you mean, that is true?'

Mara's discomfort intensified. Without meeting the eyes of her father-in-law, she said, 'My husband wished for you to wait for him.'

The Warlord set down the after-dinner sweet he had been nibbling and looked confused, the result of the odd dialogue and the wine. 'Buntokapi wished us to wait for him? Then he knew he would be late in greeting us?' Almecho sighed, as if a great weight had been lifted from him. 'Then he sent word he would be late and you were to entertain us until he arrived, is that it?'

'Not exactly, my Lord,' said Mara, her colour rising.

Tecuma leaned forward. 'What exactly, then, did he say, Mara?'

Like a gazen held pinned by a serpent, Mara began to tremble. 'His exact words, father of my husband?'

Tecuma thumped his hands upon the table, and the plates all jumped with a clink. 'Exactly!'

Belatedly alerted to his master's tension, Chumaka sat blinking like a night bird caught in bright light. Even inebriated, he sensed something amiss. His instincts came to the fore. Levering himself forward, he attempted to reach for his master's sleeve. The manoeuvre overbalanced him; he caught himself short of a fall with an undignified whoosh of breath. 'My Lord –'

Tecuma's eyes remained locked upon his daughter-in-law.

The image of nervous innocence, Mara said, 'My Lord husband said, "If the Warlord arrives, he can damn well wait upon my pleasure." '

Chumaka sank his fist to the wrist in embroidered pillows, frozen in the act of reaching for Tecuma's dangling sleeve. Helpless now to intervene, he watched Tecuma's face drain slowly of colour. Chumaka looked across a room that held no movement, and through the delicate steam rising from a dozen rare dishes he regarded the reaction of Almecho.

The Warlord of all Tsuranuanni sat motionless, his still features deepening to red. All his inclination towards tolerance vanished as his eyes became burning coals of barely managed rage, and his reply cut like sharpened flint. 'What else did my Lord of the Acoma say of me?'

Mara gestured helplessly, and directed a desperate glance at Nacoya. 'My Lords, I . . . I dare not speak. I beg that you wait for my husband, and let him answer for himself.' Straight, small, and pathetically fragile in her formal robes, the girl seemed lost in the cushions she sat upon. Hers was an image to evoke pity; except that the Game of the Council allowed none. As a maid with a basin hurried to her side to dab her forehead with a damp towel, the Warlord glared at Tecuma of the Anasati.

'Ask her the whereabouts of your son, Lord, for I require a messenger sent at once to summon him into our presence. If he intends insult, let him speak in my presence.'

Mara dismissed her maid. She rallied with the formality of a Tsurani warrior facing a death sentence, though such control taxed her visibly. 'My Lord, Buntokapi is in his town house in Sulan-Qu, but no messenger may go there, by his explicit command. He vowed to kill the next servant sent to trouble him.'

The Warlord heaved to his feet. 'The Lord of the Acoma is in *Sulan-Qu*? While we wait upon his pleasure? And what, will you tell us, does he expect us to do in the meantime? Speak, Lady, and leave nothing out!'

Tecuma rose also, a serpent ready to strike. 'What nonsense is this? Surely my son . . . not even Bunto could be so rude.'

The Warlord silenced him with a gesture. 'Let the Lady of the Acoma speak for her husband.'

Mara bowed. Her eyes seemed too bright, the delicate shades of her makeup harsh against her pallor. With stiff ceremony, she formed a triangle with her thumbs and fingers, the ancient gesture which signified that honour must be compromised by the command of a superior. All present in the room knew that her news would bring shame. The priests who had blessed the repast silently arose and departed. The musicians and servants filed out after them, and soon the chamber held only the guests, their advisers, and the Warlord's honour guard. Papewaio stood immobile as a temple icon behind the Lady of the Acoma's shoulder, and Nacoya, equally still, waited by her side. Quietly Mara said, 'My tongue will not compromise the honour of this house. My First Adviser was present when Buntokapi delivered his orders. She will answer for him, and for me.' She waved weakly towards Nacoya.

The old woman arose, then bowed with extreme respect. Servants had helped her dress for this occasion, and for the first time Mara could recall, the pins that held her white hair were set straight. But the incongruous humour of that observation fled as the old nurse spoke. 'My Lords, by my oath and honour, what the Lady says is true. The Lord of the Acoma did say those words as she repeated them.'

Out of patience with delays, even ones of courtesy, the Warlord of Tsuranuanni focused his irritation upon Nacoya. 'I demand once more: what else did the Lord of the Acoma say?'

Nacoya stared blankly ahead and answered in a voice that stayed low and flat. 'My Lord Buntokapi said, "If he," meaning yourself, Lord Almecho, "does not wish to wait here, he can sit in the needra pens, if he prefers. And if I don't get back the day he arrives, he can sleep in needra shit, for all I care." '

The Warlord paused as if carved from stone, the sheer force of his fury rendering him without volition. A long, torturous minute passed before he spoke to Tecuma. 'Your son chooses a swift destruction.' Light trembled in the jewels on Almecho's collar and his voice rumbled with menace. His tone rose to a shout as the enormity of his rage took flight. Like a scarlet-banded killwing climbing high before swooping to impale its prey, he whirled to face the father of the man who had insulted him. 'Your young upstart begs to beget a legacy of ashes. I will call upon clan honour. The Oaxatucan will march and grind Acoma bones into the very ground they walk upon. Then we shall salt the earth of their ancestors so that nothing shall grow upon Acoma soil for the length of the memory of man!'

Tecuma stared woodenly at the spread of congealing delicacies. The shatra crest painted upon the dishes seemed to mock him by repetition, for Buntokapi's rash words, which he himself had forced the wife to repeat, had swept politics aside in an instant; now matters of honour lay at stake. Of all things, this unwritten code of Tsurani civilization could prove the most dangerous.

Should Almecho call the Oaxatucan, his family, to battle on a matter of honour, all other families of the Omechan Clan would be bound to support that assault, just as all members of the Hadama Clan were honour-bound to answer any call the Acoma made. This sworn duty to give aid was the primary reason open declarations of war were avoided; most conflicts were conducted and resolved within the framework of the Game of the Council. For as no other disruption could, open warfare between clans brought chaos to the Empire – and stability within the Empire was the first duty of the Great Ones. To begin a clan war was to invite the wrath of the Assembly of Magicians. Tecuma shut his eyes. The smell of meats and sauces made him feel ill; in vain he reviewed the list of permissible responses, while Chumaka fumed helplessly by his side. Both of them knew Tecuma's options were nonexistent. Almecho was one of the few Lords in the Empire with both the power and the intemperate nature to touch off an open clan war. And by the mores of tradition, Tecuma and the other families of the Hospodar Clan would be forced to stand aside and impartially observe the bloody warfare; his own son and grandson would be obliterated and he would be helpless to intercede.

The wine sauces in the dishes suddenly seemed symbolic of the bloodshed that might soon be visited upon the house of the Acoma. For the sake of a son and his infant son, war must not be permitted to happen. Mastering his urge to shout, Tecuma spoke calmly. 'My Lord Almecho, remember the Alliance. Open clan warfare means an end to your conquest on the barbarian world.' He paused to give that concept time to register, then seized upon the next available expedient to divert the Warlord's wrath: the senior Subcommander of the Warlord's invasion force upon the barbarian world was nephew to the Lord of the Minwanabi, and should there be need to elect a new Warlord in the High Council, Jingu of the Minwanabi's claim upon the succession would be strengthened, since the invasion army was already under his family's command. 'The Minwanabi especially would be pleased to see another upon the white and gold throne,' he reminded.

Almecho's colour remained high, but his eyes lost their madness.

'Minwanabi!' he nearly spat. 'To keep that dung eater in his place, I would endure much. But I will have your son grovel for my forgiveness, Tecuma. I shall have him belly down and crawling through needra soil to beg at my feet for mercy.'

Tecuma closed his eyes as if his head ached. Whatever had caused Bunto to utter such a destructive instruction was thoughtlessness and not any overt attempt to bring ruination upon himself and his family. Aching with shame and tension, he turned to Mara, who had not moved since the moment Lord Almecho had uttered his threats against her house. 'Mara, I do not care what orders Buntokapi left concerning the sending of messengers. Send for your litter and bearers, and tell your husband that his father demands his attendance here.'

Night was falling behind the screens, but no servants dared enter to light lamps. In the half-dark of twilight, Mara stirred and directed a look of open appeal at her father-in-law. Then, as if the gesture exhausted her, she nodded to Nacoya. The old woman said, 'My Lord Tecuma, my master Buntokapi expressed himself upon that possibility as well.'

Tecuma felt his heart sink. 'What did he say?'

Nacoya complied without drama. 'My Lord of the Acoma said that should you come and wish to see him, we were to tell you to go piss in the river, but away from Acoma lands so that you don't soil his fish.'

There was a moment of utter silence; astonishment, anger, and naked shock moulded Tecuma's thin features. Then the stillness was rent by the Warlord's explosive laughter. 'Don't soil the fish! Ha! I like that.' Looking hard at the Anasati lord, Almecho said, 'Tecuma, your son has insulted his own father. I think my need for satisfaction will be answered. There is only one possible atonement for Buntokapi.'

Tecuma nodded stiffly, grateful that the deepening shadows hid his grief. By insulting his own father in public, Buntokapi had forever denied himself honour. Either he must expiate his shame by taking his own life, or Tecuma must renounce all blood ties and prove his loyalty was ended by destroying the disinherited son and all his family and retainers. What had begun as a political struggle between Tecuma of the Anasati and Sezu of the Acoma, resolved by Sezu's death, might now become a generational blood feud, one to match that which already existed between the Minwanabi and the Acoma. To separate the honour of the father from the transgressions of the son, the Lord of the Anasati would be obliged to kill not only Buntokapi, but the newborn Acoma heir, the grandson he had never seen, as well. The thought set him utterly at a loss for speech.

Aware of Tecuma's dilemma, Almecho spoke softly in the rapidly falling darkness. 'Either way, you lose your son. Better he takes the honourable path and chooses to die at his own hand. I will forgive his insults if he does, and will seek no further vengeance upon your Acoma grandson. I would not see our alliance further strained, Tecuma.' No words remained to be said. Turning his back on Mara, Nacoya, and the Lord of the Anasati, the Warlord signalled to his honour guard. The six white-clad soldiers snapped to attention, then wheeled and escorted their lord out of the great dining chamber.

Stunned to immobility, Tecuma did not immediately react. He stared unseeing at his half-eaten meal. It was Chumaka who briskly took charge, sending a summons to the barracks to ready his warriors to march. Slaves fetched the Anasati litter, and lanterns within the courtyard splashed the screens with brightness. Tecuma stirred at last. His jaw was hard and his eyes bleak as he looked to the Lady of the Acoma. 'I go to Sulan-Qu, wife of my son. And for the sake of the grandson I have not seen, may the gods favour Buntokapi with courage in proportion to his foolishness.'

He departed with a pride that hurt to watch. As he vanished into the shadows of the hall, Mara's exhilaration evaporated before a deep chill of fear. She had set a clever trap; now the jaws would close in whatever manner the gods decreed. Thinking of Bunto, by now half-drunk and laughing on his way to his evening's amusements in the gambling halls with Teani, Mara shivered and called for servants and light.

Nacoya's face seemed ancient in the new light of the lamps. 'You play the Game of the Council for high stakes, my Lady.' This once, she did not chide her charge for taking foolish risks, for Buntokapi had been no favourite among the Acoma retainers. The nurse was Tsurani enough to relish the discomfort of an enemy, though her own plight might be dire as a result.

Mara herself felt no triumph. Shaken, worn thin with the stress of month after month of manipulation, she relied on Papewaio's stolid presence to steady her inner turmoil. 'Have the servants clear away this mess,' she said, as if the ceremonial plates and dishes had been brought out for an ordinary meal. Then, as if impelled by primal instinct, she half ran to Ayaki's chambers to see that the boy slept safely on his mat. Sitting in the gloom by her baby, she saw in the shadowed features of her son the echo of the father, and for all the causes Buntokapi had given her to hate, still she could not escape a deep, brooding melancholy.

Mara waited in Buntokapi's quarters, passing a restless night in the chamber which once had been Lord Sezu's, but which now reflected the tastes and preferences of one who, by marriage to his daughter, had succeeded him. Now the continuance of the Acoma relied upon this man's honour; for if Buntokapi remained true to the oath he had sworn upon the Acoma natami, he would choose death by the sword and spare his house from retribution. Yet if the loyalty of his heart remained with the Anasati, or if cowardice drove him from honour to mean-spirited vengeance, he might choose war and carry Mara and his infant son to ruin along with him. Then would the natami fall into the hands of Almecho, and the Acoma name be obliterated in shame.

Mara rolled restlessly on her side and tossed tangled sheets aside. Grey light glimmered through the screens, and although the needra herders had not yet stirred to drive the herds to meadow, daybreak was not far off. Without waiting for the assistance of her maids, Mara rose and slipped on a day robe. She lifted Ayaki from his basket and, shushing his sleepy wail, hastened alone into the corridor.

A large shadow moved, almost under her feet. Mara started back, her arms tight around her infant; then she recognized the worn, wrapped leather that covered the hilt of Papewaio's sword. He must have spent the night seated outside her chambers.

'Why are you not in the barracks, with Keyoke?' Mara demanded, relief sharpening her tone.

Papewaio bowed without offence. 'Keyoke suggested I stay by your door, Lady. Rumours had reached the barracks, through servants who overheard the Warlord's honour guard speaking among themselves. The anger of the mighty is never to be taken lightly, and I accept the wisdom of such advice.'

Mara began a heated reply, but recalled the assassin and stopped herself. Upon second consideration, she realized that Keyoke and Papewaio were trying to warn her, without breaking loyalty. Early on, they had recognized the possibility that Buntokapi might return home in a rage during the night. Had he done so, anger might have driven him to violence against her, a shameful act but not out of the question for a man who was quick-tempered, and young, and accustomed to wrestling and working out daily with arms. If such happened, and a warrior dared intercede between his mistress and his sworn Lord, Papewaio's life would instantly have been forfeit, all of his honour surrendered at a stroke. Yet Pape wielded a fast sword, and his memory of events in the marriage hut had not faded; at the least move against Mara, the Lord Buntokapi would have died between breaths. And no dishonour to the servant who had done the deed could reverse the grip of the Red God.

Mara smiled through her strain. 'You've earned the black rag once already, Pape. But if you choose to tempt the wrath of the gods a second time, I will be in the contemplation glade throughout the day. Send my Lord there if he arrives home and does not arm the Acoma garrison for war.'

Papewaio bowed, inwardly pleased by his mistress's tacit acceptance of his guard. He shifted his post to the arched entry of the contemplation glade and remained there as dawn gave way to sunrise and morning brightened over the rich holdings of the Acoma.

The noon heat came and went in sultry stillness, much as it always had. The sacred pool reflected a stone-bordered square of cloudless sky and the trailing foliage of nearby shrubbery. Ayaki slept in his basket beneath the tree by the Acoma natami, unaware of the dangers that hedged his young life. Unable to match his ignorant peace, Mara meditated and paced by turns. Even her temple discipline could not dispel recurrent thoughts of Buntokapi, in whose hands lay the fate of all things Acoma. Since he was born Anasati but sworn to uphold the honour of ancestors who had been enemies of his father, there was no knowing where his true loyalty lay. Through Mara's own machinations, his affections had been given over to his concubine, Teani; and Keyoke, Nacoya, and Jican all detested him for his excesses. The estate house had been his demesne and his dwelling, but his town house in Sulan-Qu was his home. Biting her lip, Mara stopped by the natami, where not even two years past she had sworn over stewardship of her father's name. She had then laid an intricate snare, whose bindings were that oath and the Tsurani concept of honour. These were fragile foundations upon which to base hope; for all his shortcomings, Buntokapi was no fool.

The shadows swelled, and slanted, and the li birds began to sing in the slightly cooler air of afternoon. Mara sat by the sacred pool and fingered a flower plucked from a nearby shrub. The petals were pale, delicate in the extreme; like her, they could be bruised and crushed with a clench of the hand. The servants might believe she had retired to the sacred glade to pray for deliverance from the shame brought upon her house by her husband. In fact, she had gone there to escape the fear in their eyes, for if the Lord of the Acoma chose war, their fates also hung in the balance. Some might die fighting, and they would be the fortunate ones. Others might lose all honour by hanging, and many would become slaves; a few might turn to the hills as outlaws and grey warriors. If the natami were stolen, all would know the gods' disfavour.

The shadows lengthened, and the flower wilted in Mara's hand, poisoned by the salt of her own nervous sweat. Ayaki wakened in his basket. At first content to bat his fat hands at the insects that flitted to feed on the blossoms above his head, he later grew fussy. The time for his midday meal had long passed. Mara tossed the dead flower away and arose. She plucked a ripened fruit from one of the ornamental jomach trees and peeled it for her infant. The boy quieted as he chewed the sweet fibre. Only then did Mara hear the footsteps approaching from behind.

She did not turn around. With Papewaio on guard at the gate to the glade, this would be no assassin. Priests of Chochocan did not enter unasked; gardeners did no work while master or mistress used the glade; and no other could enter without earning a sentence of death. The only person living who could walk these paths at this hour with impunity was the Lord of the Acoma. The fact that he had arrived home from his town house in Sulan-Qu without fanfare told Mara only one thing: he had seen his father, and his disgrace in the eyes of the Warlord and his insult to the house of his birth had caught up with him.

Mara eased the last bit of jomach into Ayaki's eager mouth. Aware that her hands were shaking, she made a show of blotting her sticky fingers just as Buntokapi reached the far side of the sacred pool.

He stopped on the walk, his sandals showering a fine spray of gravel into the water. Reflections shattered into a thousand fleeing ripples, and the li birds fell silent in the branches overhead. 'Wife, you are like the pusk adder of the jungles, whose markings are pretty enough to be mistaken for a flower when it lies at rest. But its strike is swift and its bite is fatal.'

Slowly Mara rose. She turned reluctantly, her fingers stained red with jomach juice; and she looked upon the face of her husband.

He had come from town at speed, without his litter of state, for his broad features were whitened with a thin layer of dust from the road. He wore a simple day robe, probably the same he had donned when his father's knock had roused him from bed; this, too, was filmed with dust, which hid the wine stains that spoiled the embroidery on one cuff. Mara's gaze followed the knotted cords of his belt, the well-worn leather of his sword, and the slice of muscled chest revealed through the opened collar of his robe. She saw the marks of Teani's passion still visible on the skin over his collarbone, and the hard set of his lips. Lastly she looked into his eyes, which showed a mixture of thwarted anger, childlike confusion, and longing.

Unaware that in the eyes of her husband she was beautiful and, in a strange way, untouchable, Mara bowed. The only words she could think to utter felt wrong.

Buntokapi stared at her with an intensity that hurt to witness. 'And like the pusk adder, my wife, your venom stops the heart. You play the Game of the Council with masterful precision. How could you know which face I would wear, the Anasati, whose blood and birth were mine, or the Acoma, whose honour I pledged to preserve with a vow?'

Mara willed her rigid posture to relax. But her voice shook ever so slightly as she said, 'The Acoma family is ancient in honour. No Lord of that name has ever lived in shame.'

Buntokapi stepped sharply forward, his legs easily spanning the breadth of the ceremonial pool. Towering over the slight form of his wife, he bent and caught her wrists. 'I could change that, proud woman. At a stroke, I could make the honour of your forebears as dust in the wind.'

Forced to look into his angry eyes, to feel the strength of a man she had not cherished, Mara needed all her will to hold steady. A minute passed heavy with threat. Then the darting play of the insects that fed among the flowers inspired Ayaki to spontaneous laughter. Buntokapi looked down and noticed the weals his handling had left on Mara's flesh. He blinked in embarrassment and let her go, and it seemed to her as she watched that something vital drained from him. Then he straightened, and a look that she had never known crossed his face.

'Perhaps I was wrong, the day we married,' said Buntokapi. 'Perhaps I am indeed as stupid as you and my father and my brothers believed. But for the sake of my son, I will die bravely as an Acoma.'

Mara bent her head. Suddenly she had to fight to suppress tears. For one brief instant she had perceived the man her husband might have been had he been raised with the love and the care that had all fallen to his elder brothers. The Lord of the Anasati might have done little to foster the potential of this, his third, son; but she had played upon Buntokapi's inadequacies until she achieved the end she had desired. Mara felt pain within; when she should feel triumph, she instead knew grief. For in this one moment she saw that Buntokapi's potential for greatness, now glimpsed like the hint of sunlight through clouds, should be wasted so soon in death.

But the poignancy of the moment lasted only a second. Buntokapi caught her arm in the bruising grip of a warrior and pulled her roughly to his side. 'Come, wife. Fetch our son from his basket. Before the sun sets this day, you shall both see what it takes to die like a Lord of the Acoma.'

Unthinkingly Mara offered protest. 'Not the child! My Lord, he's too young to understand.'

'Silence!' Buntokapi pushed her roughly, and distressed by his shout, Ayaki began to cry. Over the child's wails, the Lord of the Acoma said, 'I die for the honour of my son. It is right that he should remember. And you.' He paused, his lips curled in malice. 'You shall witness what you have wrought. If you would engage in the Game of the Council, woman, you must know that the pieces you manipulate are flesh and blood. For the future, if you continue, it is right that you should remember.'

Mara picked up Ayaki, hiding her distress in concern for her child. As Buntokapi's steps retreated from the grove, she paused, battling a strong urge to weep. She had thought she understood the stakes of her position when she grieved after the murder of her father and brother. But now Buntokapi had shown her the scope of her ignorance. Feeling humbled, and inexplicably dirtied, she held Ayaki closely. Her husband's command must be obeyed. Somehow she must find the resilience to weather the final, bitter fruits of her victory. If she did not, the Minwanabi waited with plans to ruin her, even as ruthlessly as she had plotted the downfall of Buntokapi to secure herself immunity from Anasati treachery.

The soldiers of the Acoma stood rigidly in a square, the plumes of the officers' ceremonial helms tugged by the gentle breeze that sometimes blew before sundown. Within the formation waited Keyoke, Papewaio, and another warrior sent by the Anasati to act as witness; and between them, clad in the red robes of ritual, bound with a sash of Acoma green, Buntokapi lifted a sword that was also red, and sharpened to the keenest edge Tsurani armourers could fashion.

Outside the square, but afforded a clear view by the slight rise of ground, Mara shifted Ayaki's warm weight to her other shoulder. She wished the proceedings were done with. Ayaki was wide awake and playful, tangling small fists in her hair and gown, and exclaiming brightly over the warriors in their colourful lacquered armour. Like all things Tsurani, even death had an element of ceremony. Buntokapi stood statue-still in the centre of the square, the blade that awaited his end in his hands, while Keyoke recited the list of the honours he had earned as Lord of the Acoma. The account was very short: one battle and a dozen wrestling matches. Mara swallowed stiffly, aware as never before how young her husband really was. Tsurani faces aged slowly, which made it easy to forget that Buntokapi was barely twenty, a scant two years older than herself.

Straight, still, every inch the warrior despite his bandy legs, he showed no weakness in his bearing, but something about his eyes reflected the desperate determination needed to see this moment through. Mara swallowed again and gently pried Ayaki's fingers off the lobe of her ear. He shrieked with laughter, ready for more of such play.

'Hush,' scolded Mara.

In the square, Keyoke finished his speech. He bowed deeply and said, 'Go in honour, Lord of the Acoma. Let all men remember your name without shame.'

As he straightened, each warrior simultaneously removed his helm. The breeze pushed damp locks back from sweating faces; emotionless eyes watched the sword Buntokapi lifted above his head.

Mara swallowed again, her eyes stinging with salty tears. She tried to think of Lano, sprawled and bloodied under the hooves of barbarian horses; but the sight of Buntokapi, standing in failing sunlight with his sword raised in final tribute to the gods of life, was far too real to put aside. Except for his crudeness in bed, and his explosive temper, he had not been an oppressive husband – had Mara used the same manipulations to mould him instead of destroy him . . . No, she commanded herself, there can be no regret. She called upon the discipline she had learned in Lashima's temple and banished such thoughts from her mind. Without expression she watched Buntokapi turn the sword and set the blade point against his stomach.

He offered no final words. But the eyes that met Mara's were dark with irony and a strange admiration mixed with the triumph of knowing she must live with this moment for all her living days.

'Before the sun sets this day, you shall both see what it takes to die like a Lord of the Acoma,' he had said to her in the grove. Mara's hands clenched reflexively in the folds of Ayaki's clothing as Buntokapi lowered his head. Large hands, clumsy on the body of a woman but capable in wrestling and war, closed on the red-laced leather of the sword. Lowering sunlight gilded the sweat on his wrists. Then his knuckles tightened. He took a swift, running step and dived forward. The pommel of the weapon rammed cleanly against the earth. The blade drove through his body. Hands and hilt struck his breastbone, and he grunted, his body gone rigid with agony.

He did not cry out. A sigh left his lips while the life bled swiftly through his fingers and mouth. As the spasms of his muscles slowed, and almost stopped, he turned his head. Lips caked with dust and blood framed a word that no man heard, and dead eyes stilled upon the figure of the woman and child who stood on the hillock above.

Ayaki began to wail. Mara loosened hands that gripped his young body too tight, and by the ache in her chest realized she had stopped breathing. She drew a painful breath. Now, mercifully, she could close her eyes. But the image of her husband's sprawled body seemed inscribed in the inside of her eyelids. She did not hear Keyoke pronounce the Lord of the Acoma dead, with all honour; instead, the phrases Buntokapi had spoken in the grove returned to haunt her. *'If you would engage in the Game of the Council, woman, you must know that the pieces you manipulate are flesh and blood. For the future, if you continue, it is right that you should remember.'* Confronted by a rising tide of implications, Mara did not notice the men who replaced their helms upon their heads and bowed to the departed. Time and events seemed frozen upon the moment of Buntokapi's death, until Nacoya's wiry grip caught her elbow and steered her purposefully back towards the estate house. The old nurse did not speak, which was a mercy, though Ayaki cried for what seemed a very long time.

Once she had donned robes of mourning, Mara retired, not to her bedchamber, as Nacoya preferred, but to the west-facing room that had been her father's study. There she watched the shatra birds fly across a sky brilliant with sunset. But the crimson colours only reminded her of Buntokapi's robes, and of the bloodied sword that had taken his life. As twilight fell, the servants lit the glass-shuttered lamps and closed the screens against the dew. Mara regarded the chamber that, as a child, she had considered to be the heart of her father's financial empire; the sanctum was no longer the same. The desk lay piled with documents pertaining to Buntokapi's gambling and betting exploits: most would be debts, as Mara knew from the woebegone manner assumed by Jican these past weeks. The screens bore new paintings, ones the late Lord had preferred to the hunting scenes Mara's great-grandfather had commissioned. These showed wrestlers and war scenes, and one, near the desk, showed a woman with ruddy hair.

Mara bit her lip in distaste. At first she had thought to restore the decor to the one she had known when her father and Lano were still living. Now, with the dust of the barracks unwashed from her feet, and Buntokapi's suicide still stark in her mind, she decided otherwise. Her childhood was behind her. Now, if the Acoma name were to survive, she must accept changes in herself, for the Game of the Council elevated the strong, while the weak perished or fell into ignominious obscurity.

A tentative knock sounded at the screen. Mara started, turned, and said, 'Enter.'

Jican hastened through the screen. For the first time in weeks, he carried neither documents nor needra tallies; his hands were empty, and in agitation he bowed and touched his forehead to the floor at the feet of the Lady of the Acoma. Startled, Mara said, 'Hadonra, please rise. I am in no way displeased with you or the way you have handled your duties under the rule of my late husband.'

But Jican only trembled and bent lower, a figure of abject misery huddled on the fine tiles of the floor. 'Mistress, I beg forgiveness.'

'For what?' Puzzled and trying to set the servant at ease, Mara stepped back and settled herself on the cushions where she and the hadonra had sustained many a lengthy discussion of estate finances in the past. 'Jican, please rise and speak plainly.'

The hadonra raised his head but did not leave his knees. He did his best to assume the proper Tsurani restraint, yet managed only to look contrite. 'Mistress, I bring shame to the Acoma. Strive as I might, I cannot –' He broke off and swallowed uncomfortably. 'Lady, grant me mercy, for I cannot feel grief as I should for the death of the great Lord. He passed with honour and bravery and deserves to be mourned. Yet, in honesty, I cannot feel other than relief.'

Mara lowered her eyes, discomforted by the hadonra's distress. She picked at a tassel that had torn loose from the corner of one cushion, and reflected soberly that she felt no true grief for Buntokapi. But the shock of the realities of the stakes she had manipulated left her shaken, unbalanced, and confused. Her conscience might sting for her deed, but she felt none of the tortures of cultural loyalty displayed by the man before her. In an analytical vein, she wondered whether this diminished her spirit.

The hadonra shifted uncomfortably, and Mara realized she must react, if only to speak some words of comfort that she could not genuinely believe. 'Jican, all know that you suffered great tribulations under the command of my late husband. He did not appreciate your virtues, and he did not heed the wisdom of your advice. You served in perfect loyalty while Buntokapi was alive. Now he is your ruler no longer, and I say wear the red wristbands of mourning. Act in seemly fashion, for tradition must be honoured, but trust your heart. If you cannot mourn, then at least honour Buntokapi's memory.'

Jican bowed low, his nervous manner reflecting profound relief. A harder mistress, he knew, might have asked him to take his life. But with time he had come to appreciate that Mara saw more than most rulers when it came to interpreting the mores of culture. And even her most dedicated adversaries must admire the boldness with which she had dispatched the Anasati threat.

Mara sat alone for long hours after her hadonra left. The feelings in her heart were far more difficult to sort than those of her servant. She watched the lamps burn low, and pondered, and sometimes dozed. Dreams came to her, of Lanokota wearing red, and of her father spitted on the points of barbarian weapons. Sometimes his body changed, became that of Buntokapi, and sometimes Lano lay in the dust while Keyoke pronounced him dead with all honour. At other times her mind was anguished by the sound of Ayaki's crying, which seemed to go on and on with no end. Towards dawn she woke, sweating and chilled. The candles had burned out, and moonlight streaked the screens, throwing silver-grey patterns on the tile. Mara lay still and, through the debris of her emotions, analysed the one fact that mattered. She felt sorry for Buntokapi, but she did not regret her choices. Service within the temple of Lashima might once have preserved the peace and purity of spirit she had known during girlhood; but having tasted power, and the thrill of the Game of the Council, she now knew she could never give them up.

Breeze rustled the akasi bushes, wafting the soft scent of flowers over the smells of ink and parchment. Mara lay back against her cushions, her eyes half-closed. In solitude, she granted her husband the one parting tribute she could believe in: he had shown her a moment of greatness, that afternoon in the glade. His own father had squandered that potential, and she had pandered to Buntokapi's faults, for her own selfish gain. Those things could not be changed. But the future lay like a blank parchment. Mara could ensure that Ayaki was raised differently, that the courage and strength of his father never soured into stubbornness. Once she had vowed to train out of Ayaki anything of Bunto, and to foster whatever was Acoma. Now she knew that Ayaki had gifts from

Buntokapi that would be foolish to waste. By loving him, and nurturing him, and letting him develop his gifts, she could raise a son of the Acoma that would make even the Anasati proud; and that she vowed would be so.

11

Renewal

Mara listened to the water.

The tiny stream that ran from the pool in the Acoma contemplation glade splashed softly as it rippled over rocks along its course. The wind gusted through the tree branches, a fitful sound that matched Ayaki's fussy mood. He looked on unsmiling as his mother raised the urn containing his father's remains. The ceremony of mourning was too much for his young mind to encompass; he knew only that the breeze chilled him, and his mother wouldn't let him crawl off to play.

Mara experienced neither sorrow nor regret as she poured Buntokapi's ashes into the hollow beneath the Acoma natami. Her husband was dead, and the Lord of the Anasati mourned a son, even if only a poorly loved third son. Tecuma's bitterness would be doubled, for Buntokapi's end had been contrived by one beyond reach; as mother of the only Anasati grandson, Mara was exempt from reprisal. Yet the girl herself felt no victory. Wind gusted sharply, tearing at her robe. Mara shivered. She must never allow herself to regret. What had been done was past, and necessary; to think otherwise was to be troubled by worse than her husband's angry shade. If doubts, even uncertainty, were permitted to grow, she risked paralysing her ability to make decisions in the future. That would surely consign the Acoma to eventual obliteration at the hands of enemies, for the Game of the Council would go on. Regret must be banished, despite her momentary sorrow, and indecision must be forever kept at bay.

For the second time in less than two years, Mara performed the ritual of mourning. Only now, instead of pain locked deep within, there was sadness. Sezu had taught that death was a part of politics, but now she understood that the forms were simply a rationale to justify murder. That awakening left her uneasy.

Mara sought comfort in a silent prayer, addressed to the shade of her husband. Buntokapi, she thought, for whatever rest it will bring your spirit, at the last you died with dignity. For a moment, no matter how briefly, you were worthy of the name Lord of the Acoma. For that I honour you. May your journey around the Wheel bring you better reward in your next life.

Now Mara rent her clothing, cut her arm, and placed ashes between her breasts. Ayaki stirred restlessly at her side, having tossed away the beads Nacoya had loaned to keep him occupied. Mara tore the baby's wrap and smudged ashes on his tiny chest. He looked down and made a face. Tough as his father, Ayaki would not cry when Mara pinched him; instead he stuck his lower lip out and scowled belligerently. With the ceremonial dagger Mara pricked the boy's forearm, earning a wail of protest to complete the ritual. She held Ayaki's arm over the pool, letting his blood mix with her own in the water.

Tears came easily then. Alone and free from the scrutiny of hovering advisers and servants, Mara admitted her inner fear: that she was not equal to the next round of the Game of the Council. The humiliation and pain she had suffered at Buntokapi's hands, the doubt and the anguish as she plotted his downfall, and each danger endured to survive the murder of her father and brother – all these might still be as nothing, blown away by the winds of circumstance and political fortune. The Minwanabi never slept in their hatred of the Acoma. Sometimes Mara felt helpless beyond hope.

Seeking the stability of the practical, she dressed Ayaki in the tiny ceremonial gown left for him. Then she donned her own white robe, silenced her wailing son, and carried him through the gusty afternoon to the grove's entrance.

The noise warned her first that visitors had arrived. Armour clanked in the yard, and the excited voice of a servant carried over the sigh of wind through leaves. Mara tightened her fingers around Ayaki's solid warmth, earning a wiggle of protest. Tense with apprehension, she stepped around the shielding hedges and almost collided with Keyoke's weaponed bulk. The old Force Commander had positioned himself squarely across the entrance, and by the keepers left loose on his buckles, Mara realized he had pulled his ceremonial armour on with the greatest haste. The visitors, then, would be significant.

'Anasati?' she queried softly.

Keyoke returned a terse nod. 'Papewaio and Nacoya await you, Lady. And Lujan oversees the arming of two companies at the barracks.'

Mara frowned. Keyoke would hardly have mentioned such precautions if Tecuma had come with peaceful intentions; her fears were confirmed as the Force Commander deliberately raised a hand and scratched his chin with his thumb.

Mara took a deep breath, ducking as Ayaki swung a playful fist. 'Lashima reward your foresight, Keyoke,' she murmured. And her pulse quickened as she stepped past the hedge, into view.

The yard was jammed with an assemblage of courtiers, warriors, and servants, all dusty from travel by road and wearing armour that was serviceable and plain, not the fancy enamelled style worn on state visits. A loud patch of colour in his house colours and plumes of mourning, the Lord of the Anasati sat patiently upon his litter, his adviser Chumaka at his right hand. Silence fell as Mara approached, Nacoya and Papewaio falling into step one pace behind. The Anasati soldiers assumed formal poses and formation as the Lady of the Acoma bowed, as slightly as possible without giving offence to one of Tecuma's rank.

'Welcome, father of my husband.'

'Greetings, *daughter*,' he said bitterly. 'I see the son of my son in your arms. May I view him?'

Mara felt a momentary pang of guilt. The presentation of a grandson should have been an occasion for joy. Instead, in a moment tense with unspoken antagonism, Ayaki was passed into his grandfather's outstretched arms. Engulfed in scented cloth and the sharp edges of gemstone decorations, the infant squirmed but did not cry. Tecuma regarded this stolid little face and said, 'He looks like Bunto.'

Mara nodded in agreement.

After a long moment of cuddling the child, Tecuma returned him in cold silence. Mara immediately relinquished him to the custody of Nacoya, who settled him as she had the boy's mother, after a mourning ritual many years before.

'Take my son to his nursery,' said the Lady of the Acoma. As the old nurse departed, Mara regarded the hostile face of her father-in-law. 'I offer the hospitality of the house.'

'No, daughter.' Tecuma qualified the word, all tenderness gone with Ayaki. 'I will not set foot in the house of my son's murderess.'

Mara almost flinched. With great effort she managed an impassive reply. 'Your son took his own life, my Lord, to satisfy the demands of honour.'

Tecuma bowed his head once, swiftly, in salute. 'I know, Mara. But I also knew my son. Despite his ineptness as a ruler, even he would never have contrived that insult to the Warlord and his own father. Only you could have brought such a thing to pass.' Something akin to respect coloured his manner for a brief instant. 'I salute your brilliance in the Game of the Council, Mara of the Acoma' – then his voice turned flint-hard – 'but for this one bloody victory you shall pay in kind.'

Mara measured Tecuma and realized that grief and anger were making him say more than he might under normal circumstances. Inwardly she cautioned herself. 'My Lord, I merely obeyed my husband and Lord and repeated to you the commands he gave me, before witnesses.'

Tecuma waved away the objection. 'Enough. It does not matter. My grandson inherits the mantle of the Acoma, and he shall ensure a loyal tie between my house and his.' At this a man stepped forward from the Anasati retinue, a thin, predatory fellow with shrewd eyes and a belt of enamelled caro hide. The Lord said, 'This is Nalgara, who shall act on my behalf until Ayaki is of age.'

Mara was not caught off guard. 'My Lord, no.'

Tecuma's eyes narrowed. 'I did not hear you say that.'

Mara resisted showing weakness by offering justification. 'You will take this man with you when you leave.'

Armour rattled among the Anasati warriors as hands reached for weapons, and Tecuma's arm trembled, ready to signal an attack. 'Woman, you dare?'

Hoping that Lujan had had time to arm her own companies, Mara held her ground. 'No, my Lord. I demand.'

Tecuma abandoned his pretence of politeness. 'I shall decide how Ayaki's legacy is to be managed. I am Lord of the Anasati.'

'But these are Acoma lands,' Mara interrupted, her voice ringing with an anger all her own. 'My Lord of the Anasati seems to forget that his son was Lord of the Acoma. *And the Acoma have never been, are not now, and shall never be vassals to the Anasati.* Your grandson is now heir to the title of Lord. As his mother, I am again Ruling Lady of the Acoma until the day he comes of age.'

Tecuma's face twisted with suppressed rage. 'Woman, do not seek to anger me!'

'It appears my Lord is already angry, so that what I say could have little consequence.' Stalling for time, Mara searched for a glimpse of green between the weaponed ranks of the Anasati guard. But the retinue pressed too closely together to allow any view of Lujan's men. She had no choice but to continue. 'When Bunto assumed Acoma Lordship, he ceased to have any obligations to you save those he freely chose, as you must have known, Tecuma, *for your son could not swear oath before the Acoma natami until you released him from fealty*. Show me a document, any document, appointing you as guardian for Ayaki in the event of Bunto's death and denying me my right to inherit. Then I will step aside. But without lawful evidence, you are not ruler of the Acoma.'

The slightest twitch of Tecuma's lips revealed a frustration he dared not express.

Mara hastened to drive home her point, before the confrontation turned to violence. 'We are not of the same clan, so you have no call upon the Acoma. You don't even have a political claim on our loyalty. Bunto never sought to change our alliances, so the Acoma are still members of the Jade Eye Party, not the Imperial. You have no authority here, Tecuma.' She motioned with her hand then, on faith, and to her immense relief Lujan and three dozen Acoma soldiers stepped forward, ready to defend their mistress. To the rear of Tecuma's party, another fifty soldiers had gathered in battle armour, ready for instant action should there be cause. Mara finished with a smile of irony. 'Once again I rule the Acoma, until Ayaki is twenty-five years of age.'

The Lord of the Anasati prepared to speak, but his adviser, Chumaka, intervened. 'My Lord, she is correct. Such is the law.'

Balked, Tecuma paused a long minute, his eyes distant with calculation. 'Then what of the boy if you die?'

In even tones Mara said, 'Then Ayaki is ruler of the Acoma, as I was before the age of twenty-five, ready or not.'

Tecuma made a subtle gesture, indicating that Mara was once again a woman alone against enemies. 'The boy will surely die.'

But the threat failed to move the young Lady, who stood defiantly straight. 'At the hands of the Lord of the Minwanabi, or some other seeking to rise over Acoma bodies, perhaps.'

Tecuma conceded defeat. 'Very well, *daughter*. You have made your point. I shall endeavour to keep you alive, at least until Ayaki comes to his majority. But if you make any move that I judge a menace to the Anasati –'

'Do not threaten me in my own house, father of my husband,' Mara warned. 'I could end this here and now.' She pointed to Lujan and the soldiers who waited ready to answer their mistress's command. The odds against Tecuma were now overwhelming, with only a score of soldiers to protect him against the possibility of attack by two companies. Were he to press the issue, he could die very quickly.

Mara regarded the stiff features of her father-in-law. 'I have no wish to be at odds with you, Tecuma. Your differences with my father were strictly political.' With a sigh more eloquent than words, she shook her head. 'We both know that what I have done was also a matter of politics.

'Should you die here . . . Jingu of the Minwanabi would be without any real rival in the game. No, I do not ask you to be my ally. I just wish you not to be my foe.'

The fist Tecuma had raised to signal his soldiers relaxed and lowered. He regarded Mara keenly. 'Minwanabi . . . yes. Already he thinks himself powerful enough to move against me.' The Lord of the Anasati sighed, at last acknowledging the quiet strength in Mara's stance. 'Perhaps you can make some difference.' He shook his head. 'I underestimated you. Perhaps Jingu will do likewise.'

After a silent minute he bowed to take his leave. 'Very well, Mara. You have my word on this, then; so long as Ayaki lives, I will not oppose you when you seek to discomfort the Minwanabi. But I make no such assurances where Anasati interests are concerned. We still have many differences. But once my grandson inherits the mantle of the Acoma, Lady, you shall find my memory is long. Should any harm befall him before then, from that instant your life will be measured in minutes.'

Curtly Tecuma signalled his retinue to assemble for the journey back to Sulan-Qu. Wind tugged at the officers' plumes, and streamed through Mara's dark hair as she watched the Anasati lord and his followers muster and march from the yard. The first part of her plan had been successful. For a time the second most powerful of her father's enemies had been neutralized; even more, made a reluctant ally. There were not many in the Empire who would tempt Tecuma's wrath by harming his grandson; only the Lords of the Keda, Xacatecas, and Minwanabi, and perhaps one or two others. Most would refrain, if only to see that the Lord of the Minwanabi did not grow too powerful. As Jingu's enemy, Mara had value, if only to keep him occupied. And despite the protection she had garnered from Tecuma, Mara knew the blood feud would go on. She had only forced her family's greatest foe to move cautiously. No more bungled assassinations, of that she was certain. Attack would come, but for the first time since Keyoke had fetched her from the temple, the Lady of the Acoma felt that she had gained a measure of time. She must be diligent about how she used it.

Turning her mind to the tasks before her, Mara dismissed Lujan and his warriors. With Keyoke and Papewaio at her side, she returned to the cool and the comfort of her chamber. First upon her agenda the next day was a journey to Sulan-Qu, for if Arakasi's information was correct, a Minwanabi spy resided in the town house owned by the Acoma. Buntokapi's concubine, Teani, must be dealt with at the earliest opportunity.

The erstwhile Lord of the Acoma had avoided the fashionable quarter of town for his dwelling. The side street where it lay was tidy and quiet, removed from the noisy thoroughfares of commerce, but still an easy walk to the public wrestling arenas. Mara stepped from her litter, sandals crunching gently over ulo leaves, which shed seasonally during the dry months. Accompanied by a retinue that included both Papewaio and Arakasi, she stepped up to the wide doorway whose posts were carved into the decorative forms of warriors in battle array. A strange servant opened the screen.

He bowed deeply. 'I bid the Lady of the Acoma welcome.'

Mara acknowledged the greeting with the barest wave of her hand and stepped across the threshold into shadow tinged scarlet by the sunlight that filtered through the hangings. An aroma of sweet spices filled the air, mixed with furniture oil and a woman's perfume. The house staff, numbering four, sank to their knees, awaiting Mara's command as she surveyed the fine rugs, a shell-inlaid weapons rack, and chests enamelled and set with red gems.

Her husband's town house was a cosy enough nest, she decided. But the taste and the decor of the place were influenced by a mind other than that of her late husband. Buntokapi would never have set marble statues of nymphs by the doorway, and the paintings on the screens were of flowers and graceful birds, not the battle scenes he invariably chose for himself.

Mara waited until Papewaio and Arakasi reached her side. The sword carried by the former was not for show, and the latter wore an officer's plumes, to disguise his true purpose; but in the end Mara did not require the Spy Master's guidance to spot the woman who had won her husband's heart, all for the motive of spying for the Minwanabi. Though Teani bowed submissively with the other servants, she could never be mistaken for other than Buntokapi's mistress.

Mara studied her profile and understood her husband's obsession. The concubine was a truly beautiful woman, with unblemished skin and hair touched by sun-gold and red – though Mara suspected that effect might have come from artifice rather than nature. Even though she was kneeling, the light silk of the concubine's robes draped a ripe, soft figure with breasts that were high and well formed despite being large, a small waist, and flaring hips. Mara's own body seemed boyish in comparison, and for no good reason the fact rankled. For every minute Buntokapi had been gone from the estate, his wife had thanked the gods; yet now the stunning beauty of the woman he had preferred irked Mara. A voice remembered from the temple warned, 'Beware vanity and false pride.' Mara almost laughed. Yes, she was feeling wounded vanity and injured pride. And yet fate had been kind in an odd and unexpected way.

Jingu of the Minwanabi had sent this woman to further his plot to destroy the Acoma. But instead, Teani only managed to distract Buntokapi, enabling Mara to realize her plans more quickly. And the ultimate aim of those plans was the strengthening of House Acoma . . . and the destruction of the Minwanabi. Mara savoured the irony in silence. Teani must go back to her master ignorant that her true role had been uncovered. Let Jingu think this woman had been banished by a jealous wife.

Prudently, Mara motioned for two of her soldiers to stand guard by the door. Then, stepping ahead of her bodyguards, but keeping carefully beyond reach of a knife thrust, she spoke to the kneeling concubine. 'What is your name?'

'Teani, mistress.' The woman kept her eyes cast downward.

Mara distrusted her subservience. 'Look at me.'

Teani raised her head, and Mara heard a slight stir from the warriors who looked on. The concubine's golden, heart-shaped face framed lovely eyes, almost amber in colour. Her features were perfect, and sweet as the honey in the hives of the red-bee. But beyond beauty, Mara saw something that made her hesitate. This woman was dangerous, as much a threat as any player in the Great Game. Yet the Lady of the Acoma spoke no hint of her conclusion aloud. 'What are your duties?'

Still upon her knees, Teani said, 'I served your husband as a maid, mistress.'

The Lady of the Acoma almost laughed at the woman's brazen act. To call herself a maid while sitting upon her heels in a robe more costly than any Mara owned save for her ceremonial attire was an insult to human intelligence. Brusquely Mara said, 'I think not.'

Teani's eyes narrowed slightly, but she said nothing. Then Mara understood: for the briefest instant the concubine had wondered whether her role as spy was discovered. To disarm any suspicion, Mara enquired after the other servants. 'What are your duties?'

The staff identified themselves as a cook, a gardener, and a maid, facts Mara already knew from the intelligence given her by Jican. She ordered the three of them to the estate and told them to ask the hadonra for new duties. They left quickly, glad to be avoiding the coming confrontation between their late Lord's wife and his mistress.

When the room was empty save for Mara, Teani, and the soldiers, Mara said, 'I think we shall have no need for your services at the estate house.'

Teani's poise remained admirably unbroken. 'Have I displeased my mistress?'

Mara stifled an urge to smile. 'No, on the contrary, you spared me a great deal of pain, inconvenience, and irritation over the last few months. Yet I am not as adventuresome in my tastes as some ladies of great houses; my appetites do not turn towards members of my own sex.' She glanced at the fading bruise that mottled the skin over Teani's collarbone. 'You seem to have shared my husband's taste for . . . rough sport. Your talents would go to waste on my estates – unless you think you would care to entertain my soldiers?'

Teani's head jerked, ever so slightly; she managed not to expel her breath in a hiss of anger, and Mara was forced to admiration of her action. The insult was great; as a courtesan or mistress, Teani would have a certain legitimacy in Tsurani society. In ancient times there had been little difference between a lord's courtesan and wife in Tsurani culture. Had Mara died before her husband, any real courtesan of Buntokapi's might have been permanently installed in the Acoma house. And if Teani survived both wife and master, a Ruling Lord's resident mistress had certain legal rights and privileges of inheritance. A woman of the Reed Life was considered a craftsperson or even an artist in the ways of pleasure. But a camp follower was a woman of the meanest class. Anywhere but in a camp of war, the women who followed the armies of the Empire were shunned and despised. And they had no honour. Teani had been named a whore, and if the women had been warriors, Mara would now be fighting for her life.

The concubine only glared at Mara. Struggling with her self-control just enough to convince, she pressed her forehead to the floor, red-gold hair almost brushing the toes of her mistress's sandals. 'My Lady, I think you misjudge me. I am an accomplished musician and am skilled in the arts of massage and conversation. I know the seven ways to rid the body of aches and pain: by pressure, by stroking, by rubbing, by herbs, by smoke, by pins, and by realignment of the joints. I can quote passages of the sagas from memory and I can dance.'

No doubt the woman was capable in all the named skills, though Buntokapi had probably availed himself of little other than an occasional massage, or a song before indulging in sex. But Teani was also an agent and, likely as not, a trained assassin. With Buntokapi dead, she needed only one opportunity to rid her Minwanabi master of both Mara and Ayaki, ending the Acoma forever.

Dread of Jingu's plots caused Mara to respond sharply. Not allowing Teani the courtesy of rising from her knees, she said, 'You'll have little difficulty finding yourself another position. A maid blessed with such talents as yours should easily catch the fancy of some great Lord, one who would be eager to have you at his side.

Within the hour a factor will arrive to close down this house in preparation for selling it and all the furnishings. Take whatever gifts my husband left you and depart, for nothing of the Acoma shall remain here.' She paused and regarded Teani's ripe curves with contempt. 'And of course no trash shall be left behind for the new owner.'

Mara spun and walked through the door, as if the concubine she had dismissed were now beneath her notice. Only the observant eyes of Arakasi saw Teani release the iron control she had exercised for the deception of her mistress. An expression of naked hatred settled upon the young woman's face; her beauty became a cruel thing, black and twisted and murderous to behold. And in that moment Arakasi observed that the insults of Mara of the Acoma would be carefully remembered, that each might be separately avenged.

Borrowing the authority of his officer's plumes, the Spy Master seized the initiative and assigned two warriors to remain on the premises to see his Lady's orders carried out. Then, before Teani had bridled her rage enough to remember his face, he slipped swiftly through the door.

Outside, as he hurried into place beside his mistress, Mara said, 'Is she the one?'

Arakasi unhooked the chin strap of his helm so he could speak without being overheard. 'Indeed, my Lady. Teani is the spy. Until she arrived in the city, she was a favourite with the Lord of the Minwanabi and shared his bed on a regular basis. Why she was chosen to spy upon Lord Buntokapi is not clear, but she must have convinced her master she could serve his interests.' They reached the litter, dead leaves obscuring the conversation from chance eavesdroppers. Even on the quietest side street, Arakasi exercised his customary caution. As he helped Mara onto her cushions, he whispered, 'What Teani did before she came to Minwanabi service our agent there cannot say.' He directed a meaningful glance at the town house. 'I will rest easier when my men have had the chance to discover more about her, for I think you have made an enemy, Lady. Only I saw the expression in her eyes as you left. It was murder.'

Mara rested her head back, eyes half-closed. Wisely or not, she dismissed the issue, for the next step in her plans demanded all of her attention. 'Kill me for duty, kill me for personal reasons, the risk is no more.'

Her slender body stiffened against the jostling motion as the slaves lifted the litter. Arakasi fell into step, with Papewaio on the other side. Over the tramp of marching feet he murmured, 'There you are wrong, mistress. Some might falter in their resolve if they are motivated solely by duty. But to avenge a personal slight, many care nothing if they perish, as long as their foe dies with them.'

Mara opened angry eyes. 'You are saying I acted the fool?'

Arakasi did not flinch from her regard. 'I suggest that in future my Lady weighs her words with more caution.'

Mara sighed. 'I shall take your advice to heart. If Keyoke had been with me, he would probably have been frantically scratching his chin with his thumb.'

'That's Papewaio's habit,' said Arakasi, obviously puzzled.

His mistress smiled. 'Your observation is very keen. One day I shall have to explain that warning sign to you. Now let us go home, senior officer, for the heat grows even as we speak, and much business remains to be attended to.'

Arakasi saluted smartly. Playing the part of an Acoma Strike Leader brazenly, for all present knew of his inept swordplay, he ordered the guards to surround the litter bearing the Lady of the Acoma during her return to the estates.

As late afternoon painted purple shadows across the paving, another litter set out through the north gate of Sulan-Qu. Once on the Imperial Highway, the bearers wearing the badge of the Guild of Porters turned towards the Holy City. They maintained a leisurely pace, as if the client behind the curtains wished their services for sightseeing and a breath of fresh air in the countryside. When, after two hours, she ordered a stop for rest, the bearers gathered by a roadside well a short distance off. They were all freemen, members of the Commercial Guild of Bearers, hired by those who needed to travel but without a retinue of slaves to carry them. Granted rest an hour ahead of contract, they munched upon the light fare carried in their hip bags and whispered admiringly of the woman who had commissioned them for this journey. Not only was she stunningly beautiful, but she had paid them fine metal for what so far had proved an exceedingly easy job.

Presently a pot seller stepped out of the general flow of traffic, his wares dangling from thongs that affixed them to a long pole balanced across his shoulder. He halted beside the litter, apparently to catch a breather. His angular face was red from exertion, and his eyes beady and quick. Attracted by the rattle of his crockery, the woman behind the curtains motioned him closer. Pretending to examine a pot, she said, 'I am glad you had not reached Sulan-Qu yet. It would have complicated things.'

The trader mopped his brow with a fine silk cloth. 'What has passed?'

The woman curled her pretty lip and let the pot fall with a sour clank. 'As I suspected. The Acoma bitch would not allow me into her household. Jingu was a fool to think she might.'

The pot seller who was not a merchant exclaimed in annoyance and examined his piece for chips. When he found none, his manner appeared to ease. 'The Lord of the Minwanabi listens to his own counsel first.'

The woman traced the fancy enamel ornamenting a slop jar with an exquisitely manicured nail. 'I will return to Jingu's side. He will regret this setback in getting an agent into the Acoma house, but he will have missed me.' Her lips shaped a dreamy smile. 'I know there are things he misses about me. None of his other girls have my . . . skills.'

Drily the pot seller said, 'Or perhaps they simply lack your tolerance for abuse, Teani.'

'Enough.' The concubine tossed tawny hair, and her robe fell open. A glimpse of what lay beneath made the pot seller smile at the contradiction between the astonishing beauty and the unexpected cruelty in this woman. Misreading his expression as male lust, and amused by it, Teani spoke, recovering his attention. 'Buntokapi was never of use to Jingu. Mara was truly in control, though she was clever in not letting her Lord discover that until too late. Inform our true master that I shall return to the Minwanabi house once again, and send him whatever information I may.'

The merchant nodded, rubbing uncalloused fingers over the wood of his pole. 'That is good. I have carried these damned ceramics since I left our Lord's river barge this morning, and I am glad to end this charade.'

Teani focused on him, as if enjoying his discomfort. 'Give me the slop jar,' she murmured. 'The bearers must believe I had a reason to speak with you.'

The man unhooked the item. Enamel flashed gaudily in the sunlight as he handed it to the woman, his attitude one of undisguised irony. 'One less to carry.'

'Why did you come yourself?'

The merchant grimaced, for the pole bore down unmercifully and he could not reach around it to scratch an itch. 'I dared trust no one else with the task. When my Lord's barge left the city last night, we simply poled upriver a few miles and tied up. He supposed you would still be at the town house; hence my disguise. None of us guessed the Lady Mara would be so quick to rid herself of Bunto's city property. She only quit the contemplation glade yesterday.'

Teani glanced towards the well where the bearers sat gossiping. She inclined her head in their direction. 'I think you had better order them all killed. One might mention this encounter.'

The merchant considered the eight men by the well. 'It will be messy, but worse if we risk discovery. Besides, if you are attacked by robbers along the highway, how can the Commercial Guild of Bearers fault you? I will make arrangements just before you reach the Minwanabi estates, so you can rush to the safety of Jingu's arms. Now, our master's instructions: despite all that has transpired, the Lady Mara is to be left untroubled.'

Teani stiffened in surprise. 'After Buntokapi's murder?'

'Our master commands this. We must not speak longer.' With an unfeigned grimace of distaste, the merchant shifted his clanking wares to his other shoulder.

Teani sat silently as he left, her professional detachment lost. Mara of the Acoma inspired a personal rage and hatred deeper than any she had previously known. The concubine did not trouble to analyse the cause. Born to a woman of the Reed Life, and cast into the streets at the age of six, she had survived by wits alone. Her unusual beauty had brought her quickly to the attention of men and she had barely escaped slavers on several occasions, despite having committed no crime to warrant such a conviction; in the dirtier alleys of the Empire, the niceties of the law might occasionally be put aside for enough money. Teani discovered early that to some men honour was negotiable. She learned abuse before love, and at twelve sold herself for the first time, to a man who kept her in his home for two years. He had been a twisted soul who took pleasure inflicting pain upon beauty. Teani had struggled at first, until suffering taught her to ignore her discomfort. In time she had killed her tormentor, but the memory of pain stayed with her, a familiar thing she understood. After that she had used beauty and natural wit to rise up society's ladder, choosing one benefactor after another, each more rich and powerful than the last. For seven years she had served her present employer, though never in bed as with previous masters. Beneath her soft beauty and cruel passions this Lord saw the stony hatred that motivated Teani; he had set those qualities to use against his enemy, the Lord of the Minwanabi, never once tempted to make the relationship other than professional for his own use. For this the concubine conceded her loyalty, for this master was unique among those she had met along the road of her life.

But only Buntokapi had touched her as a person. Before him Teani had taken little personal interest in the men she slept with or murdered. Though the Lord of the Acoma had been like a porina boar in a wallow, even to the point where he stank like one, rushing to take her with the sweat from his wrestling still rank on his body, he had understood her. Buntokapi had given her the pain she needed to survive, and the love she had never known in all twenty-eight years of her life. Teani shivered slightly at the memory of his hands, tearing at her soft flesh at the height of his passion; she had dug her nails into his back, even taught him to enjoy the pain himself. But Mara of the Acoma had ended that.

Teani's fingers tightened on the bright enamel of the slop jar, while anger built in her heart. Buntokapi had been tricked to his death, ruined by his natural tendency to count honour over life. Teani understood nothing of honour . . . but rivalry, that was a thing she knew well. That she-dog of a wife – innocent as a babe, Teani thought in disgust. How easily abuse would crack the cool façade of the Lady! What pleasure the concubine would find in humiliating Mara for hours, days perhaps, before giving her to Turakamu. Teani licked her lips, sweating lightly in the heat. The pleasure of dominating the Lady of the Acoma promised more than she could imagine from sex with any men she had known. But the ignoble way that Mara had evicted her from the town house cut off any immediate avenues of vengeance. Now Teani had no recourse but to resume her post as spy in Jingu's household. The obese Lord of the Minwanabi revolted her, and his fawning would be difficult to endure; but he and the Acoma were sworn enemies. Through him Teani thought to arrange her satisfaction. Mara would die, slowly and in torment, or shamefully if no other option availed. That the concubine's true master now wished otherwise affected nothing. Teani had changed employers many times in the past.

On that thought she tossed the slop jar violently among the cushions and signalled her bearers to return. As they crossed the road, the powerful, coarse body of the one in the lead caught her eye. He had fine muscles and a bullying manner to his walk. Excited by prospects of violence and vengeance, Teani decided to stop in a secluded glade down the road. She would have some sport; the man and his companions were going to die anyway, and not to use them for pleasure would be a waste of fine meat. Besides, a few extra marks on her face and body would convince Jingu that bandits had indeed molested her, and keep him from becoming suspicious. So thinking, Teani shivered in anticipation as the bearers lifted her litter and resumed their journey towards the Holy City.

Down the road to Sulan-Qu, the pot seller halted, as if to count whatever payment the fine lady had given him. From under a broad-brimmed hat he watched the litter depart, while silently pondering what made the woman dally before calling her bearers. The likely daydreams of a creature like Teani were not pleasant to contemplate. With a grunt of disgust he shifted the weight of his pots. He had been the one to convince their Lord her talents went beyond the bedchamber, and a dozen times in the past her work had born out his judgment. But lately she had been showing signs of independence, a tendency to interpret directions to her own liking. Alone in the dusty road, amid the noise of passing traffic, the sham merchant debated whether that trait signalled a growing instability. He soothed his uncertainty in his usual economical manner: either way, Teani could only bring trouble to the Minwanabi. If she exchanged loyalties, at best Jingu would gain a servant of questionable reliability. Besides, she could be removed if she became a problem.

Irritated by the weight of the pole as it bit into his shoulder, Chumaka, First Adviser to the Lord of the Anasati, turned towards

Sulan-Qu. Benefits would come of sending Teani back to the Minwanabi household; though she had surprised them all by turning up in Buntokapi's town house, Chumaka considered that things had turned towards a better course. His master would disagree, but then his master had just lost a son. Chumaka counted that for little. He had never much cared for Bunto, and while the Acoma girl was more talented than anticipated, Minwanabi was the real menace. Things were stirring in the High Council, and the game gained intensity as the Warlord's campaign on Midkemia continued. The ins and outs of intrigue always quickened Chumaka's blood. Gods, but I love politics, he thought as he walked down the road. Feeling almost cheery, he began to whistle over the rattle of his crockery.

Following her return from Sulan-Qu, Mara called a meeting. Her closest advisers gathered in her chamber while cool twilight veiled the fields and thyza paddies of the estate. Nacoya sat to her right, a red scarf tied over her hair in deference to Turakamu, into whose domain the late master had passed. Baskets of red reeds had been placed by every door in the estate house, in recognition of mourning, that the Red God might avert his eyes from those who grieved.

Mara wore traditional robes of the same colour, but her manner showed nothing of sorrow. She sat straight and proud as Jican, Keyoke, Papewaio, Lujan, and Arakasi made their bows and chose seats upon cushions arranged in a circle upon the floor.

When the last of them had settled, the Lady of the Acoma met the eyes of each in turn. 'We know what has occurred. None need ever again speak of it. But before we lay the memory of Buntokapi to rest for all time, I wish to say this. What has passed, what is to come as a result of what has passed, all responsibility rests upon my head. None who serve the Acoma need fear for one moment that they have acted without honour. If others in the Empire whisper of dishonour in corners, the shame is mine alone to bear.' With that, Mara closed the tally sheet on her dead husband. None would ever again wonder if they had betrayed their lawful Lord.

Almost briskly Mara turned to other matters. Though red as a colour flattered her, a frown marred her forehead as she addressed Keyoke. 'We must speed up recruitment of soldiers. The Minwanabi are temporarily thwarted, and we must use what time we have available to us to consolidate our position.'

The Force Commander nodded in his usual spare manner. 'That is possible, if we call every available young son, and if all of them respond. Some will answer the summons of other houses. My Lords of the Minwanabi and Kehotara are still trying to replace the three hundred soldiers they sent against us several months ago. I think we can add another two hundred safely, within the next two months – though they will all be unseasoned boys. The other three you ask for might take as long as another year to recruit.'

Mara had to be satisfied with this; Buntokapi had left some sizeable debts, and Jican had mentioned that time would be needed to rebuild the estate's capital. By the time the recruiting was completed, finances should have recovered enough to underwrite the expense of the new warriors' training. And with the reluctant alliance with the Anasati, few would dare attack, and none openly.

As always, Nacoya broke in with a warning. 'Mistress, as the Acoma gain allies and garrison strength, you must be especially cautious of indirect attacks.'

Arakasi agreed. 'Mistress, on the day your official mourning ends, you will surely receive invitations carried by marriage brokers on behalf of one suitor or another. When some of those worthy sons of noble houses come to call, agents of the Minwanabi are most certain to be among their retainers.'

Mara considered this with a hard expression. 'Then we shall have to ensure that such agents find nothing noteworthy to report back to their masters.'

The meeting went on, with Mara confidently assimilating her former role as ruler of the Acoma. As darkness deepened and lamps were tended by silent slaves, decisions were made and fresh information discussed; through the interval between nightfall and midnight, more business was conducted than during the entire tenure of Buntokapi as Lord of the Acoma. At the end Jican arose with a sigh of evident satisfaction. And whatever private guilt or relief the others might have felt at Buntokapi's passing was hidden as they arose to depart. There were too many new problems to confront.

As Nacoya, who was slowest, began stiffy to rise from her cushions, Mara gestured impulsively for her to remain. The others had nearly reached the door, but they stopped deferentially as she requested one thing more.

A mischievous glint lit the Lady's eyes as she studied the expectant faces of her senior staff. 'What would you think if I officially appointed Nacoya as permamént First Adviser to the Acoma?'

The old nurse gasped aloud, and Keyoke broke into a rare grin.

'The post has stood empty since Jajoran's death,' Mara said. Her amusement deepened as Nacoya, who never lacked for chatter, opened and closed her mouth soundlessly, like a fish.

Arakasi was first to respond, offering the aged woman a gallant bow. 'The promotion and the honour go well with your years, old mother.'

Lujan offered a rakish comment, but Papewaio had known Nacoya since he was a small boy, and his memories of her kindness ran deep. In total abandon of decorum, he lifted the old woman off her feet and spun her full circle through the air.

'Go and celebrate,' Mara called over her former nurse's startled yelp of delight. 'For never has a servant of the Acoma better deserved a promotion.'

'I'll have to survive the experience first,' said a breathless Nacoya. Papewaio set her down, delicately, as if she were made of cho-ja crafted glass; and as Keyoke, Arakasi, Jican, and a laughing Lujan crowded around to embrace the new First Adviser, Mara reflected that she had not seen such joy in the house since before her father's death. Lashima grant me wisdom to make it last, she prayed; for the Minwanabi threat was not ended, but was only forced back by an unstable alliance.

The traditional period of mourning came to an end, and the priests of Turakamu came to burn the red reeds that had sat in the baskets by the doors for three continuous weeks. Smoke still lingered over the Acoma fields when the first of the marriage brokers arrived, and within a day three ornately calligraphed petitions with wax seals lay piled in the study. Glad to be wearing a colour other than red, Mara called Nacoya and Arakasi into attendance and reviewed the top parchment. A thoughtful expression crossed her face. 'It seems our friend Minwanabi's favourite lapdog has an unmarried son. What do you know of him?'

Seated by her knee, Arakasi took the document she offered. The parchment had been perfumed, and the scent warred with that of the akasi blossoms beyond the screen. 'Bruli of the Kehotara. His father, Mekasi, has tried to marry him off twice, and both courtings have failed. Now the boy serves as a Patrol Leader in his father's army, though he's not a brilliant tactician, apparently. His company has drawn only garrison duty since he took command.' The Spy Master tapped the parchment, a faint smile on his face. 'I would not, however, count him a fool. We can expect he is a mask for another Minwanabi agent in his retinue, or an assassin in his own right.'

Mara recovered the parchment from Arakasi, her lip pinched tightly between her teeth. To refuse to consider the petition of Bruli of the Kehotara would be a public admission of weakness. 'They intend to shame me, or kill me,' she said, but the sick feeling of fear in her heart could not be heard in her voice. 'I say we take the bait and turn it sour.'

The slightest bit shy in her new role as First Adviser, Nacoya offered no comment; but Arakasi sat utterly still. 'That could be perilous, mistress. Bruli's father, Mekasi, is a gambler and not a good one. He lost enough that his estates are heavily mortgaged. His son is a vain boy who insists that everything he wears or uses be only of the costliest work, and his two older sisters and older brother were similarly indulged. Their spending on top of existing debts has nearly ruined their father. The Minwanabi cleared the accounts, but not out of charity. What makes Mekasi of the Kehotara truly dangerous is that his family tradition is sworn to the ancient code of Tan-jin-qu.'

Mara's hand tightened on the parchment, for she had not been aware of this detail. The code of Tan-jin-qu – the name was ancient Tsurani for 'lifelong' or 'until death' – meant that Mekasi had bound the Kehotara to the Minwanabi in an ancient form of vassalage, almost forgotten except as an historical oddity. By its terms, any pledge made was impossible to revoke, amend, or modify. If Mekasi of the Kehotara vowed obedience to the Lord of the Minwanabi, he would murder his children without hesitation upon Jingu's order. As betrayed alliances were common fare in the Game of the Council, Tan-jin-qu made the Kehotara as dependable as if they were part of the Minwanabi household, even more dependable than families in the same clan. Only when Mekasi died and his eldest son assumed the mantle of Lord could the family negotiate a new beginning. Until then the Kehotara could not be threatened, bullied, bought, or bribed to betray the Minwanabi.

'Well then,' said Mara, a determined set to her shoulders, 'we must make sure this Bruli is entertained in a manner befitting his station.' Arakasi looked keenly at his mistress.

Trying to seem bland, for Mara's suggestion was no trifle, Nacoya said, 'I assume you intend to grant this petition a hearing?'

'Of course.' Mara seemed distant. 'We must not be hasty in rebuffing this overture. Do we wish to offer insult to so august a personage as the Lord of the Kehotara?'

'Then you have a plan.' Arakasi smiled slowly.

Mara responded without humour. 'No. But I will have, by the time this minion of Jingu's presents himself – that is, if your agents can gather me all the information they have on Bruli and his family, before his retinue arrives.'

Forced to admire her boldness, Arakasi leaned forward. 'It will be costly. You shall have to cover the expenses of the fastest runners in the Guild of Porters, and these must be sworn and bonded, so that their messages cannot be intercepted or tortured from them.'

'Of course,' answered Mara, though Jican would howl. Men willing to die for the integrity of the messages they carried could not be hired for other than cold metal. 'See to this at once, Arakasi.'

The Spy Master rose swiftly, his steps buoyed by exultation. This was what his network was intended for! A bold player of the game who was unafraid to carve out the advantage; and the bonus was that Mara's target was an ally of the Minwanabi. Suddenly the day seemed perfect.

Darkness sprang into light as the screens were thrown open, admitting the petitioner for marriage into the great hall of the Acoma. Bruli of the Kehotara was almost beautiful in his black-trimmed red armour; and from the dais at the head of the hall, under the weight of her massive ceremonial costume, Mara saw at once that Arakasi's agents had reported accurately. The man was vain as a calley bird. He had good reason to be; slender yet muscular, whereas the majority of men in the three central nations of the Empire tended towards the stocky, he moved with the grace of a dancer. His blue eyes were a rare and startling counterpoint to his almost black hair, and he had a warm smile. That he would happily murder as soon as marry the woman he approached on the dais was not far from Mara's mind as she wistfully considered, for just a moment, how different Bruli was from Bunto.

As if reading her mind, Nacoya leaned close and whispered. 'He'd spend more time looking at himself in the mirror than looking at you, daughter.'

Mara resisted a smile. Her pose remained outwardly formal as she welcomed the second son of the Kehotara to her house.

Two unprepossessing Kehotara warriors accompanied Bruli's litter, while another six were housed with Acoma soldiers. Mara was certain the honour guard had been picked for their homely appearance, to heighten the contrast to their master's handsome features as they marched into the Lady of the Acoma's presence.

One of the soldiers stepped forward, acting as Bruli's First Adviser. 'Lady Mara, I have the honour to introduce Bruli of the Kehotara to you.'

Nacoya returned the ritual reply. 'The Lady Mara welcomes so honoured a guest as Bruli of the Kehotara into our presence.'

At that moment the small form of the runner slave appeared through a side door. He carried a baton marked with white ribbons, signalling the arrival of a message. Mara feigned a struggle to hide relief. 'Bruli,' she said quickly, 'you are welcome in our home. Please ask for whatever you wish from our servants. They will see that you are comfortable. Now, if you will excuse me, the press of business cannot be long ignored by the Lady of the Acoma. I will see you again, perhaps tomorrow?'

She rose, revealing a slenderness hidden until now by the elaborate ceremonial dress. Her bow was peremptory, and she stepped precipitously through a side screen, leaving Bruli of the Kehotara with memorized words of poetry unsaid and a befuddled expression on his face.

Nacoya took over smoothly, according to plan. Knowing vanity to be the great weakness of this young noble, she stepped to Bruli's side, taking his arm and patting it in a motherly manner.

Bruli's gaze hardened, still fixed upon the doorway through which Mara had departed. 'Mother of wisdom, the Lady's behaviour borders on insult. What matter of business could not wait for my humble words of praise?' Bruli paused and touched his hair to reassure himself that he had not mussed it when he removed his helm for his bow. 'Surely something more has caused the Lady Mara to rebuff me in so abrupt a manner. Tell me, what is amiss?'

Nacoya resisted a smile while steering the pretty man towards a side chamber prepared with tables of wine and fruit. 'Young sir, come take some refreshment. Then I will tell you what I have mentioned to no other, for I think you handsome and well mannered. Lady Mara is a young girl, despite being a widow. Her father, brother and husband were all warriors, fine warriors, but they are all she has ever known. She is weary of men in armour. If you wish to court her favour, return at once to Sulan-Qu and seek the best tailors there. Have them fashion lovely robes of soft weave and jaunty colours. I think if you appeared tomorrow with the look of the scholar or poet, not the warrior, that is more likely than anything to change her cold reception to your advances.'

Bruli's forehead knitted in thought. To be a warrior was the highest goal of any Tsurani male, but women had all sorts of odd notions. His blue eyes came alight. 'Thank you, ancient mother. Your advice is sound.' He sighed in self-reproach and accepted the wine Nacoya offered. 'Had I wits, I would have anticipated this. Of course, it is now obvious. I shall return tomorrow and Mara shall see how gentle I can be, a man of refinements and grace, with no need of armour and arms to proclaim my manhood. Thank you.'

Nacoya patted Bruli's sleeve, her brow disingenuously furrowed. 'And music, I think. My lady would be impressed with any man who showed interest in the fine arts.' Bruli nodded and handed his empty glass to a servant. 'My thanks, old mother. Now, you will understand if I do not tarry. If I am to have new robes from the tailors, I must depart for Sulan-Qu on the hour.'

'You are a diligent suitor, worthy of the Lady's attention.' Nacoya clapped for servants to summon Bruli's litter and his guardsmen. There followed a comical bustle as Bruli rearranged his honour guard by height, that the picture they made while marching should seem bold and harmonious to the eye. When he had departed from the estates, for the first time in memory Nacoya couldn't contain herself. She crossed the hall to the door to Mara's quarters, doubled over. Then her laughter could no longer be stifled. Clapping a withered hand to her mouth in helpless desperation, she hurried to meet her mistress. Who but a Ruling Lady would have seized upon Bruli's vanity and worked that weakness into a plan? The Lords Jingu of the Minwanabi and Mekasi of the Kehotara would learn that matters of honour were not always settled with weapons.

Still chuckling, Nacoya entered Mara's quarters, where Jican and Arakasi were already meeting with the Lady of the Acoma. Mara looked up from a scroll and noticed the hand still pressed tightly over her First Adviser's mouth. 'You seem amused.'

Nacoya sat, slowly, her disarranged hairpins sliding further to one side. 'If a foe can be bested without bloodshed, what harm if a little entertainment can be derived from the act?'

Mara's interest sharpened. 'Then our plan is working, mother of my heart?'

Nacoya returned a spirited nod. 'I think I can keep Bruli busy for a week or so and spare you the need to insult the Kehotara. The idea we discussed looks promising.'

Mara nodded her approval, resuming her interrupted conversation with Jican. 'Did you say that Hokanu of the Shinzawai requests permission to call upon the Acoma?'

The hadonra consulted the parchment in his hand, which was of quality penmanship but not an ornamented petition for marriage. 'The Lord of the Shinzawai sends word that his son will be passing through on his way from their town home in Jamar to the main estates in the north. He begs leave to have Hokanu call upon you.'

Mara remembered Hokanu from the wedding, a striking, darkly handsome man about her own age. She did not need Nacoya's prompting to remind her that he had been one of the choices for her consort before she had selected Buntokapi.

Aware of Arakasi's intent expression, Mara asked the Spy Master's opinion.

'Hokanu's interest might be a wise thing to foster. The Shinzawai are among the oldest and most influential families in the High Council; the grandfather was Clan Kanazawai Warchief until he retired, then Kamatsu was. Two Warchiefs in succession from the same family shows rare deftness in clan politics. And they are not vicious players of the Game of the Council, but have gained position through skill and intelligence, with no blood feuds under way, and no debts. And they are the only major family beside the Xacatecas not in alliance with the Warlord, the Minwanabi, or the Anasati. But they are enmeshed in some plot of the Blue Wheel Party.'

So Arakasi, too, thought an alliance through marriage would benefit the Acoma. But Mara's interest was political only. 'What plot?'

'I don't know.' Arakasi gestured in frustration. 'My agents are not well placed for getting inside information on the Blue Wheel. I deduce a move is afoot to blunt the influence of the Warlord, since Blue Wheel sentiment within the council holds that Almecho commands too much power. Still, since Almecho's invasion of the barbarian world, that movement has all but ceased to exist. Even the Shinzawai provide support. Kamatsu's oldest son, Kasumi, is a Force Leader of the Kanazawai forces upon Midkemia' – the Spy Master frowned as he pronounced the foreign names – 'facing the armies of Crydee in the westernmost province of what the barbarians call the Kingdom of the Isles.'

Mara was always astonished at the amount of information Arakasi could remember, even down to seemingly trivial details. He never made notes or kept lists; other than coded messages disguised as normal business documents, he never permitted his agents to write their reports. And his intuitive guesses were uncanny.

'Do you think the Blue Wheel Party has changed alliance?' she asked.

'No.' Arakasi seemed certain. 'The world of Midkemia holds too many riches for one man's gain, and Kamatsu is too crafty a player of the game. I expect the Blue Wheel will withdraw support from the Alliance for War at a critical moment, leaving the Warlord dangerously overextended. If so, the aftermath should prove interesting.'

Mara reconsidered the note from the Lord of the Shinzawai in the light of this information and reluctantly decided to decline. Her plans for Bruli and the snarled state of Acoma financial affairs would prevent her from honouring Hokanu with the hospitality he deserved. Later, perhaps, she would send him an invitation to make up for the regret she must send now. 'Jican, instruct the scribes to answer with a polite letter informing the younger son of the Lord of the Shinzawai that we will be unable to offer our hospitality at this time . . . My Lord's death has left much confusion in the affairs of the estate, and for this we must humbly beg understanding. I will sign the parchment personally, for Hokanu is one I earnestly wish not to offend.'

Jican made a note on his tally slate. Then his brow furrowed with more than usual resignation. 'There is the matter of the late Lord Bunto's gambling debts, Lady.'

Tired of sitting, Mara rose and wandered over to the screen that opened onto the garden. Staring at the flowers, said, 'How much did he lose?'

The hadonra answered without hesitation, as if the numbers had haunted his sleep for some nights. 'Seven thousand centuries of metal, twenty-seven dimis, and sixty-five cintis . . . and four tenths.'

Mara turned to face him. 'Can we pay it?'

'Certainly, though it will limit capital flow for a season, until the next crop is sold off.' As if the matter pained him, Jican added, 'We shall have to deal in some credits.'

But the cho-ja craftsmen were starting to produce marketable jade; the time of debt would be short. Mara said, 'Pay them now.'

Jican made another note. 'Then there is the matter of the debt of the Lord of the Tuscalora.'

'What debt?' The Tuscalora lands bordered the Acoma holdings to the south, and to Mara's knowledge there had been no ties of business with the Ruling Lord for several generations.

Jican sighed. 'Your husband was a poor gambler, but at wrestling he excelled. He defeated the Tuscalora champion on four occasions, and Lord Jidu lost heavily each time. He wagered thirty centuries on the first bout, and paid in gems. The second bout was for five hundred centuries, and this he noted in a paper contract he since chose not to honour, for the next two bets were wagered double or nothing. His champion was beaten; it was the talk of Sulan-Qu for a week. At present the Lord of the Tuscalora owes the Acoma a total of two thousand centuries.'

'Two thousand! That would ease our finances considerably.'

Jican shrugged. 'If he has assets to pay – I have sent two polite reminders and received no answer at all, probably because the Lord has extended himself on credit until this season's crops are harvested for market.'

'Send a strongly worded demand, over my personal chop.' Mara looked away a moment, thoughtfully, then added, 'Much good will be lost if anyone thinks he may take advantage because a woman is again ruling House Acoma. Let the Lord of the Tuscalora know I require an immediate answer.'

Jican nodded. Mara allowed him to withdraw and, alone, considered the uneasy feeling that had arisen within her over the Tuscalora debt to the House of the Acoma. Her neighbour to the south had been of no consequence, neither ally or enemy. But his army was large enough to threaten Acoma safety should the matter of debt turn into contention between the two houses. But not to demand her rightful due was to invite gossip about Acoma weakness in every marketplace within the Empire. Mara sighed. The Lord of the Tuscalora was known for his touchy and belligerent temperament. He disliked backing down, which was why Buntokapi had led the man so far into debt to begin with. Mara hoped this one time Jidu of the Tuscalora would prove a reasonable neighbour.

Mara read the parchment, her throat tightening with anger and no small amount of fear. Arakasi, Keyoke, Papewaio, and Nacoya all waited silently as she finished the return message from the Lord of the Tuscalora. She sat silently for a long time, tapping the scroll against her fingers. Finally she said, 'We cannot ignore this. Keyoke, what would my father have done with a message like this?'

The Force Commander said, 'The men would be arming, even now.' He studied Sezu's daughter and added, 'I can march at your word, mistress.'

Mara sighed, taking no pains to hide her distress from these, her four closest advisers. 'I cannot accept this defiance and insult as a declaration of war, Keyoke. For us to engage in conflict with the Tuscalora would mean our destruction.'

Keyoke regarded her levelly. 'We can take his measure.'

Mara's brown eyes were unflinching as she met her Force Commander's stare. 'At what cost? The Tuscalora forces are not so inferior that we can march in and not suffer.' She shook her head. 'Shall we find ourselves where we were after Father and Lano died? This time our enemies will not be so slow to strike.' Her voice became thick with frustration. 'Everything I have built, all that I've endured, would be as nothing.'

Nacoya's old hand cut down in emphasis as she said, 'Then do nothing, Lady. The amount is not so large as to warrant putting yourself and Ayaki at risk. Deal with this insulting little man when you are better able.'

Mara became very still. 'No, I must do something. For us to ignore this rejection of our claim would be to announce to every house in the Empire that we are unable to answer insult to our honour.' She dropped the parchment on a side table, as if it were poisonous. 'This must be answered.

'Keyoke, have the entire garrison ready to march at first light. I wish the men marshalled as close to the border of the Tuscalora estates as possible without alerting his sentries.'

Keyoke inclined his head. 'The terrain there is unfavourable for a charge. We would need twenty minutes to reach the estate house should trouble arise.'

Mara stared grimly at the flower bed beyond the screen. 'It shall be as nothing to me if the assault takes five minutes or five hours. By the time you arrive, I would already be dead. No. We must carve our advantage through other things than strength of arms alone.'

There followed a discussion of tactics that extended long past dusk. Servants brought a repast that went largely untouched; even Arakasi's appetite seemed off. And in the end, when Keyoke and Papewaio had exhausted their knowledge of warcraft, Mara suggested another plan, the one that offered a dangerous hope.

Nacoya grew silent and white-faced. Papewaio sat stroking his chin with his thumb, over and over again, while Keyoke simply looked grim. But only Arakasi truly understood Mara's bitterness as she excused her advisers, saying, 'I will travel tomorrow to confront Lord Jidu. And if the gods are ill disposed to the Acoma, then our ruin will not be due to the plottings of the Anasati or the treachery of the Minwanabi, but to an honourless man's seeking to renege on a debt.'

12

Risks

Mara frowned.

She concealed her worry behind a fan of stiffened lace and voiced her desire to halt. Papewaio signalled the one other officer and fifty men in her retinue, and the bearers set her litter down in the dooryard of the Tuscalora estate house.

Mara pulled aside the curtains to gain a better view of her unwilling host. Jidu of the Tuscalora was a fat man, his face and jowls moon-round, and his eyelids long-lashed as a woman's. Both plump wrists were covered with jade bracelets, and the bulging cloth of his robe was sewn with discs of shell. He clinked like a tinker when he moved, and perfumes hung around him in a nearly visible cloud.

From Jican, Mara had learned that Jidu's profits came only from chocha-la bushes. The rare variety of chocha beans provided the most costly and desired confection in the Empire, and because of a freak concentration of minerals in his soil, the Tuscalora were blessed with the most outstanding plantation in the Empire. Had Jidu the wits to operate in an organized fashion, he would have been a wealthy man. Instead, he was merely affluent.

But poor estate management was no reason to presume the Tuscalora ruler was ineffectual. Lord Jidu's argumentative reputation had more than once led to bloodshed with his neighbours to the south. Only the Acoma strength, before Sezu's death, had blunted the man's aggressive nature. Mara came expecting trouble and hoping to avoid conflict. Even as she greeted Lord Jidu, her entire garrison, save a few guards along the outer perimeter of her property, were moving into place a short distance from the Tuscalora border. If the matter came to battle, Tasido and Lujan would lead a combined assault upon the Tuscalora, while Keyoke held the reserves to protect the home estate house. If Mara's contingency plan failed – if the battle went against her and the Acoma could retreat in time to minimize their fatalities – enough strength remained to keep Ayaki alive until his Anasati grandfather could rescue him. Mara put aside such thoughts. Under such circumstances, she would be dead and all would be in the hands of the gods – or Tecuma of the Anasati.

Warned of his visitor by a runner from his border guard, Lord Jidu bowed without stepping from the shade of his foyer. That Mara's honour guard came armed for battle did not ruffle him as he leaned casually against his doorpost and said, 'Lady Mara, your arrival is an unexpected pleasure. To what do I owe the honour?' His face became instantly impassive as his visitor ordered her warriors to stand at ease around her litter. The Lady clearly intended to stay, despite the fact that the Lord of the Tuscalora pointedly scanted courtesy by not inviting her inside for refreshments.

Chilled by the man's calculating eyes, Mara forced herself to begin. 'Lord Jidu, I have a note signed by you promising the sum of two thousand centuries in metal to my late husband. My hadonra has communicated with your hadonra regarding this matter several times in the last few weeks. When another request, *personally made by me*, was delivered to you, you took it upon yourself to answer with insult. I came to speak of this.'

'I'm not certain I take your meaning,' said the Lord of the Tuscalora. He made a show of tossing aside a fruit rind and, with a curt motion of his head, sent one of his servants swiftly into the house. The next instant the runner flashed out through a side entrance, sprinting for what surely would be the soldiers' quarters.

'I mean this,' said Mara with all the forcefulness she could muster. 'When you say you do not feel obliged to respond to my message and would be pleased if I would cease "nagging at you," you insult my honour, Lord Jidu.' Pointing an accusatory finger, she looked more the image of her father than she knew. 'How dare you speak to me like some fishwife by the riverside! I am the Lady of the Acoma! I will not abide such instruction from any man! I demand the respect I am due.'

The Lord pushed away from the doorpost, his manner no longer languid. Speaking as if to a child, he said, 'Lady Mara, betting debts are not usually settled so directly. Your late husband understood.'

Mara snapped her fan shut, certain the man was stalling her. The instant his garrison received the call to arms, his mockingly paternal solicitude would end. She swallowed, bitterly resolved, and answered with the pride of her ancestors. 'My late husband no longer rules, but I can assure you, had Lord Buntokapi received such impolite demands to "cease nagging," he would be challenging you over the point of his sword. Don't think I will do less if you do not apologize at once and make good the debt.'

Lord Jidu stroked his plump waistline like a man just rising from a feast. He watched Mara keenly, and his confidence warned her before the rattle of armour and weapons that a squad of Tuscalora soldiers hurried into view. Papewaio went tense by her side. These were not slack household guards but soldiers well seasoned by extended duty on the border. They stationed themselves at either side of the doorway, in an advantageous formation: in the event of attack, the Acoma bowmen would be forced to fire uphill, and into the glare of the sun.

Pulling himself up to the limit of his squat stature, Lord Jidu stopped stroking his stomach. 'If I avow that your demand for payment is an affront, what then, Lady Mara? To pester me for the sums due you implies I will not pay my debt. I think you may have insulted Tuscalora honour.'

The accusation caused the soldiers by the door to clap hands to their sword hilts. Their discipline was faultless; and their readiness to charge, a palpable tension in the air. Papewaio signalled the Acoma retinue, and as smoothly the Lady's green-armoured guard closed protectively about the litter, shields angled outward. Surrounded by men who sweated with nerves and determination, Mara resisted the need to blot her own damp palms. Had her father felt the same fear as he charged on the barbarian world, knowing his death awaited? Fighting to maintain an outward appearance of calm, Mara looked between the shield rims of her bodyguard and locked stares with the Lord of the Tuscalora. 'Then we agree we have a cause to settle.'

Sweat sparkled on Jidu's upper lip, yet his eyes were not cowed. He flicked his fingers, and instantly his line of soldiers crouched in preparation for a charge. Almost inaudibly Papewaio murmured for his own men to hold steady. But his heel scuffed backward in the gravel, and behind the litter Mara heard a faint rustle. The archer crouched there, beyond the view of the estate house, had seen the signal. Surreptitiously he strung his bow, and Mara felt fear like a blade in her heart. Papewaio was preparing to fight, and his instincts in matters of war were uncanny.

Still, Lord Jidu's reply all but unnerved her. 'You speak boldly, for one who sits deep in the heart of Tuscalora lands.'

Mara arose from her litter and stood motionless in the sunlight. 'If Acoma honour is not satisfied, blood must answer.'

The two rulers measured each other; then Lord Jidu flicked a glance over Mara's fifty guards. His own squad was three times that number, and by now his reserves would be armed and awaiting orders from their Strike Leaders, to rush the estate borders where scouts had earlier reported the presence of soldiers in Acoma green. The Lord of the Tuscalora lowered his brows in a manner that caused his servants to duck quickly inside the estate house. 'The blood spilled will be Acoma, Lady!' And the man's plump hand rose and signalled the charge.

Swords scraped from scabbards, and the Tuscalora archers snapped off a flight of arrows, even as their front ranks rushed forward. Mara heard battle cries from the throats of her own soldiers; then Papewaio shoved her down and sideways, out of the line of fire. But his action came too late. Mara felt a thud against her upper arm that turned her half around. She fell back, through gauze curtains and onto the cushions of her litter, a Tuscalora arrow with its pale blue feathers protruding from her flesh. Her vision swam, but she made no outcry.

Dizziness made the sky seem to turn above her as the shields of her defenders clicked together, barely an instant before the enemy closed their charge.

Weapons clashed and shields rang. Gravel scattered under straining feet. Through the haze of discomfort, Mara concentrated upon the fact that the one Acoma archer who mattered had not yet released his round. 'Pape, the signal,' she said through clenched teeth. Her voice sounded weak in her own ear.

Her powerful Strike Leader did not answer. Blinking sweat from her eyes, Mara squinted through sunlight and whirling blades until she found the plumed helm. But Papewaio could not come to her, beset as he was by enemies. Even as Mara watched him dispatch one with a thrust to the neck, two others in Tuscalora blue leaped over their dying comrade to engage him. Plainly, Jidu's orders had been to cut down the one Acoma officer, in the hope that his death might throw Mara's guard into disarray.

Through her pain, Mara admired the merit of such tactics. With the high number of newcomers among the Acoma guard, and little to no encounters on the battlefield, many of these men were fighting with shieldmates who were strange to them. And against the relentless, concentrated attack of Jidu's finest warriors, even Papewaio was hard-pressed. Mara gritted her teeth. Only minutes remained before the enemy overwhelmed her guard, and the plan she had devised to avoid their massacre had yet to be put into effect.

She gripped the side of the litter, but even that small movement caused the arrow in her arm to grate against bone. Agony shot through her body; she whimpered through locked teeth and struggled not to faint.

Blades screeched in a bind, seemingly over her head. Then an Acoma guard crashed back and fell, blood spraying through a rent in his armour. He shuddered, his opened eyes reflecting sky. Then his lips framed a parting prayer to Chochocan, and his hand slackened on his sword. Mara felt tears sting her eyes. Thus her father had died, and Lano; the thought of little Ayaki spitted on an enemy spear turned her sick with fury.

She reached out and caught the sweat-damp grip of the fallen soldier's sword. Using the blade as a prop, she dragged herself to her knees. The sun fell hot on her head, and her eyes swam with pain. Through waves of faintness, she saw that an unlucky arrow had managed to dispatch her precious archer. He lay moaning with his hands clenched over his gut. And the signal arrow that would summon Lujan and Tasido to action sparkled unused at his feet.

Mara groaned. Shouts beat against her ears, and the clash of blade on blade seemed like drum rolls in the temple of Turakamu. Papewaio called an order, and the Acoma still able to fight closed ranks, stepping back of necessity over the still-warm bodies of their comrades. Mara prayed to Lashima for strength and reached out with unsteady hands for the fallen archer's bow.

The horn bow was heavy and awkward, and the arrow slippery in her sweaty hands. Mara notched the shaft with raw determination. Her hand faltered on the string, and the arrow tilted, sliding. She managed to recover it, but the rush of blood to her head momentarily blackened her vision.

She willed herself to continue by touch. Sight cleared in patches; another man crashed against her litter, his blood pattering into streaks across white gauze. Mara braced the bow and strove against weakness and pain to draw.

Her effort failed. Tearing agony laced her shoulder, and her lips drew back in a cry she could not stifle. Weeping tears of shame, she closed her eyes and tried again. The bow resisted her like iron-root. Tremors shook her body, and faintness stifled her awareness like dark felt. As the cries of the men and the clatter of weapons dimmed in her ears, still she strove to pull a bow that probably would have defeated her strength when she was in perfect health.

Suddenly someone's arms supported her. Sure hands reached around her shoulders and closed firmly on the fingers she held clenched to leather grip and string. And like a miracle, a man's strength joined hers, and the bow bent, paused, and released.

With a scream audible through the noise of battle, the signal arrow leaped into the sky; and the Ruling Lady of the Acoma passed out into the lap of a man with a leg wound, who, but for the grace lent by her cunning, would have died a condemned criminal in the wilderness. He eased his mistress's slender form onto the stained cushions of her litter. The strip he should have used to bind his own hurt he pressed to staunch the blood from the arrow wound in Mara's shoulder, while around him the Tuscalora pressed in for the victory.

Lord Jidu ignored the chilled fruit at his side as he sat forward eagerly upon his cushion. He motioned for a slave to fan cool air upon him while he sat watching the finish of the battle in his dooryard. Perspiration from excitement dripped off his forehead as he regarded his imminent victory – though it seemed to be longer in coming than he had expected. Many of his best warriors bled upon the gravel walk, no small few felled by the black-haired Acoma officer who fought with his hands drenched red to the wrists. He seemed invincible, his blade rising and falling with fatal regularity. But victory would come to the Tuscalora, despite the officer's aptness at killing. One by one the ranks at his side diminished, overwhelmed by superior numbers. For a moment Jidu considered ordering him captured, for his worth in the arena would recover the cost of this battle. Then the Lord of the Tuscalora discarded the thought. Best to end this quickly. There was still the matter of the other force of Acoma soldiers on his border, now attacking, no doubt, upon the release of that signal arrow. At least one Tuscalora archer had struck the Lady. Perhaps she bled to death even now.

Lord Jidu took a drink from the tray. He drew a long sip, and sighed in anticipation. The question of this debt he had incurred while gambling with Lord Buntokapi was coming to a better conclusion that he could have hoped. Perhaps he might gain the Acoma natami, to bury upside down beside the bones of Tuscalora ancestors. Then the Lord Jidu considered Tecuma of the Anasati, ignorant of this battle. A laugh shook his fat throat. Capture the Acoma brat and force Tecuma to terms! The boy in exchange for withdrawal of Anasati support from the Alliance for War! Jidu smiled at the thought. The Great Game dealt blows to the strong as well as the weak; and any ally of the Warlord's was to be balked, for war inevitably bent the monkeys of commerce away from chocha and into the pockets of armourers and weapons masters.

But all would depend on this victory, and the Acoma soldiers were showing an alarming reluctance to die. Perhaps, thought Jidu, he had ordered too many to attack the force on the border. Already both sides had been reduced, but now the odds were little better than two to one in favour of the Tuscalora. Again the green plume of the Acoma officer fell back, and the First Strike Leader of the Tuscalora shouted to his men to close. Now only a handful of soldiers remained, crowded against Mara's litter with their swords swinging in tired hands. Their end was certain now.

Then a breathless messenger raced up to the estate house. The man prostrated himself at his master's feet. 'Lord, Acoma troops have penetrated the orchards and fired the chocha-la bushes.'

Jidu bellowed in fury for his hadonra; but worse news followed. The messenger took a gasping breath and finished his report. 'Two Acoma Strike Leaders with a force of three hundred warriors have taken position between the burning crops and the river. None of our workers can get through to battle the blaze.'

The Lord of the Tuscalora leaped to his feet. Now the situation was critical; chocha-la bushes matured with extreme slowness, and a new field would not mature to yield sufficient harvest to recover his loss within his lifetime. If the bushes burned, the proceeds from this year's crop could not pay off the creditors. Ruin would be visited upon Jidu's house, and Tuscalora wealth would be as ashes.

Gesturing for the exhausted messenger to move clear of his path, the Lord of the Tuscalora shouted to his runner. 'Call up the auxiliary squads from the barracks! Send them to clear a way for the workers!'

The boy ran; and suddenly the fact that Mara's escort were nearly defeated lost its savour. Smoke turned the morning sky black and evil with soot. Plainly, the fires had been expertly set. Lord Jidu almost struck the second messenger, who arrived panting to report that shortly the crops would be ablaze beyond hope of salvage – unless the Acoma force could be neutralized to allow water brigades access to the river.

Jidu hesitated, then signalled a horn bearer. 'Call withdraw!' he ordered bitterly. Mara had set him to select between hard choices: either surrender honour and admit his default as a dishonour, or destroy her at the price of his own house's destruction.

The herald blew a series of notes and the Tuscalora Strike Leader turned in open astonishment. Final victory was only moments away, but his master was signalling him to order withdraw. Tsurani obedience told, and instantly he had his men backing away from the surrounded Acoma guards.

Of the fifty soldiers who had arrived upon the Tuscalora estates, fewer than twenty stood before their Lady's blood-splattered litter.

Jidu shouted, 'I seek truce.'

'Offer the Lady of the Acoma your formal apology,' shouted the green-plumed officer, who stood with sword at the ready should combat resume. 'Satisfy her honour, Lord Jidu, and Acoma warriors will lay down their weapons and aid your men to save the crops.'

The Lord of the Tuscalora jiggled from foot to foot, furious to realize he had been duped. The girl in the litter had planned this strategy from the start; what a vicious twist it set upon the situation. If Jidu deliberated, if he even took time to dispatch runners to survey the extent of the damage to determine whether his force had a hope of breaking through, he might forfeit all. No choice remained but to capitulate.

'I concede the honour of the Acoma,' shouted Lord Jidu, though the shame gripped him as though he had eaten unripe grapes. His First Strike Leader called orders for the warriors to lay down their arms, with reluctance.

The Acoma soldiers left living unlocked their shield wall, weary but proud. Papewaio's eyes flashed victory, but as he turned towards the litter to share victory with his Lady, his sweat-streaked features went rigid. He bent hastily, the bloody sword forgotten in his hand; and for a last, vicious instant, the Lord of the Tuscalora prayed that fortune favoured him. For if the Lady Mara lay dead, the Tuscalora were ruined.

Mara roused, her head aching, her arm aflame. An Acoma soldier was binding it with a torn shred of litter curtain. 'What . . .' she began weakly.

Papewaio's face suddenly loomed over her. 'My Lady?'

'What has passed?' she asked, her voice sounding small.

'As you hoped, Jidu ordered a withdrawal when his fields were threatened.' He glanced over his shoulder, where his battered and weary squad stood ready, and said, 'We are still in danger, but I think you hold the stronger position for the moment. But you need to speak with Jidu, now, before matters turn for the worse.'

Mara shook her head and allowed Papewaio and another soldier to lift her from her litter. Her feet seemed to betray her. She was forced to cling to her Strike Leader's arm as slowly she made her way over blood-spattered gravel to where her line of remaining soldiers stood. Mara's vision was blurred. She blinked several times to clear it, and noticed an acrid smell in the air. Smoke from the fired fields drifted like a pall over the estate house.

'Mara!' Jidu's shout was frantic. 'I propose a truce. Order your men to stand away from my fields and I'll admit I was wrong in not acknowledging my obligation.'

Mara regarded the fat, anxious man and coldly moved to turn the situation to Acoma advantage. 'You attacked me without provocation. Did you think, after admitting you were wrong, I would forgive the slaughter of good men for payment of a debt you owe me anyway?'

'We can settle our differences later,' cried Jidu, his colour turning florid. 'My fields burn.'

Mara nodded. Papewaio motioned with his sword point and a

soldier sent another signal arrow overhead. Mara tried to speak, but weakness overcame her. She whispered to Papewaio, who shouted, 'My mistress says our workers will put out the fires. But our men will maintain position with lit torches. Should anything here go amiss, the chocha-la fields will be reduced to ashes.'

Jidu's eyes went feral as he struggled to think of a way an advantage might still be gained. A ragged, smoke-stained runner raced into the dooryard. 'Master, Acoma soldiers repulse our men. The auxiliaries failed to open a way to the river.'

The Lord of the Tuscalora lost his resolve. Painfully resigned, he sank to his cushions and rubbed his hands on chubby knees. 'Very well, Mara. I accept the inevitable. We shall abide by your wishes.' He said to his First Strike Leader, 'Put up your arms.'

The Lord of the Tuscalora looked on uneasily while Mara shifted her weight to ease her wounded arm. The Lady of the Acoma had refused Jidu's offer to let his healer tend her; instead she had settled for a field bandage contrived by Papewaio. Acoma soldiers still held position amid the chocha-la, and the Tuscalora Force Commander confirmed the worst. The Acoma could fire the fields again before they could be forced back.

Jidu sweated and strove desperately to pass the matter off as a misunderstanding. 'It was an agreement between men, my Lady. I had many wagers with your late husband. Sometimes he won, sometimes I won. We let the sums accumulate, and when I won a bet, the amount was deducted. If later I chanced to gain the advantage, I let the debt ride in turn. It's . . . a gentleman's agreement.'

'Well, I do not gamble, Lord Jidu.' Mara turned dark, angry eyes upon her unwilling host. 'I think we shall simply settle for payment . . . and indemnity for the damage done my honour. Acoma soldiers died this day.'

'You ask the impossible!' The Lord of the Tuscalora flung pudgy hands in the air in an un-Tsurani-like display of distress.

Mara raised her eyebrows. 'You still choose not to honour this debt?' She glanced pointedly towards the Acoma soldiers who clustered close at hand, an archer in their midst ready to launch another signal arrow. Jidu stared at the shell sequins ornamenting his sandals. 'Ah, my Lady . . . I'm sorry to cause you inconvenience.

But threats cannot change the fact that I am unable to honour the debt at this time. Of course, I will meet my obligation in full the instant my circumstances permit. On this you have my uncompromised word.'

Mara sat very still. Her voice held a hard and bitter edge. 'I am not presently inclined towards patience, Lord Jidu. How soon may I expect payment?'

Jidu looked abashed as he admitted, 'I have recently suffered personal reversals, Lady Mara. But I can safely promise compensation when this year's crop goes to market.'

If it goes to market, Mara thought pointedly. She sat back. 'The chocha-la harvest is not due for another three months, Lord Jidu. You expect me to wait until then for two thousand centuries of metal – and my indemnity?'

'But you must,' the Lord of the Tuscalora exclaimed miserably. He motioned in distress to the short, thin man who sat at his master's side. Sijana, the Tuscalora hadonra, shuffled scrolls in a hasty review of the estate's finances. He whispered furiously in his master's ear and paused, expectant. Lord Jidu patted his stomach with renewed confidence. 'Actually, Lady, two thousand centuries can be paid now – plus another five hundred to repair the damage you've suffered. But a single payment of that size would prevent me from expanding the planting for next year. Lord Buntokapi understood this and promised to allow a favourable repayment schedule, five hundred centuries a year for the next four years – five years to cover the restitution.' The hadonra's nod of satisfaction turned to dismay; a deep flush rose from Jidu's collar as he realized his words had contradicted his earlier insistence that his debt was to be left to wait upon the outcome of future wagers. Since Mara was certain to seize upon this small but shameful lie, he quickly added, 'I'll pay interest, of course.'

Heavy silence fell, punctuated by Jidu's heavy breathing and a near-imperceptible creak of armour as Papewaio shifted his weight to the balls of his feet. Mara used her good hand to open her fan, her manner poisonously sweet. 'You argue like a moneylender, while Acoma soldiers lie dead outside your door? If my late Lord chose to offer terms on the debt, so be it. Produce the document and we shall abide by the terms.'

Jidu blinked. 'But our agreement was spoken, Lady Mara, a promise between noblemen.'

The fan vibrated in the air as Mara reined back rage. 'You have no proof? And yet you haggle?'

With his fields held hostage, Jidu shied from bringing up matters of honour again. 'You have my word, my Lady.'

Mara winced. The Lord of the Tuscalora had created a situation where she could only call him forsworn, an insult no ruler could ignore. Etiquette demanded that the Lady of the Acoma accept the agreement, thereby gaining nothing for the next three months, and then only a fifth of what was due, or resume the useless slaughter.

The fan poised motionless in her hand. 'But this debt is overdue already, Lord Jidu,' she said. 'Your hadonra's failure to acknowledge inquiries in timely fashion brought about this impasse. I will brook no more delays, or your fields will be put to the torch.'

'What do you propose?' he asked weakly.

Mara rested her pretty fan on her knee. Though her wound obviously taxed her, she judged her moment perfectly, offering a counterbargain before Jidu's wits could recover. 'My Lord, you own a small strip of land between my northern and southern needra fields, cut down the middle by the dry stream bed.'

Jidu nodded. 'I know the land.' He had once offered to sell that same acreage to Mara's father; Sezu had declined, because the land was useless. The banks of the dried stream were rocky and eroded and much too steep to cultivate. A crafty expression crossed the features of the Lord of the Tuscalora. 'Have you a need for that land, my Lady?'

Mara tapped her fan, thoughtful. 'We recently gave the use of our upper meadow to the cho-ja. Now, Jican might find it useful for those lower fields to be connected, perhaps with a plank bridge so the needra calves can cross without injuring their legs.' Recalling the stray note Sezu had left penned in one corner of a very tattered map, Mara stifled a smile. As if conceding a favour, she added, 'Lord Jidu, I am willing to cancel your debt in exchange for the land and all privileges granted along with it. Also, you will vow not to oppose the Acoma for the remainder of your life.'

The wizened hadonra stiffened in poorly hidden alarm; he whispered in his master's ear. The Lord of the Tuscalora heard him, then smiled unctuously at Mara. 'As long as the Tuscalora are allowed access to the Imperial Highway for our wagons, I'll agree.'

The Lady of the Acoma returned a gracious wave of her fan. 'But of course. Your workers may drive your wagons down the gully to the highway anytime they wish, Lord Jidu.'

'Done!' Lord Jidu's cheeks bulged into a smile. 'My word upon it! And gladly.' Then in an attempt to reduce tensions, he bowed low. 'I also salute your courage and wisdom, Lady, that this unfortunate confrontation has brought a closer bond between our two families.'

Mara gestured to Papewaio, who helped her rise. 'I'll have your vow, Jidu. Bring out your family sword.'

For a moment there was tension in the air again, for Mara was publicly demanding the most sacred oath in place of a simple assurance. Still, until the Tuscalora fields were clear of Acoma warriors, Lord Jidu dared not protest. He sent a servant to fetch the ancient sword of his forefathers, one as old as any in the Empire, precious steel wrapped in a simple sheath of cane wood. While Mara and her officer looked on, the Lord of the Tuscalora gripped the hilt and pronounced his oath to abide by his promise in the name of his ancestors.

At last satisfied, Mara gestured to her soldiers. They helped her back into her bloodstained litter. Her face seemed pale as she lay back in her cushions. Gently her retinue lifted her onto their shoulders. As they prepared to carry their wounded mistress home, Mara nodded at the Lord of the Tuscalora. 'The debt is met fairly, Jidu. I will gladly tell anyone who asks that the Lord of the Tuscalora is a man of honour who meets his obligations without flinching.' Then she added, pointedly, 'And abides by his promises. All will know your word is your bond.'

The Lord of the Tuscalora stood unflinching under the sting of her sarcasm. He had underrated her and had lost a great deal of prestige through the mistake. But at least the breach of honour would not become public knowledge, and for that small grace he thanked the heavens.

When the Acoma retinue was safely away from the Tuscalora house, Mara closed her eyes and hid her face in her hands. Alarmed, Papewaio stepped closer to the litter. 'You took a very great risk, my Lady. Yet you triumphed.'

Mara's reply came muffled through her hands. 'Many brave men were killed.'

Papewaio nodded. 'But they died like warriors, mistress. Those who gained honour at your command will sing your praises before the gods.' He fell silent then, for the litter seemed to be shaking. 'My Lady?'

Papewaio looked to see what ailed his mistress. Behind the shield of her palms, Mara was weeping with anger. Papewaio left her to her own release for a time, then said, 'If the gully is flooded, the Lord of the Tuscalora will have no easy way to take his crops to market.'

Mara's hands came down. Despite red eyes and a white face, her expression showed crafty triumph. 'If Jidu is forced to use the long pass around the gorge to reach the Imperial Highway, his chocha-la will spoil with mould by the time it reaches Sulan-Qu. That will cause hardship for my Lord of the Tuscalora, for I doubt he'll be able to pay the toll I will impose upon use of my needra bridge.' When Papewaio turned curious eyes upon his mistress, she added, 'You heard Jidu vow never to oppose the Acoma? Well, that is a start. That fat dog will be my first vassal. Within the season, Pape, within the season.'

The Acoma Strike Leader marched along, considering what this young woman had accomplished since he had accompanied Keyoke to the temple to bring her home. He nodded once to himself. Yes, Jidu of the Tuscalora would bend his knee before Mara or else forfeit his harvest. Such were the ways of the game, and Mara had gained the victory. There could be no doubt.

The brightly painted litter sitting in the dooryard of the Acoma estate house confirmed that Bruli of the Kehotara awaited the Lady of the Acoma. Mara reined in her irritation. Returned from the hive of the cho-ja, whose growing Queen had offered wonderful balms for healing Mara's shoulder, the young woman dismissed her bearers and escort. She must at last offer her personal greeting before giving Bruli an excuse to quit her presence, or else risk insult to the Kehotara. Which, Mara considered, might just be one of the reasons the Lord of the Minwanabi had dispatched his vassal's handsome son to the Acoma estate.

Misa, the prettier of her personal maids, waited just inside the door. She held a comb and brush, and one arm was draped with a richly embroidered overrobe whose colours would set off her mistress's dark eyes. Recognizing the hand of Nacoya in the appointing of the welcoming committee, Mara submitted without comment. With the slightest of frowns marring her brow, she stood while Misa's hands expertly arranged her hair into a knot fastened with jewelled pins. The overrobe fastened in front with a row of flimsy ribbons, yet hid the white bandage that dressed the wound on her upper arm. Questioning Nacoya's taste, Mara nodded briskly for Misa to retire, then made her way to the great hall where Nacoya was entertaining her guest in her absence.

The young son of the Kehotara rose and bowed formally on her entrance. He wore a costly robe buttoned with sapphires, the high cut of the hem and sleeves showing his legs and arms to good advantage.

'Bruli, how pleasant to see you again.' Mara sat on the cushions opposite the young man, bemused by his changed appearance. He *was* a good-looking man. Inwardly, she considered that most young ladies would have been flattered, even anxious, to be the focus of this suitor's attention. His smile almost glowed and his charm was undeniable. In some ways it was a pity he was born to a noble house, for he could easily have been a master of the Reed Life and retired wealthy from the rewards of sharing his charms with powerful clients.

'My Lady, I am pleased to see you again.' Bruli seated himself, neatly tucking his sandals beneath his calves. 'I trust the business with your neighbour went well?'

Mara nodded absently. 'Merely a small debt from Jidu to my late Lord Buntokapi that needed settlement. The matter has been resolved.'

A flicker of interest stirred in the eyes of the young man, at odds with his languid expression. Reminded that Bruli might himself be an agent for the Minwanabi, Mara steered the conversation away from her contention with Lord Jidu. 'My outing this morning has left me tired and hot. If you will join me, I will have my servant bring wine and cakes to the garden.' To allow her tactic time to have effect, she seized upon the simplest excuse. 'I will meet you there after I change into a more comfortable robe.'

Nacoya nodded almost imperceptibly, telling Mara that her delay had been opportune. The young suitor bowed. While a servant led him away, the First Adviser to the Acoma hurried to her mistress's side, her usual grouchy manner replaced by solicitude. 'Did the cho-ja ease your pain?'

'Yes.' Mara fingered the ribbons on the overrobe. 'Now, mother of my heart, will you explain to me what this silly frippery has to do with our plans for young Bruli?'

Nacoya's eyes widened with evil delight. 'Ah, Mara-anni, you have much to learn of the ways of men!' Taking her charge firmly by the hand, she towed her off to her private quarters. 'This afternoon you must do your best to be the temptress, my Lady. I have selected appropriate raiment for you to wear after your bath.'

Crossing the threshold, Nacoya displayed a conspirator's excitement. Servants could be heard pouring bath water behind the small folding partition, and several items of clothing had been neatly laid out upon the sleeping mat. Mara regarded her adviser's chosen outfit with a sceptical eye. 'Nacoya, several pieces seem to be missing.'

Nacoya smiled. She gathered up the skimpy lounging robe, commonly worn by ladies in the privacy of their own quarters. Nudity, per se, was not a social difficulty. Adults and children of both sexes bathed together and a small loincloth for swimming was optional. But like most things involved with courtship, provocation was a condition of the mind. Worn in the garden in the presence of a stranger, this slight gown would prove more alluring than if Mara had invited Bruli to swim naked with her.

Nacoya ran old fingers over the gauzy fabric, her manner suddenly serious. 'For my small plan to work, Bruli must become motivated by more than the wish to please his father. If he comes to desire you, he will do things he otherwise would never consider. You must act as flirtatiously as you are able.'

Mara almost winced. 'Shall I simper?' She turned sideways, surrendering the lace fan to one of the servants who arrived to remove her travelling robes.

'That might not hurt.' Nacoya stepped over to a chest and fished out a small vial. Then she hummed softly over the splash of the bath water; the song was an ancient courting tune she remembered from her youth. Presently Mara emerged from behind the screen, swathed in soft towels. The old woman waved the servants aside and dabbed an exotic essence upon the girl's shoulders and wrists, and between her breasts. Then she lifted the towels aside; regarding the nude form of her mistress, she resisted an impulse to cackle. 'You've a fine, healthy body on you, Mara-anni. If you could practise a little more grace and elegance in your movement, you could have all the blood gone from his head in a minute.'

Not at all convinced, Mara turned towards the reflecting glass, a costly gift from a clan leader on her wedding day. Against its dark patina, a dimmer shadow returned her gaze. Childbirth had left a minimum of stretch marks, the result of constant ministration of special oils during her pregnancy. Her breasts were slightly larger than before Ayaki's conception, but her stomach was as flat as ever. After giving birth to her son she had begun the practice of tan-che, the ancient formal dance that strengthened the body while keeping it limber. But Mara found little attractive in her slender form, particularly after having seen Teani's charms.

'I'm going to feel terribly silly,' she confided to her image in the glass. Nevertheless, she allowed the servants to dress her in the skimpy robe, with several pieces of flashing jewellery and a ribbon upon her right ankle. Billowy sleeves concealed the dressing on her upper arm. Humming loudly now, Nacoya stepped behind her mistress and gathered her hair on top of her head. Binding it with ivory and jade pins, she fussed and allowed a few wisps to dangle artfully down around Mara's face. 'There; men like the slightly dishevelled look. It puts them in mind of what ladies look like in the morning.'

'Bleary-eyed and puffy-faced?' Mara almost laughed.

'Bah!' Nacoya shook her finger, deadly serious. 'You have yet to learn what most women guess by instinct, Mara-anni. Beauty is as much attitude as face and form. If you enter the garden like an Empress, slowly, moving as if every man who sees you is your slave, Bruli would ignore a dozen pretty dancing girls to take you to his bed. As much as managing your estates, this skill is necessary for a Ruling Lady. Remember this: move slowly. When you sit, or sip your wine, be as elegant as you can, like a woman of the Reed Life when she struts on her balcony over the streets. Smile and listen to Bruli as if everything he says is stunningly brilliant, and should he jest, for the gods' sake laugh, even if the joke is poor. And if your robes move and part a little, let him peek a bit before you cover up. I wish this son of the Kehotara to be snorting after you like a needra bull at breeding time.'

'Your plan had better prove worthwhile,' said Mara with distaste. She ran her fingers through jingling layers of necklaces. 'I feel like a merchant's manikin. But I will try to act like Bunto's little whore, Teani, if you think advantage will come of it.' Then her voice gained an edge. 'Understand this, though, mother of my heart. I will not take this young calley bird to bed.'

Nacoya smiled at her reference to the finely plumed birds kept by many nobles for their beauty. 'A calley bird he is, mistress, and my plan requires that he show us his finest plumage.'

Mara looked heavenward, then nodded. She started her usual brisk walk, but remembered to move out the door with her best imitation of a woman of the Reed Life. Attempting to be languid in her approach to the young suitor, Mara blushed with embarrassment. She thought her entrance was exaggerated to the point of silliness, but Bruli sat up straight upon his cushions. He smiled broadly and jumped to his feet, bowing deferentially to the Lady of the Acoma; all the while his eyes drank in her image.

Once Mara was installed upon her cushions, the young man might even have poured her wine himself, but the servant, who was actually Arakasi, accomplished the service before him. His manner showed no trace of distrust, but Mara knew he would never let his mistress accept any cup touched by a vassal of the Minwanabi. Aware, suddenly, that Bruli had ceased talking, Mara flashed him a brilliant smile. Then, almost shyly, she lowered her eyes and pretended intent interest. His conversation seemed trivial, concerning people and events of seemingly little consequence. But she listened to the gossip of the court and cities as if the subjects fascinated her, and she laughed at Bruli's attempts at wit. Arakasi directed the house slaves, who came and went with trays of wine-soaked fruit. As Bruli's breath smelled more and more strongly of spirits, his tongue loosened, and his laughter boomed across the garden. Once or twice he rested his fingers lightly on Mara's wrist, and though she was not in the least bit intoxicated, his gentleness sent a thrill through her body. Idly she wondered whether Nacoya was right and there was more to love between man and woman than Buntokapi's rough handling had shown.

But her inner barriers stayed raised. Though to Mara the act was laughable, so awkward did she feel in the role of seductress, the detached observer within her noted that Bruli seemed entranced. His gaze never left her. Once, as she waved Arakasi back to pour more wine, the front of her robe parted slightly. As Nacoya had advised, she hesitated before closing the gap. Bruli's lashes widened, and his pretty eyes seemed nailed to the slight swell of bosom revealed. How odd, she thought, that a man so handsome should be moved by such a thing. He must have had many women; why should another not bore him? But Nacoya's wisdom was ancient. Mara followed her adviser's lead and a little later allowed her hem to creep upward slightly.

Bruli stumbled over his words. Smiling, sipping wine to hide his clumsiness, he still could not help staring at the slowly increasing expanse of her thigh.

Nacoya had been right; testing further, Mara said, 'Bruli, I must beg your leave to retire. But I hope you will have time to return to us in' – she pouted, as if thought were very difficult for her, then smiled – 'say, two days.' She rose with all the grace she could muster, artfully allowing her robe to fall more open than before. Bruli's colour deepened. To Mara's gratification, he returned an emphatic assurance that he would return upon her pleasure. Then he sighed, as if two days seemed a long period.

Mara left the garden, aware that he watched her until she disappeared into the shadows of the house. Nacoya waited at the first door, the glint in her eyes revealing that she had observed the entire hour's conversation.

'Do all men have their brains between their legs?' Mara inquired. Frowning, she compared Bruli's behaviour to what she remembered of her father's stern manner and her brother's rakish charm.

Nacoya hustled her mistress briskly away from the screen. 'Most, thank the gods.' Pausing before the door to Mara's quarters, she added, 'Mistress, women have few means to rule their own lives. You have the rare fortune to be a Ruling Lady. The rest of us live at the whim of our lords or husbands or fathers, and what you have just practised is the mightiest weapon at our command. Fear the man who doesn't desire a woman, for he will see you only as a tool or a foe.' Almost gloatingly, she patted Mara's shoulder. 'But our young calley bird is smitten, I think, as much as working on his father's behalf. Now I will hurry to reach him in the outer courtyard before he takes his leave. I have a few suggestions on how he may win you.'

Mara watched the old woman hurry energetically away, hairpins leaning precariously to the left. Shaking her head at the follies of life, she wondered what Nacoya would advise this silly young suitor from the Kehotara. Then she decided she would consider that in a hot tub. This display of womanly charms for the purpose of inflaming Bruli had left her feeling slightly soiled.

13

Seduction

The boy's eyes opened wide.

Seated on his mat before the outer screen, the runner turned towards his mistress with a wondering look upon his face. The boy was new to his post, and Mara guessed his expression portended an impressive arrival in the dooryard. She dismissed the new warriors, both recruited only that morning. They took their bows, and as a servant arrived to show them to their barracks, Mara inquired of her runner, 'Is it Bruli of the Kehotara?'

Young and still easily impressed, the slave boy nodded quickly. Mara stretched briefly and arose from amid stacks of parchments and tallies. Then she, too, stared in amazement. Bruli approached the great house in an ornate litter, obviously new, with ribbons of pearl and shell inlay gleaming in the morning sunlight. He had dressed in silk robes, bordered in elaborate embroidery, and his head covering was set with tiny sapphires, to enhance the colour of his eyes. Kehotara vanity did not end there. As if watching a pageant from a child's tale, Mara noticed that his litter bearers were uniformly matched in height and physical perfection; with none of the ragged, beaten look of toil, these slaves were like young gods, tall and muscular, with bodies oiled like athletes. A full dozen musicians accompanied the Kehotara honour guard. They played well and loudly upon horns and vielles as Bruli made his entrance.

Bemused, Mara waved for a servant to tidy the scrolls, while Misa helped her refresh her appearance. Nacoya had been up to her own machinations. On his last three visits the Acoma First Adviser had fended the boy off, warning of her mistress's impatience with a suitor who did not display his wealth as a sign of ardour. Twice Bruli had dined in the garden, Mara again feeling like a piece of meat on display at a butcher's stall. But each time she laughed at some stupid joke or feigned surprise at some revelation about one or another Lord in the High Council, Bruli was genuinely pleased. He seemed totally infatuated with her. At their last meeting, Mara had briefly allowed him to express his passion with a parting kiss, deftly disentangling herself from his embrace as his hands closed around her shoulders. He had called out an entreaty, but she ducked through the doorway, leaving him aroused and confused in the dappled moonlight of the garden. Nacoya had seen him to his litter, then returned with the certainty that the young man's frustration served to fan his desire.

Scented and wearing tiny bells on her wrists, Mara slipped into a shamelessly scanty robe – where was Nacoya finding them, she wondered. Misa patted her mistress's hair into place and fastened it with pins of emerald and jade. Then, her appearance complete, Mara left with mincing steps to greet her suitor.

When at last she appeared, Bruli's eyes widened with glowing admiration. He stepped somewhat awkwardly from his litter, his back stiff and his weight centred carefully over his sandals. Mara had to suppress a laugh; his costly robes and headdress were obviously heavy and uncomfortable. The ties on the sleeves looked as if they pinched mightily, and the wide belt with its coloured stitching surely was constricting and hot. Yet Bruli bore up with every appearance of enjoying himself. He smiled brilliantly at Mara and allowed her to lead him into the cool shadow of the estate house.

Seated in a room overlooking the garden with its fountain, Mara called for wine with fruit and pastries. As always, Bruli's conversation bored her; but at his usual post by the wine tray Arakasi gleaned some useful bits of information. The Spy Master had connected several of Bruli's remarks to things already learned by his agents. Mara never ceased to be astonished at the information her Spy Master was able to divine from seemingly trivial gossip. In private talks that followed Bruli's visits, Arakasi had fashioned some interesting theories about activities in the High Council. If his speculation was correct, very soon the Blue Wheel Party would unilaterally withdraw from the war upon the barbarian world. The Warlord's grandiose campaign would be seriously hampered. Should this occur, the Anasati, the Minwanabi, and Almecho's other allies would certainly be pressured by demands for more support. Mara wondered if Jingu would step up his attempts to eliminate her before the Minwanabi were forced to turn their energies elsewhere.

Bruli's chatter faltered, and belatedly Mara realized she had lost the thread of his conversation. She filled in with an endearing smile, unaware that the expression made her strikingly pretty. Bruli's eyes warmed in response. His emotion was entirely genuine, and for a moment Mara wondered how she would feel in his arms, compared to the unpleasantness she had endured with Buntokapi. Then Arakasi leaned to slap an insect, and his clothing jostled the wine tray. The unexpected movement caused Bruli to start, one hand flying to the dagger hidden in his sash. In an instant the solicitous suitor was transformed into a Tsurani warrior, all taut muscle and cold eyes. Mara's moment of sentiment died. This man might be more civilized in his manner, more charming in his speech, more beautiful in body and face than the brute she had once married, but his heart was stern and commanding. Like Buntokapi, he would kill or cause pain on the impulse of the instant, without even pausing for thought.

That recognition angered Mara, as if for an instant she had longed for something from this man; any man. That this longing was a vain hope roused an irrational instinct to fight back. Feigning discomfort from the heat, Mara fanned herself, then pulled her bodice open and exposed most of her breasts to Bruli's view. The effect was immediate. The young man's battle instincts relaxed, like the claws of a sarcat sheathed in softness. Another kind of tension claimed him, and he shifted closer to her.

Mara smiled, a ruthless gleam in her eyes. The small bells on her wrist sang in perfect sevenths as she brushed the young man's arm with a seemingly casual touch. 'I don't know what is wrong with me, Bruli, but I find the warmth oppressive. Would you care to bathe?'

The young man all but tore his finery in his haste to rise to his feet. He extended a hand to Mara, and she allowed him to raise her from the cushions without rearranging her clothing. Her robe gaped further, and Bruli caught a teasing glimpse of small but nicely formed breasts and the hint of a taut stomach. Mara smiled as she noted the focus of his attention. With slow, provocative movements, she rebound her sash, while small beads of perspiration sparkled into being beneath Bruli's headdress. 'You look very hot,' she observed.

The young man regarded her with unfeigned adoration. 'I am always aflame with passion for you, my Lady.'

This time Mara encouraged his boldness. 'Wait here one moment,' she said and, smiling in open invitation, stepped out to find Nacoya.

The old woman sat just out of sight behind the screen, a piece of embroidery in her lap. Mara noticed incongruously that the stitches were remarkably incoherent. Grateful to see that her First Adviser required no explanation of what had passed in the chamber by the garden, she relayed swift instructions.

'I think we have our young jigabird cock ready to crow. Order the bath drawn. When I dismiss the attendants, allow us fifteen minutes alone. Then send in my runner with a message coded urgent, and have Misa ready.' Mara paused, a flash of uncertainty showing through. 'You did say she admired the man?'

Nacoya returned a regretful shake of her head. 'Ah, daughter, do not worry for Misa. She likes men.'

Mara nodded and started to return to her suitor. But Nacoya touched her wrist, the chime of tiny bells muffled in her wrinkled palm. 'Lady, be cautious. Your house guards will see to your safety, but you play a dangerous game. You must judge carefully how far to push Bruli. He may become too impassioned to stop, and having Pape kill him for attempted rape would do the Acoma great harm at this point.'

Mara considered her meagre experience with men and chose prudence. 'Send the runner ten minutes after we enter.'

'Go now.' Nacoya released her mistress with a pat of her hand. The old nurse smiled in the shadow. Thank the gods she had not needed to lie; Misa was Mara's prettiest maid, and her appetite for handsome men was a subject of shameless gossip among the servants. She would play her part with unfeigned joy.

Attendants emptied the last pitchers of cool water into the tub, bowed, and retired, closing the screen. Mara released Bruli's hand. The bells on her wrists tinkled sweetly as, with dancelike movements, she unfastened her sash and allowed her robe to slide off her shoulders. Beaded ornaments concealed the scar of her wound, and the silk sighed over her ivory skin, slipping past her waist and over the curve of her hips. As it drifted around her ankles to the floor, Mara lifted one bare foot, then the other, at last stepping free of the folds. She mounted the steps to the top of the wooden tub, remembering to hold her stomach flat and her chin up. At the corner of her vision she saw Bruli frantically shedding costly clothing; her game with the robe had brought the young man close to the point of losing decorum. When he tore off his loincloth, she witnessed the proof of her effect upon him. Mara refrained from laughing by only a signal act of will. How silly men could look when excited.

Bruli stretched. Confident that his body was worthy of admiration, he bounded to the tub, submerging his slender hips with a satisfied sound, as if he simply wished to soak. Mara knew better. Bruli had hoped for this moment, fretting with keenest anticipation for the better part of the week. He opened his arms, inviting Mara to join him. She smiled instead and took up a vial and a cake of scented soap. The priceless metal bells on her wrists chimed with her movements as she poured fragrant oils upon the surface of the water. Rainbows shimmered into being around Bruli's athletic form. He closed his eyes in contentment, while the bells moved behind him and small hands began to soap his back.

'You feel very nice,' murmured Bruli.

Her hands melted away like ghosts. The bells sang a last shower of sound and fell silent, and the water rippled, gently. Bruli opened his eyes to find Mara in the tub before him, soaping her slender body with sensuous abandon. He licked his lips, unaware of the calculation in her pretty eyes. By the sloppy smile on his face, Mara guessed she was acting the part of the seductress convincingly.

The man's breathing became nearly as heavy as Buntokapi's. Unsurprised when Bruli seized another cake of soap and reached out to help, Mara twisted gracefully away and sank to her neck in the water. Suds and rainbows of oil veiled her form, and as Bruli stretched powerful hands towards her, the Lady forestalled him with a smile. 'No, let me.' Bath oils lapped the brim of the tub as she came to his side and playfully pushed his head under. The young man came up sputtering and laughing, and grabbed. But Mara had slid behind him. Tantalizingly, she began slowly to wash his hair. Bruli shivered with pleasure as he imagined the feel of her hands on other parts of his body. The hair washing worked downwards, became a gentle massage of his neck and back. Bruli pressed backwards, feeling the twin points of Mara's breasts against his shoulders. He reached over his head for her, but her elusive hands slithered forwards, caressing his collarbones and chest. Aware of the quiver in his flesh, Mara hoped her runner would appear promptly. She was running out of ploys to delay, and in an odd way she had not anticipated, her own loins had begun to tighten. The sensation frightened her, for Buntokapi's attentions had never made her feel this way. The scented soap filled the air with blossom fragrance, and the light of afternoon through the coloured screens made the bathing room a soft, gentle place for lovers. But Mara knew that it could just as easily be a place for killing, with Pape waiting with his hand on his sword, just out of sight behind the screen. This man was a vassal of the Minwanabi, an enemy, and she must not lose control.

Tentatively she rubbed her hand down Bruli's stomach. He shivered and smiled at her, just as the screen swished back to admit the breathless form of her runner.

'Mistress, I beg forgiveness, but your hadonra reports a message of the highest importance.'

Mara feigned a look of disappointment and raised herself from the tub. Servants rushed in with towels, and Bruli, tormented by lust, stared dumbly at the last glistening patches of nude flesh to disappear into the linens. Mara listened to the imaginary message and turned with open regret. 'Bruli, I am most apologetic, but I must leave and tend to an unexpected matter.'

She bit her lip, ready with an excuse should he ask what had arisen, but his mind was so preoccupied with disappointment, he only said, 'Can't it wait?'

'No.' Mara gestured helplessly. 'I'm afraid not.'

Water sloshed as Bruli raised himself to object. Mara hastened solicitously to his side and pressed him back into the bath. 'Your pleasure need not be spoiled.' She smiled, every inch the caring hostess, and called to one of her attendants. 'Misa, Bruli has not finished his bathing. I think you should stay and tend him.'

The prettiest of the towel bearers stepped forward and without hesitation stripped off her robe and undergarment. Her figure was soft, even stunning, but Bruli ignored her, watching only Mara as she donned her clean robes and left the room. The door closed gently behind her. The son of Lord of the Kehotara drove a fist, splashing, into the bath water. Then, reluctantly, he noticed the maid. His frustration faded away, replaced by a hungry smile.

He dived through suds and broken patches of sweet oils and grabbed her by the shoulders. Hidden beyond the door, Mara did not wait to see the finale but eased the slight crack in the screen soundlessly closed. Nacoya and Papewaio followed her a short way down the corridor. 'You were right, Nacoya. I acted the empress, and he hardly noticed Misa until after I left.'

A faint splash echoed from the bathing room, punctuated by a girlish squeal.

'He seems to have noticed her now,' Papewaio ventured.

Nacoya brushed this away as unimportant. 'Misa will only whet his appetite all the more. He will now burn to have you, daughter. I think you have learned more of men than I had judged. Still, it is good Bruli remained calm in your presence. Had Pape had to kill him . . .' She let the thought go unfinished.

'Well, he didn't.' Irritable and strangely sickened, Mara dismissed the subject. 'Now I will go and shut myself away in the study. Tell me when Bruli has finished with Misa and departed.' She dismissed her First Strike Leader and First Adviser with a wave. Only the runner remained, his boy's legs stretching in imitation of a warrior's long stride. For once his antics did not amuse. 'Send Jican to the study,' Mara instructed him curtly. 'I have plans concerning that land we acquired from the Lord of the Tuscalora.'

Mara hurried purposefully forward, but a screech of infant laughter melted her annoyance. Ayaki had awakened from his midday nap. Indulgently smiling, Mara changed course for the nursery. Intrigue and the great Game of the Council could wait until after she had visited her son.

When next he arrived to court Mara, Bruli of the Kehotara was accompanied by a dozen dancers, all expert in their art, who spun and jumped with astonishing athletic grace as a full score of musicians played. The litter that followed this procession was yet another new one, bedecked with metal and fringed with beaded gems. Mara squinted against the dazzle of reflected sunlight and judged her suitor's style was approaching the pomp favoured by the Lord of the Anasati.

She whispered to Nacoya, 'Why does each entrance become more of a circus?'

The old woman rubbed her hands together. 'I've told your young suitor that you appreciate a man who can proudly display his wealth to the world, though I wasn't quite that obvious.'

Mara returned a sceptical glance. 'How did you know he would listen?'

Nacoya waved airily at the the young man who leaned hopefully out of his litter, that he might catch a glimpse of the Lady he came to court. 'Daughter, have you not learned, even now? Love can make fools of even the best men.'

Mara nodded, at last understanding why her former nurse had insisted she play the wanton. Bruli could never have been coerced into spending such a fortune simply to carry out his father's wishes. That morning Arakasi had received a report that the boy had come near to bankrupting the already shaky financial standing of the Kehotara. His father, Mekasi, would fare awkwardly if he had to appeal to Jingu's good graces to save his honour.

'To get between your legs, that boy would spend his father centiless.' With a shake of her head Nacoya said, 'He is to be pitied, a little. Serving up Misa in your stead has done what you wished: only heightened his appetite for you. The fool has fallen passionately in love.'

The First Adviser's comment was nearly lost in a fanfare of horns. Vielle players ripped into a finale of arpeggios as Bruli's party mounted the steps to the estate house and entered the garden. The dancers simultaneously twirled, dropping in a semicircle of bows before Mara as Bruli made his appearance. Now his black hair was crimped into ringlets, and his arms bore heavy bracelets of chased enamel work. As he came over to Mara, his strut faltered. Instead of the skimpy robe he had come to expect, she was wearing a formal white robe, with long sleeves and a hemline well below her knees.

Though he sensed some difficulty, he managed his bow with grace. 'My Lady?' he said as he waved his retinue aside.

Mara motioned for her servants to stand apart. Frowning a little, as if she struggled with disappointment too great to hide, she said, 'Bruli, I have come to understand something.' She lowered her eyes. 'I have been alone . . . and you are a very handsome man. I . . . I have acted poorly.' She finished the rest in a rush. 'I have let desire rule my judgment, and now I discover that you think me another silly woman to add to your list of conquests.'

'But no!' interrupted Bruli, instantly concerned. 'I think you a paragon among women, Mara.' His voice softened almost to reverence. 'More than that, I love you, Mara. I would never consider conquest concerning a woman I wish to wed.'

His sincerity swayed Mara for only a second. Despite his beauty, Bruli was but another vain young warrior, with little gift for thought or wisdom.

Mara stepped back as he reached for her. 'I wish to believe you, Bruli, but your own actions deny your pretty words. Just two nights ago you found my maid an easy substitute for . . .' How easily the lie came, she thought. 'I was ready to give myself to you, sweet Bruli. But I find you are simply another adventurer of the heart, and I a poor, plain widow.'

Bruli dropped immediately to one knee, a servant's gesture, and shocking for its sincerity. He began earnestly to profess his love, but Mara turned sharply away. 'I cannot hear this. It breaks my heart.' Feigning injury too great to support, she fled the garden.

As the tap of her sandals faded into the house, Bruli slowly rose from his knees. Finding Nacoya by his elbow, he gestured in embarrassed confusion. 'Ancient mother, if she will not listen to me, how may I prove my love?'

Nacoya clucked understandingly and patted the young man's arm, steering him deftly through musicians and dancers to his dazzlingly appointed litter. 'Girls have little strength, Bruli. You must be gentle and patient. I think some small gift or another, sent with a letter, or, better, a poem, might sway her heart. Perhaps one a day until she calls you back.' Touching the fringes with admiring hands, Nacoya said, 'You had her won, you know. Had you shown restraint enough to leave that maid alone, she surely would have become your wife.'

Frustration became too much for Bruli. 'But I thought she wished me to take the girl!' His rings rattled as he folded his arms in pique. 'The maid was certainly bold enough in the tub and . . . it is not the first time I have been given a servant for sport by my host.'

Nacoya played the role of grandmother to the limit of her ability. 'Ah, you poor boy. You know so little about the heart of a female. I wager no woman you paid court to ever sent her maids to warm your bed.' She wagged her finger under his nose. 'It was another man who did so, eh?'

Bruli stared at the fine gravel of the path, forced to admit she was correct. Nacoya nodded briskly. 'See, it was, in a manner of speaking, a test.' As his eyes began to narrow, she said, 'Not by design, I assure you; simply put, had you dressed and left at once, my mistress would have been yours for the asking. Now . . .'

Bruli flung back crimped locks and groaned. 'What am I to do?'

'As I said, gifts.' Nacoya's tone turned chiding. 'And I think you should prove your passion may be answered only by true love. Send away those girls you keep at your hostelry in the city.'

Bruli stiffened in immediate suspicion. 'You have spies! How else could you know I have two women of the Reed Life at my quarters in the city?'

Though Arakasi's operatives had indeed provided that fact, Nacoya only nodded in ancient wisdom. 'See, I guessed right! And if an old, simple woman such as myself can guess, then so must my Lady.' Short and wizened beside the proud warrior, she ushered him to the dooryard where his litter waited. 'You must go, young master Bruli. If your heart is to win its reward, you must not be seen talking overlong with me! My Lady might suspect me of advising you, and that would never please her. Go quickly, and be unstinting in the proof of your devotion.'

The son of Mekasi reluctantly settled onto his cushions. His slaves shouldered the poles of his gaudy litter, and like clockwork toys, the musicians began to play the appointed recessional. Dancers whirled in joyful gyrations, until a carping shout from their master ended their display. The vielles scraped and fell silent, and a last, tardy horn player set the needra bulls bellowing in the pastures. How fitting that his send-off came from the beasts, Nacoya thought as, in a sombre band, his cortege departed for Sulan-Qu. The hot sun of midday wilted the flower garlands on the heads of the dancers and slaves, and almost the Acoma First Adviser felt sorry for the young man. Almost.

The gifts began to arrive the next day. A rare bird that sang a haunting song came first, with a note in fairly bad poetry. Nacoya read it after Mara had laid it aside, and commented, 'The calligraphy is well practised. He must have spent a few dimis hiring a poet to write this.'

'Then he wasted his wealth. It's awful.' Mara waved for a servant to clear away the colourful paper wrappings that had covered the bird's cage. The bird itself hopped from perch to reed perch, singing its tiny heart out.

Just then Arakasi bowed at the entrance of the study. 'My Lady, I have discovered the identity of the Kehotara agent.'

As an afterthought, Mara directed the slaves to carry the bird to another chamber. As its warble diminished down the corridor, she said, 'Who?'

Arakasi accepted her invitation to enter. 'One of Bruli's servants hurried to send a message, warning his father of his excesses, I think. But the odd thing is another slave, a porter, also left his master's town house to meet with a vegetable seller. Their discussion did not concern produce, and it seems likely he was a Minwanabi agent.'

Mara twined a bit of ribbon between her fingers. 'Has anything been done?'

Arakasi understood her perfectly. 'The first man had an unfortunate accident. His message fell into the hands of another vegetable seller who, it so chances, hates Jingu.' The Spy Master withdrew a document from his robe, which he gravely offered to Mara.

'You still smell like seshi tubers,' the Lady of the Acoma accused gently, then went on to read the note. 'Yes, this proves your suppositions. It also suggests that Bruli had no idea he had a second agent in his party.'

Arakasi frowned, as he always did when he read things upside down. 'If that figure is accurate, Bruli is close to placing his father in financial peril.' The Spy Master paused to stroke his chin. 'With Jican's guidance, I convinced many of the craftsmen and merchants to delay their bills until we wish them sent. Here the Acoma benefit from your practice of prompt payment.'

Mara nodded in acknowledgment. 'How much grace does that leave the Kehotara?'

'Little. How long could any merchant afford to finance Bruli's courtship? Soon they will send to the Lord of the Kehotara's hadonra for payment. I would love to be an insect upon the wall watching when he receives that packet of bills.'

Mara regarded her Spy Master keenly. 'You have more to say.'

Arakasi raised his brows in surprise. 'You have come to know me very well.' But his tone implied a question.

Silently Mara pointed to the foot he tapped gently on the carpet. 'When you're finished, you always stop.'

The Spy Master came close to a grin. 'Sorceress,' he said admiringly; then his voice sobered. 'The Blue Wheel Party has just ordered all their Force Commanders back from Midkemia, as we had suspected they might.'

Mara's eyes narrowed. 'Then we have little time left to deal with this vain and foolish boy. Within a few days his father will send for him, even if he hasn't discovered the perilous state of his finances.' She tapped absently with the scroll while she considered her next move. 'Arakasi, watch for any attempts to send a messenger to Bruli before Nacoya convinces him to make me a gift of that litter. And, old mother, the moment he does, call him to visit.' Mara's gaze lingered long upon her two advisers. 'And hope we can deal with him before his father orders him to kill me.'

Bruli sent a new gift each of the next four days. The servants piled them in one corner of Mara's study, until Nacoya commented sourly that the room resembled a market stall. The accumulation was impressive – costly robes of the finest silk; exotic wines and fruits, imported to the central Empire at great cost; gems and even metal jewellery. At the last, on the fifth day following the afternoon she had sent the young man away, the fabulous litter had arrived. Then Mara ordered Arakasi to send Bruli the second message, one intercepted scarcely the day before. The Lord of the Kehotara had at last received word of his son's excesses and sternly ordered the boy home at once. In his instructions the angry old patriarch had detailed exactly what he thought of his son's irresponsible behaviour.

Mara would have been amused, if not for Arakasi's agitation over how word of the incident had got through to the Kehotara lord without his agent's knowledge. The Spy Master had touchy pride, and he regarded any failure, however slight, as a personal betrayal of his duty. Also, his discovery of the Minwanabi agent in Bruli's train had him concerned. If two agents, why not three?

But events progressed too swiftly to investigate the matter. Bruli of the Kehotara returned to the Acoma estate house, and Mara again attired herself in lounging robes and makeup to further confuse her importunate suitor as he bowed and entered her presence. The musicians were conspicuously absent, as were the fine clothes, the jewellery, and the crimped hair. Red-faced and ill at ease, the young man rushed through the formalities of greeting. With no apology for his rudeness, Bruli blurted, 'Lady Mara, I thank the gods you granted me an audience.'

Mara forestalled him, seemingly unaware that his ardour was no longer entirely motivated by passion. 'I think I may have misjudged you, dear one.' She stared shyly at the floor. 'Perhaps you were sincere . . .' Then, glowing with appeal, she added, 'If you would stay to supper we might speak again.'

Bruli responded with an expression of transparent relief. A difficult conversation lay ahead of him, and the affair would be easier if Mara's sympathies were restored to him. Also, if he could come away with a promise of engagement, his father's rage would be less. The Acoma wealth was well established, and a few debts surely could be paid off with a minimum of fuss. Confident all would end well, Bruli waited while Mara instructed Jican to assign quarters for Bruli's retinue. When the son of the Lord of the Kehotara had been led away, Mara returned to her study, where Arakasi waited, once more in the guise of a vegetable seller.

When she was certain of privacy, Mara said, 'When were you planning to leave?'

Arakasi halted his pacing, a shadow against shadow in the corner made dim by the piles of Bruli's gifts. The songbird sang incongruously pretty notes through his words. 'Tonight, mistress.'

Mara threw a cloth over the cage, reducing the melody to a series of sleepy chirps. 'Can you wait another day or two?'

He shook his head. 'No longer than first light tomorrow. If I do not appear at a certain inn in Sulan-Qu by noon, and several other places over the next week, my replacement will become active. It would prove awkward if you ended up with two Spy Masters.' He smiled. 'And I would lose the services of a man very difficult to replace. If the matter is that vital, I can find other tasks for him and remain.'

Mara sighed. 'No. We should see an end to this nonsense with the Kehotara boy by then. I want you to identify the Minwanabi agent in his retinue to Keyoke. And tell him I will sleep in Nacoya's quarters tonight.' The songbird stopped its peeping as she finished. 'What would you think if I have Pape and Lujan keep watch in my quarters tonight?'

Arakasi paused. 'You think young Bruli plans to pay a late visit to your bed?'

'More likely an assassin from his retinue might try.' Mara shrugged. 'I have Bruli where I want him, but a little more discomfort on his part would serve us well. If someone roams the corridors tonight, I think we shall make it easy for him to reach my quarters.'

'As always, you amaze me, mistress.' Arakasi bowed with irony and admiration. 'I will see your instructions reach Keyoke.'

In one smooth movement the Spy Master melted into the shadows. His departure made no sound; he passed from the corridor unseen even by the maid who came to tell Mara that her robes and her bath awaited, should she care to refresh herself before dinner. But one more item remained. Mara sent her runner for Nacoya and informed the old woman that Bruli should now receive his father's overdue messages. In the gathering gloom of twilight she added, 'Be sure to tell him they have just arrived.'

An evil gleam lit Nacoya's eyes. 'May I carry them myself, mistress? I want to see his face when he reads them.'

Mara laughed. 'You old terror! Give him the messages, with all my blessing. And don't lie too extravagantly. The letters were delayed from town, which is more or less the truth.' She paused, hiding a moment of fear behind humour. 'Do you think this will spare me his simpering during dinner?'

But Nacoya had already departed on her errand, and the only answer Mara received was a sleepy twitter from the songbird. She shivered, suddenly, needing a hot tub between herself and thoughts of the play she was about to complete against the Lord of the Kehotara.

The oil lamps burned softly, shedding golden light over the table settings. Carefully prepared dishes steamed around a centrepiece of flowers, and chilled fish glistened against beds of fresh fruit and greenery. Clearly, the Acoma kitchen staff had laboured to prepare a romantic dinner for lovers, yet Bruli sat ill at ease on his cushions.

He pushed the exquisite food here and there on his plate, his thoughts obviously elsewhere. Even the deep neckline of Mara's robe failed to brighten his spirits.

At last, pretending confusion, the Lady of the Acoma laid aside her napkin. 'Why, Bruli, you seem all astir. Is something amiss?'

'My Lady?' The young man looked up, his blue eyes shadowed with distress. 'I hesitate to . . . trouble you with my own difficulties, but . . .' He coloured and looked down in embarrassment. 'Quite frankly, in my passion to win you, I have placed too large a debt upon my house.' A painful pause followed. 'You will doubtless think less of me and I risk losing stature in your eyes, but duty to my father requires that I beg a favour of you.'

Suddenly finding little to relish in Bruli's discomfort, Mara responded more curtly than she intended. 'What favour?' She softened the effect by setting down her fork and trying to seem concerned. 'Of course I will help if I can.'

Bruli sighed, his unhappiness far from alleviated. 'If you could find it within your heart to be so gracious, I need some of those gifts . . . the ones I sent . . . could you possibly return them?' His voice dropped, and he swallowed. 'Not all, but perhaps the more expensive ones.'

Mara's eyes were pools of sympathy as she said, 'I think I might find it in my heart to help a friend, Bruli. But the night is young, and the cooks worked hard to please us. Why don't we forget these bothersome troubles and enjoy our banquet? At the first meal tomorrow we can resolve your difficulties.'

Though he had hoped for another answer, Bruli gathered his tattered pride and weathered the rest of the dinner. His conversation was unenthusiastic, and his humour conspicuously absent, but Mara pretended not to notice. She called in a poet to read while servants brought sweet dishes and brandies; and in the end the drink helped, for the unfortunate son of the Kehotara eventually took his leave for bed. Plainly he left without romantic advances so he could pass the night painlessly in sleep.

Mist rolled over the needra meadows, clinging in the hollows like silken scarves in the moonlight. Night birds called, counterpointed by the tread of an occasional sentry; but in the Lady's chamber in the estate house another sound intruded. Papewaio pushed one foot against Lujan's ribs.

'What?' came the sleepy reply.

'Our Lady doesn't snore,' Papewaio whispered.

Yawning, and scowling with offended dignity, Lujan said, 'I don't snore.'

'Then you do a wonderful imitation.' The First Strike Leader leaned on his spear, a silhouette against the moonlit screeen. He hid his amusement, for he had come to like the former grey warrior. He appreciated Lujan for being a fine officer, far better than could have been hoped for, and because Lujan's nature was so different from Papewaio's own taciturnity.

Suddenly Papewaio stiffened, alerted by a soft scuff in the corridor. Lujan heard it also, for he left the rest of his protest unspoken. The two Acoma officers exchanged silent hand signals and immediately came to an agreement. Someone who did not wish his movements to be overheard was approaching from the hallway outside. The stranger walked now not six paces from the screen; earlier Papewaio had placed a new mat at each intersection of the corridor beyond Mara's chamber; anyone who approached her door would cause a rustle as he trod across the weave.

That sound became their cue. Without speaking, Lujan drew his sword and took up position by the door. Papewaio leaned his spear against the garden lintel and unsheathed both a sword and dagger. Moonlight flashed upon lacquer as he lay down upon Mara's mat, his weapons held close beneath the sheets.

Long minutes went by. Then the screen to the hall by the garden slid soundlessly open. The intruder showed no hesitation but leaped through the gap with his dagger drawn to stab. He bent swiftly over what he thought was the sleeping form of the Lady of the Acoma.

Papewaio rolled to his right, coming up in a fighter's crouch, his sword and dagger lifted to parry. Blade sang on blade, while Lujan closed in behind the assassin, his intent to prevent him from bolting.

Faint moonlight gave him away, as his shadow darted ahead of him across the floor. The assassin's blade cut into pillows, and jigabird feathers sailed upon the air like seed down. He rolled away and spun to his feet to discover himself trapped. Though he wore the garb of a porter, he responded with professional quickness and threw his dagger at Papewaio. The Strike Leader dodged aside. Without sound, the intruder launched himself past, twisting to avoid the sword that sliced at his back. He crashed through the paper screen and hit the pathway beyond at a full run.

Hard on his heels, Lujan shouted, 'He's in the garden!'

Instantly Acoma guards hurried through the corridors. Screens screeched open on all sides, and Keyoke strode into the turmoil, calling orders that were instantly obeyed. The warriors fanned out, beating the shrubs with their spears.

Papewaio regained his feet and moved to join the search, but Keyoke lightly touched his shoulder. 'He got away?'

The First Strike Leader muttered a curse and answered what he knew from long experience would be the Force Leader's next question. 'He's hiding somewhere on the grounds, but you must ask Lujan to describe him. The moonlight was in his favour, where I saw nothing but a shadow.' He paused while Keyoke sent for the former bandit; and after a moment Papewaio added thoughtfully, 'He's of average size, and left-handed. And his breath smelled strongly of jomach pickles.'

Lujan concluded the description. 'He wears the tunic and rope belt of a porter, but his sandals are soled with soft leather, not hardened needra hide.'

Keyoke motioned to the two nearest soldiers and gave curt orders. 'Search the quarters given to the Kehotara porters. Find out which one is missing. He's our man.'

A minute later, two other warriors arrived with a body slung limply between them. Both Papewaio and Lujan identified the assassin, and both regretted that he had found time to sink his second, smaller dagger into his vitals.

Keyoke spat on the corpse. 'A pity he died in honour by the blade. No doubt he received permission from his master before undertaking this mission.' The Force Commander sent a man to call in the searchers, then added, 'At least the Minwanabi dog admitted the possibility of failure.'

Mara must receive word of this event without more delay. Brusquely Keyoke waved at the corpse. 'Dispose of this carrion, but save a piece by which he may be identified.' He ended with a nod to his Strike Leaders. 'Well done. Take the rest of the night for sleep.'

Both men exchanged glances as the supreme commander of the Acoma forces stepped away into the night. Keyoke was seldom free with his praise. Then Lujan grinned, and Papewaio nodded. In complete and silent understanding the two men turned in the direction of the soldiers' commons to share a drink before well-earned rest.

Bruli of the Kehotara arrived at breakfast looking wretchedly out of sorts. His handsome face was puffy, and his eyes red, as if his sleep had been ridden with nightmares. Yet almost certainly he had been agonizing over his predicament with the gifts rather than knowledge of the assassin his retinue had admitted to the Acoma household; after his loss of self-control at dinner, Mara doubted he had skill enough to pretend that no attempt had been made upon her life.

She smiled, half in pity. 'My friend, you seem ill disposed. Didn't you care for your accommodations last night?'

Bruli dredged up his most engaging smile. 'No, my Lady. The quarters you gave me were most satisfactory, but . . .' He sighed, and his smile wilted. 'I am simply under stress. Regarding that matter I mentioned last night, could I ask your indulgence and forebearance . . . if you could see your way clear . . .'

Mara's air of cordiality vanished. 'I don't think that would be prudent, Bruli.'

The air smelled, incongruously, of fresh thyza bread. Numbly conscious that breakfast foods cooled on the table, Bruli locked eyes with his hostess. His cheeks coloured in a most un-Tsurani fashion. 'My Lady,' he began, 'you seem unaware of the distress you cause me by denying this petition.'

Mara said nothing but signalled to someone waiting behind the screen to her left. Armour creaked in response, and Keyoke stepped into view bearing the bloody head of the assassin. He laid the trophy without ceremony on the platter before the young suitor.

'You know this man, Bruli.' The words were no question.

Shocked by a tone of voice he had never heard from the Lady of the Acoma, but not by the barbarity upon his plate, Bruli paled. 'He was one of my porters, Lady. What has occurred?'

The shadow of the officer fell across him, and the sunny chamber suddenly seemed cold. Mara's words were metal-hard. 'Assassin, not porter, Bruli.'

The young man blinked, for an instant blank-faced. Then he slumped, a lock of black hair veiling his eyes. The admission came grudgingly. 'My father's master,' he said, naming Jingu of the Minwanabi.

Mara granted him a moment of respite, while she bade her Force Commander to sit at her side. When Bruli summoned presence enough to meet her gaze, she nodded. 'The man was without a doubt a Minwanabi agent. As you were for your father.'

Bruli managed not to protest what he knew to be futile. His eyes lost their desperate look and he said, 'I ask a warrior's death, Mara.'

Mara set her two hardened fists upon the tablecloth. 'A warrior's death, Bruli?' she laughed with bitter anger. 'My father and brother were warriors, Bruli. Keyoke is a warrior. I have faced death and am more of a warrior than you.'

Sensing something he had never known in a woman, the young man pushed gracelessly to his feet. Cups rocked on the table. With Minwanabi involvement, the grisly remnant of the porter became doubly significant. Bruli pulled a dagger from his tunic. 'You'll not take me to hang like a criminal, Lady.' Keyoke's hand shot to his sword to defend his Lady, but as Bruli reversed the dagger, pointing it at his own breast, the Force Commander understood that the Kehotara son intended no attack.

Mara shot upright, her voice a whip of command. 'Put away that dagger, Bruli.' He hesitated, but she said, 'No one is going to hang you. You're a fool, not a murderer. You will be sent home to explain to your father how his alliance with Jingu led his house into jeopardy.'

Shamed, silent, the handsome suitor stepped back before the impact of her statement. Slowly he worked through its implications, until he reached the inevitable conclusion: he had been used, ruthlessly, even to his innermost feelings. Deadly serious, with no hint of his former affection, he bowed. 'I salute you, Lady. You have caused me to betray my father.'

If his impulsive nature were permitted to run its course, he would probably restore his damaged honour by falling on his sword the moment he crossed the border of Acoma land. Mara thought quickly; she must forestall him, for his suicide would only inflame the Kehotara to more strident support of the Minwanabi lord's wish to obliterate all things Acoma. She had plotted, but not for this boy's death. 'Bruli?'

'My Lady?' He delayed his departure more from resignation than from hope.

Mara motioned for him to sit and he did so, albeit stiffly. The smell of food faintly sickened him, and shame lay like a weight upon his shoulders.

Mara could not sweeten the bitter taste of defeat; Buntokapi had taught her not to gloat when the game brought her victory. Gently she said, 'Bruli, I have no regret for doing what is needed to protect what is mine to guard. But I have no wish to cause you undue difficulty. That your father serves my most hated enemy is but an accident of birth for both of us. Let us not be contentious. I will return most of your exotic gifts in exchange for two promises.'

In his difficulty, Bruli seemed to find himself. 'I will not betray Kehotara honour.'

'I will not ask that of you.' Mara leaned earnestly forward. 'Should you succeed your father and brother as Lord of the Kehotara, I ask that you not embrace the tradition of Tan-jin-qu. Will you agree to keep your house free of Minwanabi vassalage?'

Bruli gestured depreciatingly. 'The chances of that happening are slim, Lady Mara.' His elder brother was heir, and his father enjoyed robust health.

Mara indicated herself, as if that answered his observation; who, among mortals, could know what fate would bring?

Ashamed of the hope that quickened his breath, Bruli asked, 'And the second condition?'

'That if you do come to rule, you will owe me a favour.' Mara elaborated with the care of a diplomat. 'Should I die, or should I no longer wear the mantle as Ruling Lady, your promise shall not pass to my successor. Yet if I live and you sit as Lord of the Kehotara, then once, and only once, you must do as I bid. I may ask you to support some action of mine, in commerce or in matters of arms, or in the Game of the Council. Grant this, and you shall be free of future obligations.'

Bruli stared blankly at the tablecloth, but the tension in his pose betrayed the fact that he was weighing his options. Mara waited, motionless in the glow of sunlight through the screen. She had added the second condition on impulse, to distract the young man's thoughts from suicide; but as he sat thinking the matter through, her own mind raced ahead; and she saw that she had opened yet another avenue of possibilities for gain in the Game of the Council.

Given the choice of death and financial shame for his family, or respite from his folly and the possibility of a promise he might never be required to keep, Bruli chose swiftly. 'Lady, I spoke impulsively. Your bargain is a hard one, yet I will choose life. If the gods bring me the mantle of Kehotara lordship, I shall do as you require.' He stood slowly, his manner changed to scorn. 'But as the possibility of my inheriting in place of my brother is remote, you have acted the fool.'

Hating the moment for its cruelty, Mara silently motioned to the servant who waited by the screen. He bowed and set a paper with a torn seal in her hand. 'This has come to us, Bruli. It was meant for you, but since your father saw fit to send assassins in your retinue, out of need for my personal safety my hadonra chose to read it.'

The paper was bound with ribbons of red, the colour of Turakamu. Cold, suddenly, as he had never thought to be in life, Bruli raised an unwilling hand. The paper seemed too light to carry the news he read penned in the script of his father's chief scribe. Cut to the heart by new grief, Bruli crumpled the parchment between shaking fists. Somehow he retained his self-control. 'Woman, you are poison, as deadly and small as that of the keti scorpion that hides under the petals of flowers.' She had known when she bargained that Mekasi's eldest son had been killed upon the barbarian world, victim of the Warlord's campaign. She had shaped her snare for Bruli, aware he had already inherited the title of heir. Now honour forbade him to take back his sworn word.

Shivering now from anger, Bruli regarded the woman he had once been fool enough to love. 'My father is a robust man with many years before him, Acoma bitch! I gave you my promise, but you shall never live long enough to see the keeping of it.'

Keyoke stiffened, prepared to reach for his sword, but Mara responded only with soul-weary regret. 'Never doubt I shall survive to exact my price. Think on that as you take back the gifts you sent. Only leave me the songbird, for it will remind me of a young man who loved me too well to be wise.'

Her sincerity roused memories now soured and painful. Cheeks burning from the intensity of his warring emotions, Bruli said, 'I take my leave of you. The next time we meet, the Red God grant that I view your dead body.'

He spun on his heel, aware that every Acoma soldier within earshot stood ready to answer this insult. But Mara placed a restraining hand on Keyoke's arm, silent while the young man departed. In time the tramp of the Kehotara retinue faded from the dooryard. Nacoya came in looking rumpled, her mouth a flat line of annoyance. 'What an importunate young man,' she muttered and, seeing Mara's stillness, changed tack in the same breath. 'Another lesson, child: men are easily injured over matters of the heart. More often than not, those wounds are long in healing. You may have won this round of the game, but you have also gained a deadly enemy. None are more dangerous than those in whom love has changed to hate.'

Mara gestured pointedly at the head of the dead porter. 'Someone must pay the price of Minwanabi's plotting. Whether or not Bruli finds other passions to occupy his mind, we have gained. Bruli has squandered enough of his father's wealth to place the Kehotara in a vulnerable position. Jingu will be prevailed upon to offer financial assistance, and anything which discomforts that jaguna is a benefit.'

'Daughter of my heart, fate seldom works with such simplicity.' Nacoya stepped closer, and for the first time Mara looked up and saw the scroll clutched between her old hands. The ribbons and seal were orange and black, colours she never thought to see under her roof in her lifetime. 'This just arrived,' said her First Adviser. With an air of stiff-backed reluctance, she passed the parchment into the hands of her mistreess.

Mara snapped the ribbons and seal with hands that trembled beyond control. The scroll unrolled with a crackle against the silence that gripped the chamber. Mara read, her face expressionless as an image in wax.

Nacoya held her breath; Keyoke found what comfort he could in his statue-still military bearing; and at last Mara raised her eyes.

She rose, suddenly seeming fragile in the glare of the sun. 'As you guessed,' she said to the two oldest retainers in her service, 'the Lord of the Minwanabi requests my attendance at a formal celebration of the birthday of our august Warlord.'

The colour drained slowly from Nacoya's withered skin. 'You must refuse,' she said at once. No Acoma in uncounted generations had set foot onto the territory of the Minwanabi, unless accompanied by soldiers armed for war. For Mara to enter Jingu's very house and mingle socially with his allies was a sure invitation to die. Nacoya finished lamely, 'Your ancestors would forgive the shame.'

'No!' the Lady of the Acoma bit her lip, hard enough that the flesh turned white. 'I risk grave insult to Almecho if I refuse, and after this betrayal by the Blue Wheel Party, his acclaimed temper will be short.' Her voice trailed off, but whether from regret that she must confront Jingu before she was ready or out of fear for her own safety was unclear. Stress made her face an unreadable mask. 'The Acoma must not bow to threats. I shall go into the stronghold of the enemy who most wishes me dead.'

Nacoya made a small sound of protest, then desperately turned her back. Torn by the sight of her adviser's bowed shoulders, Mara tried against hope to offer comfort. 'Mother of my heart, take courage. Remember that if Turakamu reaches out for my spirit, the Lord of the Minwanabi cannot triumph unless he also murders Ayaki. Do you think he would challenge the combined might of the Acoma and the Anasati to take the life of my son?'

For this Nacoya had no answer; at last she shook her head. But her heart told her that Jingu would dare even this to see his ancient enemies destroyed. Worse had been done, and for far less reason than blood feud, in the history of the Game of the Council.

14

Acceptance

The runner left.

Mara pressed clenched hands on the edge of her writing desk and desperately wished him back. Too easily, the dispatch he carried to the Guild of Porters might bring her death and the final ruin of the Acoma. But the alternative was to live without honour, shame her ancestors, and defile the ancient code of her house. Mara allowed herself a momentary stretch to ease her tense back, then summoned Nacoya, to tell the old woman that she had sent formal acceptance to Minwanabi's invitation.

Nacoya entered with grim deliberation, sure sign she had seen the runner leave the estates. Age had not blunted her shrewdness; she already guessed that the sealed wooden cylinder he carried did not hold instructions for the factors signed by Jican.

'You have many preparations to make, Ruling Lady.' The erstwhile nurse's demeanour was all that a First Adviser's should be; but long years of intimacy could not be shed with a change of office. Mara read acerbity in the ancient woman's tone and knew that fear lay behind it: fear for her mistress, and for all on the Acoma estates whose lives were sworn to her natami. To enter the household of the Minwanabi lord was to challenge the monster while stepping between the teeth of its jaws. Only the most powerful might survive, and Acoma stock in the council had recovered very little since the deaths of Lord Sezu and his heir.

Yet Mara gave no opportunity for her chief adviser to embark on such recriminations. No longer the untried girl who had left Lashima's temple, she was determined not to seem overwhelmed by Minwanabi threats. Panic would only hand Jingu a victory; and his impulsive nature might make it possible to wrest some unseen advantage for her house. 'See to the necessities of travel, Nacoya, and have maids assemble my wardrobe. Papewaio must be told to choose warriors for my honour guard, ones who are trustworthy and proven in service, but whom Keyoke will not need in key positions to safeguard the estates in my absence.' Pacing the polished floor before a shelf of scrolls, Mara paused a moment to tally days. 'Has Arakasi returned?'

A week had passed since Bruli and Arakasi had both departed the Acoma estates, one to deal with a father's anger, the other to keep his mistress's network of agents running smoothly. Nacoya pushed a drooping hairpin straight. 'He returned less than an hour ago, mistress.'

Mara turned with a frown of intense concentration. 'I will speak with him after he has bathed and refreshed himself. In the meantime, send for Jican. Much business remains to be discussed before we leave for the Warlord's birthday celebration.'

Nacoya bowed with evident reluctance. 'Your will, Lady.' She rose silently and left; and in a room emptied of all but the waiting presence of a few servants, Mara stared at the afternoon sunlight that embellished the screens of the study. The artist had painted his hunting scenes with masterful vigour, the trained grace of a killwing impaling swift game birds. Mara shivered. Feeling little stronger than a bird herself, she wondered whether she would ever have the chance to commission such art again.

Then Jican arrived, his arms burdened with parchments and tally slates, and a long list of decisions to be made before her departure. Mara put aside her disquiet and made herself concentrate on matters of commerce. Particularly troublesome was a note in Jican's neat script objecting to her wish to purchase Midkemian slaves to clear new meadows for the needra displaced by the cho-ja hive. Mara sighed and rubbed the frown creases from her forehead.

Under too much stress to insist on her decision, she put off the purchase until after the Warlord's birthday. If she survived the gathering at the Minwanabi estates, she would have ample time to deal with Jican's reluctance. But if Jingu of the Minwanabi realized his ambitions, the entire question would become academic. Ayaki would gain an Anasati regent or be killed, and the Acoma would be absorbed or obliterated. Restless and irritable, Mara reached for the next list. This one occasion, she would be relieved when Jican finished and departed.

*

The afternoon had fled by the time Jican bid his mistress good-bye. Limp in the evening shadows, Mara called for chilled fruit and drink. Then she sent her runner for Arakasi, and a servant to fetch his updated report detailing the Minwanabi household from the numbers of his kitchen scullions to the names and backgrounds of his concubines.

Arakasi entered, and Mara said, 'Is all in order?'

'Mistress, your agents are well. I have little of importance to add to that report, however, as I amended it before I bathed.' He cocked his head slightly, awaiting his mistress's pleasure. Noticing that the rigours of travel had left him gaunt and fatigued, Mara motioned to the cushions before the fruit tray.

As Arakasi seated himself, she informed him of the Warlord's birthday celebration at the Minwanabi estates. 'We will have no chance for missteps,' she observed as the Spy Master chose a bunch of sā berries.

Quieter than usual, and free of all airs, Arakasi twisted the fruit one by one from their stems. Then he sighed. 'Appoint me a place among your honour guard, my Lady.'

Mara caught her breath. 'That's dangerous.' She watched the Spy Master keenly, aware that the man's hunger for vengeance matched her own. If prudence did not desert him, he would be seeking to turn the tables on this trap and gain a victory.

'There will indeed be danger, Lady. And there will be death.' Arakasi pinched a berry between his fingers, and juice ran red over his palm. 'Nonetheless, let me go.'

Slowly, carefully, Mara banished uncertainty from her heart. She inclined her head in acquiescence, though unspoken between them remained the fact that Arakasi was as likely to get himself killed as protect the life of his mistress. Though he could wear a warrior's trappings well enough, the Spy Master had poor skill with weapons. That he had asked to accompany her at all bespoke the extreme cunning and treachery she could expect from the Minwanabi Lord. It did not escape her that if she failed, Arakasi might wish to wrest one last chance to fulfil his desire while Jingu was within his reach. For the cho-ja, and for all he had added to the security of the Acoma defences, she owed him that much.

'I had planned to take Lujan . . . but he could be needed here.' Keyoke had come to admit grudgingly that, beneath his roguish manner, Lujan was a gifted officer. And if Keyoke was forced to defend Ayaki . . . Mara turned her thoughts away from that course and said, 'Go to Pape. If he trusts you with the loan of an officer's plume, you can help him select my retinue.' Mara managed a brief smile before fear returned to chill her. Arakasi bowed. The instant he left, Mara clapped sharply for servants, that the tray with the mangled berry be removed at once from her presence.

In failing light, Mara regarded the screen one final time. The waiting was at last over, and the killwing stooped to its prey. Though Minwanabi was proud, and confident, and strong, she must now seek a way to defeat him on his own territory.

The late summer roads were dry, choked with dust thrown up by the caravans, and unpleasant for travel. After the short march overland to Sulan-Qu, Mara and her retinue of fifty honour guards continued their journey to the Minwanabi estates by barge. The bustle of the town and the dockside did not overwhelm Mara; the nakedness of the slaves barely turned her head, caught up as she was in the meshes of enemy intrigue. As she settled with Nacoya on the cushions beneath the canopy, she reflected that she no longer felt strange to be ruling the house of her father. The years since Lashima's temple had brought many changes and much growth; and with them came determination enough to hide her dread. Keyoke arrayed his soldiers on board with a reflection of that same pride. Then the barge master began his chant, and the slaves cast off and leaned into their poles. The Acoma craft threw ripples from its painted bow and drew away from familiar shores.

The journey upriver took six days. Mara spent most of these in contemplation, as slaves poled the barge past acres of mud flats and the sour-smelling expanses of drained thyza paddies. Nacoya slept in the afternoons; evenings she left the shelter of the gauze curtains and dispersed motherly advice among the soldiers, while they slapped at the stinging insects that arose in clouds from the shores. Mara listened, nibbling at the fruit bought from a barge vendor; she knew the old woman did not expect to return home alive. And indeed each sunset seemed precious, as clouds streamed reflections like gilt over the calm surface of the river and the sky darkened swiftly into night.

The Minwanabi estates lay off a small tributary of the main river.

Beaded with sweat in the early morning heat, the slaves poled through the muddle of slower-moving merchant craft. Under the barge master's skilful guidance, they manoeuvred between a squalid village of stilt houses, inhabited by families of shellfish rakers; the river narrowed beyond, shallows and shoals giving way to deeper waters. Mara looked out over low hills, and banks lined with formally manicured trees. Then the barge of her family entered waters none but the most ancient Acoma ancestors might have travelled, for the origins of the blood feud with Jingu's line lay so far in the past that none remembered its beginning. Here the current picked up speed as the passage narrowed. The slaves had to work furiously to maintain headway, and the barge slowed almost to a standstill. Mara strove to maintain a façade of calm as her craft continued towards an imposingly painted prayer gate that spanned the breadth of the river. This marked the boundary of Minwanabi lands.

A soldier bowed beside Mara's cushions and pointed a sun-browned hand at the tiered structure that crowned the prayer gate. 'Did you notice? Beneath the paint and decorations, this monument is a bridge.'

Mara started slightly, for the voice was familiar. She regarded the man closely and half smiled at the cleverness of her own Spy Master. Arakasi had blended so perfectly among the ranks of her honour guard, she had all but forgotten he was aboard.

Restoring her attention to the prayer gate, Arakasi continued, 'In times of strife, they say that Minwanabi stations archers with rags and oil to fire any craft making its way upriver. A fine defence.'

'As slowly as we are moving, I would think no one could enter Minwanabi's lake this way and live.' Mara glanced astern at the foaming current. 'But we certainly could flee quickly enough.'

Arakasi shook his head. 'Look downward, mistress.'

Mara leaned over the edge of the barge and saw a giant braided cable strung between the pillars of the gate, inches below the shallow keel of the barge. Should trouble arise, a mechanism within the gate towers could raise the cable, forming a barrier against any barge seeking exit. Arakasi said, 'This defence is as lethal to fleeing craft as to any attacking fleet.'

'And I would be wise to bear that in mind?' Mara untwisted damp fingers from the fringe of her robe. Trying to keep her uneasiness within balance, she made a polite gesture of dismissal. 'Your warning is well taken, Arakasi. But do not say anything to Nacoya, or she'll squawk so loudly she'll disrupt the peace of the gods!'

The Spy Master rose with a grunt that concealed laughter. 'I need say nothing at all. The old mother sees knives under her sleeping mat at night.' He lowered his voice. 'I've watched her flip her pillows and blankets six times, even after Papewaio inspects her bedding.'

Mara waved him off, unable to share his humour. Nacoya was not the only one who had nightmares. As the barge pressed on, and the shadow of the 'prayer gate' fell across her, a chill roughened her flesh like the breath of Turakamu.

The sounds of their passage echoed off stone foundations. Then sunlight sliced down, blinding and intense after darkness. Mara looked out of the gauze-curtained canopy to a sight entirely unexpected.

The vista beyond was breathtaking in its beauty. Located in the neck of a broad valley, at the head of a wide lake, the estate house across the water looked a magic place from a child's tale, each building perfect in design and colour. The centremost structure was stone, an impossibly ancient palace built high up on a hill overlooking the lake. Low walls wound down the hillside amid terraced gardens and lesser buildings, many two and three stories tall. The estate of the Minwanabi was in truth a village in its own right, a community of servants and soldiers, all loyal to Jingu. But what a magnificent town, Mara thought. And she knew a brief stab of envy that so bitter an enemy should live in such splendour. Breezes off the lake would cool the house through even the hottest months, and a fleet of small orange and black punts trawled for fish, so that the Lord of the Minwanabi might dine upon fresh-caught koafish. As the slaves exchanged poles for oars to convey the barge across the lake, a more sober thought occurred to Mara: the valley was a bottleneck, easily defended, and easier to seal. Like the poisoned flask plant that devoured insects by luring them with sweet scents, the layout of this valley foreclosed any chance of swift, unnoticed escape.

Papewaio perceived this also, for he called his warriors to present arms as another craft approached. Quickly heaving into view, the large barge contained a dozen Minwanabi archers, a Patrol Leader at their head. He saluted and motioned for them to dress oars. 'Who comes to Minwanabi lands?' he called out as the barges closed.

Papewaio called an answer. 'The Lady of the Acoma.'

The officer of the Minwanabi saluted. 'Pass, Lady of the Acoma.' He signalled his own contingent of rowers, and the Minwanabi barge resumed its patrol.

Arakasi pointed to three other such barges. 'They have companies of archers all over the lake.'

Clearly no escape was possible from the Minwanabi lord's home. There remained only victory or death. Feeling her palms grow damp, Mara resisted the impulse to blot them on her robe. 'Let us make best speed to the house, Pape.'

Papewaio signalled the barge captain, and the slaves resumed their stroke.

The barge headed dockside, and the Minwanabi estate proved as beautiful upon close inspection as it had looked across the water. Each building was delicately painted, pastel colours dominating over the usual white. Gaily coloured streamers and brightly shaded lanterns hung from roof beams, twisting in the breeze. The soft sound of wind chimes filled the air. Even the gravel paths between buildings had been lined with tended shrubs and flowering plants. Mara expected that the courtyard gardens within the estate might prove more sumptuous that any she had seen.

The Acoma rowers shipped oars, and one threw a line to a worker upon the docks, where a welcoming party of notables waited. Foremost of these was Desio, the elder Minwanabi son, crowned with the orange and black headdress denoting his rank as heir of the house.

Liveried attendants caught other lines as the barge bumped gently against the pilings. Minwanabi house guards stood at attention, and Desio strode forward to meet Mara's litter as slaves conveyed her ashore.

The Minwanabi heir nodded stiffly, a pretence of a bow that bordered on insult. 'In the name of my father, I welcome you to our celebration in honour of the Warlord, Lady of the Acoma.'

Mara did not trouble to raise the gauze curtains of her litter. Studying the fat, pouched features of Desio, and finding little intelligence in his slate-coloured eyes, she returned a nod of precisely the same proportion. For the longest moment nothing was said, then Desio was forced to acknowledge Mara's superior social rank. 'Are you well, Lady Mara?'

Mara nodded slightly. 'I am well, Desio. The Acoma are pleased to honour Lord Almecho. Tell your father that I acknowledge this welcome.'

Desio raised his chin, nettled to admit his inferior rank. Too proud to accept rejoinder from a girl who seemed, through the gauze, to be barely more than a child, he said, 'The reception for the banquet of greeting will begin in the hour past noon. Servants will show you to your quarters.'

'Servants keep the honour of the Minwanabi?' Mara smiled sweetly. 'That's a fact I shall remember, when I greet the Lord your father.'

Desio reddened. To arrest the awkwardness that developed, a Minwanabi Patrol Leader stepped forward. 'My Lady, if you will permit, I will convey your soldiers to the place set aside for them.'

'I will not permit!' Mara said to Desio. 'By tradition I am allowed fifty soldiers to provide protection for my person. If your father wishes otherwise, I shall depart at once, and he can explain my absence to the Warlord. Under such circumstances, I expect the Acoma will not be the only great house to return home.'

'Too many families come to honour Almecho.' Desio paused to quell a smile of malice. 'If we quartered every Lord and Lady's honour guard in the house barracks, the estate would be jammed like a war camp, you must understand. Almecho likes tranquillity. To do him homage, all soldiers will stay at the head of the valley, where our main garrison is quartered.' Here Desio gave an effete shrug. 'No one is exempted. All will be treated alike.'

Without hesitation, Nacoya said, 'Then your father offers his honour as surety?'

Desio inclined his head. 'Obviously.' To gain such a concession from guests in this situation, the host was expected to offer his personal honour to guarantee the safety of his guests. Should violence come to any visitor under such an arrangement, Lord Jingu of the Minwanabi could not expiate his shame with anything less than his own life. The heir to the Minwanabi mantle said to a servant, 'Show the Lady, her First Adviser, a pair of maids, and her bodyguard to the suite of rooms prepared for the Acoma.'

He snapped his fingers to the orange-plumed presence of an officer. 'Strike Leader Shimizu and a welcoming party of warriors will see that your soldiers are comfortably housed at the main garrison barracks.'

Shocked, angered, but not entirely surprised that the Minwanabi had seen fit to separate her from her honour guard, Mara shot a glance of reassurance at Arakasi. She would not break the peace of hospitality by causing a fuss, particularly since many of the house servants present showed the scars of old campaigns beneath the flowing sleeves of their livery. No, the Acoma could not triumph here by force, but only by guile, if survival was even possible at all. With a look of acceptance, Mara chose Papewaio for her personal guard. Then she, Nacoya, and the most skilful of her warriors obediently followed the servant to the suite assigned to the Acoma.

The Minwanabi great house was ancient, saved from the burning and the ravages of forgotten raids and half-remembered wars by its superior location in the valley. The square with interior courtyard of most Tsurani houses had been altered, built upon, expanded, and sub-divided many times over the years. Descending the hillside as new additions were constructed, the heart of the Minwanabi estate had grown over the centuries until it was a warren of corridors, enclosed courtyards, and linked buildings that bore little resemblance to order. As Papewaio helped her from her litter, Mara realized with dismay that she would need servants to conduct her to and from her chambers, as a structure so complex could not possibly be learned at one pass.

The corridors crooked and twisted, and each courtyard seemed the same as the last. Mara heard the murmur of voices through half-opened screens, some belonging to familiar notables of the Empire, but more of them strange to her. Then the voices seemed to fall behind, and silence like that before the strike of a jungle predator fell over the elegant hallway. By the time the servant slid wide the screen that led to her suite, Mara knew that Jingu intended murder. Why else would he place her in an obscure corner of his house, where isolation was almost total?

The servant bowed, smiled, and mentioned that additional maids awaited her pleasure if the Lady of the Acoma or her First Adviser required assistance with their bath or dress.

'My own servants will suffice.' Mara said tartly. Here of all places, she wished no strangers near her person. The instant the bearers had deposited the last of her baggage, she clicked the screen closed. Papewaio needed no prompting to begin a swift and thorough inspection of her chambers. Nacoya, however, seemed all but in shock. Then Mara remembered. Except for one brief trip when she had presented Mara's petition for betrothal with the Anasati son, the old nurse had probably never left the Acoma estates in all her long life.

Memories of Lano lent Mara the insight to manage. The instant Papewaio had determined the rooms were safe, she stationed him to guard the door. Nacoya looked at her mistress, a hint of relief in her eyes. 'With Jingu making surety for the safety of his guests, I think we may expect the peace of a state function to apply.'

Mara shook her head. 'I think wishing has fogged your sharp eyes, old mother. Jingu offers his life as guarantee against violence by his people, and by other guests, that is all. He makes no guarantees against "accidents".' Then, before fear could get the best of her, she commanded Nacoya to draw a bath and make her ready for the banquet and her first personal confrontation with the Lord of the Minwanabi.

Unlike the great hall of the Anasati, which was dark and airless and musty with old wax, the gathering chamber of the Minwanabi was all space and light. Mara paused in the gallery-style entrance to admire the view before joining the guests who gathered like so many plumed birds below. Built in a natural hollow at the very crest of the hill, with entrance and dais at opposite ends, the room itself was immense. A high, beamed ceiling was spaced with screens that opened to the sky, overhanging a deep-sunken main floor. Several small observation galleries dotted the rim of the hall, allowing a view of floor below and, through doors to balconies outside, the surrounding countryside. Stone pillars supported the centre tree, while a pebbled brook trickled through squares of flowering trees, tile mosaics, and a small reflecting pool beneath the dais. Somewhere, sometime, the Minwanabi had patronized an architect and an artist who had possessed uncommon genius. The gifted artisans must have served an earlier generation of Minwanabi Lords, for the most garish clothing in the crowd was that worn by the Lord and the Lady on the dais. Mara winced, less impressed than most

Tsurani by the gown of green and orange worn by the wife. Mara almost wept at the thought of all this surrounding beauty wasted upon an enemy like Jingu.

'The gods may have blessed this house with extreme wealth,' muttered Nacoya. 'But the divine ones left little room for common sense, I say. Think how many insects those sky ports let in, not to mention dust and dirt and rain.'

Mara smiled indulgently on her old nurse. 'Would you try to mother even a nest of serpents? Besides, I'm sure the Minwanabi cover their roof well when the weather is bad. Jingu's wife wears too much makeup to get wet unexpectedly.'

Nacoya subsided, with a comment that her eyes were not that good, nor had they been since she was youthful. Mara patted her adviser's hand in reassurance. Then, resplendent in a gown embroidered with seed pearls, her coiled hair laced with green ribbons, she began her descent to the main floor. Papewaio followed her in dress armour; although he escorted his mistress and her First Adviser to a social occasion, he moved with a vigilance more common to the battlefield. In most ways, state gatherings of Tsurani were more dangerous. Beneath the manners and the finery, ambitions changed; as alliances shifted within the Game of the Council, any Lord present could become the enemy. Few would hesitate to damage the Acoma, if his own stock might rise as a result. And on Minwanabi territory, others not normally at odds with Mara's house might bend with the prevailing political wind.

Simple in her tastes, Mara was neither overwhelmed nor impressed by displays of great wealth. Her restrained clothing reinforced the impression already formed by the Lords and Ladies in the hall around her. Most believed her a young, inexperienced girl who had sheltered her house under the marriage to the more powerful Anasati. Now, with Buntokapi dead, she was fair game once again. Mara was content to allow this misapprehension to continue as she passed by; it increased her chances to pick up a scrap of information, a comment, or a remark that could prove useful. As she reached the foot of the stairs and made her way towards the dais to greet the Minwanabi lord, she watched the expressions of her peers and took stock of who stood gossiping with whom. Her temple-taught poise served her well. She responded politely to those who greeted her, but was not lulled by sweet smiles and warm words.

Jingu of the Minwanabi noted her approach with the ravenous interest of a jaguna. Mara saw him cease conversation with his adviser as she mounted the steps to accept his welcome. The moment gave her pause also, as for the first time she looked upon the face of her family's oldest enemy. The Lord of the Minwanabi was a corpulent man. He had clearly not worn armour since his youth, but cunning and malice still glinted in his eyes. Pearl bands encircled his wrists, and shell ornaments dangled at his collar, shiny with the sweat that beaded his neck. His bow of greeting was slightly less than that due a Lady of ruling rank. 'My Lady of the Acoma,' he said, his voice as thick and unctuous as his appearance, 'we are so pleased you chose to join us in honour of the Warlord.'

Aware the eyes of every noble in the room were turned to see how she handled this slight, Mara responded in kind, her own bow shallow and of short duration. 'We thank the Lord of the Minwanabi for his kind invitation.'

Irritated by Mara's poise, Jingu beckoned someone to the fore of the dais. 'There is one here I believe you know.' Then his lips curled into a hungry smile of anticipation.

The Lady of the Acoma showed no reaction to the woman who came at his call. The presence of Teani somewhere in the Minwanabi household was something Arakasi had forewarned her of: he had long since informed Mara that the concubine was a Minwanabi agent. But the fact that Buntokapi's former lover had insinuated herself in Jingu's innermost circle gave Mara pause. The woman was perhaps more clever than anyone had guessed. She was obviously a favourite, swathed as she was in rare silks and jewels, a chain of rarest metal encircling her slim neck. But ornaments and beauty could not entirely hide the ugliness of her character. Hatred for Mara burned in her pretty eyes, chilling in its intensity.

To acknowledge the look of a woman of her station would be an unnecessary courtesy, and too easily interpreted as an admission of weakness. Mara addressed her words and attention solely to the Minwanabi lord who sat at Teani's left hand. 'My adviser and I have just arrived after a long and tiresome journey. Would my Lord show us our places, that we might take some refreshment before the banquet and the festivities begin?'

Jingu rearranged the fringe on his costume with the flick of a pudgy finger. Then he called for a cool drink; while he waited for servants to fill his need, his hand absently stroked Teani's arm, a gesture his wife ignored. When none might mistake the fact that he deferred the wishes of his Acoma guests until his own pleasures were satisfied, he nodded sweetly to a servant. 'Escort the Lady Mara and her servants to the table third from the end, nearest the entrance to the kitchens, so that her party may more quickly be served.' His fat girth jiggled as he openly laughed at the ingenuity of his insult.

A Lady of rank might find such placement degrading; but to Teani this gesture was not enough. Viciously piqued that Mara had ignored her, she interrupted. 'You ought to seat this woman with the slaves, my Lord. All know the greatness of the Acoma rests upon the goodwill of the Anasati, and that even Lord Tecuma's protection wore thin after the death of his son.'

This affront was too great to disregard. Still disdaining to answer Teani directly, Mara pointedly rose to the bait Jingu had dangled before her. She directed a gaze like flint to his fat, laughing face. 'My Lord of the Minwanabi, all know of your . . . generosity, but surely even you can find little benefit in keeping another man's leavings in your service.'

Jingu rested an arm around Teani's shoulders and drew her slim body against his own. 'But you confuse circumstance, Lady Mara. This woman was cast off by no man, but was only a mistress who survived her late master. I'll remind you but once. Teani is a valued and worthy member of my household.'

'Of course.' Mara sketched a negligible bow of apology. 'Given your widely known tastes, she should serve you well, Jingu. Indeed, my late husband had no complaints' – Mara gave Teani the barest glance – 'but then again, Bunto's appetites were rather coarse.'

Teani's eyes flashed sparks. The fact that Mara made no effort to respond directly to her insult made the courtesan furious. The Lord of the Minwanabi was in no way amused; this small near-virgin from Lashima's temple had shown no sign of being cowed by treatment that demeaned her. Indeed, she had held her own through this first exchange of words. And since his house servant already hovered by her elbow to escort the Lady and her retinue to their places, Jingu had no graceful recourse other than to dismiss her.

The festivities passed slowly for Mara. The food, the musicians, and the dancers were all the finest, but the table nearest the kitchen was hot, noisy, and beset by the constant bustle of servants passing by. The heat and the odours from cooking caused Nacoya to feel ill, and well before the first course of the banquet had been laid Papewaio looked strained. The incessant movement of strangers to and from the kitchen kept him on edge, particularly since every passing tray contained items that were weapons to a trained hand. He had overheard Mara's remark to Nacoya about 'accidents'. And while it was unlikely the Lord of the Minwanabi would attempt to stage a murder in this public setting, Teani's venomous gaze never left Mara. The Acoma Strike Leader's caution remained on a knife edge. When the rare ices served for dessert were cleared away, Papewaio gently touched his mistress's shoulder. 'Lady, I suggest you retire to your chambers before dark. The hallways are strange, and if you await the Minwanabi's pleasure, the servant he assigns you might have other instructions.'

Mara returned from what seemed a long period of concentrated thought. Her hair was perfectly coiled and her manner alert, but dark circles of fatigue underlined her eyes. 'We must find a way to send word to the barracks, that Arakasi will know which suite to leave messages at if the need should arise.'

Papewaio answered grimly. 'We can do nothing without risking discovery, Lady. Trust Arakasi. His agents can reach him without danger, and he will find you himself if there is need.'

Unable to be heard over the scrape of tables as servants cleared the hall for an exhibition of tumblers, Mara only nodded. She patted Nacoya's arm, then arose to make her excuses to the Lord of the Minwanabi. The headache that plagued her was real enough, and since the Warlord would not make his appearance until the morrow, her departure would cause no offence. If anything, she wished to leave the impression that she was young, inexperienced, and lacking in subtlety. An early retirement would reinforce that impression with the guests, perhaps granting her a breather to formulate a defence. Minwanabi would have a difficult time completing his plots with the eyes of every rival seeking an opening to exploit ahead of him.

Mara sent the servant who cleared away the plates to inform the Lord of her departure. By the time the news reached the dais, and the huge, self-satisfied smile creased the jowls of the great Lord's face, the chairs where the Acoma had dined stood empty. Infatuated with that small triumph, Jingu did not notice that Teani had also vanished. Weary of badgering her master for the chance to torment the Lady of the Acoma before the end, she had left to pursue her own means of realizing her goal, knowing that drink and the indulgences of entertaining would satiate the appetites of her Lord.

The blue silk scarf that covered Teani's hair fluttered behind her as she hastened down a back corridor of the Minwanabi estate house. She did not trouble to replace it, nor did she pause to retie the fall of tawny hair that tumbled over her shoulders. Strike Leader Shimizu's quarters lay across the next courtyard, and the need for stealth was past; the only person likely to be about at this hour was the slave who lit the oil lamps. Teani slipped through the last screen with a secretive smile. Tonight the slave would be late, preoccupied as he was with the needs of Jingu's guests. The old jaguna could be niggardly when it came to looking after his staff. Politics always came first in the great Lord's mind, a trait his ranking officers sometimes came to resent.

Golden in the moonlight that flooded the courtyard, Teani paused to unhook the collar of her robe. She loosened the fabric enough to reveal a provocative expanse of breast, and her teeth flashed white in a smile. Tonight, if she was skilful, the skinny little Acoma bitch would die. How sweet it would be to hear her screams.

Across the courtyard the screen to Shimizu's quarters rested ajar. Lamplight burned beyond, throwing the distorted silhouette of a man hunched on his cushions with a flask. He's drinking again, Teani thought in disgust, and all because she had delayed in the great hall, striving with no success to get Jingu to reassign the plotting of Mara's execution. The concubine wished that pleasure for herself. The fact that her Lord did not care to delegate that task to Teani left her no choice but to outwit him.

Tossing her hair over now almost bare shoulders, the concubine resumed her walk towards the open screen. She entered so silently that for an instant the dark-haired man within did not notice. Teani stole that moment to study him.

Shimizu, First Strike Leader of the Minwanabi, was known to his fellow soldiers as a man of fierce loyalties, passionate beliefs, and forthright personality. His quick reflexes and near-infallible judgment on the battlefield had earned him early promotion; his face was young for his post, unlined except for the scars acquired through his profession. His only flaw was a thin skin, giving him a temper that could erupt without warning. His eyes were hooded, his moods difficult to read except when he drank. In the petulant thrust of his lower lip, Teani saw frustration – the sulky, explosive sort given to men who are balked by a lover. Teani congratulated herself on a task well performed. She knew this man for a fool, sick inside with longing for her body, and the sort of emotional juvenile who mistook longing for love. And by the sweat that shone on his muscled chest, Teani knew that Shimizu was hers to use at will, a tool perfectly tempered to do her bidding; as so many others had been, male and female.

Except Mara. The Lady of the Acoma had escaped her. For that, Teani assembled her most inviting smile and, from behind, raised a hand to touch the sweating flesh of Shimizu's shoulder.

He started violently, and his hand grasped and drew the sword he kept always by his knee. The blade sang from beneath the sheath, turning to kill even as he recognized his lover. The edge caught in soft silk and stopped, barely short of bloodshed.

'Woman!' Shimizu's face paled, then flushed with anger, both at the lateness of Teani's arrival and the stealth of her entry. As he recovered his poise, he noticed a queer brilliance in her eyes. Her lips were slightly parted, as if the sword had been a lover to embrace. Her nipples hardened as she breathed deeply, excited by the brush of the razor-sharp edge against her flesh. Recognition of her twisted passions soured his welcome slightly; he sheathed his weapon with a show of disgust. 'You're mad, woman, sick in the mind. I might have run you through.'

But the anger, the disgust, never lasted. When Teani tipped her face upward, her breasts pressing firmly through his tunic, Shimizu lowered his head like one starving and savoured the kiss made hot for him by a slight brush with death. She had solved him like a puzzle. Every touch seemed to melt him to the marrow of his bones. Unable to suppress his surge of joyous welcome, Shimizu caught his fingers in the ties that closed her gown. 'You can stay, my love? Tell me that Jingu is preoccupied with his guests, and that you will not have to return to his bed this night.'

Teani brushed his ear with her tongue and answered, her breath hot against his neck. 'Jingu does not expect me back to his chambers,' she lied. Then, waiting for his fingers to grip more insistently at her clothing, she fended him off. 'But tonight I may not stay.'

Shimizu frowned, his eyes suddenly hard in the light of the single oil lamp. 'Why not? Do you share your affections elsewhere?'

Teani laughed, letting him dangle a moment before she slipped her robe from her shoulders and bared her lovely breasts. Shimizu tried to remain stern, but his attention was clearly engaged. 'I love no other, my fine warrior.' She shaded her tone with just enough hint of sarcasm to leave him a bit in doubt. 'It is state business that takes me from your side this night. Now, will you waste what time we have, or will you . . .' And she moaned, biting softly as he stopped her words with his lips.

Yet this time, deliberately, she held back enough that he did not lose his train of thought.

His hands roughened on the bare silk of her skin, and his tone grew demanding. 'Why, then, did you delay so long in coming to me?'

Teani whipped back her honey-streaked hair in a show of pique. 'How distrustful you are. Do you fear that your sword is not enough to please a woman?' She moved away, both to tease and to allow him a better view of her half-nude body.

Shimizu frowned, and his hands caught her shoulders. But now Teani softened like butter against him. Her fingers slid skilfully through the slit in his robe. He tensed in delicious apprehension as she scratched her nails along the inside of his thigh.

'And such a mighty sword,' she murmured, eyelids drooping as her mouth formed a pouting smile. 'My Lord of the Minwanabi detained me with tiresome instructions. It seems he wants the Acoma bitch dead, and I'm the one chosen for the filthy chore.'

But even as her hands found their mark and stroked in the manner he most preferred, Shimizu pulled back. Instantly Teani knew she had pushed too fast; or perhaps erred in her manner of presentation. She bent instantly, her hair trailing across his thighs, and teased his flesh with her tongue.

Shimizu took a moment to respond; then his hands tightened against her back, and his voice, dreamily, resumed above her. 'That's most strange, my love, that my Lord gave such instructions.'

Teani's interest sharpened. She straightened and set her hands to untie the laces of his sandals. 'Gods, do you always have to wear your studded soles in the house?'

Shimizu shifted impatiently, but the concubine continued with his laces. The hardened tip of her breast brushed the inside of his knee as she worked, driving him wild to the point where he answered her next lazy query without thinking.

'Why? Oh, my Lord told me yesterday that the Acoma girl was to die, but he intends to break her spirit first. Terrify her, he said, by killing off her servants and retainers so that when he strikes, she will be utterly alone.' Here Shimizu stopped and flushed, aware that his tongue had become loose. He tangled one fist in red-gold hair, drawing Teani away from the sandal as yet left fastened. 'I think you lie, woman. You do not go to kill Mara, but to couple with another this night.'

Teani's eyes flashed, partly in excitement, for violence aroused her; and also because men were so laughably predictable. She did not deny the accusation, but provoked further by saying, 'What makes you think that I lie?'

Shimizu caught her wrists, jerking her body against him. 'I say you lie because my orders for tomorrow night are to stage a false raid by a thief and see that Papewaio, Strike Leader of the Acoma, lies dead on Mara's doorstep. Why then, without cancelling such orders, should my Lord of the Minwanabi tell you to give the girl to Turakamu tonight?'

Heated by his handling, and loosened by the ridiculous ease with which she had goaded his ego and caused him to spill his confidence to her, Teani raised her chin in challenge. 'How should I know the ways of great men?' She met his eyes to assure herself that his hunger was still kindled. 'My love, you are jealous beyond rational thought. Shall we strike a bargain to salve your feelings? I will lie here with you tonight, and tell Minwanabi that I tried and failed to reach Mara of the Acoma with my knife. But in exchange, you must restore my honour by killing the girl along with Papewaio tomorrow.'

Shimizu did not speak but gathered Teani close. His fingers moved impatiently, working the robe free of her body. She wore no clothing beneath, and by the feverish way he pulled off his own robe and tunic, the concubine knew she had him. His preoccupation was answer enough. He would do her will on the morrow, to ensure she was his, and his alone, for the duration of the night. Shimizu mistook her shiver of delight for passion. As he claimed her, his thoughts were solely of love; but the beautiful courtesan he coupled with responded with cold-blooded skill, her purpose to ensure that Mara, Lady of the Acoma, would lie dead with a blade in her heart.

Mara wakened unrefreshed after a long and restless night. Her maids sensed her tense mood. They fetched her robes and braided silk ribbons into her hair without speaking, while Nacoya grumbled as she always did in the early hours of the morning. Too restless to wait for the meal offered by the Minwanabi house staff, Mara hurried Papewaio through his daily ritual of sword sharpening, then suggested a stroll by the lakeside. This provoked her First Adviser to sour silence.

But until Mara knew the extent of her peril, she preferred to avoid any set pattern. Before she had a chance to mingle with the guests, and observe which alliances were strong and which had grown weak, she could not hope to assess how powerful the Lord of the Minwanabi had become.

Mara breathed deeply, trying to enjoy the fresh air and flash of the sun on the water. The breeze chased ripples over the shallows, and the fishing boats bobbed on moorings, awaiting hands to man their oars. Still, the calm of the lake lent no comfort. Aware that Nacoya's steps were not so spry as they might be, Mara at last suggested they return to the estate house.

'That is wise, mistress,' Nacoya said in a tone that suggested the Lady should not have gone walking where sand and dew might spoil the silk ties of her sandals. But the old woman's rebuke lacked spirit. Her eyes were sad, and her heart felt empty so far from the Acoma estates. As she turned back to the palatial home of the Lord of the Minwanabi, with its gardens, and its banners, and its deadly gathering of guests, Papewaio took her arm and steadied her without asking leave.

The reception to welcome the Warlord, Almecho, began at midmorning, though the dignitary it was intended to honour would probably not arrive until afternoon. When Mara arrived at the festivities, most of the nobles of the Empire had gathered, plumed and jewelled and hungry with ambition. The Game of the Council permeated all aspects of Tsurani life, yet none more so than extravagant affairs of state. The guests might stroll beneath fringed canopies, eating exquisitely prepared foods, and exchanging gossip and tales of ancestral valour, or occasionally making wagers or trade bargains. But every Lord present watched his peers with sharp eyes, seeing who curried favour with whom and, notably, who was retiring, silent, or, more telling, absent altogether. Mara studied the faces and the house colours along with the rest, aware she was observed in turn. The Lord of the Techtalt and his son gave her barely a nod in greeting, which indicated that already many would delay being seen with her until the standing of the Acoma had stabilized.

Mara adroitly made the issue seem trivial by leading Nacoya to a table and sending a servant for refreshments. She took care to ask only for dishes she had seen on the plates of other guests, and when the food arrived, she and her First Adviser were observed to eat well, as if nerves did not trouble their appetites. Papewaio saw, and would have smiled if the protocol expected of an honour guard did not constrain him. Mara handled even the subtleties with fineness, for only by missing her breakfast could the fussy Nacoya be induced to take refreshment under this much stress. The effect was not lost on those guests who watched. A few nodded in covert admiration, and others whispered in corners. Still others were oblivious to the affairs of the Acoma, being embroiled in plots of their own.

Mara heard the Lord of the Xacatecas laugh low in his throat; he said something that caused the third son of the Ling Family to wince and turn pale. The offspring and cousins of the Xosai seemed everywhere one turned, and the northern-born wife of the Kaschatecas flirted shamelessly with the First Adviser of the Chilapaningo. That dignitary looked as stiff as cured needra hide; quite probably he was mortified by her attentions, but she spoke too fast and gripped his sleeve too tightly for him to excuse himself.

Mara scanned the crowd, noting the wide variety of fashions and house colours. She counted the guests in two categories: those who were allies or not strong enough to challenge her, and those who were threats or wished some vengeance upon her. Since the Minwanabi were numbered among the Five Great Families of Tsuranuanni, every powerful house in the Empire had sent some representative. Mara noted the Keda, the Tonmargu, and the Oaxatucan, each with their circle of flatterers. Lesser Lords kept their distance, or sought to wheedle favour. The Ekamchi lord's purple headdress bent close to his First Adviser, while the red robes of the Inrodaka clashed with the garb of two servants whose livery Mara did not recognize. Having studied those guests who were present, she felt a sudden chill. Nowhere did she see a tunic of scarlet and yellow.

As if sensing her uneasiness, Nacoya pushed aside the jigabird bones that remained of her repast. 'I do not see the Lord of the Anasati,' she said pointedly. 'Unless the gods have delayed him, my daughter, you and your young son are in the gravest danger.'

Nacoya did not elaborate upon the obvious: that the absence of a prominent family was of political significance, the least aspect of which was that Tecuma's vow to protect the Acoma for the sake of Ayaki would give no shelter unless he or his eldest son was in attendance. Without Anasati protection, Mara had only fifty warriors, who were quartered in barracks beyond her reach. Now the coldness of the Techtalt's greeting gained a new significance; for it seemed possible that Buntokapi's slight against the Warlord had damaged the Anasati name more than Mara had anticipated. Her danger grew in proportion. The Lord of the Minwanabi might think himself strong enough to obliterate the Acoma, then win the war that would result when Tecuma sent armies to defend Ayaki's title.

'You should not have accepted this invitation,' Nacoya whispered.

Mara gestured sharp denial. Not even the fact that two houses now stood in peril could change her resolve. She would survive, turn defeat into triumph if chance lent her the appropriate weapons. But the absence of an ally she had depended upon worried her enough that she failed to notice that Teani came late to the reception, a secretive, self-satisfied look on her face whenever she glanced at Mara. Neither did the Lady of the Acoma rise from the table fast enough to avoid the Lord of the Ekamchi, who appeared, leering, at her elbow.

'Good day, Lady of the Acoma. What a surprise to see you did not bring any of your new cho-ja warriors to watch out for your health.'

Mara bowed stiffly, reading an uncharacteristic boldness in the pudgy man's manner. 'My health is in sunlight, Lord of the Ekamchi. And I do not lack protection with Papewaio at my side.'

The Lord of the Ekamchi grimaced, having good cause to

remember the courage and prowess of the Acoma First Strike Leader. Still, some purpose kept him persistent, revealing to Mara that he knew of some shifting alliances before she did. Unwittingly emulating her father, she chose the bold course and provoked the issue before it could be broached under less favourable circumstances. 'You have perhaps spoken with Tecuma of the Anasati lately?'

'Ah!' The Lord of the Ekamchi was taken aback. Still, his eyes flashed briefly in triumph as he recovered his poise. 'I regret to tell you that our host, the Lord of the Minwanabi, did not invite Tecuma of the Anasati to this festival. He wished not to remind the Warlord of the late unpleasantness, indeed, the slight visited upon that worthy man by the son who married the Acoma.'

'Buntokapi died with honour,' Mara said acidly. 'You demean yourself by speaking ill of the dead.' Her words were a warning, and a challenge to Ekamchi honour if the subject was not dropped.

The Lord who had insulted her withdrew with a barb of his own. 'Still, I know that Tecuma could not have come, if circumstances permitted. He is otherwise occupied, I have heard, since an attack on his richest trade caravan left its defenders dead to a man. He lost his goods, and two hundred warriors as well, to a most vicious band of thieves.' The Ekamchi Lord smiled, for he knew, as would Mara, that such a slaughter had not been achieved by lawless men. Some great house moved boldly against the Anasati; and of them all, only one had sworn blood feud against the Acoma, who had contrived Tecuma's unwilling alliance.

'Pray to the gods for the health of your son,' sneered the Lord of the Ekamchi.

He walked off, and Mara missed the chance for a rejoinder. The fact that so small a Lord would dare to insult her came as a shock, and also served to remind her that in the eyes of the pettiest enemies her death was considered certain.

15

Arrival

The Warlord appeared.

He entered to a fanfare of flutes, his robe of gold-trimmed white dazzling in the sunlight. Stark in contrast, two black-clad figures walked at his side. Seeing them, the guests fell instantly silent. Even the Lord of the Minwanabi hesitated before greeting the man who was second in power to the Emperor. When Jingu did step forward to bow, his manner was subdued and deferential rather than boisterous. The presence of the black-robed Great Ones often had that effect on people. The minds of magicians were unknowable, and their ways beyond question. They existed outside the law, their only task to serve the Empire. That Almecho had brought two of them to his birthday celebration affected every guest present; no plot could be certain, and no alliance completely dependable, with the presence of magic like a wild thing in their midst. Some whispered that Almecho had won several of the Black Robes to his cause; others said much of this Warlord's policy was being decided in the City of Magicians.

Mara watched the proceedings of formal greeting from an unobtrusive place in one corner. She was somewhat relieved to see the Great Ones at Almecho's side, for the attention of the guests would now be diverted by something besides her plight . . . at least for a while. She was tired of dealing with the biting observations of the other guests, and sick of having the Lord of the Ekamchi repeatedly point out Tecuma's absence. The Great Ones would cast long shadows across the interplay of intrigue; they could bring magic arts to play, render judgment swiftly and without appeal – their words were as law. They could obliterate Jingu in his own house if they felt he threatened the Empire, and Desio would only bow and intone the ritual phrase 'Your will, Great One.'

Yet traditionally the Great Ones remained aloof from the Game of the Council; some other gambit brought the two magicians. Mara smiled to herself. Whatever the reason for their arrival, the result was two-edged: her enemies had other concerns, but then Minwanabi gained a freer hand to work her demise as the guests' concerns focused elsewhere.

Yet even as Mara weighed the implications, the guests began to assemble, each family according to rank, to pay their respects to the Warlord. Mara and Nacoya would soon be required to leave the obscurity of their corner, for the Acoma were one of the most ancient names of the Empire, first among those that followed the original Five Great Families. Still the Lady delayed, while the Keda and Tonmargu gathered ahead of her. Then, as the Lord of the Xacatecas strode forward in turn, she threaded her way through the crowd.

'Go slowly,' she instructed Nacoya. Where other families moved in groups of sons, daughters, in-laws, and cousins, each relative of the blood being permitted an honour guard, her own contingent consisted only of a First Adviser and Papewaio. Other Lords and their advisers often did not notice her presence until she had passed them by, since greatness and power seldom moved without fanfare. Quite often Mara could overhear enough of their conversations to catch the drift of their concerns before the speakers were aware of her proximity. More than one group of whisperers identified the Great Ones as the same two who had engineered support in the Assembly of Magicians for Almecho's campaign on the barbarian world. Several other magicians had come to be seen regularly with the Warlord, earning them the sobriquet 'Warlord's pets'. The hoods shaded the faces, making it difficult to recognize which two wizards attended. But if these were Ergoran and his brother Elgahar, more than one Lord's plots might suffer a setback.

As the Xacatecas began their opening bows, Mara responded to Nacoya's motherly prompting and made her way towards the dais. Kamatsu of the Shinzawai and his son fell in behind her as she ascended the stairs; and then the Xacatecas took their leave and she found herself confronting Almecho and her host, Jingu of the Minwanabi.

The Great Ones remained to one side, their unique social rank setting them apart from any formal role in the greeting ceremony.

But as she took her bow, Mara caught a clear look at one of them and recognized the hooked nose and thin lips of Ergoran beneath the black hood. The Warlord took her hand as she rose, a slight twist of sarcasm marring his smile as he returned the ritual greeting. He had evidently not forgotten their last meeting, when she had dutifully repeated the words of Buntokapi concerning needra pens. Etiquette prevented his raising the topic, since ritual suicide had absolved the stain on Acoma honour. But nothing prevented the Warlord from initiating an exchange that caused Mara some social discomfort.

'Lady Mara, what an unexpected delight. I'm pleased to see you bear as much personal courage as your father – to walk into this nest of relli.' Still holding her hand, and stroking it in a patronizing display of attention, he turned to Jingu of the Minwanabi. His host stood biting back his anger, as distressed by the last remark as was Mara. 'Jingu, you're not planning to spoil my birthday celebration with bloodshed, are you?'

The Lord of the Minwanabi's flush deepened as he spluttered a denial, but Almecho cut him off. To Mara he added, 'Just have your bodyguard sleep lightly at your door, Lady. Jingu knows if he doesn't observe the proper form in killing you, he'll make me very angry.' He glanced at his host. 'Not to mention that he's given sureties to his guests and it wouldn't be profitable to eliminate you if he had to take his own life as well, would it?'

The Warlord laughed. In that instant Mara knew that the Great Game was, truly, only a game to this man. If Jingu could murder the Lady of the Acoma in such a way that he could disavow responsibility publicly, the Warlord would not only take no umbrage, but would silently applaud Jingu for his cleverness. Even if Jingu failed, to Almecho the whole situation would become a diverting amusement. Sweat dampened Mara's back. She trembled despite her effort at self-control, and almost at her elbow the second son of the Shinzawai whispered something to his father. Almecho's eyes narrowed; Mara's colour must have gone ashen, for the Warlord squeezed her hand.

'Dont be upset, little bird; Jingu might surprise us all and behave himself.' With a wide grin, Almecho added, 'The betting odds right now are that you might have a slight chance of leaving alive at the end of the celebration.'

He still showed no sign of releasing her, but before he could derive further pleasure at her expense, a polite voice intruded.

'My Lord Almecho . . .' Kamatsu of the Shinzawai inserted himself into the conversation. Experienced through a lifetime spent in court intrigue, the former Warchief of the Kanazawai Clan changed the subject with a charm few present could have equalled. 'Only a few minutes ago the Lady Mara pointed out that I had no opportunity to introduce my younger son to you at her wedding.'

Almecho's attention was diverted enough for Mara to disengage his fingers. She half stepped to the left, and without breaking rhythm, Kamatsu moved likewise. Almecho had no graceful alternative but to acknowledge the Shinzawai lord standing directly before him. A handsome young man accompanied his father. Kamatsu smiled and said, 'May I present to you my second son, Hokanu?'

The Warlord frowned, momentarily off balance. He inclined his head towards Hokanu, but before his famous temper could invent a disparaging remark, Kamatsu continued. 'His elder brother, Kasumi, you've met. I'm sure you remember, Almecho – he is the Force Leader of the second army of the Kanazawai Clan in your campaign.'

Again the smooth remarks denied the Warlord more than a polite mumble. Both Shinzawai moved onto the dais, causing others behind them to move towards the Warlord. As Almecho cast one last glance at Mara, Kamatsu said, 'We will take up no more of your time, Lord, for you have many others waiting to greet you. May the gods smile down upon this celebration of your birthday.'

The Warlord had no choice but to face the next of his guests. By then Mara had regained some of her composure. She silently thanked the gods for the return of her wits and inclined her head in grateful appreciation to the Lord of the Shinzawai. Kamatsu was moving away from the receiving line, but he returned a slight nod. His manner reflected something she had not seen since she had entered the boundaries of the Minwanabi estates: sympathy. The Shinzawai lord might not be an ally, but he had showed himself no enemy either. He had risked much by interrupting Almecho's sport, yet the act had been boldly accomplished. While the father departed, Mara saw that the son lingered, his dark eyes following her. She gave the young man a subtle smile but dared not voice her thanks, lest the Lord of the Minwanabi come to believe the Acoma and the Shinzawai held pact against him. Nacoya urgently tugged her sleeve, hastening her steps towards the relative obscurity of a corner.

'You must leave this place, Mara-anni,' the First Adviser urged as soon as they had a moment to themselves. While Papewaio positioned himself between his mistress and the assembly of guests, she qualified. 'You have no allies here, with the Warlord making sport of the Acoma. If you stay, you will lose your life, and Keyoke will face a war to protect Ayaki. Better the shame of flight than to risk the loss of the natami.'

Mara sat on an embroidered cushion and fought the weariness that dragged at her shoulders and back. 'We cannot leave now.'

'Girl, we must!' Closer than she had ever come to a public expression of fear, the old woman sank down by her mistress's knee. 'The continuance of the Acoma is at stake.'

Mara gently patted her First Adviser's hand. 'Mother of my heart, we cannot run from this confrontation. Not only would our stock in the game fall far enough that we would deserve to become the butt of Almecho's humour, but I doubt we would escape alive. If we somehow could flee over the borders of the Minwanabi estates, we would find ourselves vulnerable to open attack by "bandits" with no risk to Jingu. Here, with his surety, we have a chance of preserving our lives.'

'Don't count on this, mistress,' Nacoya said sourly. 'Jingu of the Minwanabi would never have brought the daugher of Sezu here if he thought to let her escape. For you this place is like a nest of poisoned thorns, filled with a hundred deadly traps. With even the gods' favour, you could not avoid them all.'

Mara straightened, stung by a spark of anger. 'You think me a girl still, old mother. That is a mistake. Jingu's threats and even the Warlord's ridicule will not make me shame my ancestors. Somehow, by cunning or by politics, we will escape this trap and triumph.'

Though as frightened inside as Nacoya, Mara managed the words with conviction. The elderly woman heard, and was comforted, while across the room Hokanu of the Shinzawai observed the proud bearing of Mara of the Acoma. She had admirable courage for one so young. If Minwanabi wished her dead, his plot would need to be deviously woven, for this girl was a true daughter of her father.

The afternoon progressed tediously after that. Jingu of the Minwanabi had arranged for musicians, tumblers, and a one-act farce in the Segumi style. Yet even with the Warlord's Great Ones in attendance, the Tsurani love of the arts could not completely eclipse the lure of politics. Several Lords had hoped to exploit the fact that Almecho had overextended his position in the wars on the barbarian world. Now, with the two magicians who controlled all passage between Kelewan and Midkemia seated like the shadows of midnight in their midst, even the boldest Lords dared not seek support for their plots. Mara overheard many expressions of annoyance that Almecho should flaunt his ties with the Great Ones at what should have been a celebration in his honour.

As the curtains fell following the actors' final bows, Desio of the Minwanabi stepped onto the wooden platform erected for the performance. His tread echoed hollowly on the boards as he strode to centre stage, his arms raised for silence.

Heads turned, and whispered conversations stilled. Desio lowered his hands with a ruffle of feathered cuffs and made his announcement. 'Minwanabi scouts have brought word of an outbreak of trouble on the river. A band of water pirates has swept down from the north, and two barges have been robbed and burned near the borders of this estate.' A murmur swept the hall, then stilled as the heir of the Minwanabi added more. 'Lord Jingu has heard the Warlord's request that his birthday celebrations not be spoiled by bloodshed. To this end, he has ordered the chain beneath the prayer gate raised, cutting off the inlet from the lake. Any barge attempting passage from the river will be burned on sight, and any guests wishing to leave this celebration early should inform us of their intention, that the warriors on duty can let them out.' Desio finished with a deferential bow, and a pointed smile at the Lady of the Acoma. Then tumblers replaced him on the stage, and the party for the Warlord resumed.

Mara managed not to show resentment at this latest plot of Minwanabi's. Not only had he managed to make any attempt at departure a public admission of cowardice, but he had neatly given himself an excuse if a guest chanced to be slaughtered on the river beyond his gates. Not even a messenger could be sent to the Acoma estates without Jingu's knowledge. Mara glanced at Papewaio and knew by his tired eyes that he understood; even Keyoke could not be warned. The stakes were now higher than any of her advisers had anticipated. If she died, very likely an attack on Ayaki would occur before word of her demise reached the Acoma estates.

An old friend of her father's, Pataki of the Sida, passed near her table, and bowed politely. In a voice that only Mara and Nacoya could hear, he said, 'You would be wise to send your bodyguard away to rest.'

'Your advice is sound, my Lord.' She smiled and tried to look less tired. 'But I suggested the same thing earlier, and Papewaio said he did not care to sleep.'

The aged Lord nodded, aware as they all were that the warrior's dedication was not misplaced. 'Be wary, daughter of Sezu,' Pataki said. 'Almecho has little love for Jingu. He would enjoy seeing Minwanabi ambition blunted, but he needs their support in his little war on the barbarian world. So should Jingu manage to kill you without shame, Almecho would do nothing against him.' For a moment the Lord of the Sida regarded the dais where the guest of honour sat dining. Almost reflectively he added, 'Still, should Jingu be caught breaking his oath of surety for guests, Almecho would happily observe the ritual suicide.' As if they had been speaking pleasantries, Pataki smiled. 'Many here have a stake in what befalls the Acoma, my Lady. But none will act against you save the Minwanabi. At least you know your enemy.'

With sudden warmth, Mara returned a nod of respect. 'I think I also know my friend as well, Lord Pataki.'

The old man laughed, feigning reaction to a witty remark. 'The Sida and the Acoma have dealt honourably with each other for many generations.' He glanced to his own table where two grandsons sat waiting. 'Your father and I had even spoken of a possible alliance from time to time.' His old eyes turned shrewd. 'I would like to think you and I may someday speak of such things. Now I must return to my family. May the gods protect you, my Lady.'

'And may the gods protect the Sida,' Mara returned.

Nacoya leaned closer to Mara and whispered, 'At least one here is a man like your father.'

Mara nodded. 'Yet even he will not lend a hand when Jingu acts.'

The weak had been known to die in public with no outcry from observers, so long as the forms were observed. Minwanabi would strike. The only question was when.

Beyond the opened screens, dusk shadowed the shoreline, and the lake gleamed like a sheet of hammered silver in the afterglow. Stars pricked the zenith one by one, while slaves with wicks and oil jars made their rounds to light the lamps. Soon full darkness would fall, and then the danger would increase. Mara followed the other guests to the banquet hall, doing her best to match their mood of gaiety and enjoyment. But with all her heart she wished for a warrior's role, to fight with armour and sword until death found herself or her enemies; to walk in fear through a crowd who smiled and laughed was to be undone one strand at a time, until dignity became a mask to conceal madness.

The repast served by Jingu of the Minwanabi to honour the Warlord was prepared by some of the finest cooks in the Empire; yet Mara ate without tasting what she took from dishes ornamented with rare metal rims. She strove throughout the meal to ease Nacoya's strained nerves, all the while aware that Papewaio struggled not to fall asleep in his tracks. Without asking, she knew that he had stood guard the past night without rest, and though he was a strong man, keen of mind and determined of will, he could not be expected to maintain his façade of vigilance much longer. Mara excused her party from the festivities at the earliest opportunity.

Black shadows thrown by deep hoods made the expressions of the Great Ones unreadable, but their eyes followed Mara as she rose. To their right, Almecho smiled broadly, his elbow digging the Lord of the Minwanabi in the ribs. And from every part of the hall eyes watched with contempt as the Lady of the Acoma helped her aged First Adviser to her feet.

'I wish you pleasant dreams,' murmured Desio of the Minwanabi as the small party moved off towards the hallway.

Mara was too weary to respond. A moment later, when the Lord of the Ekamchi detained her in the doorway for one last jab at her expense, Papewaio saw her shoulders stiffen. The idea that his mistress should suffer even one more slight from this fat little man ignited the tall warrior's temper. Before Mara could speak, and before the other guests could become aware of the situation,

Papewaio grasped the Lord of the Ekamchi by the shoulders and moved him forcibly through the doorway, out of view of the diners.

The Lord of the Ekamchi gasped in astonishment. Then his plump cheeks quivered with outrage. 'Wrath of the gods!' he swore as the tall warrior towered over him. 'You ignorant oaf, do you think you can handle me without penalty?'

Behind him, his own bodyguards rattled weapons, but they could not strike past their master's fat bulk to reach Papewaio.

To all this bluster the Strike Leader of the Acoma returned a bland indifference. 'If you trouble my Lady any more, I will do more than handle you,' he warned. 'I will handle you with *violence!*'

Ekamchi spluttered. His guards half drew their swords, restrained only by the fact that Papewaio could harm their master long before they could move.

'Step aside,' said Mara clearly to the Lord who blocked the passage. 'Even you would not dare to mar the Warlord's birthday celebration with bloodshed, Techachi of the Ekamchi.'

The fat Lord reddened further. 'For a servant to lay hands on a man of my rank carries a death sentence,' he carped.

'I see,' said Mara, nodding sagely.

Papewaio raised his helmet, revealing the black rag of shame already tied to his brow. He smiled.

The Lord of the Ekamchi paled and stepped aside, mumbling a hasty excuse. He could not demand the execution of a man already condemned; and if he ordered his guards to attack, he only granted the wretch an honourable death by the blade. Caught in his quandary, and hating Mara the more for it, he stalked back into the banquet.

'Hurry along, old mother,' Mara whispered to Nacoya. 'The corridors are not safe for us.'

'Do you think our suite is any less of a trap?' the old woman returned, but she hastened her steps according to her mistress's wishes.

Yet as Mara had guessed, privacy and quiet did much to restore Nacoya's wits. Changed into more comfortable lounging robes, and seated upon cushions, the old woman began dryly to instruct her mistress in the ways of survival in a hostile court.

'You must set lamps outside, opposite each of the screens,' she insisted. 'This way, an assassin trying to enter will throw a shadow against the paper, and you will see him coming. Also, lights inside should be placed between you and the windows, so that your own form will not show up as a silhouette to anyone lurking outside.'

Mara nodded, wisely allowing Nacoya to ramble on. The tricks with the lamps she had learned from Lano, and upon entering her suite, she had detailed one of her maids to arrange things accordingly. Soon she and the old woman sat bathed in light, the stolid bulk of Papewaio on guard at the entrance.

With nothing else to distract her, Mara felt the pressure of her own concerns. She confided those worries to her First Adviser. 'Nacoya, what of the fifty warriors stationed at the barracks? The Minwanabi oath of surety does not include our retinue and I fear their lives may be threatened.'

'I think not.' The old woman's confidence was unexpected after her daylong siege of insecurity.

Mara restrained the urge to be angry. 'But to kill them would be so easy to arrange. A false claim that a plague of summer fever had broken out in the barracks – on even a suspicion of disease, the bodies would be burned. No man could prove how our soldiers had died . . .'

Nacoya touched Mara's wrists. 'You fret for the wrong causes, Mara-anni. Minwanabi will not trouble himself with the lives of your warriors. Mistress, all he has to do is strike you and Ayaki down, and every man who wears Acoma green will become a grey warrior, masterless and cursed by the gods. That fate would suit Jingu's tastes better, I am thinking.'

Here the First Adviser paused. She sought her mistress's eyes but found them closed. 'Mara, listen to me. Other dangers await, like relli coiled in the darkness. You must be aware of Teani.' Nacoya sat straighter, as yet showing no inclination to retire. 'I observed her all day, and she watched you tirelessly while your back was turned.'

But Mara was too weary to remain alert. Propped on one elbow in the cushions, she let her mind drift without discipline. Nacoya regarded her with ancient eyes and knew the girl had reached the limits of her endurance. She must not be permitted to sleep, for if an assassin struck, she must be ready to snuff out the lamp and retire quickly to the corner Papewaio had designated for emergencies, so that he would not inadvertently strike the wrong mark with his sword.

'Did you heed?' Nacoya asked sharply.

'Yes, mother of my heart.' But with the Warlord himself finding amusement in the Acoma predicament, Teani was the least of Mara's worries. Or so she thought, as the light threw shadows like death over the carry boxes that held her gowns and jewellery. How would Lano or her father, Lord Sezu, have handled the Acoma honour in this situation? Mara frowned, trying to guess how those who had died at the hand of Minwanabi treachery might have advised her to act. But no voices answered. In the end she had only her wits.

That conclusion haunted her into a fitful sleep. Though instinct warned against rest, she looked too much like a thin, tired child. Nacoya, who had raised her from infancy, could no longer bear to badger her. Instead, she arose from the cushions and delved into the clothing in the carry boxes.

Mara was deeply asleep by the time the old woman returned, her hands draped with a gauzy collection of silk scarves. These she arranged near the lamp by the sleeping mats, one last-ditch preparation before she herself succumbed to exhaustion. What would be would be. Two women, two maids, and one overburdened warrior were no match for the entire household of the Minwanabi. Nacoya hoped only the attack would come soon, that Papewaio might retain awareness enough to fight back.

But the night wore on without incident. The old nurse nodded and slept while the warrior on guard beyond the screen struggled against a numbing haze of exhaustion. Overtired nerves caused him to see movement in the garden, odd shapes suggesting lurking dangers. He blinked, and over and over again the shapes resolved into a bush or tree, or simply a shadow moving as the copper face of the moon dimmed and brightened behind a cloud. Sometimes Papewaio dozed, only to snap erect at the slightest suggestion of a sound. Yet the attack, when it came, caught him napping.

Mara jerked awake, sweating, confused, and uncertain of her surroundings. 'Cala?' she murmured, naming the maid who normally attended her at home.

Then a terrible tearing of paper and the sound of snapping wood jabbed her fully alert. Bodies struck the tiles not far from her cushions, followed by a man's grunt of pain.

Mara rolled out of her cushions, banging against Nacoya in the process. The old woman woke with a shrill scream of terror, and while Mara fumbled in the darkness to seek the safe corner Papewaio had prepared, Nacoya delayed. Her hands raked up the scarves and tossed them in panic over the lamp. Fire bloomed like a flower, blazing and banishing the dark. Mara blundered to a halt, her shins bruised against an unfamiliar side table. Horrible, coarse gasps sounded in the darkness beyond the torn screen.

Crying now, and praying for Lashima's guidance, Mara squinted through the conflagration around the lamp. She saw Nacoya lift a cushion and sweep the whole into the damaged screen, igniting the torn paper.

Flames leaped up, shedding golden light over the twisted features of a stranger, flung full length across the threshold with his arms locked in struggle with Papewaio. The Acoma First Strike Leader sat astride the man, hands clutching his throat. The combatants seemed a match in size and strength, but few could equal Papewaio's fury in battle. Each man sought to choke the other. Papewaio's face was a red mask of agony, matching his opponent's. Then Mara gasped. Horrified, she noticed the dagger stuck through the armhole of Papewaio's armour.

But even though he was wounded. Papewaio's strength was great. The fingers gripping his throat weakened and slipped. With a final jerk he brought the assassin's head up, then pulled with both hands, snapping bones with an audible crack. Limp arms fell from Papewaio's throat and the body convulsed. Papewaio released his grip, and the corpse fell to the floor, the neck twisted at a terrible angle. Dim shadows moved in the courtyard beyond. Nacoya did not wait to identify them but raised her voice in the loudest scream she could muster.

'Fire! Awake! Awake! There is fire in the house!'

Mara caught her idea and repeated the cry. In the droughts of summer, a Tsurani estate house might burn to the ground as a result of a mishandled lamp. And the flames Nacoya had started already chewed hungrily at the framing that supported the roof tiles. Minwanabi, his servants, and his guests must all respect the threat of fire. They would come, but all too likely too late to matter.

As the light brightened, Mara saw Papewaio cast around for his sword. He glanced over his shoulder and moved out of sight, reaching for something. Sounds followed that froze Mara to the heart: the smack of a blade cutting flesh and a grunt of pain. She rushed forward, calling for Papewaio. Guided by a glint of green armour, she saw her honour guard twist and fall heavily. Beyond him the plumes of a Minwanabi officer flared orange in the glow. Strike Leader Shimizu straightened with a bloodied sword, and in his eyes Mara read murder.

Yet she did not flee. Beyond, lights bloomed in the windows. Screens slid back, and robed figures ran forth, wakened by Nacoya's cry of fire.

Saved by the presence of witnesses, Mara confronted Papewaio's killer. 'Would you murder me before the eyes of all the guests and condemn your lawful Lord to death?'

Shimizu glanced quickly to either side and saw the running figures who converged across the courtyard. Flames ripped rapidly up the roof line, and Nacoya's cries were joined by a chorus of others. The alarm was spreading rapidly through the estate house, and soon every able man would appear upon the scene with buckets.

The chance to kill Mara was lost. Shimizu might love Teani, but a warrior's code would never value a courtesan above honour. He bowed and sheathed his fouled blade. 'Lady, I just aided your honour guard in dispatching a thief. That he died at his duty is the will of the gods. Now you must flee the fire!'

'Thief?' Mara all but choked on the word; at her feet, Papewaio lay sprawled with a black-handled dagger in his shoulder. That thrust could never have killed him, but the gaping wound through his heart surely had.

The first, shouting guests reached the scene of the fire, and taking no further notice of Mara, the Minwanabi Strike Leader called orders to clear the halls. Already the flames reached the corner supports, and fumes boiled white from the varnish, filling the air with an acrid odour.

Through the guests pushed Nacoya, clutching a few belongings as the two whimpering maids hauled the biggest carry box out of harm's way. 'Come, child.' Nacoya caught her mistress's sleeve, trying to pull her down the hall to safety.

Tears and smoke stung Mara's eyes. She resisted Nacoya's efforts, motioning for the Minwanabi servants who arrived to assist. Nacoya indulged in a rare blasphemy, but her mistress refused to move. Two servants took the carry box from the struggling maids. Others raced to gather the rest of Mara's property from the rapidly spreading flames. Two burly workers took Nacoya by the arm and led her out of danger.

Shimizu caught at Mara's robe. 'You must come, Lady. The walls will soon fall.' Already the heat of the blaze was becoming unbearable.

The bucket bearers began their job. Water hissed onto flaming timbers, but on the opposite side of the room from the place where the dead thief lay. His clothing had begun to blaze, eradicating any evidence of treachery he might have provided. Dully Mara responded to necessity. 'I will not leave until the body of my Strike Leader has been carried from the field.'

Shimizu nodded. Without emotion he bent and shouldered the corpse of the warrior he had just run through with a sword.

Mara followed through halls choking with smoke as a murderer bore brave Papewaio's body to the coolness of the night. She stumbled past servants who struggled with slopping buckets to battle the blaze, lest their master's estate house become totally engulfed. Mara implored the gods to let it burn, let it all burn, so that Jingu might know a tenth part of the loss she felt at Pape's death.

She might have wept then for the loss of a loyal friend; but amid a cluster of sleep-rumpled guests Jingu of the Minwanabi awaited, his eyes bright with the joy of victory.

Shimizu deposited Papewaio's body on the cool grass and said, 'Master, a thief – one of your servants – sought to use the confusion of new guests in the house to cover his escape. I found him dead at the hands of the Lady of the Acoma's honour guard, but that brave warrior was also slain in turn. I found this on the dead man.' Shimizu gave over a necklace of no particular beauty but fashioned from costly metal.

Jingu nodded. 'This belongs to my wife. The culprit must be a house servant who pilfered our quarters while we dined.' With an evil grin, he turned to face Mara. 'It is a pity that such a worthy warrior had to give his life to protect a trinket.'

No evidence or witness existed to refute such obvious lies. Mara's wits returned like a cold rush of wind. Before Jingu of the Minwanabi she bowed with icy poise. 'My Lord, it is true that my

Strike Leader Papewaio died bravely, defending the wealth of your wife from a thief.'

Taking her agreement for capitulation, and a salute to his superiority in the game, the Lord of the Minwanabi expansively offered commiseration. 'Lady, your Strike Leader's valour in behalf of my house shall not be unremarked. Let all present know that he conducted himself with highest honour.'

Mara returned a level stare. 'Then honour Papewaio's spirit as he deserves. Grant his memory due ceremony and provide him a funeral in proportion to his sacrifice.'

The shouts of the bucket brigade filled an interval as Jingu considered refusing Mara's request. But then he noticed the Warlord grinning at him through an opened screen across the courtyard.

Almecho was aware that Papewaio's death had been murder; but the contrived excuses did not upset protocol, such nuances amused him hugely, and since Mara had not cried for mercy, or otherwise flinched from the brutalities inherent in the Great Game, she was due this recompense from her enemy. Almecho called out to Jingu in a show of camaraderie, 'My Lord host, your wife's metal jewellery is worth many times the cost of such a rite. Give the Acoma man his funeral, for the gods' sake, Jingu. His death leaves you a debt of honour. And since he lost his life at my birthday celebration, twenty of my own Imperial Whites shall stand in salute around the pyre.'

Jingu returned a deferential nod to Almecho, but his eyes showed cold annoyance in the light of the flames that still burned through one of his finer suites. 'Hail to Papewaio,' he conceded to Mara. 'Tomorrow I shall honour his shade with a funeral.'

Mara bowed and retired to Nacoya's side. Supported by her maids, she watched Shimizu retrieve the limp form of Papewaio and toss him indifferently to the strangers who would prepare him for his funeral. Tears threatened her composure. Survival did not seem possible without Pape. The hands dragging lifelessly across the damp grass had guarded her cradle when she was first born; they had steadied some of her first steps and defended her from murder in the sacred grove. The fact that the Lord of the Minwanabi was now obliged to pay for an extravagant ceremony to honour the warrior of an enemy house seemed a hollow victory, and meaningless. No more would the flamboyant red shirt with its tassels and embroidery bother anyone's eyes on festival days; and right now that loss seemed more important than any power gained in the Game of the Council.

16

Funeral

The drums boomed.

The guests of Jingu of the Minwanabi gathered in the main foyer of the estate house for Papewaio's funeral. Foremost among them, and veiled in red in deference to the God of Death, Mara of the Acoma led her temporary honour guard, one of the Warlord's Imperial Whites. The drumbeat deepened, the sign for the procession to begin. Mara held a frond of ke reed in her hands, the raising of which would signal the marchers forward. Now was the timc. Yct shc closed her eyes, hesitant.

Weariness and grief left an ache inside that no ceremony would assuage. The Acoma were warriors, and Papewaio had given his life to serve his mistress, earning him an honourable death, but Mara still ached for him.

The drums boomed again, insistent. Mara lifted the scarlet reed. Feeling more alone that ever before in her life, she led the procession through the wide doorway to honour the shade of Papewaio, First Strike Leader of the Acoma. Jingu of the Minwanabi and the Warlord came after her, followed by the most powerful families of the Empire. They moved without speaking into a daylight turned gloomy with clouds. Mara's steps were heavy, her feet reluctant to continue, yet each time the drum beat, she managed another stride. She had slept safely the night before in the Warlord's suite; but her rest had been the drugged sleep of total fatigue, and she had not awakened refreshed.

A rare storm had blown in from the north, bringing misting rain. Low-hanging tendrils of fog curled across the surface of the lake, stone-grey in the subdued light. The damp made the air chill after weeks of arid heat, and Mara shivered. The earth under her sandals seemed dank as death itself. She thanked the Goddess of Wisdom that Nacoya had not insisted upon attending the funeral ceremony. By agreement with her mistress, the old woman had pleaded illness from the smoke and the sorrow of the last night's events; for the moment she lay safe on her mat in the suite of the Warlord, Almecho.

Mara led the procession down the gentle slope to the lakeside, grateful that only her own safety should concern her; for the guests who walked in pairs behind her were edgy, unpredictable as caged beasts. Not one of them believed the fiction that a servant had stolen the jewels of the Lady of the Minwanabi. No one had been impolite enough to point out that Shimizu had the alleged booty in his possession while the thief's body was consumed by fire before anyone could reach him. The possibility that Jingu had violated his pledged oath of guest safety could not be questioned without proof. Hereafter Mara and her retinue might not be the only targets for such plotting; no Lord present dared relax for the remainder of the gathering, for a few among them might react to the uncertainty in the atmosphere and strike at enemies of their own.

Only the Warlord seemed amused. Since he was the Emperor's voice within the Empire, the conspiracies and the setbacks of the rival factions beneath him offered as much enjoyment as the festivities honouring his birthday – which Papewaio's funeral had deferred until tomorrow. While his host, the Lord of the Minwanabi, fixed his attentions on Mara of the Acoma, Almecho knew Jingu was not plotting to wear the white and gold – at least not this week.

Though most guests marched in proper silence, Almecho whispered pleasantries in the ear of Jingu. This landed the Lord of the Minwanabi in a prickly mesh of protocol: whether he should remain serious, as was proper for a Lord who attended the funeral of one who had died defending his property; or whether he should defer to the mood of his guest of honour, and smile at the jokes, which in all likelihood were presented to provoke precisely this same dilemma.

But Mara drew no satisfaction from Jingu's discomfort. Ahead, on a finger of land past the piers, rose the ceremonial pyre of the Acoma First Strike Leader. He lay in his plumes and ceremonial armour, his sword upon his breast; and across the blade, his crossed wrists were bound with scarlet cord, signifying death's dominance over the flesh. Beyond him, at attention, stood the fifty warriors of the Acoma retinue. They were permitted at the gathering to honour their departed officer; and from their number Mara must choose Papewaio's successor, one soldier to stand as her honour guard throughout the remainder of the celebration for the Warlord. Almost, her step faltered on the path. To think of another in Pape's place brought pain past bearing; yet the more practical side of her mind kept functioning. Her next stride was firm, and her choice already made. Arakasi must wear the honour guard's mantle, for she would need any information he might have gathered to counter the Minwanabi threat.

Mara stepped up to the bier. She lowered the scarlet reed, and the guests fanned out, forming a circle around Papewaio's body, leaving small openings at the east and west. The neat lines of Acoma warriors waited behind Papewaio's head, each holding his sword point down in the earth to symbolize a warrior fallen.

The drums boomed and fell silent. Mara raised her voice to open the ceremonies. 'We are gathered to commemorate the life deeds of Papewaio, son of Papendaio, grandson of Kelsai. Let all present know that he achieved the rank of First Strike Leader of the Acoma, and that the honours that earned him this position were many.'

Mara paused and faced east; and the small gap left in the circle was now filled by a white-robed priest of Chochocan, who wore armlets woven of thyza reed, and whose presence symbolized life. The Lady of the Acoma bowed in deference to the god, then began to recite the memorable deeds of Papewaio's service, from the first day of his oath to the Acoma natami. As she spoke, the priest shed his mantle. Naked but for his symbols of office, he danced in celebration of the strong, brave warrior who lay in state upon the bier.

The list of Papewaio's honours was a lengthy one. Well before the recitation ended, Mara had to struggle to keep her composure. Yet as her account faltered, the guests did not fidget or show boredom. Life and death, and the winning of glory according to the code of honour, were a subject central to the Tsurani civilization; the deeds of this particular servant of the Acoma were impressive. Rivalry, hatred, even blood feud did not extend past the borders of death, and so long as the priest danced in remembrance of Papewaio, the Lord of the Minwanabi and every distinguished guest acknowledged the renown of the deceased.

But no warrior's prowess could accomplish immortality. Eventually Mara reached the night when the blade of a thief had ended a brilliant career. The dancer bowed to the earth before the bier, and the Lady of the Acoma turned west, where a red-robed priest stood in the small gap in the circle. She bowed in respect to the representative of the Red God; and the priest in the service to the Death God threw off his mantle.

He was masked with a red skull, for no mortal might know the face of death until his turn came to greet the Red God, Turakamu. The priest's skin was dyed scarlet, and his armlets were woven of serpent skins. Again Mara raised her voice. She managed the last with flawless poise, for her life now balanced upon her ability to play the Great Game. In ringing tones she described the death of a warrior. And with true Tsurani appreciation of theatre and ceremony, she made her account an accolade to the honour of Papewaio.

The priest of Turakamu danced a warrior's death, with bravery, glory, and honour that live on in memory. When he finished, he drew a black knife and slashed the scarlet cords that bound Papewaio's wrists. The time for flesh was ended, and the spirit must be freed from its bondage to death.

Mara swallowed, her eyes dry and hard. From the priest of Turakamu she accepted the flaming torch that burned at the foot of the bier. This she raised skyward, with a silent prayer to Lashima. Now she must name Papewaio's successor, the man who would assume his former duties so that his spirit would be free of mortal obligation. Saddened, Mara strode to the head of the bier. With trembling fingers she fixed the red reed to the warrior's helm. Then she plucked away the officer's plume, and turned to face the still ranks of the Acoma soldiers who closed the north end of the circle.

'Arakasi,' she said; and though her summons was barely above a whisper, the Spy Master heard.

He stepped forward and bowed.

'I pray to the gods I have chosen wisely,' Mara murmured as she gave the torch and the plume into his hands.

Arakasi straightened and regarded her with dark, enigmatic eyes. Then, without comment, he turned and cried out for his companion at arms, Papewaio. The priest of Chochocan re-entered the circle with a reed cage that contained a white-plumed tirik bird, symbol of the spirit of rebirth. As the flames touched the kindling stack beneath Papewaio's muscled corpse, the priest slashed the reed constraints with a knife. And Mara watched, her eyes misted, as the white bird shot skyward and vanished into the rain.

Fire hissed and cracked, smoky in the dampness. The guests waited a respectful interval before they filed slowly back to the estate house. Mara remained, along with her fifty warriors and her newly chosen honour guard, waiting for the fire to burn out and the priests of Chochocan and Turakamu to gather Papewaio's ashes. These would be enclosed within an urn and buried beneath the wall of the Acoma contemplation glade, to honour the fact that Papewaio had died in loyal service to the family. For a time, Mara was alone with Arakasi, away from the scrutiny of the guests.

'You did not bring Nacoya with you,' Arakasi murmured, his words barely audible over the snap of the pyre. 'Mistress, that was clever.'

His choice of words pierced the lethargy left by grief. Mara turned her head slightly, studying the Spy Master to analyse the reason for the edge of sarcasm she had detected in his tone. 'Nacoya is in the estate house, ill.' Mara paused, waiting for a reply. When none came, she added, 'We shall be joining her within the hour. Do you think you can keep us alive until evening?' The remainder of the day had been set aside for contemplation and remembrance of Papewaio. But she referred to the fact that, once away from the bier, the guests would reassume the ongoing machinations of the game; and Arakasi, though competent, was not her most proficient swordsman.

The Spy Master accepted the implication with the barest indication of a smile. 'Very wise, indeed, my Lady.'

And by his tone of relief, Mara understood. He had thought she intended to flee the Minwanabi, now, while she was reunited with her warriors. Nacoya would have agreed to remain behind towards this end, an intentional sacrifice to blind Minwanabi to her mistress's intention to break and run for home. Mara swallowed, pained again by grief. How readily the old woman might have embraced such a ruse, her abandonment in an enemy house a gambit to ensure Acoma continuance.

'Papewaio was sacrifice enough,' Mara said, sharply enough for Arakasi to know that flight was the last of her intentions.

The Spy Master nodded fractionally. 'Good. You would not have survived, in any event. Minwanabi has ringed his estates with his armies, with the appearances of safeguarding the presence of his guests. But over their drink and their dice, his soldiers admit that many others without colours wait outside the estate borders, posing as pirates or roving bands of outlaws, to trap the Lady of the Acoma.'

Mara's eyes widened. 'And how did you know this? By borrowing an orange tunic and mingling with the enemy?'

Arakasi chuckled, very low in his throat. 'Hardly that, my Lady. I have informants.' He regarded his mistress, studying a face that was pale but for the faint flush lent by the heat of the fire. Her slight frame was straight, and her eyes afraid but determined. 'Since we stay and confront the Lord of the Minwanabi, there are things you should know.'

Now Mara showed the slightest indication of triumph. 'Loyal Arakasi. I chose you because I trusted you to hate the Lord of the Minwanabi as I do. We understand each other very well. Now tell me all you know that will help me to humble this man who murdered my family and a warrior who was most dear to my heart.'

'He has a weak link in his household,' Arakasi said without preamble. 'A relli in his nest that he does not know about. I have discovered that Teani is an Anasati spy.'

Mara drew a startled breath. 'Teani?' She assessed this and suddenly felt more than the chill of the rain. All along, Nacoya had insisted that the concubine had been more dangerous than Mara credited; and Mara had not listened, a mistake that might have cost her everything she had struggled to gain, for here was a Minwanabi servant who had no concern should Mara's death cost Jingu his life and honour. In fact, to arrange such a pass would no doubt please Tecuma, as it would avenge Buntokapi's death and remove the man most likely to cause little Ayaki harm. Mara wasted no time on recriminations but at once began to calculate how this information might be used to her advantage. 'What else do you know of Teani?'

'The news is very recent. Word just reached me last night.' Arakasi lifted the plume and, by tilting his head to affix it to his helm, managed to speak directly into Mara's ear. 'I know the concubine shares her favours with one of the higher-ranking officers, which the Lord suspects but has not proven. Jingu has many women he calls upon, but she is his favourite. He does not care to do without her . . . talents long.'

Mara considered this, gazing into the flames of Papewaio's pyre; and a memory returned, of fire and dark, when Pape had lain still warm in the courtyard at her feet. Teani had accompanied the Lord of the Minwanabi. While Jingu had made a show of surprise, Teani seemed genuinely startled by Mara's presence. Jingu had spoken briefly to Shimizu, who had surely been Pape's executioner, while Teani's eyes had followed the Minwanabi Strike Leader with contempt of a startling intensity. Mara had been preoccupied with Papewaio at the time, and the concubine's twisted hatred had not seemed significant. Now, though, the memory gained importance, particularly since Teani's reaction had caused Shimizu discomfort. 'What is the name of Teani's lover?' Mara inquired.

Arakasi shook his head. 'I don't know, mistress. But when we reach the estate house, I can send my agent there to find out.'

Mara turned her head away as the flames consumed Papewaio's body. Watching was too painful, and the gesture gave her a better chance to speak to Arakasi over the loud crackle of the flames. 'I will wager a full year's harvest it's Shimizu.'

Arakasi nodded, his expression set with sympathy as if his Lady expressed some thought on the valour of the departed. 'No bet, mistress; he's the most likely candidate.'

The oil-soaked wood beneath Papewaio finally caught, and flame erupted skyward, hot enough to consume even bone and hardened hide armour. Only ashes would remain when the pyre cooled.

'Pape,' murmured Mara. 'You will be avenged along with my father and brother.' And now, while the sky wept cold drizzle, the fires consumed all that was mortal of the staunchest warrior Mara had known. She waited, no longer cold, her mind preoccupied with the beginning of a plan.

Mara returned to the Warlord's suite following Papewaio's funeral. Soaked to the skin, and accompanied by an honour guard who also dripped wet on the waxed wooden floor, she found Nacoya up from her sleeping mat. In a waspish frame of mind, the old woman ordered Mara's two maids to stop fussing over the carry boxes for the move to new quarters and attend their mistress at once.

The Lady of the Acoma fended off the attentions of the maids, sending them back to their packing. Though aware that Nacoya was overwrought, she saw little sense in rushing the process of changing and refreshing herself after the funeral. For now she needed the security of the Warlord's suite.

Mara paused long enough to shake her dripping hair loose from its coil. Then she nodded to Arakasi, who placed the urn containing Papewaio's remains by the carry boxes and stepped forward.

'Go and seek Desio,' Mara instructed the man who now played the role of warrior. 'Tell him we will need servants to conduct us and our belongings to the new suite the Lord of the Minwanabi has seen fit to assign the Acoma.'

Arakasi bowed, showing no sign that his orders would be taken any way but literally. He left in silence, knowing Mara would understand that he would find Desio, but not by the most direct route. The Spy Master would seek his contacts and, with luck, return with the information Mara needed on Teani.

The weather cleared by sunset, and with the passing of the rain the guests of the Lord of the Minwanabi grew restless with the inactivity of contemplation. A few of them gathered in the larger courtyards, to play mo-jo-go, a gambling card game, while others staged bouts of mock combat between the more skilled warriors of their honour guards, with heavy betting. With Papewaio's recent death, Mara understandably did not participate; but the casual mingling of Minwanabi's household staff and the informality of the Lords present offered an ideal chance for Arakasi to gather intelligence. Watching him through the slightly parted screen door of her new chambers, Mara could not guess whether the Spy Master had contacts in every major Lord's retinue, or whether the man's acting ability enabled him to lure even loyal men into casual conversation. However he garnered his news, by sundown when Arakasi returned with the second of his reports, his information about Teani was astonishingly detailed.

'You were right, Lady. Shimizu is certainly Teani's lover,' Arakasi accepted thyza bread and delicately smoked meats from a tray offered by Nacoya. Mara had chosen to eat supper in her rooms and had invited the Spy Master to share her meal.

The Lady of the Acoma watched with unreadable eyes while Arakasi arranged strips of needra on thyza pastry. His clever fingers rolled the result into a twist, which he ate with the manners of a born noble. 'More than that,' he resumed, knowing Mara would take his meaning. 'Teani has the Minwanabi Strike Leader netted like a fish. He follows along as she pulls, though his better instincts might be inclined otherwise.'

Here the Spy Master paused in his repast. 'Last night the two lovers quarrelled.' He grinned. 'The servant lighting lamps overheard and stayed around cleaning wicks – he found the conversation fascinating. The man was reluctant to speak to my agent, as the name of their Lord had been mentioned, but whatever the final disposition, Teani has been snappish as a bitch ever since. Shimizu can be expected to do anything to regain her favour.'

'Anything?' Bored with eating, Mara waved to Nacoya, who brought damp cloths to wipe her face and hands. 'That does offer possibilities, does it not?' While Arakasi ate freely, Mara considered: Shimizu had slain Papewaio by treachery; Teani might be forced into manipulating him to admit his Lord had ordered the death of the Acoma officer. As an Anasati spy, Teani had no true loyalty to Jingu. She would be the only servant in his house unwilling to die for Minwanabi honour. Mara made up her mind. 'I wish you to have a message delivered to Teani,' she said to Arakasi. 'Can this be done in secrecy?'

Now it was the Spy Master's turn to lose his appetite. 'If I could presume to guess what plan you have in mind, it is risky, no, dangerous in the extreme. By my assessment, the concubine cannot be depended upon to protect her true master, the Lord of the Anasati. She has betrayed a master before, perhaps more than one, and I suspect she may have murdered another.'

Mara, too, had studied Teani's background, that of an abused street prostitute who had grown to love her profession, and one thing more: twisted ambition. In the past the woman had sold out lovers and friends and even done murder upon men who had visited her bed. At first these acts had been ones of survival; but later she had continued out of greed, and a hunger for power. That Mara shared Arakasi's opinion of the concubine's reliability mattered little at this point. 'Arakasi, if you have a better plan, I will embrace it.'

The Spy Master gestured in the negative; and deep in his eyes Mara read approval as she said, 'Very well. Fetch me parchment and pen, and have my message sent to this woman by nightfall.'

Arakasi bowed and did as he was bid. Inwardly he admired the boldness of Mara's intentions; yet his sharp eyes did not miss the slight tremble of her hand as she penned the note that would begin her attempt to redress the power-hungry rapacity of the Minwanabi lord.

The lamp flame flickered in the draught as Teani paced to the screen and spun around, the mantle fanning an agitated breeze across the cheek of Strike Leader Shimizu. 'You should not have summoned me at this hour,' he said, disappointed with himself because already his annoyance was fading. 'You know that I cannot shirk my duty to attend you, and I am due on watch in an hour.'

Poised in lamplight with her gold-streaked hair laced with ribbon, Teani took his breath away. The curve of her breasts beneath her thin robe made duty seem unreal. 'Go on to your watch, then, soldier,' the concubine said.

Shimizu lowered his eyes, perspiration glistening on his forehead. If he left now, his mind would not be on his post, and the Lord of the Minwanabi might as well have no guard on his door at all. Trapped between honour and the burning need of his love, the Strike Leader said, 'You may as well tell me why you asked that I come.'

Teani sat as if strength and confidence had suddenly deserted her. She turned the frightened eyes of a girl to her lover; but the robes shifted as she leaned forward, showing a calculated amount of flesh. 'Shimizu, I did not know who else to ask. Mara of the Acoma wishes to have me assassinated.'

She seemed vulnerable enough to wrench the heart. Shimizu's hand gripped his sword by instinct. As always, her beauty overwhelmed the honest instinct that warned her words might deceive. 'How do you know this, my love?'

Teani lowered her lashes as if fighting despair.

Shimizu removed his helm, abandoned it hastily on a side table, then bent at her side. Enclosing her shoulders in his embrace, he spoke into her scented hair. 'Tell me.'

Teani shivered. She buried her face in his strength and allowed his hands to stroke her, coaxing away the fear that prevented speech. 'Mara sent me a note,' the concubine managed at last. 'She claims that her late husband left me some jewels as an inheritance. To avoid calling my indiscretion to the attention of my Lord, she demands that I go to her chambers tonight when all are asleep to claim them. Only I know that Buntokapi left me no gifts. That night he left me in Sulan-Qu he knew he was going back to the estate to die, and he arranged for my comforts before he departed.'

Shimizu shook her gently, as if to disrupt a childish fit of sulks. 'You're in no danger, precious. No demand of the Lady of the Acoma can force you to complete such an errand.'

Teani raised her head, her breasts pressed against the Strike Leader's side. 'You don't know her,' she whispered, afraid still, and appealing to the edge of pain. 'Mara is clever, and cold-hearted enough to arrange the death of her own son's father. If I refuse this invitation, how long do I have before an assassin visits my sleeping mat and plunges a knife through my heart? Shimizu, I shall live each day in terror. Only in your arms do I feel safe from this woman's wicked plots.'

Shimizu felt that the smallest breath of cold touched his flesh. He drew taut, as if the woman in his arms had touched a nerve. 'What do you wish of me?' Her insecurity prompted a warrior's desire to protect; yet he could not strike Mara without breaking the Minwanabi surety that the safety of all guests was secure under his roof. In warning Shimizu added, 'Even for your sake, I cannot betray my Lord.'

Not in the least distressed, Teani reached under Shimizu's tunic and traced the muscles of his thigh with her fingers. 'I would never ask you to dirty yourself with an assassin's work, love. But as my man, would you permit your woman to enter the lair of a dangerous beast without protection? If I answer the appointment after your guard duty ends, would you go as my escort? If Mara intends me harm, and you defend me, then our Lord will have nothing but praise. You'll have slain the enemy of his heart and done so without risk of shame. If you are right' – she shrugged, as if the possibility was faint – 'and there is some truth to the woman's message, what harm is done by my bringing an escort?'

Shimizu relaxed utterly, and her caress flushed his skin like fine wine. That a member of the Minwanabi household should bring an honour guard to her appointment with a guest was entirely proper, even expected; and as such, he could lawfully defend the safety of his charge if her life were threatened. Loosened by relief, he kissed her. And in the fervency of his response Teani sensed that the warrior she manipulated wavered in his resolves like a reed in a gale. If she had asked for Mara's death, Shimizu would have been deeply unsure which would claim his first loyalty: his obligations to his Lord or his devotion to the woman in his arms.

Teani pushed Shimizu away with all the caution she would have used while sheathing a deadly weapon. No trace of satisfaction showed in her eyes, but only resignation and bravery as she lifted the plumed helmet from the side table and set it in Shimizu's hands. 'Honour our Lord, my love. Then meet me here when your guard duty is over, and we shall go to meet Mara of the Acoma.'

Shimizu placed the helm of his head. With the strap still swinging loose, he bent and kissed her fiercely. 'If Mara dares try to harm you, she shall die,' he whispered. Then he broke away and strode swiftly through the screen.

As Shimizu vanished into the twilight, Teani rubbed the red marks his armour had pressed into her flesh. A wild joy shone in her eyes; and she blew out the lamp, that no observer should share this moment of triumph. All she had to do was provoke an attack from Mara, or fake one if the bitch did not rise to insults. Then, by the warrior's code, Shimizu must strike a blow in Teani's defence; and if in the greater game Mara's death came to be judged a shameful act, what did damage to the Minwanabi matter to a concubine whose loyalty belonged to Tecuma of the Anasati? Buntokapi's murderess would be meat for jagunas, and to Teani that triumph was beyond any other consideration.

Beyond the balcony rail, moonlight spilled gold across the wind-ruffled waters of the lake. But Mara did not step up to the screens to admire the view. Arakasi had cautioned against this when she first entered the new suite. The guardrails of the balcony, as well as the supports and some of the planks near the edge, were old, almost ancient wood, but the pegs used to fasten them were new, lacking the dullness chican wood gained when weathered. Someone had prepared the way for an 'accident'. A walkway of glazed stone tiles lined the garden three floors below this window. No one falling from the balcony could possibly survive. Few questions would be asked if her body were found lying broken there in the morning, with the old railing above having obviously collapsed as she leaned upon it.

Night darkened the corridors and suites of the Minwanabi estate house, few guests remained awake. Missing Papewaio, and aching for sleep and the security of her own estate, Mara settled restlessly on the cushions beside Nacoya.

Dressed in simple robes, and enamelled shell bracelets crafted by the cho-ja, the Lady of the Acoma rested her head on her palms. 'The concubine cannot be much longer in coming.'

Nacoya said nothing; but from his post beyond the entry screen, Arakasi returned a dubious shrug. His gesture indicated that he thought Teani unpredictable in the extreme; yet her note had stated she would come after the midnight change of the guard. Mara felt cold, though the night was warm. She wished for Papewaio, whose skill in battle was legendary. Arakasi might wear the armour of an honour guard, but his talent with weapons was nothing to boast about. Still, without the Spy Master's network she would have no plan at all. Steadying her nerves with temple discipline, Mara waited and at last heard footsteps in the corridor.

She turned a self-satisfied smile to Arakasi; then abruptly banished the expression from her face. The footsteps drew nearer, and above the expected jingle of expensive jewellery, Mara heard the squeak of armour and weaponry; Teani had brought a warrior for company.

Nacoya blinked sleepily, hard of hearing enough that she did not detect the party approaching down the corridor. But she straightened as Mara glanced through the doorway, warned by Arakasi's bow. He could always be counted upon to affect the manners appropriate to his station; analysing the extent of his deference, Nacoya muttered, 'The concubine has brought an honour guard, as is her right.' She fell silent. The hour was too late to caution Mara that any act which might be interpreted as aggressive behaviour towards Teani might be constituted an attack upon a member of the Minwanabi household. The honour guard would then be justified in defending Jingu's concubine, even duty-bound to do so.

Though Mara assumed her most regal posture and her sternest self-control, she could not repress a small start of fear as the warrior attending Teani stepped around the screen into view. He wore the orange plumes of a Minwanabi Strike Leader, and his features were those of the officer Mara had seen sheathe his bloody blade over the body of Papewaio.

The concubine walked behind, draped in dark silk. Costly metal ornaments pinned her tawny hair, and bracelets sparkled on her wrists. As she stepped up to the screen, Arakasi positioned himself smoothly before her escort. 'We both wait here . . . against any need.'

That no armed warrior might approach his Lady save by her leave was protocol. He waved Teani over the threshold, and the lamps flickered, winnowed by a draught off the lake.

Mara watched with stony eyes as Teani made her bow. Though endowed with a well-curved figure, close up Teani was not soft. She moved with a predator's grace, and her eyes reflected cunning and confidence. Mara searched the woman's form with practised eyes, but cleverly placed folds of silk revealed nothing but seductive triangles of bare skin. Any weapons Teani might carry were well hidden.

Aware, suddenly, that the concubine was assessing her in return, Mara nodded a stiff greeting. 'There are matters between us to discuss.' She waved at the cushions opposite.

Teani accepted the invitation and sat. 'We do have much to discuss.' She scraped a fleck of dust from her cuff with a sharp-edged fingernail, then added, 'But nothing to do with gifts from your late husband, Lady. I know the real reason you asked me to come here.'

'Do you?' A short silence developed, which Mara extended by sending Nacoya to heat a pot of aub petal tea. Controlled enough not to break first, Teani added nothing more. Mara met the hatred in her eyes with calm. 'I doubt you know all that I have to say.'

While Nacoya bustled back with the pot, the officer who had accompanied Teani watched their every move; since Arakasi had confirmed Mara's suspicion that Shimizu was the concubine's lover, she was able to interpret his fanatical expression. He waited like a relli coiled to strike.

Nacoya set cups and strips of spice bark before the cushions. As she began to pour the tea, Teani spoke again. 'You surely do not expect me to drink in your chambers, Lady of the Acoma.'

Mara smiled, as if the accusation that she might poison a guest were no insult at all. 'You accepted Acoma hospitality readily enough before.' And as Teani bridled, she sipped neatly from her own cup and began her opening move. 'I observe that you have brought Strike Leader Shimizu as your honour guard. That is good, for what I have to say concerns him.'

Teani said nothing, but in the doorway Shimizu shifted his weight onto his toes. Arakasi rested his hand lightly on his sword, though he was no match for a true warrior.

Mara concentrated solely upon the beautiful courtesan before her. In a voice low enough that the soldiers by the door could not hear, she said, 'My honour guard Papewaio was murdered last night, but not by a thief. I say to you that your honour guard, Shimizu, ran a sword through his heart, thereby forfeiting the surety of the Minwanabi.'

A breeze off the lake dimmed the lamp. Teani smiled in the shadow and abruptly waved Nacoya over to pour her tea. 'You are no threat to the Minwanabi, Lady Mara.' Contemptuously, as if her presence were warmly welcome, she crumbled spice bark into the cup, raised it to her lips, and drank. 'Papewaio cannot return to life to testify.' Teani had not troubled to lower her voice, and now Shimizu's eyes were fixed upon the Lady of the Acoma.

Sweat sprang along Mara's spine. For her father, for her brother, and for Pape, she made herself continue. 'That is true. But I say that your master is guilty, and your warrior companion was his instrument. You both will swear to the fact . . . or else Jingu will watch his pretty lover die by the rope.'

Teani stiffened. Without spilling her tea, she set down her cup. 'That's a threat to frighten children. Why should my master order me a shameful death, when I do nothing but please him?'

Now Mara let her reply ring across the breadth of the room. 'Because I know that you are a spy for Tecuma of the Anasati.'

For a moment surprise, shock, and naked calculation warred on the concubine's face. Before Teani could recover her poise, Mara completed her gambit and hoped the gods of chance would support her lie. 'I have documents that prove you are Tecuma's sworn servant, and unless you do as I wish, I will have them sent to the Lord of the Minwanabi.'

Arakasi watched Shimizu with the single-minded intensity of a killwing. At first the tall officer seemed stunned by betrayal. Then, as Teani visibly struggled for words to deny the accusation, Shimizu stirred in the doorway and slowly drew his sword.

The concubine strove to patch the tear in their relations.

'Shimizu! Mara lies. She speaks falsely of me to make you betray our master.'

Shimizu hesitated. Reflections from the lamp trembled along the razor edge of his lacquered blade as, tortured with self-doubt, he debated.

'Attack her,' Teani goaded. 'Kill Mara for me. Kill her now!'

But her voice rang too shrill. Shimizu straightened his shoulders. Fear, and regret, and painful resolve all mingled on his features as he slowly shook his head. 'I must inform my Lord Jingu. He shall judge.'

'No!' Teani sprang to her feet. 'He'll hang us both, you fool!'

But the protest served only to seal her guilt in the eyes of the warrior who had loved her. He spun away from the doorframe. Arakasi moved to overtake him, and sounds of a struggle arose from the corridor. Plainly the Acoma Spy Master attempted to block Shimizu's way, to grant Mara time to obtain proof of Minwanabi treachery against Papewaio.

Teani whirled, her eyes narrowed with fury. 'You'll never get what you want from me, you sexless bitch.' She drew a knife from the waistband of her robe and sprang from the cushions to murder.

Mara had seen the shift of the concubine's weight. Already rolling as Teani piled into her, she dropped her shoulder under the thrust. The knife struck harmlessly into cushions.

As the concubine twisted the weapon free, Mara recovered her breath. 'Shimizu! Help! For your master's honour!' She rolled again, the flash of the blade a hairsbreadth from her groin.

Teani uttered a furious curse and slashed at her enemy's throat.

Mara blocked with a wrestler's move, but only for a moment. The concubine was larger than she, and anger lent her strength. Sliding, twisting, struggling for her life upon the floor, Mara managed a desperate cry to Nacoya. 'Get help. If I die in front of witnesses, Jingu is ruined and Ayaki will survive!'

The old nurse fled. Teani shrieked wordlessly in frustration. Possessed utterly by hatred, she rammed Mara backwards against the tiles. The knife dipped. Mara's grip began to give, and the blade trembled lower, nearer and nearer to her exposed throat.

Suddenly a shadow loomed overhead. Armour flashed in the moonlight, and hands seized Teani from behind. Mara's hold broke with a jerk as the concubine was yanked backward, the knife still in her hand.

Shimizu hauled his lover up by the hair, like a hunter's kill. 'You must be an Anasati spy,' he said bitterly. 'Why else would you harm this woman, and see my master shamed beyond redemption?'

Teani met her lover's accusation with a glare of sultry defiance. Then she twisted like a serpent and rammed the knife towards his heart.

Shimizu spun and took the blade against the wristband on his arm. The edge glanced off, opening a slight wound. Wild with rage, he flung away the concubine who had betrayed him. She staggered gracelessly backwards and caught a heel on the track that secured the screens. The balcony lay beyond, the railing a silhouette against the moonlit surface of the lake. Teani flailed, off balance, and stumbled against supports already weakened for murder. The railing cracked and gave way with the softest whisper of sound. The concubine twisted, horror robbing her of grace, as she clawed to regain the balcony. Mara's breath caught in her throat, even as the weakened boards splintered from under Teani's feet. The sound was a death knell. Teani knew, as she tottered, that the glazed tiles of the courtyard awaited below; the body found broken in the morning would be hers, and not that of her enemy.

'No!' Her shout echoed over the lake as the last board collapsed beneath her. She did not scream. As she plunged through the darkness, she cried, 'I curse you –' and then her body struck the tiles. Mara closed her eyes. Still clenching a drawn sword, Shimizu stood stunned and tormented. The woman he had cherished lay dead below.

The moonlight shone uninterrupted across a vacant expanse of balcony, framed by broken supports. Mara shivered and stirred, then raised stunned eyes to the warrior, who seemed locked like a statue in grief. 'What happened to my honour guard?' she asked.

Shimizu seemed not to hear. He turned half-dazed from the balcony and bent unfriendly eyes upon Mara. 'You will provide evidence that Teani was an Anasati spy, my Lady.'

Mara pushed damp hair from her face, too shaken and too preoccupied to react to the threat in his tone. Her goal, vengeance for her father, her brother, and even Papewaio, lay very close at hand. If only she could wring an admission from Shimizu – the

Strike Leader could not hope to hide the fact that he had been forced to kill Teani to defend the oath of guest safety. Since the concubine had initiated the attack, Jingu could be accused of betrayal; for upon Mara's arrival half the guests present had overheard his announcement that Teani was a privileged member of his household.

Shimizu took a threatening step forward. 'Where is your proof?'

Mara looked up, relief at her own survivial making her careless in her reply. 'But I have no proof. Teani was an Anasati spy, but my claim of written evidence was only a gambler's bluff.'

Shimizu glanced quickly to either side, and with a jolt of renewed dread, Mara remembered. Nacoya had left to find help. No observers remained to witness whatever happened in the room.

'Where is Arakasi?' she repeated, unable to hide the fear in her voice.

Shimizu stepped forward. His manner changed from stunned horror to resolve, and his fingers tightened on his weapon. 'You have no further need of an honour guard, Lady of the Acoma.'

Mara retreated, her feet tangling in cushions. 'Warrior, after all that has passed this night, would you dare compromise the honour of your master beyond doubt?'

Shimizu's expression remained stony as he lifted his sword. 'Who is to know? If I say that you killed Teani, and I was honour-bound to defend her, there are no other witnesses to challenge me.'

Mara kicked clear of the cushions. Shimizu advanced another step, backing her helplessly against the carry boxes. Terrified by his passionless logic, and chilled by realization that his mad, clever plan might create enough confusion to spare Jingu's honour, she tried to stall him with words. 'Then you killed Arakasi?'

Shimizu leaped across the massed expanse of cushions. 'Lady, he sought to keep me from my duty.'

His blade rose, glittering in the moonlight. Out of resources, and cornered without hope, Mara drew the small knife she kept hidden in her sleeve.

She raised her hand to throw, and Shimizu sprang. He struck with the flat of his sword; smashed from her grasp, the knife rattled across the floor and lay beyond reach by the balcony doors.

The sword rose again. Mara threw herself to the floor. Darkened by the shadow of her attacker, she screamed, 'Nacoya!' while silently beseeching Lashima's protection for Ayaki, and the continuance of the Acoma line.

But the old nurse did not answer. Shimizu's sword whistled downward. Mara twisted, bruising herself against the carry boxes as the blade sliced into the sleeping mat. Mara struggled, pinned helplessly against unyielding boxes of goods. The next cut from Shimizu's sword would end her life.

But suddenly another sword rose over Shimizu's head. This weapon was familiar, and ineptly handled as it carved a shining arc in the moonlight and crashed upon the neck of her attacker. Shimizu's hands loosened. His sword wavered, then fell from his fingers, to slash point first through the leather side of a carry box.

Mara screamed as the huge warrior toppled, his plumes raking her side as he crashed upon the floor. One pace behind, and staggering to a stop, Arakasi employed the sword he had lately used as a club for a prop to steady himself. He managed a drunk-looking bow. 'My Lady.'

Blood flowed from a scalp wound, down the side of his face and along his jaw, the result of a blow that must have knocked him unconscious in the corridor. Mara caught her breath with a soft cry, half-relief, half-terror. 'You look a fright.'

The Spy Master wiped at his face and his hand came away red. He managed the ghost of a grin. 'I dare say I do.'

Mara struggled with partial success to regain her poise. Reaction left her giddy. 'You have to be the first man to wear the plumes of an Acoma officer who does not know the edge from the flat of the blade. I am afraid Shimizu will sport a bruise as handsome as any he gave you, come morning.'

Arakasi shrugged, his expression caught between triumph and deep personal grief. 'Had he lived, Papewaio intended to improve my technique. His shade will have to be satisfied with the ruin of the Minwanabi instead.' Then, as if he had admitted a grief he might rather have kept to himself, the Spy Master silently helped his mistress to her feet.

Voices sounded in the corridor. Indignant and shrill, the words of Jingu and his son Desio carried clearly over the confused tones of the guests. Mara straightened her disarranged robes. She bent, dislodged Shimizu's sword from the carry box, and met the crowd of nobles and servants as a true daughter of the Acoma.

Jingu stamped explosively through the opened screen. 'What has happened here?' He stopped, open-mouthed at the sight of his prone Strike Leader, then glared wrathfully at the Lady of the Acoma. 'You have brought treachery to my house.'

Onlookers crowded around, their clothing disarrayed from their hasty rush from their sleeping mats. Mara ignored them. She bowed with formal grace and placed Shimizu's sword at the feet of the Lord of the Minwanabi. 'I swear by my life and the name of my ancestors that the treachery done is not mine. Your concubine Teani tried to kill me, and for love of her, your Strike Leader Shimizu lost his wits. My honour guard, Arakasi, was forced to intervene. He barely saved my life. Is this the way the Minwanabi answer for the safety of their guests?'

A murmur arose from the onlookers, the voice of the Lord of the Ekamchi loudest among them. 'The warrior is not dead! When he rouses, he might say the Acoma tell lies under oath.'

Jingu gestured irritably for silence. He glared at Mara with pale, cold eyes. 'As my servant Teani lies dead on the tiles below, I would hear what my officer Shimizu has to say upon this matter.'

Mara gave no sign that, by implying that she had lied under oath, Jingu had offered gravest insult. No honour could be gained by reacting to the words of a condemned man; and all present understood that if Mara's charge were proved, the Lord of the Minwanabi would have no standing among them. His honour would be as dust, and his influence in the Game of the Council come to nothing.

'My First Adviser, Nacoya, witnessed the attack by the concubine.' Mara summoned every scrap of poise she had learned from the sisters at the temple. 'Your own Strike Leader had to defend me to protect your honour. Had Teani not fallen to her death below, I would have had to kill her with my own hands to save myself.'

Someone by the door murmured a comment in her favour. Outraged, Desio pushed forward, only to be shoved aside by the hand of his father. Jingu dared a smile, like a dog who has stolen meat and escaped receiving the blame. 'Lady Mara, if you have no other witness, you have no accusation to make. For if Shimizu says that you attacked Teani, and he came to her defence, and you say that Teani attacked you, and Arakasi came to yours, the case rests upon the word of your First Adviser against that of my Strike Leader. They are of equal rank, and by law their word carries equal weight. Who among us can determine which of them is lying?'

Mara had no answer. Frustrated, aching, and furious to discover herself unable to prove the truth, she regarded the enemy who had ruined her father and brother, and whose ancestors had caused her ancestors generation after generation of grief. Her face showed no expression as she said, 'You balance the honour of the Minwanabi upon a slender thread, Lord Jingu. One day soon it will snap.'

Jingu laughed, a full-throated sound that eclipsed a smaller disturbance by the entrance. Mara saw beyond him and felt a moment of triumph so fierce it felt like the pain of a sword withdrawn. Through the screen, parting a way through the packed bodies of the onlookers, came Nacoya. Behind her walked Almecho with two black-robed figures at his side.

The Warlord glanced about the room, observing the mayhem that had visited the guest suite given to Mara. 'By the gods,' he exclaimed with a laugh, 'what has occurred? A storm in the house, from the look of things.'

Jingu returned a bitter smile. 'An attack, my Lord, but there seems little agreement on just who assaulted whom first.' He added a theatrical shrug. 'I'm afraid we'll never get to the heart of this, as Lady Mara's First Adviser – out of admirable if misplaced loyalty – will lie to support her Lady's tale. It will be her word against Shimizu's. I expect we'll have to let the entire matter pass.'

Almecho's eyebrows rose in malicious reproof. 'Oh, really? I don't think we need let any slight of honour pass, Jingu. Just so there is no cloud on your good name – not to mention any shame to spoil my birthday celebration – I'll ask my companions to lend a hand.' He turned to the two black-robed figures at his side and spoke to the first. 'Elgahar, can you sort this matter out?'

A dispassionate voice answered, 'Of course, my Lord.' As Jingu's face drained of colour, the magician continued, 'We can prove without doubt who is lying and who is speaking truth.'

Almecho's eyes travelled from Lady Mara's face to Jingu's with poisonous amusement. 'Good,' he said softly. 'Let us separate the guilty from the innocent.'

17

Revenge

Elgahar demanded silence.

Conversations fell to a murmur, then subsided to total stillness as the guests of the Lord of the Minwanabi crowded themselves into the room where Teani had fallen to her death. Shimizu had regained consciousness. Seated now at the feet of his Lord, he regarded the Great One with impassive eyes.

Mara sat opposite, Nacoya and Arakasi at her side. Her honour guard had cleaned the blood from his face, but he had made no other effort to refresh himself. A few of the guests had sent slaves to bring robes to cover their sleeping attire, but most had not troubled with appearances. Piqued by curiosity, all waited with keen anticipation for the demonstration of the Great One's magic.

The moon shone brightly over the broken rail of the gallery. Bathed in its coppery light, the Great One lowered his arms. 'I will require clear space around all areas where the action occurred, and no people standing in the doorway.'

Sandals shuffled on waxed wood as the guests did Elgahar's bidding. The Warlord placed himself behind the Lord of the Minwanabi, and Mara saw him lean down and whisper. Jingu returned what was meant as an offhand smile, but the result was forced and stiff. No Lord in the Empire truly understood the powers of those in the Assembly of Magicians; the ability of this Great One to cast a spell for truth seemed to bring little comfort to the Lord of the Minwanabi. The magic might easily catch Mara in a lie, and then the Acoma would be ruined, but other possibilities occurred to Jingu. Teani's unpredictable nature had been part of her appeal to him; and her hatred of Mara was no secret.

The Great One positioned himself by the door. His robes blended like ink into shadow, leaving his face and hands visible as a pale blur. When he spoke, his words rang like a voice beyond the bounds of human understanding. The innocent, the guilty, and onlookers alike shrank from the sound. 'We stand upon the site of violent acts,' Elgahar said to those gathered to witness his magic. 'Resonance of intense passion creates echoes in the otherworld, that state of energy which parallels reality. My spell shall call forth these echoes in visible form, and all eyes will see what occurred between the servants of the Minwanabi and his guest, Mara of the Acoma.'

He fell silent. The hood eclipsed his features as he stood for a moment in total stillness, then tipped his head towards the ceiling. He gestured in the air with one hand and began an incantation so low that even those standing closest could not decipher the words. Mara sat like a temple statue, barely aware of the vague rise and fall of the magician's voice. The spell he shaped affected her strangely, as if a force touched her inner self and separated a piece of her spirit. At her side, Arakasi stirred sharply, as if he, too, felt the pull of the magic.

A soft glow arose in the centre of the room, over the torn expanse of the cushions. Mara watched with wondering eyes as a vague, transparent image of herself appeared, seated as she had been in the hour of Teani's arrival. An ice-pale spectre attended her, and all recognized the wizened form of Nacoya.

The guests murmured in amazement. Nacoya, seeing herself, turned her face away and gestured a sign against evil. The Great One gave no notice. His incantation ended abruptly, and he lifted his hands; framed in the spill of the moonlight, the glowing figures began to move.

The scene unfolded in ghostly clarity, soundless, and fragile as light reflected in water. Mara saw herself speak, and a flicker of movement appeared within the doorway. The Great One stood motionless, even as the outline of Teani entered, passing clean through his body as if he had been made of air.

The nearest guests gave way in alarm, and more than one exclaimed aloud. But the spectre of the concubine remained oblivious. Ghostly in her beauty, she retraced her steps of the hour before and advanced to the cushions before Mara. The images of both women sat and spoke; Mara regarded her own form, amazed to realize how calm she had seemed before Teani. Even now, the re-creation of the scene caused her heart to beat quickly, and her palms to sweat. The recollection of her terrible doubt nearly overwhelmed her still. But none of this had showed to Teani's eyes; and the guests who observed the fruits of the Great One's magic themselves gained the impression of a supremely confident young woman confronting one of inferior rank. To Mara it was now easy to understand why the concubine had fallen for the bluff and believed evidence existed that proved she was a spy to the Anasati.

Next all in the room saw Teani call out to Shimizu beyond the door. Though her image made no sound, the lips could easily be read, and a moment later the Strike Leader appeared. The words of the exchange could not be guessed, but Teani's expression shifted, becoming so animal and basic that several guests gasped in surprise. Shimizu abruptly left the frame of the spell, and all in the room saw Teani draw a knife from her sleeve. With no visible provocation, she launched herself from the cushions, striking out at the figure of Mara. Whatever claim Jingu might offer in defence, now no doubt remained that a servant of the Minwanabi had attacked the Lady of the Acoma. The Lord of the Minwanabi's surety of safety was broken.

For the first time any Lord of the Empire could recall, Jingu showed pallor in public. Perspiration appeared upon his upper lip, while before him the drama of the hour before continued to unfold. The Strike Leader Shimizu re-entered the room, and after a brief and bitter struggle received a wound from her knife. All stared in fascination as he hurled the concubine through the doorway. Wooden railing shattered in soundless impact; and Teani fell to her death, leaving only a spectral impression of a face contorted with hatred, horror, and desperate fear imprinted in the memories of the guests. For an instant the crowded room seemed suspended and motionless. Then, assuming the drama was concluded, a few guests murmured appalled remarks. Mara stole the moment to glance at the Lord of the Minwanabi.

His expression showed calculation, and his small eyes, faint hope. If Teani had acted the renegade, then Shimizu had preserved his honour in killing her; should the image stop here, he was safe. But the face of the Great One showed neither sternness nor sympathy beneath the dark shadow of his hood. His spell continued to unreel, and in the midst of the chamber the Minwanabi Strike Leader spun into a battle crouch and advanced upon the Lady of the Acoma.

Jingu stiffened as if touched by an executioner's sword point. Shimizu's broad back prevented any in the room from seeing what Lady Mara might have said, but after a short exchange of words, the warrior's blade rose and swiftly fell. Mara could be seen rolling in the corner. And cautiously, surreptitiously, those guests beside their host began to edge away, as if his shame were a contaminant that might spread on contact. Arakasi's courageous intervention became aftermath, as around the room guest after guest turned eyes of judgment and contempt upon the Lord of the Minwanabi.

Clearly the image had said enough. Into a strangling stillness Elgahar mumbled a few phrases, and the alien blue-white light was extinguished. Mara let air back into cramped lungs, shaking still with suspense. Her danger was not over yet.

Beside the Lord of the Minwanabi stood Almecho, an evil delight in his expression. Costly embroidery flashed as he raised his shoulders in an elaborate shrug. 'Well, Jingu. That seems a clear enough assault upon your guests. First the girl, then the warrior. You have enthusiastic servants, don't you?'

Jingu showed no sign of turmoil. Racked by emotions only he could know, he glared first at Mara, then at the muscled and bleeding form of his Strike Leader. Those closest heard him whisper, 'Why? Shimizu, you were my most trusted warrior. What drove you to this act?'

Shimizu's lips curled in agony. Whatever excuse he gave regarding the machinations of Teani, his actions had already condemned his master to die to expiate the shame to his honour. 'The witch betrayed us,' he said simply, and whether he referred to Mara or Teani was unclear.

'You madman!' screamed Jingu, and his vehemence rocked all in the room. 'Stupid get of a diseased bitch, you've killed me!' Without thought, he drew a dagger from beneath his robe and lunged forward. Before any could react to his rage, he slashed backhanded across Shimizu's exposed neck. Severed arteries shot a fountain of blood, spattering fine robes and bringing a scream from a weak-nerved Lady. Shimizu tottered in uncomprehending confusion. His hands fumbled futilely as the life spurted between his fingers, and his great shoulders sagged as he realized his own death was upon him. Matters of betrayal and lies, twisted desires and misplaced love, all now became meaningless. He sank back. Almost peaceful as he welcomed the hand of Turakamu, he whispered last words to his master. 'I thank my Lord for granting me death by the blade.'

Shimizu nodded finally to Mara, a silent salute for her victory. Then his eyes went vacant, and the hands that had sought her life fell slack. Sprawled in death at the feet of the elaborately clothed guests, he seemed a fitting symbol of Jingu's defeat. In the Game of the Council, the Lord of the Minwanabi was ruined.

Almecho broke the silence. 'That was impulsive, Jingu. The warrior might have had something more to say. A pity.'

The Lord of the Minwanabi whirled. For an instant he seemed capable of striking out at the Warlord, but his fury left him and he let the dagger fall. Almecho sighed. The cowled figures of the Great Ones returned to stand at his side as he focused his regard on Desio, son and heir of the Minwanabi. 'As sunrise is considered the best time for such matters, I expect you'll busy yourself for the next few hours with preparation for your father's ritual expiation of his guilt. I'm returning to my bed. When I arise, I trust you'll somehow restore the gaiety to this shambles of a celebration . . . Lord Desio.'

Desio nodded.Unable to speak, he began to lead his father away. Jingu seemed in a trance. Deflated, his bold, brash voice utterly stilled, he turned his mind inward to the task before him. Never a brave man, he must still act the part of a Tsurani Lord. Fate had decreed his death, and somehow he must find the strength to accomplish what was expected. But as his father crossed the threshold, Desio cast a last glance backward at the Lady Mara. His look offered clear warning. Others might applaud her playing of the Game of the Council, but she had not won; she had simply passed the blood feud along to another generation. Mara read his hatred and hid a shudder of dread. She needed no reminder of the fact that she was still deep within the heart of Minwanabi strength.

She thought swiftly, and before the Minwanabi heir could escape public regard, called after him. 'My Lord Desio. Violence has been visited upon me by Minwanabi servants. I require an escort of your soldiers when I depart for home tomorrow. It would be a shame to blot the cleansing of your family name if the wronged guest was attacked by those in your service . . . or by nameless bandits or water pirates upon the river.'

Thrust painfully into the responsibilities of rulership, Desio lacked the wits to excuse the request with grace. Aware only of the anguish of his father, and hatred of the Lady who had caused it, he still observed the forms he had been raised to follow. Feud would continue between the Minwanabi and the Acoma, but in public the insult to Mara and the blight on his family name required at least a gesture of reparation. Desio nodded curt agreement and departed, to attend upon the sorrows of Jingu's ritual suicide.

Movement returned slowly to those who remained in the chamber. Guests stirred and exchanged comments, while a battered Arakasi helped the Lady Mara to her feet. Almecho and others looked upon the Lady of the Acoma with respect. No guest present believed the Lord of the Minwanabi would have sent servants to murder the Lady of the Acoma out of hand. None doubted that the Great One's magic had revealed the last act of some complex plot of Mara's, the Great Game of the Council at its subtle and deadly finest. The Lady of the Acoma had surmounted all but impossible odds to avenge a blow that had come close to ruining her house. Now all silently congratulated her for her skill in defeating her enemy in his own home.

Yet Mara had learned nothing if not to guard herself doubly against treachery where the Minwanabi were concerned. After a murmured conference with Arakasi, she stepped forward. Offering a deferential bow to the Warlord, she smiled in a manner that truly made her beautiful. 'My Lord, I am sorry that my inadvertent part in these bloody acts has cast a shadow over your birthday celebration.'

More amused than irritated, Almecho regarded her keenly. 'I place no responsibility on your shoulders, Lady Mara. Jingu is about to erase any debt that remains. Still, I suspect the affair is not ended. Even though our young Lord will provide escort for your return home – I salute that touch, by the way – you yet may face difficulties.'

Mara made light of her own danger. With all the charm at her disposal, she instead offered sympathy to the one who was the Emperor's voice within Tsuranuanni. 'My Lord, too much sorrow has passed here for your celebration to continue with grace. As much as Desio might wish otherwise, grief will leave him little heart to resume the festivities in your honour. While there are other estates closer, mine lie in the fastest direct route by river. In reparation, let me offer my home as a humble substitute for the final celebration of your birthday. Should you accept my hospitality, my staff and my artisans shall do their utmost to entertain you.' Filled with secretive plans, Mara thought of the gifted but unrecognized performers she had observed at her wedding. In return for her past courtesy they would be willing to perform on short notice, and as one who had discovered new talents for the Warlord's pleasure, her social stock would grow. And many a worthy musician and artist might gain needed patronage, putting them even deeper in her debt.

Almecho laughed. 'You're a sharp-witted one, aren't you, little bird?' His eyes narrowed. 'I had best keep an eye on you myself. No woman has ever worn the white and gold, but you . . .' He lost his serious expression. 'No, I like your bold offer.' He raised his voice to the guests who had lingered to watch the final turn of events. 'We depart at sunrise, to journey to the lands of the Acoma.'

He bowed slightly and, flanked by the dark forms of his magicians, stepped briskly through the doorway. The moment he had disappeared, Mara found herself the centre of a storm of attention. In the very chamber in which she had escaped murder by narrow margins, she suddenly had ceased to be a social outcast, a girl marked for death at a moment's notice. From the greatest families in the Empire she received congratulations, honour, and the accolades of a victor who could play the Game of the Council.

Mara's retinue of warriors was recalled from the Minwanabi barracks well ahead of daybreak; they rejoined their mistress on board the Acoma barge. While land and water still lay in darkness, the craft poled away from the docks. Too excited by the events of the night to attempt to rest, Mara stood by the rail with her First Adviser and her Spy Master. Feeling the absence of Papewaio with keen sorrow, they watched the lighted windows in the Minwanabi estate house fall astern. The aftermath of terror and unexpected triumph had left Mara both shaky and exhilarated. Yet her thoughts, as always, ranged ahead. The usual preparations would be lacking, since the Warlord and all the guests would arrive at the Acoma estates unannounced. In spite of herself, Mara smiled. Jican was surely going to tear his hair when he discovered his staff had the responsibility of conducting Almecho's birthday celebration.

The barge rocked gently as the slaves switched their poles for oars and began a steady stroke. Here and there soldiers spoke in whispers to each other; then all conversations stilled as the sky brightened over the lake. Astern, a colourful flotilla of guests' barges departed the hospitality of the Minwanabi. With the watercourses jammed with noble witnesses, Mara need not fear attack by enemy warriors disguised as bandits; and Desio in any event could hardly mastermind an attempt around the grief and the ceremony attendant upon his father's ritual suicide.

When the golden disc of the sun lifted above the valley, Mara and every other noble passenger abroad in their barges noted the small knot of soldiers upon the hillock near the Minwanabi contemplation glade. These men stood honour to Lord Jingu as he mustered the courage to fall upon his own sword. When at length men in orange armour formed up into ranks and marched in formal step to the mansion, Mara breathed a prayer of thanks to the gods. The enemy who had arranged her father and brother's murder, and nearly her own, at last was dead.

With Jingu's passing, the Minwanabi ceased their role as supreme power after the Warlord, for Desio was a young man of poor social gifts. Few considered him a worthy successor to his father; those travelling south to the Acoma lands commonly judged that the old Lord's successor would be hard pressed to preserve the alliances his father had forged, let alone increase Minwanabi power. Now Desio could expect to be closely watched. As he shepherded his family's decline, all who were once fearful of Minwanabi power would now add strength to his enemies. Unless one of Desio's more gifted cousins came to power, the Minwanabi fate was sealed. The stock of a great house had fallen far in the Game of the Council.

Mara considered this throughout the voyage by river, and beyond, as her litter wove through the crowded streets of Sulan-Qu and into the quieter countryside surrounding Acoma lands. With the Minwanabi dominance ended in the High Council, Almecho stood unchallenged, save for the alliance of those in the Blue Wheel Party and the Alliance for Progress. Mara regarded the decorated litters of the nobles who trailed after her retinue, her mind absorbed by the likely readjustments of politics. With the beginnings of a smile, she realized the wisdom of having Nacoya place Hokanu of the Shinzawai near her at least once during the feasting. Then she inwardly laughed. Just as she must once again consider marriage, the Empire would begin another round of multi-player bickering as the game entered a new phase; but it would always be the Game of the Council.

Mara turned to mention her thought to Nacoya and found the old woman napping. At last, with their return to familiar roads, the First Adviser had begun to relax the tension that had driven her throughout their stay in the Minwanabi house.

Just then Arakasi said, 'Mistress, something odd ahead.'

Nacoya roused, but her complaints died unuttered as she saw her mistress staring raptly forward. At the crest of the next hill, at the boundary of the Acoma lands, stood two warriors, one on each side of the road. To the left, upon Acoma soil, waited a soldier in the familiar green of her own garrison. On the right, on lands belonging to the Empire, the second soldier wore the red and yellow armour of the Anasati. As Mara's retinue and litter came fully into view, both men spun around and shouted almost in unison, 'Acoma! Acoma!'

Startled as her litter swerved to the left, Mara glanced back and saw her bearers pull aside to make room for the Warlord's litter to draw even with hers. Almecho shouted over the noise of tramping feet. 'Lady, you've arranged an exceedingly odd welcome.'

Caught at a loss, Mara said, 'My Lord, I do not know what this means.'

The Warlord gestured to his Imperial Whites, and side by side the two retinues crested the hill. Another pair of warriors waited beyond, some distance along, and an even more distant pair farther yet. On the crest of the last hill before the prayer gate a fourth pair could be seen. And from the waving back and forth, the cry 'Acoma' had been clearly carried ahead of the returning litters.

Mara bowed her head to Almecho. 'With my Lord's permission . . . ?'

At Almecho's brusque nod, the Lady of the Acoma instructed her bearers to quicken pace. She grabbed at the beaded handrail as, running, her slaves forged ahead. Her guard of warriors jogged with her, past the familiar, outlying fields, the needra pastures with their tawny cows and calves. Mara felt tension tighten her chest. As far as the eye could see, the fields were empty of field hands or herders, porters or cart drivers. Even the slaves were absent. Where Acoma workers should have been hard at their labours, crops and livestock stood abandoned in the sun.

Wishing she had Keyoke's staunch presence at her side, Mara

shouted to the first Acoma soldier they passed, 'What's going on? Have we been raided?'

The warrior fell in beside the trotting slaves and reported on the run. 'Anasati soldiers came yesterday, mistress. They made camp beyond the prayer gate. Force Commander Keyoke has ordered every soldier to stand ready. The lookouts he posted on the road were to call out when you returned, or report the appearance of Minwanabi soldiers.'

'You must be cautious, daughter.' Jounced breathless by the movement of the litter, Nacoya made as if to elaborate; but Mara needed no warning to spark her concern. She waved Keyoke's sentinel back to join her honour company, and called out to the Anasati warrior who had stood opposite her own man, and who now kept pace with her litter on the opposite side of the road.

Any reply would be a courtesy, since no Anasati warrior was answerable to the Lady of the Acoma. This one must have been instructed to keep his own counsel, for he ran on in silence, his face turned resolutely forward. When the litter crested the last hill, the valley beyond lay carpeted in coloured armour. Mara's breath caught in her throat.

Over a thousand Anasati warriors stood before her gate, in battle-ready formation. Confronting them, from the other side of the low boundary wall, Keyoke commanded a like number of Acoma soldiers. Here and there the green ranks were divided by wedges of gleaming black, cho-ja warriors ready to honour the treaty with their Queen, that called-for alliance should any threaten the peace of Acoma lands.

Shouts echoed down the valley the instant the litter came into view. The sight caused the Acoma forces to erupt with an uninhibited cheer; to Mara's astonishment, the Anasati war host answered them. Then a thing happened that even old Nacoya had never heard of, not in tales, or ballads, or any of the remembered historical events in the great Game of the Council: the two armies broke ranks. Throwing down weapons and unbuckling their helms, they approached her litter in a single joyous crowd.

Mara stared in wonderment. Dust blew in the grip of a freshening breeze, hazing the plain like smoke as two thousand shouting soldiers surrounded her litter and honour guard. With difficulty, Keyoke pushed a path through his Acoma soldiers. A clear space widened in the Anasati side, and a confounded Mara found herself eye to eye with Tecuma. The Lord of the Anasati wore the armour of his ancestors, bright red with yellow trim, and at his side marched the plumed presence of his Force Commander.

The multitude of warriors stilled, even as the litter bearers jolted to a stop. The hoarse gasps of their breathing sounded loud in the silence as Keyoke bowed to his mistress. 'My Lady.'

Tecuma stepped forward with the first polite bow observed by a Ruling Acoma in many generations.

'My Lord,' acknowledged Mara, a bit stiffly from her seat in the litter. With a frown of genuine confusion, she commanded her Force Commander to report.

Keyoke drew himself up and spoke loudly that all might hear. 'Sentries warned of the approach of an army at dawn yesterday, my Lady. I mustered the garrison and went myself to challenge the trespassers –'

Tecuma interrupted. 'We have not yet entered Acoma lands, Force Commander.'

Keyoke conceded this point with a stony glance. 'True, my Lord.' He again faced Mara and resumed. 'I was approached by my Lord of the Anasati, who demanded to see his grandson. In your absence, I declined to allow him his "honour guard".'

Mara regarded Ayaki's grandfather with no expression visible on her face. 'Lord Tecuma, you brought half your garrison as an "honour guard"?'

'A third, Lady Mara.' Tecuma returned a humourless sigh. 'Halesko and Jiro are in command of the other two thirds.' Here the old man seemed to falter, though he filled the moment with his usual finesse by unstrapping and removing his helm. 'Sources of mine indicated you would not survive the Warlord's celebration and' – he sighed as if he hated to make this admission – 'I feared it would be so. To prevent harm to my grandson, I decided to come visit, in case Jingu sought to end the Acoma-Minwanabi blood feud for good and all.'

Mara raised her brows in comprehension. 'Then when my Force Commander declined your attentions to my grandson, you decided to stay and see who arrived first, myself or Jingu's army.'

'True.' Tecuma's hands tightened on his helm. 'Had Minwanabi soldiers come over that hill, I would have marched in to protect my grandson.'

In even tones, Keyoke said, 'And I would have stopped him.'

Mara shared a pointed stare between her Force Commander and her father-in-law. 'Then you'd have done Jingu's work for him.' She shook her head in irritation. 'This is my fault. I should have considered an Anasati grandfather's concern might turn to war. Well then, there's nothing to worry about, Tecuma. Your grandson is safe.'

Here the Lady of the Acoma paused, as she relived the miracle of relief all over again. 'Jingu is dead, by his own hand.'

Taken aback, Tecuma jammed his helm over iron-grey hair. 'But –'

Mara interrupted. 'I know, you received no word. Regretfully for the Anasati, your "source" is dead also.' At this news, Tecuma's eyes narrowed. Plainly he ached to know how Mara had found out about Teani, but he said nothing. Very still, he waited as Mara told him her last item of news. 'We've moved the Warlord's birthday celebration here, Tecuma. Since you were the only Lord who was absent, perhaps you'd care to amend that slight and join us for the next two days? But please understand: I must insist that you restrict your honour guard to fifty men, as everyone else has.'

The old Lord nodded, at last giving way to relief and amusement. As Mara briskly ordered her own honour guard to resume their march to the estate, he stared at her slight form with something akin to admiration. 'It is well we did not see Minwanabi soldiers breasting that hill, Mara.' He considered the resolute warrior at Mara's side and added. 'Your Force Commander would have been forced to yield quickly, while most of my forces held Jingu's army at bay. I would not have wished that.'

Keyoke said nothing, only turning and signalling to where Lujan stood, at the rear of the first line of Acoma soldiers. He in turn waved to another soldier further away. When Mara looked at Keyoke with a curious expression, he said, 'I indicated that the one hundred cho-ja warriors waiting in ambush should feel free to return to their hive, mistress. Now, if you feel it appropriate, I'll order the men to stand down.'

Mara smiled, though she would not laugh at Tecuma's obvious shock at hearing of a hundred cho-ja warriors that would have met his advance guard should they have won their way past Acoma lines. 'Maintain an honour guard to meet our guests, Keyoke.' The Force Commander saluted and turned to do as he was bid. To Tecuma, Mara said, 'Grandfather of my son, when you have dealt with the disposition of your forces, please come and be my guest.' So saying, she ordered her bearers to carry her to her house.

Tecuma watched her depart. Even his smouldering hatred over Bunto's death was replaced by wonder for the moment. He looked down the road at the advancing column of guests, and was glad that the problems of food, housing, and entertainment were not his own to bear. The little hadonra – was it Jican? – was surely going to fall apart.

But Jican did not fall apart. He had heard about Mara's return before the soldiers on lookout, since the gossip had been brought by a guild runner with rush dispatches from a merchant. The man passed on rumours of vast quantities of noble barges all tied up in Sulan-Qu, the Warlord's white and gold prominent among them. In his subsequent panic, the hadonra forgot to pass the information along to Keyoke and the warriors. Instead he had requisitioned every freeman, slave, and all the craftsmen who were already gathered at the estate house to defend Ayaki if the Anasati war host broke through; these had been reassigned to work freshening linens and peeling fruits in the kitchens, and into this furious hive of activity came Mara and her honour retinue.

'So that's where all my fields hands are,' exclaimed the Lady of the Acoma, even as her bearers set her litter down in the dooryard. By now she could not contain her amusement, for her little hadonra had delivered his breathless report while still wearing cast-off bits of armour from the store sheds, his helm a pot borrowed from the cooks. The servants who bustled from the slaughtering pens to the kitchens were similarly equipped, and everywhere the hoes, rakes, and scythes they would have employed as weapons were leaning against the furniture. Mara's laughter was cut short by a carping complaint from Nacoya, who was weary of litters and barges and wished for a real hot bath.

'You may have whatever you wish, mother of my heart. We're home.'

And like a weight of stone lifted from her shoulders, the Lady of the Acoma knew this was so, for the first time since she had left for the Holy City of Kentosani.

Still tying strings from changing back to his house livery, Jican ran furiously from the estate house to the lawns, where huge pavilions were erected to house several hundred Lords, Ladies, noble children, First Advisers, honour guards, and their innumerable servants. There would hardly be room to move in the main house, jammed as the guest rooms would be with Almecho's immediate relations and Imperial Whites. Selected servants would be housed in the barracks with the soldiers, with the overflow assigned to the slave buildings. The slaves, and the unlucky freemen to draw the short lots, would sleep under the stars for three days. Mara felt her heart warm at the loyalty of her servants and soldiers; for through the chaos and upheaval of her return, no one complained. Even the house servants had stood ready to defend Ayaki, though their farm implements and kitchen knives would have proved no match for the weapons of trained soldiers. Yet their bravery was none the less for that fact; and their loyalty was beyond the bounds of duty.

Touched by their devotion, and having hastily changed into fresh robes, Mara returned to the dooryard as the Warlord's cortege heaved into sight in full splendour. The Imperial Whites were a machine of precision as they escorted their master from his litter. Trumpets blew and drums beat and Almecho, second only to the Emperor Ichindar in power, made his formal arrival before the Lady of the Acoma.

Mara bowed gracefully. 'My Lord, I welcome you to our house. May your visit here bring rest, and peace, and refreshment.'

The Warlord of all Tsuranuanni bowed slightly. 'Thank you. Now, would you keep things somewhat less formal than . . . our previous host did? Daylong celebration can be tiresome, and I would like an opportunity to speak with you in private.'

Mara nodded politely and looked to her First Adviser to welcome the two black-robed magicians and show them to their quarters. Pride had straightened the old woman's shoulders, and in her indomitable mothering manner she took the two envoys of the Assembly of Magicians under her wing as if she had dealt with their kind all her life. Mara shook her head, marvelling at Nacoya's resilience. Then she let the Warlord take her arm, and the two of them walked alone into the peaceful stillness of the garden she preferred for meditation.

Four warriors stood guard at the entrance, two wearing green and two the white of the Imperial Guard. Pausing by the rim of the fountain, the Warlord removed his helm. He sprinkled water over damp greying hair, then faced the Lady of the Acoma. Beyond the hearing of guests and servants he said, 'I must salute you, girl. You have proven your mettle in the game over the last two years.'

Mara blinked, not at all certain she grasped his intent. 'Lord, I did only what was necessary to avenge my father and brother and preserve the existence of my house.'

Almecho laughed, and his bitter humour sent small birds winging from the treetops. 'Lady, what do you think the game is, if not to remain while you dispose of enemies? While others have been flitting around the High Council nattering at one another over this alliance and that, you have neutralized your second most powerful rival – turning him into a reluctant ally, almost – and destroyed your most powerful enemy. If that isn't a masterful victory in the game, I've never seen anyone play.' He hesitated a moment. 'That dog Jingu was growing a little too ambitious. I believe he plotted to dispose of three opponents: you, the Lord of the Anasati, and then me. Tecuma and I are somewhat in your debt, I think, though you certainly didn't act on our behalf.' He trailed his fingers thoughtfully through the water; small currents rose up and roiled the surface, just as the currents of intrigue ran always beneath the affairs of the Empire. The Warlord regarded her keenly. 'Before I leave you, I want you to know this: I would have let Jingu kill you, if that was your fate. But now I am pleased you lived and not he. Still, my favour is scant. Just because no woman has ever worn the white and gold before, don't think I count your ambition any less dangerous, Mara of the Acoma.'

Somewhat overwhelmed by this endorsement of her prowess, Mara said, 'You flatter me too much, Lord. I have no ambition beyond the desire to see my son grow in peace.'

Almecho placed his helm upon his head and motioned for his guards to return. 'I don't know, then,' he reflected, half to himself. 'Who is to be more feared, one who acts from ambition or one who acts for the needs of survival? I like to think we can be friendly, Lady of the Acoma, but my instincts warn me you are dangerous. So let us just say that for now we have no reason to be at odds.'

Mara bowed. 'For that I am very grateful, my Lord.'

Almecho returned the bow, then departed to call servants to attend his bath. As Mara followed him from the garden, Keyoke saw his Lady and came at once to her side. 'Pape . . . ' he said.

Mara nodded in shared sympathy. 'He died a warrior, Keyoke.'

The Force Commander's face showed nothing. 'No man can ask for more.'

Certain that Nacoya was acting in all her glory with the guests, Mara said. 'Walk with me to the glade of my ancestors, Keyoke.'

The Force Leader of the Acoma shortened stride to match that of his slight mistress and silently opened a side door. As they left the main house, and birdsong replaced the talk of guests and servants, Mara sighed. 'We shall need a new First Strike Leader.'

Keyoke said, 'Your will, mistress.'

But Mara kept her opinion to herself. 'Who is the best for the position?'

Keyoke seemed unusually expressive as he said, 'It galls me to say it, but despite his less than seemly attitude at times, no man is better able than Lujan. Tasido has been with us longer and is a better swordsman . . . but Lujan is among the best I've seen in tactics, strategy, and leading men since' – he hesitated – 'well, since your father.'

Mara raised her eyebrows. 'That good?'

Keyoke smiled, and his humour was so unexpected that Mara stopped in her tracks. She listened as her Force Commander qualified. 'Yes, that good. He's a natural leader. That's the reason Papewaio came to like the rascal so quickly. And if your First Strike Leader had survived he'd be telling you the same. Had the Lord of the Kotai lived, Lujan would probably already be a Force Commander now.' By the hint of pain beneath Keyoke's tone, Mara understood how much like a son Papewaio had been to this old campaigner. Then his Tsurani self-discipline fell back into place and the old warrior was as she had always known him.

Glad of his choice, Mara said, 'Then name Lujan First Strike Leader, and promote a Patrol Leader to take his place.' They passed beneath the trees, where once Papewaio had knelt and begged to take his life with his sword. With a pang of sorrow for his passing, Mara considered what might have happened had she not re-interpreted tradition concerning the black scarf of the condemned.

A shiver touched her spine. How delicate was the thread of progression that had preserved her life.

Strangely abrupt, Keyoke stopped. Ahead lay the guarding hedges at the entrance to the glade, and the Force Commander traditionally might accompany her that far. Then Mara saw that a lone figure awaited her, before the contemplation glade of her ancestors. The red and yellow helm in his hands was familiar, gleaming in the copper light of latest afternoon; and the scabbard at his side held no weapon.

Mara gently dismissed her Force Commander and stepped forward to meet the Lord of the Anasati.

Tecuma had brought no honour guard. The scarlet and yellow armour of his family creaked in the stillness as he offered greeting. 'My Lady.'

'My Lord.' Mara returned his slight bow, aware that the birds in the trees had fallen silent at the coming of sundown.

'I hoped to find you here. Since the last time we exchanged words in this place, I thought it appropriate to make a new beginning on the same soil.' He glanced to the chattering throng of guests crowding the dooryard, and the bustle of the servants who attended them. 'I expected the next time I trod this grass, I'd see orange-clad warriors swarming over it, not revellers come to honour you.'

'They come to honour the Warlord,' corrected Mara.

Tecuma studied the face of his daughter-in-law, as if truly seeing her for the first time. 'No, Lady. They celebrate Almecho's birthday, but they truly honour you. There will never be love between us, Mara, but we have Ayaki in common. And I dare to think we share a respect for one another.'

Mara bowed, lower than ever before. In all sincerity she said, 'We have that, Tecuma. I have no regrets, save that good men have been made to suffer . . .' Her mind turned to her father, brother, Papewaio, and even Buntokapi, and she added, 'and to die. What I have done was for the Acoma, and all that shall be Ayaki's someday. I hope you understand.'

'I do.' Tecuma gathered himself to leave, then shook his grey head, unwilling humour showing through his poise. 'I truly do. Perhaps when Ayaki comes to his majority and rules, I may find it in my heart to forgive what you have done.'

Mara wondered at the strange way that events could turn in the

Game of the Council. 'I am glad at least that for now we have no reason to be at odds,' she said.

'For now.' Tecuma sighed with something very close to regret. 'Had you been my daughter, and Bunto Lord Sezu's son . . . who knows what could have been possible?' Then, as if the matter were forever put aside, he placed his helm on his head. The hair stuck out at odd angles over his ears, and the ornamented strap swung against his neck, but he did not look the least bit foolish. Rather he looked a ruler, with years of life behind and more yet to come, with age and wisdom, experience and knowledge, a master of his office. 'You are a true daughter of the Empire, Mara of the Acoma.'

Left no precedent upon which to model a response, Mara could only bow deeply and accept the accolade. Overwhelmed by emotion, she watched Tecuma walk back to rejoin his retinue. All alone, she entered the contemplation glade of her ancestors.

The path to the natami seemed changeless as time. Sinking down on the cool earth where many an ancestor had knelt ahead of her, Mara ran her fingers over the shatra bird carved into the stone. Quietly, but in a voice that trembled with joy, she said, 'Rest you well, my father, and you, my brother. He who took your lives is now but ashes, and your blood is avenged. The honour of the Acoma is intact, and your line preserved.'

Then tears came unbidden. Years of fear and pain lifted from Mara's spirit.

Overhead, the fluting call of a shatra bird called the flock to take wing in celebration of sundown. Mara wept without restraint, until lantern light glowed through the hedges and the distant sounds of festivities filled the glade. All her struggles had borne fruit. She knew peace for the first time since Keyoke had fetched her from the temple; and somewhere upon the Great Wheel the shades of her father and brother rested peacefully, their pride and honour restored.

Filled with the deep satisfaction of victory, Mara arose. She had a household full of guests to attend to . . . and the Game of the Council would continue.